Emma Cooper is a former teaching assistant who lives in Shropshire with her partner and four children. She spends her spare time writing novels, drinking wine and watching box-sets with her partner of twenty-four years, who still makes her smile every day.

Emma has always wanted to be a writer – ever since childhood, she's been inventing characters (her favourite being her imaginary friend 'Boot') and is thrilled that she now gets to use this imagination to bring to life all of her creations.

Praise for *It Was Always You*

'This book had me hooked from the beginning . . . Equal parts funny, sad and poignant, and as a teen of the 1990s too, I absolutely loved the nostalgia. A complete triumph'

Clare Swatman

'This book! My favourite Emma Cooper book to date. It's romantic, heart-breaking and a real page-turner. I had no idea what was going to happen and I loved every second . . . I LOVED IT!'

Olivia Beirne

'A beautiful, moving, and heart wrenching book to give you all the feels . . . Will, Ella and Cole are three brilliantly real characters who you can't help but want to spend time with, all the way to the heart stopping conclusion'

Emily Stone

'Absolutely magical! Emma always creates such wonderfully compelling characters, they jump off the page and into your heart. So romantic and heartfelt, I didn't want it to end'

Josie Silver

it was always you

EMMA COOPER

REVIEW

First published in 2022 by Headline Review
An imprint of HEADLINE PUBLISHING GROUP

First published in paperback in 2022 by Headline Review

1

Cataloguing in Publication Data is available from the British Library

ISBN 978 1 4722 8891 2

Typeset in 12.25/13.5pt Garamond MT Std by Jouve (UK), Milton Keynes

Printed and bound in Great Britain by Clays Ltd, Elcograf S.p.A.

Headline's policy is to use papers that are natural, renewable and recyclable
products and made from wood grown in well-managed forests and other
controlled sources. The logging and manufacturing processes are expected
to conform to the environmental regulations of the country of origin.

HEADLINE PUBLISHING GROUP
An Hachette UK Company
Carmelite House
50 Victoria Embankment
London EC4Y 0DZ

www.headline.co.uk
www.hachette.co.uk

Note from the Author

To the reader,

I began writing this book on 1st January 2021 during the third UK lockdown. For me and many others, this was the hardest lockdown of all. After Christmas away from family and friends, a year of being isolated and with the constant anxiety that Covid 19 brought, myself and Mr Emma were now faced with home-schooling our seven-year-old as well as supporting our three other children as they tried to complete their A levels and attend online university lectures. Because of this, and the uncertainty of how the pandemic would unfold, I decided to set this book in a world without Covid, a world where I could live through my characters who were able to visit each other, hold one another and go to restaurants, bars and supermarkets without the need for a mask.

It is my hope that you can forgive me for this indulgence, and that it also brings you some much needed escape from the pandemic, which at the time of writing this, still looms large and unescapable over our heads.

Stay safe,
Em x

For Mum . . . I forgive you for eating my Revels x

Prologue

Hindsight is a powerful illusion. It allows us to cup a memory in the palm of our hands, turn it towards the light, letting us examine the pebble-drop impact of our choices. But our memories are not perfect; they twist and turn, flicker and fade with the passing of time.

Hindsight gives us the chance to see ourselves without our imperfections, things we could have done and said differently, but none of us are perfect; perhaps we should take the time to forgive ourselves for that.

When Ella and Will remembered how their love story began, their recollections would vary, and they would think of things they could have done differently; but it began on the last Saturday night of October 1999, the night the clocks went back.

The autumnal air weaved through the crowds of the fairground, thick with the pungent smell of fried onions and the promise of mulled cider. Violet strobes lit up the sky, and passengers with rosy cheeks beneath woollen hats were strapped into metal crates, while 'Praise You' by Fatboy Slim boomed from hidden speakers. Squeals of delight leaked into the atmosphere, as the eager patrons were pushed up and down, each ride bought and paid for with a ticket and a smile.

At the back of the fairground, through a small wood, stood the remains of Dermont Abbey. Hardly anything of the building remained, just a few jagged walls falling from the sky where once they'd climbed; the archway that Henry VIII had strode through still stood, as tall as an oak, the crumbling entrance sitting quietly beneath the trees, away from the small crowd of teenagers.

Past the ditch that knights and carriages had once ridden over, beyond the burning orange-red leaves and the rough bark of the beech trees, Ella, Will and a group of friends circled a small bonfire. Their bottoms were balanced on tree stumps and logs; cheap bottles of spirits were lifted to their lips while cigarettes glowed orange between their fingertips. With mud-covered boots and tired eyes, the fairgoers had now mostly left, making their way home to the safety of their warm beds.

Ella felt the cool air lifting the stray tendrils from the plaits hanging over her shoulders, the shop-bought fire-engine-red flickering around her face like the flames of the fire. She breathed in the scent of woodsmoke clinging to the denim of her jacket as she gazed over at the boy who would become her husband.

Will's hair fell across his eyes, his head dipped as he stared into the fire, deep in thought. Flanking him, two girls and a boy. Will was the one they all radiated around: he was the boy with the clear skin, the blue eyes, the blond hair; he was the boy that the air stilled around as he walked into a room, so that the walls widened, the roof stretched high into the sky, until he, it seemed, was the centre of the room, the universe, their lives.

Will was a musician, a guitarist.

Ella had seen him play once, his fingers plucking and pulling the melody from the strings, her heart hammering in her chest as the notes seeped into her skin, into her veins, the melody pumping around her body, flowing through her heart. She'd had tears in her eyes when he finished.

Will had looked down at his fingers from where the melody flew, his expression one of confusion, of shock. How had he produced a sound so pure, good and untainted, while the grief and guilt of his brother's death still haunted his dreams?

He hadn't seen Ella: she had clasped the handle of her art case, her portfolio and her application for university nestled inside, and crept from the room, the soft melody humming inside her, along with the look in Will's eyes as he gazed down at his fingers as if they belonged to someone else.

Ella knew he was too good for her. She was plain and unremarkable, clumsy – knocking down displays in supermarkets, tripping over stray chairs in classrooms, spilling ketchup down her top in the school canteen. She was tall and solid, not dainty and pretty; her nose was too wide, she laughed too loud, her mouth was too full and she had a beauty spot at the curve of her right cheek so that even after a shower, it looked as though a spot of ink remained. Her hair was brown, neither light nor dark without the help of a packet of hair dye.

Her eyes watered from the smoke of the fire and she stole her gaze away from him, wiping under her eye with her thumb, careful not to undo the line of black eyeliner. She returned her focus to the way the flames reflected in the eyelets of her Doc Martens, bands of gold and copper circling the black thick laces, half listening to Cole as he chattered away, the way he always had since they were children.

Will studied Ella from beneath his fringe. He noticed the way she grimaced as she took a sip of whatever drink Cole was giving her.

On that night, the grimace was unfamiliar to Will, but in time to come, when she became his wife, it would be a grimace he would know and love; when she tried to swallow yet another attempt of his cooking; when he held out a spoonful of soup to her lips after she contracted glandular fever; and when he applied calamine lotion to her chicken-pox polka-dotted skin at the age of thirty.

Will wanted to go over, to grab the bottle from her hand, but instead, he nodded at the boy next to him. The boy in question was trying to get Will to join his band and was giving Will the hard sell, talking about going on tour, about leaving their town, travelling the world.

'You know we can do it,' the boy enthused.

The girl leant over and agreed. 'We should do it,' she replied, her tongue running along the bottom of her lip. She believed that it would only be a matter of time until Will Roberts saw what was right in front of him.

The members of their group seemed so important that night but after ten years of marriage, they would pale into insignificance. Will and Ella would discuss their former friends over a curry and a bottle of wine. 'Lisa, wasn't it, or Lizzie? You know, the one who snogged your face off right in front of me,' Ella would say.

Cole took another sip of gin and turned to Ella. The words he needed to say were like molten glass in his chest: he tried to mould them but the longer they stayed inside, the harder it was becoming for Cole to speak them; they were hardening. He cleared his throat and began.

'Ells?' He looked up at her, cheeks flushed, his hand scratching the back of his dark curly hair, but she was looking at Will. The liquid words hardened inside Cole's chest; they splintered, shattered, wafer-thin shards disintegrating, the glass turning into sand. He took another long swig of the gin, the alcohol in his bloodstream washing the words away.

The conversation, the stolen drinks, the excitement in the air quickened the time around them.

4

The teenagers checked their watches, mobile phones yet to become a permanent appendage: it's almost here they said, the extra hour, let's all turn our watches back at the same time.

The girl next to Will took this celebration of sorts as an opportunity, and as he turned his head to talk to her, he found himself with her on his lap, her lips on his, her arms around his neck.

Ella watched the girl's hands in Will's hair, his fingers at her waist. Cole passed the bottle back to Ella; she drank thirstily, thrust it back at Cole's chest and stood, her body swaying.

Cole reached out for her elbow, but she shook him off.

'I need some air, away from the fire.' Her words came slow and thick as she battled with her jacket, discarding it in a heap on the ground.

'I'll come with you.' Cole turned to grab the bottle and her jacket from the log they'd been sitting on.

'No, you stay here, I'm too hot, I need to . . .' – she stared back at Will and the girl – 'walk.'

'But—'

'I'm fine, Cole.'

'I'll come, just wait a sec . . .' He began to shrug his jacket on.

'I said I'm fine,' Ella snapped, guilt leaving an imprint with each step of her boots as she walked away from the hurt look on his face.

Ella swayed and stumbled as she trod through the wood, a well-worn path towards King Henry's archway.

Behind her, Cole was staring into the flames, hurt by her words, hurt by her reaction.

Will prised himself away from the girl.

'I'm sorry, I can't do this . . . it's not you.' The girl's eyebrows arched in disbelief and she shuffled herself further up the log, away from him. 'No, really, *really.*' Will reached out a hand towards her but retracted it. 'It's me.'

And it was true back then. Will was broken, his soul fractured the moment he'd climbed out of the river and seen that his brother, Jack, was missing.

Ella made her way across the hardened ground, away from the light of the fire and chatter of her peers. The darkness followed her as she stepped deeper into the forest, edging her progress along the path, branches folding around her figure as she became obscured from view.

She didn't know that with each step she was being pulled towards her future, her past, her present, the old, the new, and everything in between. The seconds passed. Ella was oblivious to the gentle rhythm of time, of the hands sliding across the clockface, the scrape of the minute and hour hands edging towards two a.m., the vibration thrumming as the hour struck: the magic hour upon her.

Ella stepped out from the edge of the forest, her boots continuing towards the brick of the archway, her figure dwarfed by age-old masonry that had been smoothed by hundreds of seasons, by thousands of hands and fingers. Her mind was tangled, twisted in knots, thoughts about Will and the girl, of Cole, swirling around as her young body tried to realign itself, battling with the alcohol she wasn't yet used to consuming.

Around her, a mist rolled in. Ella glanced back at the teenagers; she could just make out the clipped edges of their chatter, the orange of the fire flickering between the tree, the fog like a blanket wrapping around the sounds, hushing the world, pulling her close.

Her heart thumped inside her chest; she could almost feel the muscle expanding and contracting, the blood rushing in and out.

Through the blue-grey haze, she began to see the outline

of a woman on the other side of the archway. Ella suspected she should be scared, but instead, a feeling of calm surrounded her. Ella stepped forward, one hand trailing along the stonework, the other feeling through the mist.

The woman waited on the other side of the archway. Heavy air hung around her, but Ella could see she was tall, that she was wearing a red scarf, a green coat. The woman raised her hands beside her as though feeling against a mirror, head leaning forward, dark blonde hair settling over her shoulders.

'Hello?' Ella asked, unsure, stepping forward.

The woman's mouth worked but Ella couldn't quite hear the words. Ella took another step. There was an urgency about the woman's face, of desperation; her hand knocked as if there was a barrier between them. Ella watched the woman's mouth form words, but the words were scattered and broken, like a radio not quite tuned in.

Goosebumps climbed along Ella's arm, the blood draining from her cheeks as she moved closer.

The woman swallowed and appeared to compose herself, wiping her cheek with the heel of her hand. Another cloud of mist passed between the two women, some words filtering through the haze, but Ella couldn't quite grasp them.

The scene in front of Ella was becoming unbalanced, as though she was standing at the bow of a ship, the woman her horizon, tilting left then right. Ella squinted, her eyes focused on the brooch attached to the woman's green coat: amber, an oval encased in gold.

The world around Ella shifted, the cold hard ground suddenly against her cheek, her chin bruised, her lip bleeding.

The fog was gone, the scene reset, and Will was there, his hands helping her up, Cole at his back, the others from the group standing around them.

'Are you OK?' Will asked. 'Ella? Are you OK?'

'Here, have a drink of this.' Cole took out a bottle of Evian.

'Leave it, Cole, you've done enough,' Will snapped, not registering the bottle of water. Ella looked up at Will as her arms were manipulated into the warmth of his leather jacket, as it folded over her shoulders. There were green flecks in the blue of his eyes she hadn't seen before. His dark eyelashes were long, concern forming a slight groove between his eyebrows.

She didn't know it yet, but that groove would deepen into a permanent feature.

'Where is she?' Ella croaked.

'Who?' Will replied, applying the cuff of his sweatshirt against her lip, catching the blood.

'There was a woman.'

But Ella was already beginning to doubt what she'd seen. She looked around, registering that there was no longer any fog, that the night air was clear but for the aftertaste of bonfire smoke.

'Did you hit your head?' Cole asked from behind Will's shoulder. Ella's hand reached up to her temple, her fingers trailing the weaves of her plaits.

'I don't think so . . . maybe? She was right there, did you see her?'

The group shook their heads, their unease covered with sniggers and jokes about not being able to hold her drink.

Will ignored them as he looked into Ella's eyes, speaking softly. 'There's no one there. Let me take you home.'

He helped her up, Ella leaning on him for support. Tentatively, the two walked away from the group, walking towards their future.

PART ONE

THE BEGINNING

Chapter One

Now

Ella

'Sorry, sorry!' The door slams behind me and I follow the smells of chilli into the kitchen. Friday night is chilli night in my parents' home. My brothers and I have no idea where this law comes from, but the law it is, only bendable on birthdays and Christmas – and even on those law-breaking days, the holy trio of guacamole, sour cream and salsa dips will be split into thirds in a terracotta pot with a bowl of tortilla chips and will be sat somewhere within the Walkers' cluttered home.

I head into the kitchen, Mum's grand ideas transforming this generic box-shaped kitchen into something that looks like it belongs in a farm cottage: white AGA, copper pots, navy-blue Shaker-style cupboards with an eclectic array of crockery and fairy lights displayed on the Welsh dresser opposite. The Welsh dresser was passed down from Grandma Grunt, who for years I thought of as an actual Welsh lady, complete with pointy black hat, who grunted from a rocking chair. I couldn't have been further from the truth: apparently, she was a bit of a goer in the sixties and is rumoured to have shagged both Mick Jagger and David Bowie before settling down to have Mum at the ripe old age of thirty-four, positively ancient in those days. Thinking about it now, I don't *actually* know why she was called Grandma Grunt; I do hope it's nothing to do with the Jagger and Bowie legend. I rouse myself from the thought and plant a kiss on Mum's perpetually warm cheek, her auburn hair curled and piled on her head. Mum is something of an enigma: Nigella Lawson meets Emmeline Pankhurst.

'Sorry I'm late, I had an extra delivery and you should have seen her face!' I reach over and dip a tortilla chip into a bowl of homemade salsa.

'You're always late . . . Ella!' Mum admonishes my attempt at a snack, blowing a stray ringlet of hair from her forehead. 'Fingers!'

'Sorry,' I say, feeling younger than my forty years. 'It was a surprise bouquet – honestly, the way her face lit up when she read the card . . . met the guy at the pub quiz night, she said, the card was asking her out on a date. The look on her face, pure joy and hope.' I sigh. 'I can't remember the last time Will sent me flowers.'

'Ella, you're a florist, why on earth would he send you flowers?'

'Because it would be nice to be the one on the other side of the door for once.'

I have the best job in the world. I know that might be a grand statement to make, but really, I do. Of course, the best job in the world would be even better if I didn't have to wear a pair of dungarees that are constantly riding up my crotch and if I wasn't always *ever so slightly* behind schedule.

I never mean to be late – I always try to leave early, always try my best to make sure that I'm on time – but *things* just get in the way.

Take this morning. I set the alarm for six, opened my eyes, turned my alarm off – Mr Blue Sky by ELO, *guaranteed* to put you in a good mood for the day – and looked over at Will, who somehow manages to sleep deeply when it's time to get up and yet can't fall asleep until the early hours. He looked so peaceful and so handsome, and I really mean handsome: my husband is like film-star good-looking. Last week, I heard a woman in Costa telling her friend that he looked like Kevin from *This is Us. That* is how good-looking he is. Sometimes when I see photos of us, I wonder what people must think when they see us together. OK, his laughter lines are deeper than they used to be, his blond hair is a little darker, receding just a *tiny* bit and he has a permanent crease between his eyebrows that makes him look like he's constantly worrying about something and, if I'm being really honest here, he is a little *softer* around the middle than he used to be . . . then again, so am I . . . but Will still turns heads.

'Where *is* Will?' Mum asks.

'Parents' evening, the highlight of his year,' I say with sarcasm. It's the part of his job as a music teacher that he dreads. Put Will in a room full of mardy sixteen-year-olds with guitars and keyboards and he's in his element. Put him behind a desk in a tie with ambitious parents and you may as well be sealing him in with a bucket full of snakes à la *I'm a Celeb*. 'I've got to go and pick him up in an hour.'

'Oh? What's wrong with his bike?'

'He's wearing his suit,' I say by explanation. Will continues to ride a motorbike, although it's been years since I've sat behind him.

I think back to this morning. I lay on my side just looking at him, watching the rise and fall of his chest, the flickering beneath his eyelids . . . he looked so peaceful and I was just filled with this surge of love for him that I thought then would be a good time to, well, give *him* a good time. Amber, our daughter, already embedded in her new life in a different city, rarely comes home, Jamie leaves tomorrow but had stayed over at his girlfriend's for the night, so I kind of *hopped on*, you know, as a nice surprise. Things have been a bit slow in that department for a while, but Will's under so much pressure from work at the school, and he's almost forty-two, so it's to be expected, right? Although Amira, partner in crime as well as in business, is *always* at it with her husband and he's a year older than Will. Nonetheless, the surprise was kind of ruined when, startled at his rude awakening, Will bolted upright, sending me tumbling off the edge of the bed. I've got a bruise the size of a baguette on my leg. Maybe I should give him a little more warning next time; it must have come as a bit of a shock, me straddling his morning glory before he'd even had a cuppa or a whiff of marmalade.

'And Jamie?' Mum interrupts my thoughts as I absent-mindedly rub the outside of my tender thigh. 'I thought he was coming with you?'

'No, he's having drinks with Robbo before he drives to Leicester tomorrow, but he should be here soon.'

'You know I never thought he'd go to uni, it sounds so . . . *academic*.' Mum lifts the lid of the slow cooker and gives the meat a good stir. 'Jamie has always been hands-on.'

'Takes after his mother,' I grin. 'Do you remember when he was little, he would arrange his food into separate colours and then make a pattern? And he was always constructing things out of the buffet finger rolls and cocktail sticks. He would sit for hours, never in a rush, just happy to be in the moment. How time flies,' I say wistfully. Jamie often takes a more relaxed approach to things: he left his uni application until the last minute, tackled his A levels with a relaxed sense of detachment, and when it came to arranging accommodation, ended up with one of the only rooms still available on campus. Amber had booked hers the day they became available, sitting at her desk with a list of pros and cons for every accommodation listing. And then she was off to uni the first day she could, bags packed, fully committed to the years of work that lay ahead of her as a medical student.

Mum tilts her head to where *Richard Osman's House of Games* is firing questions from the flat screen sandwiched between two truly hideous *professional* photos of me squashed between my identical twin brothers. The first showcases me as an awkward top-and-bottom-braced thirteen-year-old sitting in front of Kenny and Roddy, who are two years older and both named after maternal and paternal grandparents . . . thank God Nanny Nibs was called Ella. You'd be hard pushed to notice that they're identical now: Kenny is more like an aging Joe Wicks, whereas Roddy has more than a touch of the Jack Blacks about him. Both photos are horrific. I have a huge zit on the end of my nose on the other one, my brothers flanking me this time; I look like I'm about to vomit as I give a tense smile to the camera, the reason being that beneath the aperture, Kenny had let out a fart so toxic that it was a wonder the photo was recorded at all.

'Mashard.' Mum gives herself a self-satisfied nod.

'How is that the right answer? It's not even a word!'

'It's not supposed to be a real word, it's the answer smash round . . . you have to mix the two answers together. Mash and shard.'

I snatch another handful of Doritos and duck away from the tea towel Mum is aiming at me, taking off my coat as she belts another obscure answer at Mr Osman.

My coat lands on the banister as I make my way towards the lounge. The lounge has been redecorated *again*; Mum's fingers are never far away from a pile of material. Grey and teal are the colours she has chosen for her palette this season: yet another new set of curtains hangs at the windows and matching cushion covers are scattered on the sofas. The soft furnishings may change at a head-spinning rate, but the layout has been the same since we were kids: large window, open fire, three-piece suite, sideboard, nest of tables stacked in the corner.

Kenny – the eldest of my twin brothers by two minutes and forty-three seconds – is dozing on the sofa.

I smirk.

How unfortunate to have left himself so *wide* open.

My neck flexes to the left, to the right, as I imagine one of those pleasing neck-crack sounds that I can never seem to enact. My fist clenches and I pull my forearm towards my bicep, observing the sharp point of my elbow. I begin to rub the end of the tip as one might chalk a snooker cue, stepping forward silently, stealthily, like a cat. A small snore catches in the back of Kenny's throat and I still my progress, halting mid-stride in the same way as I used to when we played musical statues at the numerous birthday parties held in this very room. But he just smacks his lips together and turns his head towards me slightly. I take another step and hover over him, checking the trajectory of my elbow, so that it will land without doing him any *real* harm. I position myself into a classic wrestlers' elbow-drop stance, a grin splitting my face; I'm about to announce my arrival to my brother with a perfectly aimed drop into his very soft stomach, a move I've perfected over the years, and which was often my only defence from my brothers' *classic* and *relentless* rugby-tackle-Ella-every-spare-moment-we-can-find routine.

A noise at the door halts my movements, and as I look up, Dad is holding back a smirk, shrugging his shoulders consensually at me in a 'go for it' motion. Dad never seems to change. He's still tall, still has a mischievous twinkle in his grey eyes, still has longish hair, thick, the same steel grey as it was through my childhood. Dad, I always think, looks like he's about to say something incredibly amusing or something incredibly profound, which is actually *quite often* the case. I return my gaze to my poor unsuspecting brother just as my mother arrives at Dad's shoulder.

'Ella!' she shouts, alerting my brother just as I'm about to land. Dad sighs in disappointment.

'Fuuuuuuuuuuuck!' Kenny shouts, reacting startlingly quickly, hooking his arm around my waist and pulling me onto the sofa, securing me against him, one hand in a cobra-like grip, the fingers of his other somehow holding both my cheeks, puckering my lips into a fish face.

'Yield!' he bellows.

'Never!' I squeak through my hollowed cheeks and fishy lips. I wriggle as best as I can but his grip is too strong.

'Yield!' he repeats.

'Ella, leave your brother alone!' Mum chastises, then leaves the room to attend to more robust chilli-stirring. I let my body slacken.

'Fine,' I say, looking at my dad in exasperation. Better luck next time, Dad's expression reads as he follows Mum into the kitchen.

Jamie arrives just as the mountain of grated cheese hits the table.

'Bonjour, ma famille!' My son strides into the dining room, tall, blond, an almost perfect replica of his father, looking red of cheek and glassy of eye. He plants an alcohol-fumed sloppy kiss on my cheek and knuckle-rubs my brothers on the crowns of their heads. Kenny doesn't correct where his thinning bowl cut of dark hair is now sticking up at all angles, whereas Roddy – arriving straight from the gym and dressed as though he's about to start a fitness regime rather than having just completed one – smooths down the disarray to his heavily conditioned curls with one smooth motion, reaching for a glass of water at the same time as Kenny lifts his red wine to his lips, a burgundy moustache now residing above them.

Just as my twin brothers are complete opposites in personality, so too are my children. Jamie, although looking just like his father at that age, embodies a very different personality. Jamie is as easy-going as they come, sure of himself, comfortable in his own skin; he turns his head to the sun and craves being the centre of attention. I sometimes wonder if that was Cole's influence on him as a child. Amber looks like her brother – both of my children favour their father's looks – but Amber is much more like Will than me; she's quiet, thoughtful, considered. As a child and come to think of it, even now, Amber has always resembled the archetypical angel: wide, innocent, blue eyes, blonde curls falling down her back, penitent and patient smile, with her head often dipped to avoid the attention that so often falls on her lap – an echo of her father.

'Had a good time, have we?' Dad asks Jamie, who slides into the seat, nudging Kenny with his elbow and signalling him to pass the wine as Roddy pours Jamie a glass of water and hands it to him. Dad rises from his seat. 'Beer?' he offers Jamie.

'Cheers, Pops,' Jamie replies, taking a polite sip of the water his uncle has handed him.

Kenny shrugs and tips the glass of red he has just poured Jamie into his own. I smile at Dad as he leaves the room; he's always been like this, always laying out boundaries to keep us safe but not restricted. He could see that Jamie embarking on red wine after he's already been down the pub would not be wise, but he also recognised that Jamie wouldn't want water *just yet*.

'I saw Uncle Cole in the pub, he says to say hi.'

I glance in Mum's direction, the raise of her eyebrows issuing questions: *Are you speaking to him? Is he any better?* I meet her eyes and give my head the minutest of shakes, then clear my throat.

'How was he?' I ask, as Jamie reaches over and loads his plate up with chilli and rice; I scoop up some cheese with a spoon and sprinkle it over my chilli. Jamie hesitates, the spoon balancing over his plate for a split second before he plummets it back into the serving bowl.

'He was OK. He'd had a few, though!'

I can almost see the image running through Jamie's mind: Cole's tattooed arms, his chin-length dark curls, his dimpled smile and lovable warm welcome. I imagine his arm thrown around Jamie's shoulders, an unlit roll-up between his fingers, his loud voice introducing him to the bar as his nephew even though there is no blood bond between them; I can smell the alcoholic haze that is never far away from him. An unattached, or more often than not, *attached* woman is invariably on his arm; for all Cole's problems, they still fall under his spell, attracted by his fun demeanour, his soft heart.

'He gave me a twenty to take with me.' Jamie's voice brings me back. 'Said not to tell Dad.' He winces as he says the words. 'Where *is* Dad?' he asks me, reaching over and dolloping a mound of sour cream at the edge of his plate along with a mountain of tortilla chips.

'Shit!' I shovel a few mouthfuls of food into my mouth, stand, and swallow down a glass of water. I glance at the cuckoo clock, which still ejects an arthritic cuckoo every hour, the croak and grind of the cogs refusing to step down. I'm late, as usual.

Chapter Two

Then

31st October 1999

The air around Will was hot, bubbling, simmering with emotion. His hair was damp against his forehead, his body in the single bed twisting and turning while the sheets billowed out from the mattress only to be sucked in again: sails fighting against a storm. Beneath the brown arc of his eyebrows and obscured by his pale eyelids, Will's eyes darted left and right.

The dream Will found himself trapped in was almost picturesque in setting. The day was warm, the sun just rising; a few white clouds skimmed across the blushing sky, ivory silk over creamy peach skin. Below, a river hurried onwards, gurgling, chattering excitedly, moving forward to its next destination.

An eight-year-old version of his brother, Jack, was reaching out to him from the river bank, kneeling beside the water, blue shorts, dirty knees, green-and-red-striped top, copper hair. But Will was in the centre of the river, the water shouting in his ears: come with us, come with us, come with us. Will pushed his legs harder; he kicked and pummelled against the current, against the sheets, fighting to keep his head above the water as it washed over him.

I'm coming, Will was trying to say to his brother, but the river became even more excited and doubled its effort, rushing inside his mouth. The weight of it filled him, and his fit, agile body began to tire, his jeans and T-shirt wrapping around him like chains, his body becoming heavy with their dead weight. The sunlight above coated the surface of the water with golds and silvers and as Will's head slipped beneath the surface, he could see the metallic light above, his long fingers grasping and reaching upwards as he tried to fight against the browns and greens that were holding his hair around his head, pulling each lock away from his scalp, stretching his limbs away from his body, suspended. The dirt beneath him shifted and stirred, a monster awakening from its slumber, yawning and opening his mouth wide. Will found himself being drawn deeper into the water, sucked in, swallowed further into the darkness that was below him. Will tried to call out again; no sound came out in his dream, but beneath the sheets, a strangled cry escaped his mouth. The light from the river's surface became further and further from his reach, the golds and silvers growing mute, tarnished into bronze and pewter; his mouth filled with silt, thick and cloying in his throat. His feet hit the bottom of the riverbed, and for a moment, hope bloomed in his chest – he might be able to push himself back up to the surface – but he hadn't seen the monster's wide jaws.

Will gasped and sat up. The remains of his bedsheets stuck to his skin, sweat running down his spine and across his top lip. His feet kicked them off, tears stinging his pale blue eyes as reality came crashing down. The red digits on his alarm clock read seven-thirty. Will swung his legs over the side of the bed, his head in his hands, his elbows on his knees, the heat of the dream clinging to his skin.

Outside the bedroom window, rain sprayed against the pane like a thousand fingernails tapping. Will squinted up at the blue curtains, his heart still beating hard inside his ribs. He climbed off his bed, bare feet warm against the cool laminate flooring, and opened the window, letting the rain pelt against his face, cooling the heat of his golden skin. His blond hair was wet within moments; he pushed it back from his face and tilted his chin towards the sky, closing his eyes and letting the water pound against his eyelids, fall from his eyelashes, run along the tip of his straight nose and into his mouth. Will's nineteen-year-old chest slowed; the heat from his dream seeping away as he closed the window, his breathing now calm as he listened to the sound of his house.

Silence hammered against the bedroom door.

Beneath Will's bedroom, Will's mother was standing staring at the lounge wall where her sons' and husband's faces smiled back at her, her husband's smile frozen in time after a heart attack two years ago, just a year before she lost her younger son. The kettle had boiled and there were four cups waiting on the side, each with a redundant tea bag sitting in it, the tea now thick and stagnant, waiting for milk and sugar.

Back in the bedroom, Will forced his fists into his eye sockets. He was all too aware that when he went downstairs, his mother would smile at him, rouse herself from wherever it was that she went when she stared at the photos of Jack, perpetually eight years old. She'd offer to make Will breakfast. He'd decline, but she would insist: a young man like Will needed a good breakfast. But the toast would go hard and cold in the toaster, and she'd return to the lounge with the smiles on the wall.

Will showered, threw on some clothes and walked downstairs.

Gwendoline Roberts stood with her back to her son. Her white cardigan hung from her shoulders as she gazed at the four fixed smiles on the wall: white, bobbed hair brushed and sprayed into place, straight back, face made up with pale powder and red lipstick that she blotted against a piece of tissue.

The sight of those lips imprinted on the tissue would be one of the memories that haunted Will in time to come.

Will trod quietly into the kitchen, tipped the tea down the sink and washed up the cups. His stomach growled and he opened the cupboard, took out a loaf of bread, checked its sell-by date and slid the last two pieces into the toaster rack, re-boiling the kettle to make a fresh cup of tea.

'Mum?' He placed the tea and toast onto the coffee table, twisted off the lid from the capsule, retrieved the two anti-depressants and put them next to the breakfast.

'Oh, hello, darling, I didn't hear you get up. Let me get you some breakfast, a young man like you.'

'I've already had mine, I made extra, though . . .'

'Oh, you are a darling.' She patted Will's cheek with a soft touch, smiled and shook her head proudly – such good-looking boys, her sons – and returned her focus to the wall.

'Mum?'

'Hmmm? Sorry, darling, I'm in a world of my own. Do you need some breakfast?'

'No, I'm not hungry.'

'Nonsense! Young man like yourself . . .'

'I'm off out now, Mum.'

'OK, darling, but make sure you're home for tea!' she called out as Will shoved his feet into his boots, pulled on his leather jacket, and closed the door behind him. He knew that 'tea' would be an open bag of potatoes half-peeled, cut into chip shapes, and four eggs cracked into a bowl: scrambled eggs, chips and beans, Jack's favourite.

Across town, Ella Walker rolled over, kicked off her duvet and reached for the glass of water beside her bed, replaying the memories from the night before. She tried to piece together the image of the woman she thought she'd seen: red scarf, green coat and the words echoing around her as the woman spoke. She was so sure that she had been real, but as her head thudded from the gin, from lack of sleep and the embarrassment of having passed out in front of Will Roberts, of all people, she decided that her memories of the night were sketchy at best. Ella couldn't help but smile as she began to piece together parts of the conversation from their walk home; she had some recollection of saying it felt like there was a woodpecker trapped inside her head. 'Did you know, every time a woodpecker's beak hits a tree, its head is put through one thousand times the force of gravity?' he'd asked. Her eyes had widened as she took in the way he blushed as he spoke. 'Sorry, I say stupid shit when I'm nervous.' Ella groaned; she was fairly sure she'd thrown up shortly after that, which would undoubtedly have killed the mood.

Downstairs, she could hear the usual hubbub of her family: her mum singing in the shower, the sound of the radio in the kitchen. She climbed out of bed. Sugar. That was what she needed. Ella made her way to the kitchen, opened the cupboard, reached for a French fancy and unwrapped the pink fondant, and then headed back upstairs, questioning why she didn't eat cake for breakfast every day.

Will had sat with his legs straddling his stationary motor-bike for the past half an hour, unsure of where to go as he replayed the previous night, shaking his head at the whole woodpecker conversation and wondering why he'd thought reeling off some ridiculous facts would impress her. From behind the visor of his blue helmet, Will looked on as neighbours filed out of their doors with smiles and shielded eyes from behind the box-straight hedges and immaculate lawns.

His leather gloves turned the key; he slipped it into neutral and pulled the clutch with his fingers, the same action that he and Jack would use to brake when they sped down Brattan Lane on their BMXs. He pushed the starter button and felt the bike come to life beneath him.

Before Will's father died, Will had told them over dinner that he wanted to get a bike.

'And just how do you expect to buy one of those?' Gwendoline had asked, pouring thick gravy over roast potatoes.

'I'll save up,' sixteen-year-old Will had replied through a mouthful of chicken. 'From my Saturday job in the music shop.' Gwen had met Jeremy Roberts' eyes, amusement playing in the corner of her mouth, a look that meant it would take Will over a decade to save up the money, that there was no real threat. But a few days later, Jeremy had sat Will down, grey beard, half-moon glasses, and said, 'Son, a motorbike might sound like the best option for a young man your age, but let me show you something.' It was a risk assessment: Will would be thirty-four times more likely to die in a motorcycle accident than any other form of transport. With reluctance, Will agreed that getting a nice reliable Nissan would be a better course of action.

Nine months after this conversation, Jeremy Roberts had been putting his laundry in the washing machine when he gripped his chest and collapsed, a fabric softener bottle falling from his hand, dying of a heart attack, a man who rarely ate red meat, who only drank a glass of wine with lunch on a Sunday afternoon and who jogged every day.

Will bought his blue and silver bike with his inheritance the day he turned eighteen. It was only a 125 Yamaha. But soon, he would upgrade, and for the rest of his adult life he would ride a motorbike as his main source of transportation, the red Nissan Qashqai reserved for date nights, shopping days and family outings.

The bike spluttered into life and Will left the estate. He

had no direction in mind; he just wanted to clear his thoughts. The road led him onwards, brown leaves falling from the trees, mud splattering upwards, puddles parting as he passed. Some traffic lights slowed him down; others let him continue. Will passed Cole's house, and he signalled left, turning into the road where he'd walked Ella home last night.

At the time Will's bike passed Cole's house, Cole was staring into a mirror.

The mirror in question hung at a slant on his bedroom wall. It had been there most of Cole's life; it covered a missing piece of the pale-blue painted woodchip paper behind it. There was a hairline crack that split the surface in two; the bottom corner was chipped, the surface mottled in the top right corner. The reflection showed that Cole's eyes were bloodshot, his face pallid and glazed with sweat as the alcohol from the night before escaped his pores.

He replayed the way Ella had looked at Will, the lingering hope he'd felt as she stared at him across the fire. Tears filled Cole's bloodshot eyes, frustration making his fists clench. He'd waited too long, he'd been a coward, and now it was too late. His fingernails dug deeper into his fist as he pulled his hand back, staring at his own reflection with disgust, acknowledging what he knew already: he was a failure. His fist pulled back and in a fraction of a second, it flew through the air.

If you slowed this moment down, you would have witnessed how the dust motes were scattered, dispersed, the air between Cole and the mirror displaced. You would have seen his knuckles connecting with the surface, a shockwave imploding the glass, the impact held tightly in a spiderweb of shards, held still in the tiniest fraction of time before the glass could no longer hold the frail structure in place; the pieces were too small, his reflection too fractured, and so the spiderweb disintegrated, and the silver light fell onto the brown carpet, the decade-old swirls of beige dulling it on impact.

But this didn't happen in slow motion; instead there was a flash of skin on glass, of pain and noise, holding perfect symmetry.

As Cole made his way into the bathroom and ran his hand beneath the tap, just a few doors down the street, Will's engine idled beside the road.

Will knew the estate well; Cole, Jack, Will and Tom used to play kerby just down the road in the cul-de-sac by the row of garages. They would stand on opposite kerbs, throwing the ball: if it bounced back towards them from the kerb and they caught it, they could step into the middle of the road and count points every time the ball hit the kerb; Ella would shout the word 'car!' in warning when their game was about to be interrupted. She was always there, hovering on the outside of the group like Cole's shadow.

Will glanced up at Ella's house, switched off the engine and looked towards the skyline. The houses along the street were all the same, semi-detached, 1930s ex-council. From the front they were neat, a row of two bedrooms above a front door and a large rectangular lounge window. Cole's house was the same. Before Jack died, Will had spent more time at Cole's house than he did in his own. The two boys were reflections of each other, Will's blond hair to Cole's brown, Will's sensibility to Cole's recklessness, the yin and yang. Perhaps that was why they became so unbalanced, one without the other: light scorches and dark devours. Cole's house was untidy and the rooms all needed redecorating but there was always junk food in the cupboard, and they were free to play on the PlayStation or watch horror films whenever they pleased.

From Will's view as Ella had swayed up the path last night, he concluded that her interior would be laid out in the same design: hallway, staircase to the left, kitchen ahead, lounge to the right, bathroom at the top of the stairs, three bedrooms leading off the landing.

Will was correct in his assumptions and as he contemplated this, the black roller blind at the left window was drawn up, a pale arm pushing open the window.

Ella's head leant out, turned towards the sun, her smile wide and full. A gust of wind tumbled towards her, blowing her hair around her head, *like flames*, Will observed. He took off his helmet, hooked it over the handlebars and studied Ella as she faced the sun, her eyes still closed, the beauty spot deepening as she continued to smile. When he'd first noticed it, he'd questioned whether she had drawn it on herself.

Will's face broke into a grin; the pure joy on Ella's was infectious. Ella's eyes flashed open, the smile still there, her gaze landing on Will. 'Hi!' she shouted, leaning forward slowly. Will raised his hand, hesitant, unsure of how she might react to finding him sitting outside her house; she tucked her hair behind her ear self-consciously and met his eyes. 'You hungry?' she shouted again.

This was an unexpected response and Will was thrown momentarily. Will pictured the cold toast and the anti-depressants sitting at home and cleared his throat, finding the idea of shouting uncomfortable, so instead nodded with an 'I could eat' expression.

'Give me a sec!' Ella disappeared, Will just catching the edge of a grin as she ducked away.

Will parked up his bike, contemplated how long a 'sec' was as he ran his fingers through his hair, smoothed down his top and opened the latch on the small gate. He took a deep breath as he walked up the path, raising his hand to knock on the door.

It flew open, Ella standing on the other side, her hair pulled into a bun on top of her head, a few flame-red locks hanging around her face.

'Hi,' she greeted him, beaming.

'Um, hi.' Blood fanned across Will's cheeks. 'I just wanted to check you're OK?'

She reached for the small bruise at her right cheekbone, then dropped to where her bottom lip held a slight swell. 'I'm fine. Thank you . . . for bringing me home. I bet that was just the *highlight* of your year, me stumbling all over the place, puking in next door's rhododendrons.' She winced.

Will wanted to tell Ella that actually, walking her home last night *had* been the highlight of his year.

'Is this him?' A woman, tall, large eyes, auburn hair came striding out of the lounge. Ella nodded and mouthed sorry at him. 'Will! The last time I saw you, you were only a little lad – goodness, haven't you grown into a looker?' Susan Walker stepped past Ella and drew Will into an unexpected hug, then put her hands on his shoulders and appraised him, keeping her focus directly on his eyes. Will leant himself away, finding her scrutiny and close proximity uncomfortable. 'Bill!' she shouted over her shoulder. 'Will is here! Will, we are so grateful to you, thank you for taking care of our girl last night. Pissed as a fart, she was.'

'Will?' Bill Walker stepped out of the kitchen, the smell of bacon and fried bread following closely. 'Well, don't just leave him on the doorstep! Let him in!' Bill departed but then popped his head back through the door. 'Fried or scrambled, Will?'

'Sorry?'

Ella took Will's helmet from his hands and placed it on the stairs while his jacket was dispatched from his shoulders by Susan.

'Your eggs? How do you take them?'

'Eggs?'

'Eggs! Fried, scrambled, poached?'

Will pictured the bowl with the eggs which would be waiting for him on his return. 'Oh, I, well . . . fried. Please.'

'Right oh, sir!'

And that is how Will found himself suddenly part of the Walker family.

Chapter Three

Now

Ella

9th September 2022

The rubber of my black boots hurries along the buffed and polished school corridors towards the music department. One of my insteps is slightly more worn than the other, adding an uneven thud-squeak-thud-squeak beat like the beginnings of a *High School Musical* scene. I imagine a backup troupe of red-lipped land girls striding behind me, fingers clicking, leaning forward at the waist, following my progress as I push open the double doors with a Pow! Like Beyoncé. But all that follows me is the slight aftertaste of Bunsen burner gas and magnesium as I hurry past the science department. I hurry on; Will's last appointment finished about half an hour ago.

My hand hesitates on the stainless-steel panel of the double doors to the music section; there are still parents sitting outside Will's classroom. I catch my breath, noticing as I do that I have a large reddish-brown chilli stain on the front of my dungarees, right above my left boob. *Perfect.*

I retrace my steps and head into the girls' loos. I pump the soap dispenser and grab a paper towel, white and soft, not green and rough, but the stain is stubborn and all it does is

31

make me look like I'm lactating. I turn off the tap and bin the towel, returning to the mirror. I take off my red headscarf, Amira's idea of a 'look', a 'brand' for our shop . . . land girl meets vintage chick? Or chic? Amira has lots of strong ideas about branding and image; she has mood boards and *everything*. I consider pocketing the scarf, but then look at my greasy roots; my hair is desperately in need of a cut and some highlights and so fix it back in place. I pinch my cheeks like an actual land girl and exit the loos in search of my husband.

I can see Will through the windows, his head thrown back in laughter at the father and son in front of his desk. I'm always struck by his presence: even after all these years, Will emits something, some kind of energy, some special essence, that the rest of us mortals just don't possess. He doesn't see it, he never has: he finds the interest he receives uncomfortable; I can see him shrink inside himself sometimes when he becomes the focus of a conversation, when he becomes the centre of attention. The only time I have ever seen him comfortable with it was when he was younger, when he sat behind his guitar. I'm no psychologist, but it doesn't take a genius to work out that the guitar acted as a shield, that Will found protection in the way it covered him, allowed him to be somebody else; but my God . . . the way he used to look when he played.

There are still two sets of parents, yummy mummies fringed by their protégés: same designer clothing, the same privileged posture being passed on like hand-me-downs, the mothers leaning towards each other, gossip spoon-fed into each other's eager mouths, their daughters' heads both dipped towards their iPhones, one honey blonde, the other smooth chestnut. My husband looks up and sees me as I wave. He glances at the clock discreetly as the father pumps his hand. Will follows them towards the door, catching my eye through the glass partition, mouthing 'sorry' to me. I smile back, no problem, and lift an imaginary cup and wiggle it; he nods a yes please, his knees sagging in an amateur dramatic display of exhaustion – I envision Marley's ghost, only with school reports and exercise books trailing behind him. I snort loudly, making the gossiping mothers glance up, both giving my outfit a keen eyes-up-and-down assessment, both noticing the chilli lactation stain with a derogatory twitch of their mouths.

The classroom door opens, the father and son stepping into the corridor with more laughter. The father is medium build, scruffy around the edges, loud and unashamedly proud of his son, who looks comfortable beneath the pride of his father. They are around the same height; the boy's face is pimpled with spots, but he has a kind smile below his glasses – he reminds me a little of Kenny at that age.

'Thanks again, Mr Roberts,' the father is saying. 'Honestly, you worked wonders with this boy of mine last year, we were so glad to hear you're still his teacher this year.' The boy in question flushes red as he glances towards the honey-blonde iPhone girl. My heart breaks a little for him as she looks up, her expression changing from mildly amused at whatever she is watching, to disgust as she meets the boy's eyes. Her eyebrows raise and she looks away from him towards smooth chestnut girl; I can practically hear the words 'As *if*' firing behind her as her focus is pulled back towards the boy's flushed face, his obvious discomfort going unnoticed by his father, who is still talking proudly to Will.

'Ah, well . . .' Will replies, 'the benefit of a small school. I get to work with this bunch for another year.'

I wonder how the honey blonde will feel when she looks back on this moment, when she's forty with children of her own. Will she remember the hurt in his eyes, feel a pang of guilt at the way she treated him? Will she wish that she could change her actions? Or carry on with her life, regretting nothing?

At the sight of Will, the spoon-fed gossip pauses; their heads tilt up, lips part slightly, eyes brighten. This isn't something new to me; even now that Will is approaching forty-two, he still pulls the eyes of the popular girls in the same way as he did at school.

'Becca? Do you want to come through?' Will says to the chestnut-haired girl, her mother standing and following with an arse the size of a walnut.

I bite down the pride I feel at the women's reaction to my husband, and head off in search of the coffee machine in the canteen, returning with a cup in one hand and a tentative knock on Will's classroom door with the other. Only one iPhone girl is remaining, the mother nowhere in sight. Inside Will's classroom, Becca slouches in her chair, the mother leaning forward towards the desk, smiling demurely as Will talks about the up-and-coming project and Becca's part in it.

'Hi!' I whisper, turning to the mother and daughter as I sidestep past. 'Sorry to interrupt,' I whisper again, placing the coffee on the desk. 'I'm just . . .' I nod to the coffee as it lands on Will's desk . . .'Mr Roberts can get quite grumpy without his caffeine!'

'Thanks, Ella.' Will smiles up at me. The woman's eyebrows knit together, a perfectly placed pucker between her immaculately shaped eyebrows, irritated at my interruption. I smile back and for some unexplained reason begin walking backwards from the desk in some sort of exaggerated pantomime: a court jester exiting the throne room without turning his back on the queen. Will clears his throat, wearing a quizzical *What are you doing?* expression. I shrug my shoulders. *I have no idea.* I nod my head towards the chairs in the corridor, conveying to him that I'll wait outside.

I close the door quietly, give a polite smile to the yummy mummy opposite, who has now returned with a fresh coat of lipstick, fold into a spare chair, and pull out my phone, scanning my inbox for orders and special requests. Occasionally, we will have an attentive partner who will want to include a specific flower into one of our standard bouquets. There is a particularly sweet request from an octogenarian ordering a bouquet for his wife's birthday, asking for a Ballerina Rose as she was a dancer when she was younger. I smile at the sentiment, glancing up at the sound of Will's voice getting closer. The woman opposite me, I notice, has also brushed her hair. I chew the corner of my lip, biting down the humour there.

'So . . .' She smiles brightly to her honey-blonde progeny. 'Mr Roberts . . .'

'Yeah? What about him?'

'Well, is there anything I need to ask him? About your progress?' She shifts her perky chest upwards.

'Nope.' The fingers tap on her phone screen and she sighs. Will's voice carries closer to the door and the mother's neck stretches; she reminds me of a meerkat. Her daughter's attention is drawn from her phone screen as she takes in her mother's hand pulling down her top a little.

'Oh, please don't be weird, Mum.'

'I'm not being weird.'

'Please don't do that hair flick, giggly thing you did with Mr Tomlinson.'

'I was laughing at his joke, I was being polite.'

'It was a physics joke, you don't even know what Schrödinger's cat is.'

I smirk at the irony as the door opens. Will's head is dipped, a sure sign that he feels uncomfortable.

'Seriously, Mum, don't,' the girl hisses. 'Mr Roberts is cool. Anyway, I think he's married.'

'Happily?' she asks.

'Mum!' her daughter warns as the door opens. You'd

think I'd be hurt that this conversation is happening with me right in full view of the mother with the pert boobs, but I'm not unused to the surprise on people's faces when I'm introduced as Will's wife. I'm neither surprised nor offended that she has discounted me as just another parent, and one not even worthy of forced polite conversation, it seems.

'You don't look old enough to have a daughter in university!' The conversation comes from the opening door. Will gives Walnut Arse a tight but polite smile.

'Ah, well, we started young.' He meets her eyes, fleetingly turning his attention to her daughter. 'Keep up the practising, Becca.' He smiles genuinely at the daughter as she squeezes past her mum, giving her friend a look that reads as *Oh my God why does she have to be so embarrassing?* The blonde rolls her eyes and inclines her head to her own mother: *I know, right?*

Reluctantly, the mother departs, throwing Will a smile over her shoulder and meeting her gossiping friend's eyes with a secretive smirk.

'Lizzie?' Will smiles at the honey blonde, her mother standing and offering her hand to Will. Awkwardly he accepts it, his other hand still holding the door open.

'And you must be Mrs Lloyd?' Will asks Perky Tits.

'Miss,' she corrects thrusting her hand into his. He shakes it, glancing at me, a look of guilt crossing his features even though he has nothing to feel guilty about – it's just the way things are. I flutter my eyelids at him good-naturedly, letting him know that I'm not bothered.

'I won't be long,' Will says.

'No hurry, I've got a few emails to answer.' I give him my smile, the smile he used to tell me he pictured when he couldn't sleep through the pain in his hand. 'I've saved you some chilli,' I add. Perky Tits hesitates, looking at me with fresh eyes; they widen and give me a once-over, from my boots to my stained dungarees and headscarf. Her expression isn't hostile, or jealous; I can't quite interpret the meaning.

'Great, I'm *starving*.' Will turns to Perky Tits and gestures towards the desk. 'Sorry about that, my long-suffering wife,' he says by explanation as the door closes softly behind him, but not before she gives me a look over her shoulder that I still can't quite place.

After losing myself in my inbox for a while, I stand as the door opens again and the three of them exit among praise for Lizzie's efforts and promises of a supporting letter for her application to the London School of Music. I smile politely as we say our goodbyes, sliding my arm around his waist as the doors swing behind *Miss* Lloyd.

'Long day?' My cheek is against his shirt; I close my eyes briefly and breathe him in before pulling back and looking up.

'Remind me again why I decided to be a teacher?' he asks, his bright voice sliding into a groan.

'Because you love shaping young minds?' I ask as he extracts himself from my arms and makes his way to his desk, reaching across and turning off his monitor. I follow him and perch on the end of his desk as he begins to clear a few things away.

'Maybe I should have trained as a dentist?' He bends, putting some paperwork away inside his desk drawer. 'Or a vet?'

'Do I need to remind you of our failed attempts at keeping hamsters alive?'

'Good point.'

'Although you would look hot in a set of scrubs.'

'Those blue paper things?' He pauses his movement. 'Really?' He stands; I shuffle forward. 'Maybe we could test the theory and order some off Amazon.'

I reach for his tie and pull him towards me. He carefully pulls his tie away and continues the conversation, making his way to a stray Casio keyboard and locking it in a cupboard. I sigh.

'Stockbroker?' he asks.

'Too stressful.' I hop off the desk and wander over to the display on the far wall, my fingers reaching for a ukulele.

'Explorer?'

'Spiders,' I counter. He shudders as he locks the key to the instrument cupboard away in his desk drawer and reaches for his coffee cup, draining the rest.

'Chef?'

'Now you're being ridiculous.' Will is an awful cook, even though he tries his best. He grabs his coat from the back of his chair. 'So . . .' I take a breath. 'Did Perky Tits leave you her number?'

He laughs. 'Perky Tits? Lizzie's mum?'

'Yep.' I meet his eyes, raising my eyebrow.

'Not that I noticed, although . . .' he holds his chin in contemplation, 'I could just get it from the school records.'

'Ha, ha.' I pause, my voice becoming more serious. 'Did she?' I ask again.

'Now who's being ridiculous?'

'She was all but licking your face as you held the door open.' I look over my shoulder at him demurely and put on a deep sexy voice: 'Missssss . . .' I turn, holding out my hand as if to be kissed, 'Lloyd.'

Will shakes his head at me. 'She wasn't that bad.'

He flicks off the lights one by one and holds the door open for me. I go to slip my hand in his but find his laptop case is clasped in there instead.

'Jamie's had a few down the pub,' I say as we step through the next set of double doors.

'He's driving to Leicester tomorrow!'

'Oh, shush, he's stuffing his face at Mum's, and you and I know he won't leave until late.' Jamie has always been disorganised; there *are* some things my children have inherited from me. 'I bet he'll be asleep on the sofa by the time we get there.'

'Shit.' Will taps his pockets. 'I've forgotten my fob. Wait here, I'll go back and get it.'

'I'll come with you.' I turn.

'I'll be quicker on my own, just wait for me in reception. Sorry,' he says, before taking long, determined strides along the corridor.

I head to reception, stare at the vending machine and decide to grab Will a packet of Munchies, his favourite, with the pound coin in my pocket left over from the shopping trolley. I stab the code in and wait for the metal to rotate enough to deposit my chocolate, but it seems to be one circumference short, the packet hanging tantalisingly close to falling from the bottom row of confectionery.

Bugger.

I kneel down, align my body along the side of the machine and push my hand through the flap at the bottom. I'm fairly sure if I stretch a little further, I'll be able to catch the end of the packet, but I can't quite get there. The reception is hot, and I can feel my face flushing with the effort, but it's almost within reach. I give a little grunt of energy, my fingers stretching as far as they can, my shoulder jammed up against the base of the machine.

In a moment of what can only be described as genius, I retract my hand, unwrap my headscarf and reposition myself, now trying to loop the material over the chocolate with a Frisbee throwing motion.

Success!

My tongue pokes out of the corner of my mouth as I pull the end of the scarf, the tube of chocolates inching forward.

Behind me, voices drift into the reception. I recognise Perky Tits and Walnut Arse following their daughters towards the exit, but in my almost prone position in the corner of reception, I haven't drawn their attention.

'I mean, good God, he could be a doctor in *Grey's Anatomy*, couldn't he? Those steely blue eyes. He could be McSteely.' Miss Lloyd giggles as I hold my breath. 'And did you see his wife?'

'No!' The other voice is aghast. 'Where was she?'

'She was the one in the dungarees, the Gwen Stefani wannabe,' she laughs.

'No! I thought she was the *cleaner*.'

'I *know* . . .'

I keep my head down as they make their progress towards the automatic doors.

'Mum, please can we grab a Starbucks on the way home? I will actually *die* if I don't have a caramel frappe.'

'Darling,' she says conspiratorially to her friend, 'you can have as many frappes as you want if you get Mr Roberts' number for me.'

'I heard that, Mum, you're disgusting.'

I give the chocolate an angry pull, landing it in the chute with a clatter. Miss Lloyd turns her head. Without the headscarf, and with my body crouching down, it seems to take her a moment to place me.

I stand, feeling my cheeks warm with embarrassment as Will comes through the doors. Miss Lloyd flashes him a quick look, before meeting my eyes with the same expression that I hadn't been able to place earlier.

'Ready?' Will asks a little breathlessly. Miss Lloyd and her entourage escape through the automatic doors.

'Yes, I was just getting you some Munchies.'

'Munchies?' I offer him the battered-looking tube. 'Thanks.'

'You've just missed *Miss* Lloyd . . . she was talking about you,' I say as we leave the building and cross the carpark. 'She said you could be one of the doctors in *Grey's Anatomy*, all steely-blue-eyed.'

'What does that even mean?' he asks as I point the keys towards our red Qashqai.

'That she wants you to give her an examination, I expect.'

We climb into the car, both of us pulling on our seatbelts as the radio blares out of the speakers. Will turns it down.

'What else did she say?'

'Nothing really,' I reply, pulling out of the junction.

It's as I lie next to my husband later that night, his back turned away from me, that I understand the look she had given me . . . it wasn't jealousy or confusion, but sympathy.

She could see what I had, that it was slipping away, and how much it would hurt if I lost it.

Chapter Four

Then

31st October 1999

The Walker family kitchen was warm, the windows fogged with steam, the radio playing in the background and the table covered in plates laden with a full English breakfast. To Will's right, Ella's brother Kenny was peppering Roddy's breakfast while Roddy was distracted by pouring a glass of juice. Moments later, while Kenny was distracted as he reached for more toast, Roddy dropped a mushroom to the bottom of Kenny's orange juice.

Across from Will sat Ella; she was eating heartily, her stomach recovered from its evacuation the previous night.

Soon, Will would discover that it was unusual for Ella to eat a cooked breakfast, because Ella preferred to eat cake for breakfast. 'Why do we always wait until later in the day to eat the best food?' she would question Will. She'd be wearing his burgundy The Smiths T-shirt, the neck slipping over her shoulder; her legs tanned, her natural hair colour lightened by the French sun. They would be sitting in a small French apartment, the broken shutters of the windows wide open, the plaster peeling from the walls, rich coffee resting beside the mattress on the floor. A slow smile would cross his face as he watched her take a bite out of a lavender-coloured macaron, puffs of lilac sugar falling from her mouth, her face a picture of concentration as she tried to decipher the different flavours. Her hair would be in a messy plait, hanging over her shoulders, when he told her he loved her, the words falling from his mouth as Ella's eyes flashed open. And when she sat on top of him on that summer morning in a small French town, her kisses would taste of soft sugar, of the lavender in the French hills, and he would think this is it, this is the life I want to give her, a life filled with warmth, sun, cakes for breakfast and the whole world outside waiting to meet her.

But in the Walkers' kitchen, Ella was taking surreptitious glances at Will, like a bird nipping at seed, her eyes glancing up at him then back down to her plate.

Will watched the scene before him with a look of shock and confusion. He didn't know how it had happened, how one minute he'd been taking his bike out for a ride and then the next he had ended up around this table, shoulder to shoulder with men throwing jokes at each other and passing sauce across his plate.

'So, Will . . .' Susan topped up Will's glass with orange juice, 'what are your plans now you've finished sixth form? You're a year above Ella, that's right, isn't it?'

'Mum!' Blood flushed Ella's cheeks.

'What?' Susan Walker turned to her daughter.

'I, I, haven't decided yet,' Will answered.

'Plenty of time for that yet, isn't there, Will?' Bill winked in his direction. The familiarity of this family was overwhelming for Will and he found himself questioning his every answer, his every move. His attraction to Ella kept taking him by surprise; even knowing full well that he was surrounded by Ella's fiercest protectors, he couldn't help meeting her eyes, couldn't help looking over at her.

In the past, Ella had always been 'one of the lads', always

had bruised knees and scrapes from climbing trees, more often than not from following Cole that little bit higher than the rest of the group. Will's memories of Ella never saw her in the centre of their group; she was just *around* . . . as though she was Cole's little sister. He had never really understood their relationship – after all, Ella had two older brothers of her own – but knew that it was something to do with their mothers being friends.

Will was correct about this fact. Susan and Deb Chapel were friends. It was the Walkers' door that Deb had knocked on when Cole's father cracked her rib; it was Ella's bedroom that Cole had shared when Ella was five and he was six and Deb had left the house with a split lip and Cole with a broken arm. But Will didn't know this . . . not yet.

On the days Ella had joined them, Will recalled that Cole and Ella would often arrive together, a ball under an arm, sharing a packet of pick and mix from the corner shop. Even back then, Will was aware that Ella didn't hang around with the popular girls on the swings, the ones sucking lollipops and waiting for the attention from the boys kicking a ball around on the field. It was the same in Will's last year of sixth form: Ella tended to walk the corridors alone, head-phones on, green canvas bag on her shoulder, band names and logos written on in black pen, an art case in her hand.

Will hadn't ever really given much attention to Ella, but over the last year of A-levels, he had noticed her with more regularity. He noticed the way she walked, with a kind of boyish stride; he noticed the curve of her neck and the pale brown birthmark at the top of her spine, how it resembled an ink blot. When he sat behind her in the canteen, he would sometimes think it looked like a snowflake, other days the sun; she was his own personal Rorschach test. And he noticed when she smiled, how her entire face changed: to say her face lit up wasn't enough; it was as though his whole world was illuminated. But most of all, Will noticed how *good* she was. She would pick up a dropped piece of paper and pass it back to someone, she would comment on how nice someone looked that day, she would ask if they were feeling better, she would comment on the teacher's desk photos, how cute their dog was . . . Ella was just good, funny, *happy*. Everything, Will knew, he wasn't.

Girls tended to make Will uncomfortable. Somewhere between the beginning of secondary school and year ten, girls started paying him a lot of attention. This was a huge cause of confusion for Will: he was aware that he wasn't funny like Cole, he wasn't particularly good at contact sports; instead he ran, and yes he played the guitar, but he played classical music – he was all too aware that he wasn't Kurt Cobain. And when Will received this attention, he often found that his words became stuck somewhere between his throat and his teeth.

And after Jack died, the words slunk even further away.

The girls in school couldn't help but notice Will: he was taller than most of the boys his age, broader, and his hair always fell pleasingly into his eyes; his skin was clear, always slightly golden and sun-kissed. They saw Will as mysterious, aloof, *mature*. They acknowledged that he was quiet, but when Will did speak to them, when he found the words, they were often considered, kind, clever, *deep*. And once news got out about the accident, well . . . that made him the topic of many a teenage girl's poetry assignment.

Will's friends jostled him, envied him, admired him, resented him and loved him.

'You play the guitar?' Bill asked, snatching the pepper away from Kenny. Will blinked, brought back to the table. He nodded, a little unsure, wondering how much Ella had told them about him in the small space of time between last night and this morning.

'Like an aiiiiiin-gel . . .' Kenny fluttered his eyelashes and twirled his imaginary hair. 'Ouch!' he bent down to rub his leg beneath the table where Ella's foot had just connected with his shin.

'Um, yeah, yeah I do.'

'And you work at the shop in town?' Susan asked, reaching for the ketchup. Ella's face was turning crimson; she concentrated hard on slicing up a piece of bacon. 'Music Maestro?' Susan continued. Will nodded again. 'And Ella tells me you have a motorbike?'

Ella clattered her cutlery down next to her plate.

Will found his words. 'Yes, it's a 125 Yamaha.' He tried to meet Ella's eyes, but she seemed to be focusing on a cold piece of congealed bacon fat at the side of her plate.

'Dad had a bike.' Roddy pointed to Bill across the table. 'Didn't you, Dad?'

'I did that, I used to take your mum for a spin now and then.'

Susan reached over and held the top of her husband's hand. 'He used to take me out for picnics all over the country, didn't you?' He brought her hand to his mouth and lifted it to his lips. 'I loved that feeling, the throbbing between my thighs.'

A piece of rogue sausage became lodged in Will's throat, and he started spluttering just as Kenny discovered the piece of mushroom in his juice and erupted from his seat, chasing his brother out of the room.

Ella moved around the table, crouching down by Will's side, passing him a fresh glass of water as her parents began clearing the table behind her.

'Sorry . . .' She flinched as Mr and Mrs Walker, plates now discarded in the washing-up bowl, began slow-dancing behind her, both gazing into each other's eyes. 'Don't mind them, they're always like this.'

There was a speckle of tomato sauce on the corner of Ella's mouth, just at the edge of her lips. Will found himself transfixed by her mouth, the slight swell of her lips; instinctively, his thumb touched the corner of her mouth, wiping the sauce away.

Ella's eyebrows rose in shock. He dropped his hand quickly, registering a brief flicker of disappointment or embarrassment from Ella – or perhaps it was hope he saw there?

But Will didn't know her well enough to read her expressions yet; but in time he would. He would know when she was disappointed, by the slight pull in the inside of her cheek with her molars; when she was in pain, by the rotation of her right shoulder; when she had a migraine, in the swelling of her eyelids; and he would know that the only way she would get better would be with an icepack, and one ibuprofen – not two – in a dark room with sounds of the ocean playing on her old CD player that she refused to replace with an Echo Dot.

Each part of his life with Ella would fit together, each memory a piece of the jigsaw. However, now, Will had only just opened the box; an Echo Dot didn't exist yet and neither did the rest of the pieces.

Ella mirrored Will's actions, standing, shoulders rising and falling, arms hanging waiting for a decision to be made: move or stay.

'Right, well, now you're fed and watered,' she began, 'we should let you get on. Unless—'

'Oh,' Will replied. He was hit by the realisation that he didn't want to go; he didn't want to leave this house with the rich smells and loud sounds, with the condensation fogging up the window and the radio on top of the microwave playing Christina Aguilera's 'Genie in a Bottle'. Will drank in the scene around him, surveying the disarray in the kitchen.

'Erm, should I . . . help?' He gestured redundantly at the table.

'Nah, it's the twins' turn.'

She led the way out of the kitchen. Will turned and thanked Mr and Mrs Walker as Bill spun his wife outwards, Susan laughing loudly, her husband catching her back in his arms. 'Any time, Will, and thank you again for looking after Ella. We'll see you again?' She yelped and squirmed as Bill nuzzled into her neck.

'Oh, I, errrr . . . That would be lovely,' Will replied, but his words were lost as a knock at the back door to the kitchen held their attention.

Will followed Ella through the hall, a familiar voice joining the household.

While Will and Ella had been eating breakfast, Cole had showered, waited for the rust-coloured water to run clear, picked out the shards of glass from the mirror with his mum's tweezers, then rested his hand on a frozen bag of peas until the swelling subsided. He needed to know what had happened with Will when he walked Ella home. It took Cole all the strength he could muster to go to the Walkers' house: he wanted Ella to tell him that nothing had happened, that actually, Will Roberts wasn't her type after all. But deep down, Cole knew this wouldn't be the case. He loved Will. He owed Will his life.

'I don't suppose there is any bacon going? I'm hanging like a bastard.'

'Serves you right, Cole Chapel! What were you thinking giving Ella gin?!' Susan admonished. 'You know she can't handle her drink, look at the state she got into with the Babycham at Christmas!'

'Ah, move over, Billster, you know you're too old for putting the moves on the love of my life!'

Cole had been flirting with Susan Walker ever since he

had learnt that he only had to pop his dimples and grin to get an extra couple of flying saucers in his pick and mix from Mrs Turner at the corner shop. They went through the same banter most days, Cole complimenting Susan, taking the mick out of Bill.

Cole's reaction to the female species entailed an entirely different approach to Will's. He loved girls: he loved their shape, their smell, their voice. Sanjay and Tom had jokingly suggested that the whole of their year had either shagged, or wanted to shag Cole, or were in love with Will. And although this was said in jest, there was some truth in their observations.

Of course, the group had now fractured; after Jack's death, Will found it too hard to be around Cole. He still did, how could he not? Because of Cole, his brother had died.

From over Ella's shoulder, Will watched Cole from the doorstep; he'd taken over Bill's place and was tangoing Susan across the kitchen with a drooping sunflower in his mouth. Will watched as Cole tipped Susan back: she was laughing loudly; he was slightly out of breath and smirking. He pulled her back up into an upright position, released her and discarded the sunflower, sticking out his tongue and pinching the end of it. 'Ugh, remind me *never* to do that again!'

'We're out of bacon, Cole, will a sausage sarnie do the job?' Bill asked from out of Will's view.

'You're a life-saver, Billster, I can almost forgive you for keeping Susan all to yourself.'

'Behave yourself, young man.' Will looked on as Susan shook her head and Cole beamed back, his eyes sparkling, his cheeks flushed, the dimples sunk deep into the cheeks that everyone loved.

Cole's gaze flickered through the hall towards the open front door, his expression changing. It didn't quite harden, didn't fix in place, but the sparkle in his eyes clouded over, the dimples filling out when his eyes landed on Will standing on the doorstep. Straightening himself, Cole gave Will a brief nod.

From an outsider, it would have appeared like a cordial exchange; they wouldn't have known that Cole was assessing his own reaction to Will's presence at the door. That he was feeling surprised that the pain didn't cut as deeply as he expected it to. After all, that wound was already open; what difference did it make if it tore open a little more?

Will acknowledged Cole with a lift of the chin in his direction; Cole's face tightened, the laughter falling away.

'Thanks for coming.' Ella brought Will's focus back. A lock of her hair fell forward, a bright red ringlet, and all thoughts of Cole Chapel slipped away from Will's mind.

Will's fingers twitched by his side, then moved, hooking her hair between his middle and index finger. It was softer than he'd expected: the lock caught the sun, the natural blonde and browns shining through the fake red. Will realised that he was staring, and tucked it behind her ear. She flushed again and met his eyes. He opened his mouth to speak but the words wouldn't come. From over her shoulder, Will watched Cole filling the kettle, his gaze flickering up at Will, then back to the task at hand.

'See you.' Will stared down at his black boots, taking a step back.

'See you.' Ella smiled brightly, her beauty spot sinking into the curve of her cheek as she closed the door behind her.

With her back to the door, Ella sank down to the floor, groaning with her head in her hands.

'What are you waiting for?' Cole sipped his tea from the kitchen doorframe. Ella pulled her hands away, looking up at Cole, the beginnings of a smile lifting her face. 'You've already got him to meet the family. The infamous loner *Will*

Roberts has been assaulted by the Walker family and lived to tell the tale.'

'I heard that!' Susan mussed Cole's hair and tutted in his direction.

'Go,' Cole said, nodding towards the front door.

Ella clambered to her feet, ran to Cole's side, giving him a quick peck on the cheek, then yanked open the door.

Will headed along the path, the echo of the morning rolling in his mind: the way Ella's hair had felt between his fingers, Cole dancing with Susan, the familiar flirtatious relationship accepted and returned as though he was already expected to be part of the family, already *was* part of the family. The images in Will's mind stopped, froze, shut down as the sound of soft footprints chased behind him.

He turned. Ella's smiling face was flushed as her bare feet ran along the tarmac path.

'Wait! When?' She opened the gate, her eyes alight. Will stalled, once again taken aback at how beautiful she looked.

And Ella was beautiful in that moment, her eyes bright, her hair on fire, the blessing of youth pushing back the creases of time, the sun refracting around her frame.

'You said, "See you," and, and . . . I was wondering . . . when?'

Will didn't decide to kiss her.

He didn't think *I'm going to kiss this girl*; he didn't think she *could* be the one . . . he just knew she was.

Three strides, three steps, three seconds, and a new jigsaw piece emerged: Will's hands cupping her face; her soft warm lips meeting his; the sun rising behind Ella's house; her one hand gripping the material of his white shirt and the other holding the back of his hair as if she never wanted to let him go.

Will didn't know that in the future he would replay this scene: he would imagine that he let Ella down gently; he would tell her he wasn't ready for a relationship. Her face would fall, she would be upset, but he would be strong. He would get on his bike and ride away and Ella Roberts would have the life she deserved.

But he didn't get on his bike and ride away. Instead, the jigsaw piece clicked into place and their lives changed for ever.

Chapter Five

Now

Ella

10th September 2022

'Wakey-wakey, sleepy head!' I place the tray of toast and tea on the floor next to Jamie's bed and sit on the side. 'Big day today.'

Jamie groans. 'What time is it?'

'Time for you to rewrite the stars.' I smile, my fingers smoothing his fair hair from his forehead.

'Seriously?' He opens one eye and looks at me. 'You're giving me *The Greatest Showman* wisdom before I've even got out of bed?'

'This is me.' I shrug my shoulders as he groans again and pulls the duvet over his head.

'What is the actual time?' His muffled voice comes from beneath the duvet. I cast an eye over his room, clothes thrown in a gradual progression from the door to the bed, a cup of something that looks like the remains of a Cup-a-Soup next to the pile of books stacked up by the side of his bed. A nostalgic smile tugs at the corner of my mouth: Jamie has always built things, from blocks to Lego to cereal boxes, to stones . . . always building, building, building.

'Half eleven. Now go and jump in the shower – your dad wants to go through the route with you again.'

'Jesus, why can't he just trust Google Maps like everyone else? It's not like I've got to get there for a lecture, I've got a couple of weeks before term starts and my first shift at the pub isn't until next week.'

'He just doesn't want you to get lost, that's all.'

Jamie pokes his head over the top of the duvet. 'And where is the fun in that?' He grins. 'Last time I got lost, I spent a very enjoyable night with a brunette from Birmingham.' Jamie shuffles up the bed.

'Why do you insist on torturing your poor old mother with your late-night escapades?' I pass him his tea, which he slurps noisily.

'You're the one who always says—'

'You should spread your wings, I know.' I take a bite out of his toast, which he swipes from my hand with a cheeky grin. 'He's just worried. He still doesn't understand why we couldn't drive up with you; we could fit more of your stuff in the two cars.'

'And have Dad using his "Mr Roberts" voice when we arrive?' He sprays toast crumbs all over the bed as he talks, my hand instantly swiping them from the top of the bed and onto the floor. 'No thank you.'

'He doesn't have a Mr Roberts voice!' I laugh. Jamie pulls a face which reads *You know he does*. 'OK, so he sometimes sounds the *tiniest* bit like a schoolteacher, but rather your father than me. I'm a walking disaster, food dropped down my top, half a roller still attached at the back of my hair, tripping over bags in the hallway – I'd trash your cool reputation within minutes – but with your father by your side, you'd be in like that.' I click my fingers.

'Why do you always do that?'

'Do what?'

'Make out that he's the star and you're the goofy sidekick?'

'Because I *am* the goofy sidekick.' I pull a goofy face to

emphasise my point. He shakes his head and takes another bite of his toast. 'So will you be seeing Heather any time soon?'

He shakes his head, a blond curl falling into his eyes. 'We split up.'

'What? Why? Are you OK?'

'It's for the best. I'm going to uni; we'll be on the opposite sides of the country . . .'

'I'm so sorry, Jam.' I fall back into his old nickname: when he was little Amber used to call him Jammy instead of Jamie, and it stuck. He eats around the crust and discards it onto his plate. 'It's no big deal, Mum, honest. It's not like we were ready to spend the rest of our lives together – there is a big world out there and I intend on sampling a lot of it before I do the whole . . .' he gestures around his room, 'settling down thing.'

I nod, smooth down my jeans and motion to stand.

'Are you going to be OK?' he asks quietly.

'What do you mean?'

'Well, it's going to be quiet around here with us all gone . . .'

'I'll be fine! I'm looking forward to having some proper time with your father.'

'I don't even want to think about what *that* means.'

'Your father is a very attractive man and . . .'

'Ugh! Mum! Stop, will you?'

I laugh and grab his last piece of toast. 'Now you know how it feels,' I say, heading for the door. 'Now, shower, you smell like Cole.'

'Mum?' I hesitate with my hand on the door. 'You will speak to him soon, won't you? Uncle Cole?'

'It's complicated, Jam, he's . . . he's not in a good place right now.'

'That's kind of when you need your friends, Mum, and

he's doing better. He'd had a few but he wasn't like, you know . . . Valentine's Day . . . he was just normal drunk. Friday night drunk.'

'I know, but . . .'

'Please, Mum, it's been what? Six months?'

'Seven,' I correct.

'Seven months since you've seen him and he said some stuff last night and—'

'What kind of stuff?'

'Just bullshit really, but he misses us, you and Dad and . . . I'll just feel better about leaving if I know you're going to check on him.'

'Jamie Roberts, that is emotional blackmail.' I sigh heavily. 'OK, I'll check on him, but you have to promise me something too.'

'Shoot.'

'Don't let yourself get pulled into his world. Cole has a way of making everyone around him feel like the centre of his universe, but when that universe implodes, he sucks those closest to him down too.'

'Ooh, deep. Been working on that a while?'

'A few weeks.'

'You're such a weirdo.'

'I know. Now shower. We need to pack the rest of your stuff.'

We stand outside the double-gabled house we bought four years ago: four bedrooms, two bathrooms, neat square lawn, double garage, double *mortgage* payment, a jump and a leap from the fixer-upper we'd bought when we first got married.

But time moves on and Will had his heart set on this one the minute he walked in. He breathed a sigh of relief; it was written all over his face: *At last, we can afford something that is easy to maintain.* No wonky walls, a drive we could park off road, a house that was calm, that suited our busy lives. I have grand plans for this house, the house where we will grow old, where our children and their children will come to visit. It's a blank canvas and I'm looking forward to making my mark on it; I just haven't had the chance yet. I can't argue with Will, though: life is easier when every switch you turn works, when the heating doesn't bang and clang and you don't have to immediately cross your fingers and pray that it isn't finally going to give up.

I shield my eyes against the sun and watch as Will checks the oil gauge in the engine, while Jamie slams his boot, giving me a quick eye-roll in the direction of his father.

'All set?' I ask Will, noticing Jamie's impatience to get on the road.

'Almost.' Will flicks open the window washer cavity and pours shop-bought screen wash into it. My heart melts a little: we always just use a squirt of Fairy; Will must have made a conscious effort to buy it for Jamie's car.

Jamie takes off his red hoody and chucks it on the back seat, on top of bin bags filled with clothes and a few boxes which contain crockery and kitchen appliances that will probably never get used, and comes to my side. I lean into his arms as he squeezes me against his chest.

'Drive carefully,' I say quietly. 'And if you get lost, there is a bumper-sized pack of condoms in your backpack pocket.' He snorts and pulls away.

'Love ya.' He kisses my forehead and makes his way to Will, who is wiping his hands on an old oil cloth from the garage where he spends his weekends tinkering with his bike.

'You're all set.' Will frowns at the bonnet for a minute before smiling at his son. 'Have you got everything?' Will arrives at my side, putting his hands in his back pockets.

'Probably not, but that's what student loans are for, right?'

He gives Will a quick hug – both men giving fist clenched back thumps – and climbs into the car, his Spotify playlist blaring through the speakers as soon as the ignition is turned. Jamie drops the passenger window, his hand held up in farewell. 'Laters!' He smiles, and the window retracts as he pulls off the drive; our son following in his sister's footsteps and leaving home.

We wave until the car is out of view and then I pull out my phone, opening our joint Spotify account, and flick on 'Rewrite the Stars' with a teary smile, and imagine my son laughing as Zac Efron starts belting out from his speakers as we step back into the house.

I shadow Will into the stylish fitted kitchen, all gleaming white gloss chosen by the previous owners; the absence of our children following us with loud steps and wide stretched arms. At the bottom of the kitchen, past the island and dining table, there is an extension, white walls sitting beneath a peaked glass ceiling leading towards two wide glass doors.

Until seven months ago, it had two sunflowers on either side of the doors; I had always loved Van Gogh's sunflowers and I took it as a sign. That was the feature that swayed me into agreeing to this house.

But they've been replaced now, just plain old glass. Cole took the colour from our house the last time he was here.

To the one side sits our old sofa, large, soft, the colour of champagne, and on the opposite side is one of my paintings, blues, whites and green scraped across the canvas. One of the only hints of us as a family in this immaculate show home of a house. I remember sitting on the beach in Spain, my canvas balanced against pebbles, my paints on a beach towel on the sand, as I created my version of the ocean. Sometimes, I close my eyes and allow my fingers to retrace the grooves made with the brush so many years ago; I can still feel grains of sand mixed in with the colour.

Will heads towards the tap to wash his hands as I dodge the scary-looking coffee machine that we had bought on a whim and are both too scared to use, instead spooning coffee into the decade-old percolator.

'He'll be OK, you know,' I say to Will, seeing the tension in his shoulders as the coffee begins to drip into the glass jug. 'He's more capable than you think.' I flinch, catching the sigh escaping Will's mouth. I didn't mean it to sound like a criticism, but there it is, like the smashed glass that had hit the floor. I tug my bottom lip with my teeth, grab a couple of cups, and distract myself from the tension in the room. Will is sitting at the table, his head facing to the right where at the end of our long lawn is the summerhouse. It was supposed to be my studio, but that dream was swallowed when I bought into the florist's with Amira. It's filled with old boxes that need sorting out now, with garden furniture, and BBQ tools.

I slide the coffee onto the kitchen table and sit opposite him, blowing over the rim of my cup. 'So . . .' I grin up at him, determined to fix the shard of glass that has already wedged between us within minutes of Jamie leaving. 'Where shall we have sex first? Here . . .' I rub the surface of the table, 'or the bathroom? Oh! We can get at it in the shower like we used to, it's been years since we've had daytime shower sex.'

'Ella—' Will begins, looking serious.

'You're right, you're right. The sealant around the bath needs redoing and if we're in there too long it'll leak into the kitchen, not to mention the last time we attempted it, you almost capped yourself on the hot tap, do you remember?'

'Ella,' Will repeats. I pause for a split second; I've heard him use that tone with me once before, but not for a very, very long time. 'We need to talk.'

The steam from my coffee rises between us. It licks the

atmosphere, gossamer thin flames a shadow of the heat that made it, but the flames are just ghosts of their past, waves and ribbons of energy that are trying to escape before their time runs out. The second hand on the oversized clock behind Will only clicks twice, but each sound is so loud that I feel my hands reacting, wanting to cover my ears to protect them from its toll.

'Don't say it,' I whisper, covering the top of the cup with my hand, the heat searing the inside of my palm. 'Please, Will . . . don't say it.'

'I think we should get a divorce.'

Chapter Six

Then

It was the end of the first week back after half term, and Will was waiting for Ella to come out of college. He pulled up the collar of his duffel coat and sat across the road on the bench by the bus stop, a notebook in his hand as he scribbled some more notes of a song that he hadn't been able to get out of his head since the morning at the Walkers', since the day he had kissed her. Will had been working all week at the shop, but they'd spoken on the phone, conversations that went on for hours, talking about music and art, about nothing and everything.

Ella jogged down the steps, black skirt with yellow flowers fluttering above her boots as she approached him. She hid a smirk as she listened to The Girls – her old friends who had distanced themselves from her a few years prior – making appreciative comments about Will Roberts sitting across from them. Part of her wanted to turn around to watch their faces as she skipped over to him.

'You're here,' she smiled, her chin tucked into her grey polo neck, her eyes flickering up at him through her lashes.

'I am.' He smiled at her and shoved his notebook in his back pocket.

'Do you want to grab some cake?' Ella said, the words coming fast and eager, a blush creeping across her cheeks.

Will, shy and unsure of what to say, covered his mouth and laughed.

'What?' But she was smiling too, ducking slightly, trying to look up through his hands. 'You don't like cake?'

'No, no, I, I like cake.'

'Good, because I thought we were off to a rocky start there, Will Roberts. I just don't think we can be soul mates if you have cake bias.'

'Cake bias?' he responded, his gaze fixed on Ella, ignoring the flirtatious look of the girls grinning at him from behind her.

'Yeah . . . didn't quite work, did it? I was trying to be funny. Let me try again.' Ella sat beside him and cleared her throat.

'Knock, knock?' she asked, as The Girls walked past with wide eyes and nudges.

'Who's there?' Will replied, meeting her eyes briefly.

'Nobel?'

'Nobel who?'

'Nobel that's why I'm knocking.'

Ella threw Will a wide face-splitting smile, looking up at him to see how her joke landed. Will laughed, stood, and offered her his arm.

'How gallant.' Ella linked her arm through his. 'If that's what I get for a knock-knock joke, wait until you try the custard slice at O'Malleys.'

A bubble of laughter erupted from Will's chest, taking him by surprise.

But then again, Ella always would take him by surprise.

Will slowed his pace beside her so that they matched each other's steps. She talked about her day. He was attentive, asking her about the photos she'd taken, the project she was working on; they talked about the millennium bug and what would happen if the world came to a standstill on New Year's Day, and when he sat opposite her as she devoured a custard slice, he resisted the urge to wipe the corner of her mouth when a piece of icing clung to her top lip. Will loved the swell of her bottom lip, the cupid bow of the top, and often found that his eyes were drawn to her mouth.

And when Will walked Ella home from school in the days and weeks that followed, Will's hands sat in his back pocket, or he'd hold her art case for her while she talked; he loved to listen to her talk. Ella found joy in the smallest of things. Three weeks after the fair, they'd been walking along the grey concrete shopping parade, drizzle sliding down the betting shop windows, clinging to their clothes, making them heavy with the weight.

'But can you imagine what that would have been like for him? If Michelangelo *was* gay, to paint "The Last Judgement" would have been like torture, to be standing there for days painting the fate that you thought waited for you when you died . . .' She paused briefly. 'Will, look!' She pointed to a puddle. Will's eyebrows drew together as he tried to see what was holding Ella's attention. 'Look at the reflection in that puddle of the streetlight, it looks like liquid gold, doesn't it?' And when Will blinked, he could see it, a puddle of liquid gold where a moment ago, there had just been dirty street water. 'Have you ever been to Italy? God, I would love to see the Sistine Chapel.' She continued her conversation without missing a beat, as if she hadn't just thrown gold into a world full of grey.

Will became addicted to the feeling he had when he was with Ella. He would watch her with wonder as she talked: she made everyone around her matter, telling the woman behind the counter how pretty her hair looked that day, pausing her stride to ask if she could pet a dog, pulling funny faces at a grumpy child in a supermarket queue, turning a wail into laughter, a swell of joy exploding into the room where moments ago there had been anguish. Will began to let himself believe that Ella wanting to spend this much time with him meant that she felt the same for him. That he mattered too.

Sometimes, Will's hand would burn inside his pocket with the need to touch her, but he hadn't kissed her since that first time. They walked through that very park, a few weeks after the golden puddle, when he knew he couldn't hold his feelings in any longer. It was cold, her nose pink, her hair poking out in two plaits beneath a blue beanie, yellow scarf wrapped around her throat. Ella slowed her step, linked her arm through his and pulled him to a standstill, pointing at a magpie.

'Look at the colour – it's not black, is it? More midnight blue?' Will pulled his hand out of his pocket and reached up to her cheek.

'What?' Her hand stretched up to her face. 'Do I have something on my face?' She yanked down the edge of her jacket over the heel of her hand, ready to wipe her cheek.

Will's hand reached for her then: he cradled her cold face in his palm, her cheek leaning heavily against it, like it was exhausted and needed a place to rest. Her eyes searched his, questioning him. With his other hand he traced the path of her profile, from the middle of her forehead, through her eyebrows, along her nose, her mouth, his thumb running along the fullness of her bottom lip. Then he cupped her face and kissed her gently.

And in the weeks and months that followed, Will retraced the shape of her profile on his pillow when he wasn't with her.

Chapter Seven

Now

Ella

10th September 2022

'Well, you can't have a divorce, so . . .'

'Ella, please, listen to me, you know it's the right thing to do.'

'No, I don't, Will, I don't think it's the right thing to do! And you thought that telling me this now is the right time to mention you're not happy? NOW? Now, Will? Our son has literally just left home and you're asking for a divorce, not even the next day?' My stomach flips, a bump in the road beneath speeding tyres. 'Is there someone else?'

'No. NO, Ella. How can you even ask me that?'

'How can I ask you? Well, let me see, Will, you're asking me for a divorce after being together for twenty-three years, so that's how I can ask you. Jesus Christ, it's my birthday tomorrow, your timing couldn't be worse if you tried.'

'I know it seems like the wrong time, but honestly Ella, I've replayed this so many times in my head and there is no *good* time.'

'Replayed this in your head? You've been *fantasising* about telling me you want a divorce?'

'No, Ella, that's not what I meant. You know how we

always begin our birthdays and it wouldn't be right for me to—' Tears glaze over his eyes, but my own are dry, barren, hot.

'Give me a birthday bonk? This is why you're telling me now, because you can't stand the thought of sleeping with me again?'

'That's not what I'm saying, I'm trying to do the right thing . . . I'm trying to—'

'Stop talking! Please, Will, I . . . God, I can't breathe in here!' I throw open the back door and walk to the bottom of the garden. Air that was here just a short while ago is thick, and syrupy, my lungs finding it hard to take in.

I want a divorce repeats in my head, over and over again. My eyes close as I try to think, try to make sense of the words he's saying. I think about how distant he's become recently, how he's been avoiding time together when it's just the two of us. And yeah, I know things have been quieter, I know those days when I have to try to make conversation are becoming more frequent, but that's marriage, right? Everyone goes through this once the kids leave home. It's completely normal – it's a huge thing to happen to a couple, and yet it's not really acknowledged, is it? That change in circumstance. People talk about how your life changes when you have a baby – you only have to go to the supermarket with a bump and strangers are all too happy to tell you how your life is going to change – but where is the advice when the situation is reversed? Nobody stops you when you're examining which wrinkle cream to use and your shopping trolley is suddenly filled with ready meals rather than the ingredients for slow-cooker batch cooking, when there is a four pack of loo roll instead of a twelve pack and when your shopping trolley no longer needs you to bear down on your knees to be able to manoeuvre it towards the checkout. Nobody puts a hand on your skin and asks if you've got everything you need, if you've got date nights planned. Or a new hobby, you know, to fill the gap now that you no longer have football games to drive to, boyfriend pick-ups, hour-long-concert carparks to sit in. There are no post-children departure classes, no exercises to help you breathe through the silences, to help you push through the layers of family life, as your life contracts decade by decade until you're left with just the two components that it all started with, ready to test if that couple is strong enough to survive beneath the weight of anniversaries, traditions, familiarity.

I stare over at the bird house on the apple tree, remembering Amber, Jamie and me making it as a Father's Day present. The roof is lopsided, and when I took it from our old house and brought it here, I impaled my thumb on one of the nails sticking out.

Even with the knowledge that we've got a tough time ahead of us, there hasn't been a moment where I've thought we weren't strong enough. I've never thought *Fuck, that's just done it, that's why he'll ask me for a divorce*.

But then again, maybe we never needed a moment like that, because our marriage is based on *Fuck it, that's just done it* moments. Amber. The bar fight. Jamie.

I knew what I was doing back then, of course I did. I knew that Will wasn't ready, I knew that he was still reeling from Jack's death, that he hung on to me like a life raft. And I know that if he hadn't been *that* vulnerable, *that* damaged, he would never have asked me out in the first place. Will needed me, my family. I've always known, deep down, that if I hadn't got pregnant, he would never have asked me to marry him. I've known it all my life – Christ, even Perky Tits could see why Will and I were together. I know Will loves me, I know he loves our children, and he's done a really good job of playing the part of a man in love with his wife: he tells me I'm beautiful, he makes love to me like I'm the only person in the world he wants in his arms . . . but I've always known, he's not in love with me the way I've always been in love with him.

The kitchen is empty when I return; I follow the sound of him upstairs and push our bedroom door open: white walls, oak floor, stone-coloured accents in the throw at the foot of the bed next to his open case. I take a sharp intake of breath. I was expecting a discussion, not a suitcase. I watch the muscles in his back work through the grey of his shirt as he folds a pair of jeans into the case. I bought him those jeans for his birthday last year. Had he known when he opened the present that just a year later they would be packed away?

'Why now?' I ask, my voice hitching. He hesitates, his back to me. I walk past him and sit next to the case and repeat my question, looking up at him.

'Because if I don't do it now . . .' he meets my eyes, 'I will never be strong enough.'

'When did you stop?'

The groove between his eyebrows deepens, a dark chasm of confusion. 'Stop what?'

'Loving me?'

He bites down on his lip, his eyes filling, his head shaking. Will bends and cups my face, his eyes searching mine. 'I've never stopped loving you.' He puts his forehead against mine. 'I will never stop loving you.'

'So, if you love me and I love you, then . . .' I reach up and hold my hand over his.

'Because sometimes love isn't enough.' His lips meet my forehead; they're firm, pressed against my skin like he's trying to leave an imprint of himself with me.

He steps back, running the zip around the case.

'Where are you going?'

'Mum's.'

'Will, don't go, please. Please don't go.'

'I have to. I'm sorry.'

He turns and leaves, me hurrying behind him as he carries his case down the stairs. 'Wait, Will . . . Will!'

He hesitates with his hand on the front door handle.

'Tell me what's going on!'

He turns to me, his lips trembling as he tries to hold himself together.

'Please, Will, why now? I don't understand.'

He meets my eyes, takes a deep breath and says, 'You will.'

And then he closes the door, while I sit on the stairs wondering how I have gone from having everything I always wanted to nothing at all.

Chapter Eight

Then

June 2000

As time eased forward, there was a difference in Will Roberts that people couldn't quite place. Although beautiful, his face had previously been two dimensional, a fine-art sketch on a blank piece of paper, exquisite but lifeless, his stare blank. But with each week that passed in Ella's company, his reflection started coming to life, as though brushed with watercolours, more pigment added to the blue of his eyes, an earthy depth to the peach across his skin, and as their time together continued, the watercolours deepened into oils until Will was no longer an outline but a living and breathing sculpture, radiating warmth and strength.

Gradually, Will became used to the hustle and bustle of the Walker household, to the jokes and the physical nature of them. The play fights, the elastic band flicking, the way Susan and Bill never tried to hide their attraction to each other, how they had no shame in telling the family that they were having an early night, how Ella's brothers would tease their father, telling him to watch he didn't do his back in. And although this way of life sometimes made Will uncomfortable, made him burn red to the tips of his ears, he loved being in their home. Especially the days when Cole wasn't around.

Cole's relationship with Ella co-existed beside them, both relationships on parallel tracks that never touched. It was as much a pleasure as it was a torment for Cole to see their relationship evolving, to see the one person he loved most in the world finding such happiness. So, Cole found a way to occupy his thoughts, to spend less time at Ella's house, to make some money so that he could move out. Cole had an apprenticeship at a local garage and spent his days learning how to take apart an engine, how to put it back together again. He'd started seeing Jasmine, the other apprentice at the garage. Jasmine was fun, adventurous and wanted absolutely no commitment from Cole whatsoever, which suited him perfectly; he had nothing to give.

If Cole was at the Walkers' when Will arrived, he would be courteous; they would make polite conversation when Ella tried to lead them to common ground, trying to reinstate that easy friendship that she used to see when Will and Cole would finish each other's sentences and laugh at inside jokes, but instead, now they gave polite replies and hasty goodbyes as one of them left the house.

Cole tied his checked shirt around his waist over his black T-shirt as he headed towards Ella's. It was warm and in his backpack he had a six-pack of cherry Coke straight from the fridge – Ella's favourite – and a bag of pick and mix to share. Cole had been looking forward to this day: it was going to be like old times. Ella had challenged him to a *Soul Calibur* battle on the PlayStation and then they were getting in a pizza, in time for *Big Brother*; they were hoping Nasty Nick would get his comeuppance. But as he approached the Walker house, his heart sank. Cole could see that Will was having trouble with his bike. Ella was stood by the side of the road, in a white vest and denim cut-offs, a pair of sunglasses perched on her head. Cole had always loved the way she looked in her standard summer outfit; there was something comforting in seeing her in the same style clothes as she'd worn when they used to play in the garden as kids.

'Hey.' Cole approached, stopping beside Will's bike as he tried to turn it over again. 'Want me to take a look?'

'Yeah, um, that would be great, I think it might be the battery.'

Will climbed off the bike, putting a proprietorial arm around Ella's shoulders. Cole didn't look up, instead began listening carefully to the engine as it tried to start. 'I don't think it's your battery, I think it might be a dirty carburettor.'

'Oh.'

'I mean, I'm not sure but I could clean it . . . if you want? Or . . . you can drop it off at a garage?'

'I wouldn't want to put you out,' Will began.

'Oh, it wouldn't put him out, you love that shit, don't you, Cole?' Ella's eager voice brought a smile to Cole's face.

Will couldn't help but be warmed by the affection radiating from Ella, seeing her boys on speaking terms with a potential for bridge-building.

'Tell you what, you two get started on the bike and I'll grab us a couple of bags of chips from the chippy.' Will's mouth had opened, but Ella stole the next words from his mouth with a quick kiss. 'Are you a curry sauce or gravy fan, like this weirdo?' She nodded towards Cole, who smirked at her.

'Actually, I like salad cream with mine.'

Cole and Ella both turned to Will, their noses scrunched up in the same fashion, and Will couldn't help but laugh.

The front door opened behind them with a flourish. Kenny stood there, superman pose, chin tilted upwards.

'Did I hear someone say chippy?'

They moved the bike onto the lawn and Cole took it apart piece by piece, using Mr Walker's old tools from the shed, sticking bits of tape onto each part so he could put it back together again. They ate the chips straight from the paper, swigged cans of cheap cola, Kenny and Roddy playing their version of Sumo wrestling behind them, and as the afternoon sun slid behind the house and the engine roared back into life, Will and Cole hi-fived and, for a split second, forgot that the last time they'd touched had been when Will hauled Cole out of the river.

Chapter Nine

Now

Ella

10th September 2022

The bottle of wine is empty. I drain my glass, turning my attention back to the wedding photo resting on my lap. I squint at our young faces kissing outside the church, my veil already lifted, confetti swirling around us like cherry blossom.

'Are you miserable, Will Roberts?' I ask his young face. He doesn't answer. 'Did you always know you would leave me?'

The frame slips from my hands and smashes on the cold lounge floorboards. I sob and crawl on the floor, trying to pick up the pieces, a shard nicking the curve between my thumb and index finger. Gathering myself, I stumble to the downstairs toilet, throw the glass into the stainless-steel bin, the white of the enclosed space dazzling behind my reflection as I run my hand beneath the tap, and pull out the splinter of glass. I wrap tissue around the wound, blood spreading quickly but staying in place long enough for me to retrieve a plaster from the first-aid box in the kitchen. My hand reaches for the phone; I call Amira but it switches to answerphone.

'Hey.' The tears start again. 'It's me. Will's left me and I don't know why, I mean I do know why but I didn't think,

I don't think . . . and Jamie's gone too and I'm in this fucking house that I didn't even decorate and . . . just come round when you get this, OK? Love you.' I end the call and look up at the clock. Of course she won't answer; she'll be asleep, safely wrapped in her husband's arms. But I know who will be up. I swipe the screen through my tears.

It rings six times, then his voice: 'Hello? Ells?' I can imagine his finger in his ear as he tries to hear me.

'Will's gone.' My voice catches. 'He's left me, Cole,' I manage to say as my whole body wracks with sobs.

'I'm coming, Ells,' he says. 'I'm coming.'

I've cleared the broken frame away and am staring into my glass, the amber whisky tilted to the right. Amber's name came from this, a glass of whisky catching the light streaming into the hotel function room as Dad made his toast, 'To Will and Ella!' and as his glass met his mouth, the light reflected the amber colour onto my stomach beneath the ivory dress, Amber only just a small bump beneath the surface. As the room toasted our marriage, I nudged Will's arm, getting his attention. 'Amber,' I said with a smile, 'if it's a girl?', my newly ringed fingers stroking the baby inside. Will grinned, 'It's perfect.' He kissed me as our friends and family cheered.

The doorbell chimes, and I knock the drink back. I make my way to the front door along the hallway, blank walls, punctuated by little snapshots of the family that lives here. Photos of us pulling faces at the lens, of day trips out and sunlit days on the beach. The security light outlines Cole's figure. I unlock the bolt, and then he's here and I'm in his arms, the familiar shape of him trying to shield me from the outside world. He pulls the door closed behind him, and in the safety of my friend's arms, I let my legs give and we slump onto the floor together, his back to the door, me cradled in his arms, head against his chest.

I don't know how long I've been crying, but my legs are stiff and Cole's shirt beneath my cheek is wet. His fingers release my hair as I prise myself away from him and stand, my joints aching. I rub my cheek where something inside his jacket pocket has been digging into me. 'What's in your pocket?'

'Nice try, Ells.' He looks at his watch. 'It's not your birthday yet.' He winks as I let out a breath: Cole has never forgotten my birthday once, not even when we were living in Spain; he still managed to get a gift through the post. I offer him a hand and drag him up from the floor, taking in his appearance, the crumple of his shirt, the red around his eyes. He's lost weight since I last saw him, his hair is longer, still curly, still unruly.

'Coffee?' I ask him.

'I'll make it.'

'No offence, but coffee has never been your strength. Builders' tea is where your talent lies.'

He follows me into the kitchen, his eyes lowered, but his focus flickers to the clear panes of glass, the replaced doors.

'I don't remember much.' His hand touches the wall. 'About that afternoon.'

'I know.' He returns to the table, picks up the whisky bottle and puts it back down. I should have cleared that away before I opened the door. He's already been drinking; even in my inebriated state, I can tell. The slow, considered speech, the sluggish movements; he doesn't need a hit just now, but by lunch time tomorrow it will be a different matter.

'I should never have come here that wasted.'

'No. No, you shouldn't have, but we can't change the past and you can't promise me it won't happen again.' Cole accepts my comment without retaliation. It's not a challenge; he knows it's the sad truth: until he's clean, there will always be that risk that shrouds our friendship like a toxic cloud. 'So, how have you been?' I ask, not ready to dive into the why-my-husband-has-just-asked-me-for-a-divorce conversation just yet. I pour the boiling water into mugs, adding three sugars and a small splash of milk in his. His acceptance of the coffee is a smoke screen.

'Not great, not bad.' He stares up at an old photo Roddy had taken of us. The photo is one of a collection of six, arranged geometrically in the shape of a sunflower. In the photo drawing his focus, I'm sitting in the middle, Amber – an angelic two-year-old – on my knee, Cole and Will either side. A smile lifts the corner of his mouth and I see my childhood friend emerge from beneath the years of alcohol abuse. 'I'm surprised this is still here. I thought Will would have got rid of it.'

'He did.' Cole looks at me over his shoulder. 'I put it back the next day.' I pass him his coffee. 'And your drinking . . . how's that?'

'Not bad.' He takes a sip of coffee. 'Not great. I am trying, Ells.'

'Good.'

Cole is a high-functioning alcoholic: he still works at his garage, still drinks tea throughout the day, but his afternoon drinking sessions start earlier, his late nights longer, his morning hangover and tremoring hand only fixed by a splash of whisky in his tea for elevenses.

He follows me into the lounge, the broken frame and the wedding photo on the glass coffee table.

Cole removes all the cushions with a perplexed look until we're settled, slipping back into the same positions as we always have, me at one end, him at the other, my feet on his lap.

Being friends with Cole is like sitting on a seesaw. It's familiar: I've seen it my whole life and at first look, it's safe, part of family life, unthreatening, fun. On one side it's solid, firm, sitting on the ground, secure, but then without any warning, I'm somehow up in the air, my stomach suspended somewhere between the ground and the sky. And it's heavenly up there: I can see for miles, the world is suddenly more magical, more fun . . . but I know there is no way back down without hitting the ground beneath me with a crack. Right now, the seesaw is level, our weight evenly distributed.

'Things have been . . . quiet for a while.' I begin addressing the elephant in the room. 'But you know Will, he always withdraws into his own world when something is on his mind. I thought it was his job and with Jamie hardly ever here and Amber pretty self-sufficient. It's hard for him. The kids growing up.'

'It's hard for you too, though, right?'

'Yeah, but he was always the fun one. I mean, I'd play and make cakes with them and read them a story at bedtime but Will, Will *lived* for his time with the kids. He was always the one to start the water fights, to wake them up when it was snowing, even if it was in the middle of the night. He was the one to help them up the trees so they could get the biggest conkers.' I smile at Cole.

'Yeah. He's a great dad,' he agrees, taking a sip of coffee.

'He is. I sometimes wondered if he felt like he had to make up for all the time he wasn't with them when they were little.'

'They had the next best thing though.' Cole grins at me.

'Oh, I know, and you were great with them, but it's not the same, is it? He's their dad.' I swill the dregs of the coffee around the bottom of the cup. The tears begin again. 'He said . . .' I clear my throat and take a breath, 'that sometimes love . . .' I try to focus on Cole's eyes through the tears, 'isn't enough.'

'Bullshit.'

I laugh through the tears.

'Seriously, Ells, that's bullshit. Something else is going on.'

'I asked him if there was someone else.'

Cole shakes his head and rolls his eyes. 'He would never play away, it's not Will's style. You've always been his world, anyone can see how much he loves you.'

'So, if that's true, what then? Why leave me? Throw away everything we have?'

'I don't know.'

My hands circle the mug. 'Do you think . . . that Will felt trapped? You know, when he proposed?'

'When he proposed?' He seems surprised that I'm thinking of something that happened so long ago. I nod, looking over at the now glassless wedding photo.

'No, he would have married you, Amber or no Amber. Maybe not quite as quickly, but he would have still married you.' A slow smile creeps across his face. 'Anyone with half a brain can see how much he loves you.' He pauses, his eyebrows drawing together. 'Why, do you? Think he feels trapped?'

'Well, he's just asked for a divorce, so I don't know, I mean. Maybe?'

'It was the noughties, not the nineteenth century. He didn't have to marry you.'

'I know, I just wonder if I hadn't got pregnant, would he have done things differently?'

'Would you?'

I consider this briefly. There is nothing I would change about my life up until this point. I look over to where Amber and Jamie are grinning down from a black-and-white canvas above the white stone fireplace. 'No. How could I?'

'But . . . don't you ever wonder how different it would have been if you hadn't gone with Will? Met somebody else? Become an artist? Had your own gallery?'

I shove him gently with my foot. 'I have a gallery, and I am an artist, it's just a different kind of art.'

'You know what I mean. If anyone should be regretting trapping anyone, it should be Will.'

'What do you mean by that?' My tone is defensive.

'Nothing. Forget it.'

'No, go on, what did you mean?' Cole opens his tobacco tin and pulls out a paper, inserts a filter tip and lays out a neat line of tobacco. 'You had so much fun ahead of you, and instead . . .' the paper rolls between his fingers, 'you ended up being all . . .' he licks the end of the paper and closes the cigarette, 'Stepford. Before you even had a chance to live.'

'Is that what *you're* doing? Living?'

He gives me a lopsided smile, a touché, as he stands, wiggling the cigarette.

'Sorry.' I apologise, biting the corner of my thumb.

'You don't have to apologise, remember?'

He leaves the room and heads outside to smoke.

When we were about fourteen, Cole and I had our first big row, our first argument as almost adults. It was over something so trivial that I can't even recall the details, something to do with my brother. I eventually calmed down, realised that Roddy was in the wrong and knocked on Cole's door. 'Sorry!' I blurted out, throwing my arms around his neck. I felt so lost and dramatically upset in that way that everything is heightened at that age.

When he pulled away from me, he grinned. 'Let's make a deal? We never have to say sorry to each other.'

'Why?'

'Because if you're really friends, you can forgive them anyway, so what's the point?'

I'm lost in my thoughts while I wait for Cole to come back, my eyes becoming heavy.

'Ells?' He shakes me awake gently, wiggling my foot.

I shift myself upwards, the memories of the day tripping over themselves as I'm brought back into consciousness. 'Do you want to crash in Jamie's room?' I ask him, not wanting to be left in this house alone.

'I don't think Will would . . .'

'Yeah, well, Will's not here, is he?' My stomach lurches at the words and I hold back the tears.

'OK, yeah.'

I flick off the lights behind us and hug Cole at the bottom of the stairs. 'Happy birthday,' he whispers and kisses me above my ear.

'Thank you.'

The next morning comes with a bang, a crash, an earthquake of memories shaking me awake. I want to duck and cover, to hide under the safety of my duvet: then, a clatter of teacups and saucers, the smell of toast, a knock at my bedroom door.

'Ells? You up?'

'Yeah,' I croak.

'Happy birthday tooooo you!' Cole bellows out in a treble tenor, carrying in a tray laden with tea, toast, a packet of ibuprofen and a rose from a vase in the kitchen. 'Happy birthday to you!' He continues singing loudly, as I shuffle up gingerly, my head throbbing and my eyes slit-like. 'Happy birthday, dear Elllllll-aaaaaa!'

'Please stop.'

He takes an even bigger breath and belts the last *Happy birthday to you* out until his face turns an uncomfortable shade of purple.

'You're an idiot.'

'Charming.' He places the tray onto my lap and sits at the foot of the bed, legs crossed like a child on a classroom carpet. Anger at Will rises up from my sternum. This isn't how my birthdays go. My birthdays start with sex, then cake, the kids and Will bringing it into my room with the candles already lit, my kids at the end of the bed with my presents in their hands. I look down at the tray, at the two pieces of toast cut into a rough circle with strawberry jam between them, a birthday candle on top.

'Thank you.'

'Sorry, there was no cake.'

'No, no this is lovely, Cole, thank you.' I blow out the candle and take a sip of the tea. Cole shows no sign of a hangover, which is par for the course.

'Want your pressies?' he asks. I blink.

'Pressies?'

'Yeah, hold on a min.' He jogs from the room and returns with two packages already wrapped. I lift the tray and place it next to me. I recognise Amber's handiwork – it's wrapped in delicate paper, and tied up with string, calligraphy penned tag – and on top of that, Jamie's wrapping, slapdash, probably done ten minutes before he was about to leave. 'I found them in Jamie's room last night, when I was looking for this fetching ensemble.' He gestures to the jogging bottoms which are rolled up at the foot and a long-sleeved black T-shirt which is two sizes too big. I stroke the paper on Amber's gift.

'Should I call the kids before I open them, do you think?'

'Do they know that Will's left?'

I flinch at his words and shake my head. 'Not unless Will's spoken to them. I didn't want to tell Jamie until he's settled, and he's useless at keeping things to himself, so then Amber would know and, you know Amber, she'll be here before I've had a chance to put the phone down and she's so busy . . .' I reach for my phone. There are three missed calls from Amber and a voicemail message which I play back.

'Hey, Mum! Happy birthday! Look, I'm helping out on a

double shift so I was hoping to catch you beforehand. Never mind, I've left my gift in Jam's room – I dread to think of the state it'll be by the time you open it! Anyway, I hope you like it, love you and I'll call you later! Bye. Bye.'

There's a message from Amira too, which reads, 'Just got your message. I'll be round asap. P.S. Happy birthday chicken x'. There is nothing from Will. This is the first time since I was nineteen Will hasn't been the first to wish me a happy birthday.

I take a bite of the toast, pop two pills out and swallow them down with the hot tea. Cole tucks his hand in his pocket, brings out a small box and passes it to me. His hand holds a slight tremor; he hasn't had a drink yet.

'If you're about to propose, I've gotta tell you, it's a bit too soon.'

'Pffft. You should be so lucky. This man will be tamed by no woman!' He punches his fist to his chest like Tarzan, then wags his finger at me. 'Not even you, Ella Walker.'

'Roberts.' I correct. 'For now,' I add, tears threatening again.

'Open it!'

I smile weakly and tear off the blue paper, revealing a small mustard-coloured velvet ring box which clicks open easily. Inside is an amber brooch, oval and surrounded in gold. It's old-fashioned to the point of cool. I hold it in my palm; it's heavy and cold to the touch. 'I love it, Cole, thank you.'

'You're welcome.'

The doorbell rings, startling us both.

'Open up, birthday girl!!' Amira's voice comes through the letter box. 'I'm freezing my norks off out here!'

'Well . . .' Cole claps his hands together, 'we can't have that. It would be tragic to have any damage done to those fine specimens!'

'Just hold on a sec,' I say, grabbing my white towelling dressing gown, and follow him down the stairs.

'Hurry up, Ella!' The letter box flaps. 'My nipples are the size of Maltesers!'

Cole chuckles as he skips down the stairs and opens the door.

'Oh! Hello, Cole, I wasn't expecting you.' Her brown eyes light up from behind black secretary glasses, her dreadlocks pulled into a ponytail behind her, hands busy holding the giant cellophane-wrapped gift basket. Her pierced eyebrow arches up at my dressing-gowned apparel, Cole's bare feet. Cole backs the door open further, clasping his hands at the base of his spine like a bellboy.

'Lady Amira.' He nods his head to the side.

'Mr Chapel.' She enters the house staring up at me wide-eyed and mouthing *What the fuck is going on?*

'Can I interest you in a breakfast beverage?'

'Oh, thanks but I'm driving.'

Cole chews the inside of his cheek briefly. 'I meant tea, it is only nine a.m., Lady Amira, what kind of establishment do you think this is?' He tuts and heads for the kitchen as I guide her into the lounge.

Amira shuts the door behind her with her backside, plonks the basket down on the table and spins round. 'OK, tell me quickly. What the fuck is going on? I get a garbled message telling me that Will's left you and the next thing I know, I'm opening the door to Cole Chapel and you in your negligée.'

I look down at my robe. 'It's hardly a negligée.'

'Shush, so what's going on? Not that I blame you.' She looks wistfully through the closed door. 'I came three times the night I slept with that man. I don't think I've ever had sex like that before or after.'

'Amira!'

'Well, it's true. Oh, don't look so shocked, you know I love sex with my Baz, but sex with someone you love is clean, isn't it? All arching backs and dreamy eyes and whispering *I love you*. But sex with Cole Chapel? It's dirty, it's scratch marks and grazed spines and three orgasms in one night.' She sighs, then rouses herself. 'But I have to admit, you don't look like you've just been banged up against the wall by Mr February from the World's Greatest Mechanic's calendar. Oh, come here.'

She pulls me into her arms, her heady perfume and warmth circling me as I start crying.

Chapter Ten

Then

August 2000

Will continued to work at the music shop. Ella would sit in the back of the shop, her sketchbook open, hand blurring across the page as she drew the instruments, the customers, and Will. He'd find her drawings of him folded inside his pockets, or on the doorstep in an envelope posted the day before; sometimes inside the envelope would be an origami swan or a rose, a frog . . . Ella brought a smile to him every day.

Physically, things progressed between Ella and Will. It was tentative on Will's part, and he would laugh gently as Ella tried to take off his clothes while they kissed on her bed, telling her there wasn't any rush. He would sit behind her, lifting her hair, and would trace the shape of her birthmark, telling her it was a flower one day, a bridge between two trees the next, and he would kiss the outline of it until she turned around in his arms and pulled his mouth towards hers.

The truth of the matter was that Will was afraid: he was afraid he was going to be a disappointment, that she'd see that he wasn't the boy, the man, that everyone else saw. He wasn't the leading man in a film, and he wasn't Cole, who – rumour had it – was something of an expert in that department, leaving girls panting and pining after him.

Will was grateful for Ella's patience. He could see and feel how much she wanted to take the next step with him, but she treated his trepidation physically in the same way as she did personally. She never asked probing questions, she never pushed; instead, she let him come to her. And as time went by, Will began to lower his guard little by little.

Beside the kerb, an ice-cream van parked. The vibrations of the engine ran low and deep, while excited children and worn-out parents held sticky coins in their hands. The sounds from the kerb tumbled on the breeze, seeping through Ella's open bedroom window. Condensation ran down the cans of lemonade beside the bed next to scrunched-up crisp packets and open CD cases. On the radio beneath them, Bob Dylan's 'Subterranean Homesick Blues' was playing in the kitchen.

'Dad used to love Bob Dylan.'

Ella lay on his chest, listening to the distant music as Will cleared his throat and began mimicking Bob, mixing up the medicine while he was on the paaaaay-vement thinking about a gooooor-veeer-ment. Ella laughed; this was a side to Will that not many saw, his ability to goof around and not take himself seriously. Will was actually a good singer, but he always displayed it by making fun of his talent. 'I reckon I could make some money as a tribute act, what do you think?'

'Hmmm, I'd stick to the guitar if I were you.'

Will continued: 'Don't folllllow leeed-ers, watch the parking meeeeters.'

She rolled on top of him, covering his mouth with her hands, laughing. 'No more!' She settled herself back on his chest.

'It was so unfair. When Dad died.' He ran his hand up

and down her spine. 'He did everything right and he still died.' The air grew heavy as his tone changed.

'He did do everything right. He made you.' Ella circled the button on his denim shirt with her index finger. 'You must miss him.'

'I do. At least with Dad, I can *just* miss him, though.'

'What do you mean?'

Ella propped herself up on her elbow as Will bit down on his lip; she could tell he wanted to say more. His eyes focused on the ceiling and then he closed his eyes, letting out a long breath.

Ella could see the words fighting to come out: it was in the way his fists were clenched by his sides, how his lips were pressed together. 'Do you want to talk about it?' she asked, her voice tentative. She watched his reaction, saw the tension in his jaw relax a little. She pressed on. 'About what happened?' His hand reached out for hers, entwining her fingers with his.

Ella didn't know, as she asked Will about Jack's death, that he had never talked about it before. Not to a therapist, not to Cole and certainly not to his mother. But as he met Ella's eyes looking down at him, felt her hair skimming his collarbone, he felt words forming inside his mouth and found that when he opened his lips to speak, they were able to escape.

'Well, when I think about Jack, it's different. I feel so guilty about that day, that it's hard to just remember the good times, do you know what I mean? Like, if he had died another way . . . I would be able to just miss him, you know? But the guilt just takes over. Does that make sense?'

'Yeah, it does . . . Do you want to tell me what happened?'

'We'd been playing football,' Will began, closing his eyes as Ella stroked the side of his face. Will could see Jack, strawberry-blond hair, spindly legs beneath blue shorts, green-and-red-striped top, a football being kicked between them as they made their way down the street. 'And we ran into Cole on the field by the park. He let Jack play in goal, kicking the ball deliberately so Jack could save it. I was hot and getting pissed off with Cole by then; I was sick of everyone treating Jack like a baby. Mum and Dad always let him win at board games, always let him off our chores, so I called it and we all started walking back, but it was so hot that day, Ella, like, it felt like the sky was hanging lower than usual, that the sun was closer or something. It was my suggestion to go to the river, I thought we could dangle our legs off one of the old fishing pegs. But then Cole spotted the rope swing when we got there. It sounded like a good idea, I just wanted to feel some breeze on my face, you know? I went first, to test the weight and it was fine and for a while it was fun. We took it in turns but then Cole started to push off further up the bank, trying to beat me, trying to get higher.'

'Sounds like Cole.'

Will opened his eyes and turned towards Ella. 'It happened so fast.' His voice was almost a whisper. 'One minute he was next to us and then the rope just snapped and Cole was gone.' Will paused, lost in his memories for a split second. 'I didn't know he couldn't swim. *Cole Chapel* would never have admitted to that, would he?' Ella rested her hand on his chest, letting him continue. 'I remember saying to Jack . . .' Will swallowed hard, ' "Stay here. Stay here." ' Will blinked back the tears filling his eyes, embarrassed. 'That's the last thing I ever said to him.'

'I'm so sorry, Will.'

'I slid off the bank into the water. The current was carrying Cole downstream and his head kept popping up, and each time it did he was further away. But it didn't take me long to get to him, at least it didn't seem that long. I looked up at the bank but it was too high to climb out where we were. I had to swim upstream, pulling him with me.'

Will didn't describe the burning in his arms and legs, the black scrape of water at the back of his nostrils, the feel of the reeds around his ankles.

'And when I dragged him out, Jack was gone.' Will said those three words: Jack, was, gone. Behind them, he hid the memory of screaming Jack's name, buried the image of leaving Cole coughing and gasping for air on the river bank as he pulled back branches and ran along the bank scouring for a glimpse of the green and red, how he felt when he ran home, heat in his lungs as he flew into the kitchen telling his mum what had happened. He hid the image of the police standing in the doorway, the memory of his mum offering them a cup of tea and slicing pieces of fruit cake onto plates as if they hadn't just told her that her eight-year-old son was lying in a mortuary. 'He must have jumped in after us . . . a fisherman found his body later that afternoon.'

'I'm so sorry, Will.' She brushed his hair away from his forehead, her hand resting against his cheek. 'But it wasn't your fault.'

'It *was* my fault. I was his big brother. I should have put him first. And instead, Cole Chapel gets to shag about as though nothing happened.'

Will didn't know that Cole was never the same after that day either, that sleeping around was part of how he coped.

'After he died, and this is gonna sound mad . . . but I hated the sun. Seriously, every morning after his death it would be there, hanging in the sky, it was like it was gloating and it's so . . . *yellow*.' Will laughed then, covering his face with his arm and a groan. 'I sound like a nutter.'

'No you don't.'

He shifted and reached out, drawing a line from her forehead to her chin. 'I never thought I'd be able to feel anything again. I was dead inside, Ella, it was like I didn't have a heart,

I felt like there was nothing inside my chest. I didn't feel happy or sad, or in pain . . . I was just empty.'

Ella's eyes filled and a tear rolled along the side of her cheek. Will wiped it away with his thumb. 'Until I walked you home, until I kissed you.' He smiled, his finger running along her bottom lip. 'And then there was this, this whoomph.'

'Whoomph?'

Will smiled, taking her hand and placing it over his heart. 'In here, and it felt like my body was . . . filling up. You made me feel something.'

And in that moment, everything became clear to Ella.

She kissed the mouth that had just told her the reason he was with her, that explained why right now, Will Roberts was on *her* bed with his hands in *her* hair – not someone better looking, not someone who looked like she belonged on his arm – her, Ella Walker. And she understood. She was there when he needed someone. She was in the right place at the right time. And as she pulled him closer and a small moan escaped his mouth, she was happy to accept that.

As summer continued to warm their days, there was a spring in Will's step as he adjusted the strap of the guitar slung over his shoulder and ducked beneath the green leaves of the trees that edged the park.

His growing relationship with Ella was transforming Will's world. He hadn't known how tightly his muscles had been wound, that the emptiness in his chest would ever be filled.

Will followed the familiar route to Ella's house. It was a Thursday, and he was on his way to his guitar tutoring job. Every Thursday for the past six months, Will had taught a boy who showed great promise. It wasn't surprising; the boy's father worked in the music industry, he had discovered.

The route took Will past Ella's house, and as he was early for his appointment, he decided to call on her on the way past, ask her about her day.

He was now used to using the back door to the Walker house, but he always gave a small, polite knock, even though Bill was forever telling Will he didn't need to. His fist tapped the door, but no sound came from inside. Through the window, Will could see that on the table, Ella's artwork was scattered, and steam rose from the recently boiled kettle; he opened the door and stepped inside. Will loved the way the house smelt, the feel of it, the shudder of the old fridge as it brought itself back up to temperature, the grind of the cuckoo clock on the wall, beeswax from the Welsh dresser, the after smell of cooking, rich and full.

From the lounge, Ella's voice carried into the kitchen, Will's smile freezing in place as he recognised Cole's voice in reply. Will stopped on the threshold between the kitchen and the hall, frozen, unsure what to do.

'What do you mean?' Cole asked.

'What do you think I mean? *It*, the *deed*.' The reply was undeniably frustrated.

'Oh.'

'Oh? What do you mean, "Oh"?'

'Nothing.' There was sarcasm snagging Cole's reply.

'It's not nothing though, is it? Is it me, do you think? Am I not . . .'

'It's not you, Ells.' Will could hear kindness in his tone, a little humour around the edges.

'Then what is it? We've been together nine months. You don't even wait nine hours.'

'Rude. I can't help it if the female species can't keep their hands off me.'

'Well, that's just it, I can't keep my hands off him and . . .'

'Whoa! La, la, la!'

The conversation in the lounge continued, Ella and Cole both unaware of Will standing just outside the door.

Cole's hands were covering his ears, and his laughter was momentarily dampened as Ella hit him over the head with a cushion. She sighed. 'What should I do?'

'Will is . . . Will is complicated. It's like he thinks everyone expects him to be good at everything and so he tries to meet those expectations. Even more since Jack.' Cole picked at the end of Ella's sock, resting on his lap. 'But one thing I know, Ells . . .' He avoided her eyes and rolled the piece of fluff between his fingers instead. 'It's definitely not you.' He flicked the piece of black fluff from his fingers in her direction. 'But I'd get that cherry well and truly popped before you go to uni, because the lads will be all over you like a rash.'

'You're disgusting.' She threw another cushion in his direction.

'Just keeping it real.' He lifted her ankles and put the cushion beneath them.

On the other side of the wall, Will backtracked silently through the house and closed the back door behind him.

Will arrived at his appointment slightly early. His student, Phillip, was twelve but had the confidence of an adult, his demeanour that of someone who'd never had to worry about anything. Will wondered if it was anything to do with the money and privilege the boy had been born into; he couldn't picture this boy playing kerby by the garages. Phillip led the way to the spacious kitchen. Everything in it oozed success: smooth lines, gleaming surfaces, cupboard doors that looked almost seamless.

'I came into your shop the other day.' Phillip passed him a bottle of Coca Cola, like one of the adverts Will had seen on ITV.

'Oh?'

'I got it.' Phillip clinked his bottle against Will's. Will couldn't help but meet the boy's pleased look.

'No way.'

'Yup, wanna wake her up?'

'God, yeah.'

Phillip led Will towards the study, opening it with a flourish. There, in the middle of the room, was a satin-cherry Gibson, the guitar Will had been saving up three years for, waiting for the fingers of a twelve-year-old.

Will lifted the guitar like a newborn, his fingers gentle but firm, cradling it carefully. 'May I?' he asked.

'Sure, I've been waiting for you to come over. I wanna see what she can do!'

Will sat down and began playing Eugene's 'Trick Bag', the song at the end of the *Crossroads* film. Cole and Will had watched that film so many times that they both knew the exact time where the video tape was creased so that the sound faded and returned, could repeat Ralph Macchio's lines in sync with him. The piece had taken Will months to learn. The music consumed him and when he finished, a slow clap came from the doorway.

'Impressive.' Phillip's father stood in the threshold. 'When you're finished with the lesson, Phil, show Will to my office, would you? Will, I'd like a word.'

'Um, OK.' Will raised the guitar strap over his body and passed it back to Phillip, concerned that he was in for a telling off, for using the lesson time on himself instead of the boy. 'Right then, let's put this baby to good use, shall we?' He smiled at Phillip and tried not to worry about the money he would lose if he lost his job.

The lesson went well. Phillip had just discovered grunge and Will indulged him by teaching him the first few bars of 'Jeremy' by Pearl Jam. Afterwards, Will followed Phillip's directions to the office and knocked hesitantly on the door.

'Come in!' the man of the house replied. Will's palm was sweaty as he turned the knob. The room was grey and black: grey sofa, chrome fittings, chrome picture frames holding awards. It was a masculine room. Phillip's father sat in a chrome swivel seat which spun towards Will as he stepped over the threshold. Will's eyes were drawn to the platinum record award framed on the wall.

'I managed them in eighty-six,' the man explained, noticing Will's interest. 'So, Will . . . what are your plans?'

'My plans?'

'For your future?' He sat forward, legs spread, chest leaning towards Will. His hair was scraped back, thinning, a pair of sunglasses sitting on his crown; he had the look of a man who holidayed abroad twice a year.

Will paused, unsure how and why he was being questioned by a man he barely knew.

'Well . . . I don't, that is, I'm not sure. I . . .'

'Have you thought about playing professionally?'

Will's mouth opened and closed.

'I'm a tour manager,' Phillip's father said, as if this explained everything. 'I need a session guitarist, someone who can play to your standard, who looks the part and can read music easily so that he can step in when needed. I have six tours lined up with seven different bands, starting in Spain and working across Europe at the end of September. You interested?'

'Interested?' Will parroted back at him.

'Yes. You'd have to audition, obviously, but I've heard you with Phillip, you're more than capable. Can you sing?' Will knew he could sing but it wasn't something he felt comfortable doing.

Will nodded the affirmative. 'I can, I'm not, that is—'

'In tune?'

'Yes.'

'Great. Can you pop into my studio next week?'

'I, yes.' Will cleared his throat. 'Yes, I can.'

'Good. The gigs aren't huge, a couple of hundred per venue, but it would be great to have someone of your ability, with your look.'

He opened his desk drawer and pulled out a card. 'The studio address is on the back. Call the number and speak to Alice, she'll tell you a time to pop in. Any questions?'

'Um, no, I . . . thank you, sir.'

'Sir makes me sound like my father-in-law, call me David.'

'Right, thanks . . . David.'

The chair spun back around, the mouse wiggled on the mouse mat, and Will closed the door behind him.

Chapter Eleven

Now

Ella

11th September 2022

'I just don't understand it.' Amira shifts and my head bounces on her lap. I'm bookended by my friends, I've opened my gift basket and we're working our way through a box of Lindt Lindor. 'Why would he want a divorce? You're like a coffee-advert married couple. He writes you poems and hides them in your undies, for God's sake, *and* he defrosts your bloody windscreen for you before you go to work so you don't have to do it! Baz doesn't even know what de-icer is! Why would a husband who treats you like a bloody goddess ask for a divorce?'

'I don't know.'

'Well, you need to find out! This is just fucking weird.'

'He said sometimes love isn't enough.' I screw up a wrapper in my fist.

'What the fuckity fuck is that supposed to mean? Cole?'

'No idea.'

My phone rings and Jamie's face grins up from the screen. 'Oh God, I can't tell him, I don't know what to say.'

'Why should you be the one to tell him? Let Will explain his actions, if not to you then to his son,' Amira huffs.

I go into the bedroom to answer the call and swipe the screen, putting on a bright smile.

'Happy birthday, Madre!' His grinning face bounces in time to his footsteps as he walks through a corridor and into a kitchen. There is the background noise of other students, the hissing of something in a pan, the slamming of a door.

'Thank you!'

'Did you find your presents? I forgot to tell you they're in my room, but I figured you'd have been in there with the Pledge and a bin bag by the time I hit the traffic lights. Have you turned it into your own craft room? Burnt the mattress on the lawn? Changed the locks?'

'Ha, very funny. Hold on, I haven't had chance to open it yet.' Jamie says hey to someone in the background and there's a laugh of agreement that last night was blinding. It doesn't surprise me in the slightest that Jam has already made friends. I prop my phone on my dressing table and sit opposite, putting on a bright smile. I'm hoping the soft lighting in here will be kind and Jamie won't notice the state of me.

'Have you had a good morning? Breakfast in bed?'

'Um yeah, thanks. Amira has just popped round with a gift basket . . . Lovely wrapping by the way.' I hold up Amber's gift.

'I'll have you know that I spent hours toiling over the right paper, the perfect gift tag . . .'

'A pen that wasn't running out?' I raise my eyebrows at him, holding up the tag where *Happy birth*— gives up to ghost writing. I tear open the paper and smile down at the red cashmere scarf in my hands. 'Oh, Jam, it's gorgeous!' I wrap it around my throat. 'And it goes so well with the dressing gown.'

'Oh, well open up Amber's.' Jam agrees with someone in the background that yeah, he'd love a brew. 'She organised me.' I laugh, reaching for Amber's parcel. I pull away the paper, gasping at the colour as I unfold a knee-length coat. 'She said it'd suit you and that green and red are complementary or contrary colours or something. Anyway, Mum, gotta go. Happy birthday, say hi to Dad, laters.'

'Will do. Love you.'

'You too.' And then he's gone. I lay out the coat; it's wool, bottle-green plaid, with a neat belt and double-breast. I finger the collar and smile. It has Amber's immaculate taste all over it. I shrug off my dressing gown and pull the coat over my yoga pants and T-shirt. It fits like a dream. I reach over and open Cole's brooch and fit it on the right-hand side with a gentle touch. I stand, lifting Jam's scarf and wrapping it around my neck, burying my nose in it, enjoying the luxury of its touch. Cole and Amira are waiting in the kitchen, Cole just a step outside the open door, cigarette in hand. Amira is using the scary coffee machine with ease, a throw-back from her barista years. I do a little shimmy, swishing the scarf as I step into the room.

'Oooh! Let me guess, Amber's present?'

Amira turns to me and Cole looks up, throwing me a smile. I nod.

'It's such a waste Amber is going into medicine, fashion is where she should be.'

'It's gorgeous, isn't it?' I smooth down the fabric. Cole stubs out his cigarette and closes the door behind him.

I make my way to the mirror. I chose it carefully, scouring the quirky shops in town and the internet until I found it; it's my first real mark on this blank canvas of a house. It sits horizontally, opposite my painting, reflecting back the blues of the Mediterranean Sea. Around the edges is a mosaic of sea glass, each piece scavenged: treasure from wind-swept beaches, the glass churned and moulded by the embrace and release of the sea. I step into its frame.

The woman in the mirror meets my eyes; they widen, the pupils expand, the colour from her cheeks falls away.

The air in the kitchen is filled with the smell of woodsmoke, with fried onions, the sweet smell of donuts; the sounds of my friends' chatter is swallowed by excited screams and the mechanics of fairground rides, 'Praise You' by Fatboy Slim and the crack and hiss of a fire.

My breath catches in my throat. The sounds of the room slow down, like a vinyl record on the wrong setting. My hand touches my face, smooths down my hair, trails around the curve of the scarf, follows the edge of the collar, fingers the brooch at my breast.

I have not thought of the woman now looking at me from the mirror for a very long time, and as my knees give and my reflection tilts like I'm standing on a ship navigating a storm, just as it did the last time I saw her, I think to myself . . . *What the fuck is going on?*

Chapter Twelve

Then

August 2000

Will checked his clock again, throwing his arm over his face. It had been four hours and twenty-three minutes since he'd walked out of Ella's house. Four hours and twenty-three minutes since he'd broken up with her, since he'd seen her face drain of all colour and felt his insides coil and twist, his breath snatched away. Tears scored his cheeks as he rolled over and buried his face in his pillow. His throat burned, a dry heat searing from the back of his nose, down his throat, into his chest. The pain of her loss was worse than he could ever have imagined possible.

He sat up, gulped some air. He couldn't do it. As he thought this, his body relaxed, the heat from his throat cooled, as if his body already knew. It was past one in the morning, but Will grabbed his keys regardless.

In the room next to him, his mother was sound asleep, the combination of anti-depressants and sedatives keeping her oblivious. Uninterrupted snores came from the lounge as he passed where his visiting aunt was prone on the sofa: not even Gwendoline's sister, Jean, was offered a bed in Jack's shrine. Will slipped on his jacket and closed the door behind him.

He pushed his bike along the street beneath the swollen sky, the clouds fat and bulbous, the moon swallowed by their giant form. Will secured his helmet and started his bike, the beam of his headlight leading him along the empty roads, past the row of shuttered shops, the Co-op, Chinese take-away, off-licence, leading him through the estate, past Cole's house, Cole's bedroom light still on. Will pulled up just shy of Ella's house, not letting himself think, not letting him doubt what he was about to do. He loved her, that was all that mattered. He couldn't bear the thought of the dry emptiness filling his insides again; he needed the coolness of her touch, the light of her smile.

Ella had been excited when Will told her about the job. 'Just Looking' by The Stereophonics was playing in the background as they lay side by side, hands held, looking up at the ceiling. 'Oh my God, Will.' Ella sat up, crossed her legs beneath her denim skirt and scooped her hair into a ponytail. 'This is HUGE. Touring Europe, doing what you love? Some people go their whole lives waiting for an opportunity like this.'

'I know.' Will shook his head in wonder; he couldn't quite believe it was real. His audition was the following week and already he could feel the cogs of his life turning, clicking into place, moving him forward. 'I mean, I might not get it, I've still got to audition.'

Ella sat on top of him, leaning forward, kissing him deeply. 'You can do it, I know you can.'

Will reached up and wrapped a piece of her hair around his index finger. The red was growing out, her natural colour pushing the fake away. 'Will you come and visit?' he asked quietly. 'I know you'll be busy with uni life, but—'

A bubble of laughter escaped Ella's mouth and she kissed him all over his face, his eyebrows, his cheekbones, his nose, his chin. 'I will report for girlfriend duty every chance I get.'

Will got the job.

He had sat in David's office and listened to the ins and outs of the tour, how gruelling a schedule it would be, how much travelling, how little time he would have free. He would need rehearsal after rehearsal. 'This won't be a holiday, Will, this is an up-at-dawn, gruelling circuit. The gigs will run late and you will often have to travel the next day, so if you're not up to it, you need to lay it on the line now. Because I need to know I can count on you.'

Will had reassured David, he was up to it.

When Will returned home, he had approached his mother as she sat on the sofa, just the ticking of the clock and the hum of a lawnmower outside the house breaking the silence.

'It would mean me going away, Mum.' He held her papery thin hand in his.

'Of course you must go, William! A holiday, that's exactly what you need. Your father always loved the sun so . . .'

Will cleared his throat. 'I thought you might like a bit of company while I'm away? Aunty Jean would love to come and visit?'

'Jean? Yes, yes . . . it would be lovely to see her. Is it a Thomas Cook package? They always did such a good job of looking after us.'

He had made a call to his aunt. Will had borne his mother's condition on his own since they lost Jack, but now he knew his mother needed more help. It felt like a betrayal as Will told his aunt the extent to which she had deteriorated. Up until then, he had been loyal to her, keeping up the pretence. Jean had arrived on their doorstep a day later, a suitcase in hand, holding Will in a determined and fierce hug.

But shortly after the first high of getting the job, doubts began to corrupt Will's mind, doubts about leaving Ella. He looked at the university holiday timetable; he read up on Ella's course, on her workload: he knew that she wouldn't be able to get out to see him often and that even if she could, he wouldn't be able to take time off. David had told him that if all went well, there was another tour starting up just after this one, four different bands, five different countries.

A thought had wormed into Will's head: *It won't work*. The thought was parasitic, eating away at the whispered conversations about their future, sucking on the promises to keep in touch, to write, to call, to visit whenever they could, so that there was no substance left. *It won't work*. The words coiled around the plans to phone every Sunday morning no matter what happened. *It won't work. It won't work*. He knew it was the right decision to break up with her. He knew that it wasn't fair to leave her while he went to Europe, to have her waiting for him; she should be free.

And that was why, just five hours ago, Will had told Ella they should break up.

'Why are you saying this?' she'd asked, eyes red from crying, arms hugging herself as she sat on her bed. 'Why, Will?'

'Because it's better to do it now than in six months.'

When Ella would replay this conversation back in the years to come, she would wonder how different their lives would have been if they hadn't got back together, if Will had left for Europe without her. But on that day, as Ella had heard his words, as she sat staring at the lips she had kissed so many times over the last few months, somewhere deep down she had known it would happen. She had prepared herself for it: even while they were making promises, she'd pictured Will onstage, seen the crowds, the drinks afterwards. Will would resist for a time, but eventually, he would come to realise that Ella wasn't enough. But when he'd actually spoken the words *out loud*, feeling like her insides were swallowing themselves was still somehow unexpected.

Ella was lying beneath her duvet as Will pulled up outside, her bedside lamp lit, her eyes raw, her body numb. Cole had left a few hours ago: he'd said nothing, just held her while she cried. Ella blinked, but her eyelashes felt too heavy for the action, and she idly wondered if this was how shock truly felt.

Outside, the clouds had split open, a scatter gun aiming diagonal sharp needles at the leather of Will's jacket. He could feel his white T-shirt clinging to his skin as he looked up at her window, relieved to see that she was still awake. He ran from his bike, crouching down to retrieve a handful of gravel as lightning lit up the sky. He stepped backwards on the lawn, throwing the small stones up against her window. A loud crack of thunder enveloped the sound. He tried again, the lightning flashing as the stones made contact.

Ella squinted at the window, leaning up on her elbow. Another clatter of grit hit the pane. Her stomach was filled with hope, the hard chrysalis of Will's break-up cracking, a glimmer of a pink wing emerging from within. Ella drew back her curtains and pulled up the roller blind, the reflection of her lamp blotting out half of the lawn outside, but she could see Will below, soaked from the rain. She lifted her hand.

From the lawn, Will looked up. Ella was surrounded by a warm glow, her hair loose and hanging around her shoulders. He dreaded her pulling down the blind, blocking out her light. She moved away from the window and Will waited, wiping his hair back from his face. A lozenge of light flooded the path as the front door opened, Ella waiting for him.

He stepped towards her but she held a finger to her lips, raising her eyes upwards to her parents' bedroom. Ella took Will's cold hand in hers and led him upstairs. She opened the airing cupboard gingerly, retrieved a towel and ushered him into her room, throwing it at him and resting her ear against the door, listening for sounds from the rest of the household. Satisfied that no one had heard, she sat next to Will on the bed as he rubbed his hair. He left the towel around his neck and looked at her. His gaze was intense, his face pale, his hands shaking. She took them from him and held them, waiting for him to speak.

'I don't want to lose you,' he began, searching her face, trying to read her. She squeezed his hand.

Will knew that the words he was about to say would change everything, but not being with her hurt too much. He brought her knuckles up to his mouth, breathing the words into them, his eyes trained on her wrist. 'Come with me.' His words were quiet, shaken. He kept her hand by his mouth, but this time met her eyes. 'Come with me, Ella.'

'Are you sure that's what you want?'

He nodded, tears filling his eyes. 'I know it's a lot to ask . . .'

'You want me to defer?'

He nodded and smiled. 'Come with me. You can paint Europe.'

Ella moved closer to Will, placing her forehead against his. She let her hands slide up the front of his shirt, discarding the towel and shrugging off the jacket. She reached for the bottom of his T-shirt, and pulled it up over his head, Will ducking slightly to help her. Her fingers traced the shape of his collar-bone, then dropped to the hem of her nightshirt, sliding it over her head, and dropping it to the floor. She shuffled backwards, lying flat, her hand reaching out to him. Will manoeuvred himself unsurely over her, his elbows suddenly becoming problematic in a way they never had been before. They both shifted until they were comfortable, their mouths meeting and their hands exploring each other's bodies with a new urgency. Ella's fingers found the button of Will's jeans and tried to tug them down, the denim still damp and clinging to his skin. With his cheeks flushed, he stood up and stepped out of them, Ella propped herself up on her elbows, drinking him in. Will looked down at his boxer shorts, unsurely.

'I will if you will?' Ella looked towards her knickers, her hand at her hip.

'I don't have . . . protection.'

Ella shuffled along the bed, opened the bottom drawer of her bedside cabinet and placed a condom on the top of it.

Will swallowed hard, taking a sidelong look at the red square, then back down at his boxers. Ella pinged her knicker elastic, trying to make light of the situation despite her nerves. 'On three?' Will tucked his thumb beneath the material. 'One,' she began, 'two, three.'

The room filled with the sounds of their shuffling bodies, with the electric air of nerves and anticipation as they twisted out of their underwear. Curiosity overrode their embarrassment for a second as their eyes explored the new landscapes of their bodies. Will returned to her, their hands and lips touching the new parts of each other.

Breathless, Will stroked Ella's hair. 'I've never . . .'

'I know.'

'What if I hurt you?'

'Then we'll know you're doing it right.' Ella's thumb stroked the shape of his eyebrow, a neat arc.

'Are you sure?' he asked again.

She nodded as his hand reached for the packet. 'I'm sure.'

Ella averted her eyes while the crinkle of foil and shifting of his body explained his actions. 'OK?' she asked him. He nodded and kissed her tenderly. 'My answer is yes, Will, yes, I will come with you.' Ella felt the relief in his kiss. He pulled back, and she knew it was time. 'On three?' she asked raising her eyebrows.

'On three.'

New jigsaw pieces of Ella and Will's life clicked into place: the lozenge of light from her open door, Will asking Ella to go with him, and the look in her eyes as she said yes.

And for the next twenty-three years, Ella was Will's and Will was Ella's.

Chapter Thirteen

Now

Ella

11th September 2022

'Thanks.' The glass is cold against my lips and I clink it against my bottom teeth as I take a sip. Cole crouches in front of me, the smell from the coffee machine replacing the bonfire smoke.

'Should we call a doctor?' Amira clutches a coffee cup in her hands.

'I'm fine.'

Cole's expression reads that I'm anything but fine.

'You're not up the duff, are you?' Amira clunks the coffee cup with a clatter on the glass table. She inclines her head towards the back of Cole's head, questioning my fidelity to Will. I give a sharp shake of my head; she shrugs her shoulders suggesting she was only asking.

'No. You need two to get pregnant as I understand it and we haven't, I mean not lately . . . it's complicated.'

Amira huffs. 'It's not that complicated.' She circles her index finger and thumb and pokes a finger through.

'Yes, thank you, I'm well aware of how to get pregnant, Amira.'

A rap at the door interrupts me. 'I'll get it,' I say, standing.

'I'm fine, Cole,' I reassure as he stands, letting me past. I unwrap the scarf and discard the coat, the brooch landing on the glass table. I'm still woozy as I leave the kitchen but I'm glad of the distraction, I know exactly how mad I would have sounded if I had articulated what I think I've just experienced.

The door swings open, a huge bunch of flowers hiding the face of the delivery man briefly.

'Ella Roberts?'

'Yes, thank you!' The rough wicker of the basket lands in my open palms, the pink birthday balloon impaled into the arrangement, my favourite lilies arranged in a spray of white and yellow.

'Have a good day! And happy birthday!' The man smiles, gives a wave and retreats down my drive. I nudge the door closed with my bottom and retrieve the card.

'Ella, Happy birthday. My love as always, Will x'

I return to my friends. Toast pops in the toaster, coffee cups are refilled, expectant looks meeting as I dump the flowers onto the table.

'Will,' I say in response, handing Amira the card and slumping into a chair. Cole leans over her shoulder, scanning the card. I ignore the way that Amira leans back towards his chest, just a centimetre between them; she can't help it, she's always been a massive flirt.

'What the fucking fuck is wrong with the man? He asks you for a divorce then sends you a bunch of flowers with all his love?'

'Will Roberts, always doing things by the book,' Cole says quietly, grabbing his cigarette tin from the inside of his jacket. I take in the tremor in his hands as he tries to lift the lid. Amira hands me back the card.

'Well, I think you should call him and tell him you don't want all his love, that you don't even want a sniff of it, and then I think we should burn the flowers in the garden.' I snort at the expression on her face: she looks as shocked as if the words had come from another person's mouth. 'If he's going to break your heart, then he needs to do it right. Not with fucking flowers from a low-rent florist.'

'They're from Luigi's.'

'Exactly. Low rent.'

'Do you think this is his way of telling me he's having second thoughts?' I say, thinking out loud. 'Maybe this is his way of offering an olive branch?'

'Hold on . . . please tell me you haven't just come to that conclusion by putting together clues like Miss Marple? From Luigi – who is actually Liam from Bangor with a bucketload of fake tan – to Italy, to olives to olive branch?'

I chew my bottom lip. 'Maybe.'

Amira inspects the bouquet. 'I hate to burst your bubble, babe, but these have been sitting pretty in the arrangement since yesterday morning at the least. Luigi probably had this loaded into one of his armies of white vans while Will was unceremoniously dumping you.'

'Thanks.'

Amira gives me her trademark shrug of the shoulder: just keeping it real, I am who I am. She pulls her vibrating phone out of her denim jacket.

'Oh, fuck it! Babe, I've got to go. Jas has thrown up at football practice again. I've told him a million times not to help himself to chocolate milk before practice.'

At the door, Amira pulls me into a hug, her familiar smell of patchouli engulfing me in hundreds of memories, from me sitting opposite her for my first interview, to me holding her hand while we danced on the tables at her thirtieth birthday party. She pulls back and looks deeply into my eyes. 'You sure you don't need me to take you to the doctor's?'

'No. Honestly, *really*, just too much to drink last night,'

I assure her. 'And I'm off to Chez Walker for my birthday lunch so they'll be with me the rest of the day, and you're coming later, right?'

She nods, reassured. 'Later, Cole!'

We turn to see Cole's saluting her and returning to the kitchen. Amira takes backward steps, holding up three fingers and mouthing the words *Three times*, and wafts the top of her jacket as if it's the middle of a heatwave. I shake my head at her and close the door softly behind me.

'So, want to tell me what really just happened?' Cole asks. His fingers rest loosely on the cup handle, the base of the cup lying on the kitchen side. I'm wise to all of Cole's attempts at hiding the shakes. I slump in the sofa at the end of the kitchen, pulling my knees up.

'You're going to think I'm losing my marbles.' He joins me at the other end of the sofa. 'Do you remember the night of the fair?'

'What night at the fair?'

'You know, the night I passed out after you gave me bloody straight gin, the night Will walked me home.'

'Oh *that* night.'

'Do you remember what I said when I woke up?'

'That you thought there was a woman with you?'

I nod, raking my fingers through my hair. 'Did I ever tell you what she was wearing?'

He looks up towards the glass roof, trying to recall but drawing a blank.

'I thought that I had made it up, that she was a dream while I was passed out, but . . .' I glance over at the coat and scarf at the end of the kitchen. 'Cole, she was wearing a green coat and a red scarf.'

'So what?'

'And a brooch, the same brooch that you've just given me. I remember it, Cole, I remember focusing on it.'

'What are you saying?'

'What if it was me? Me that I saw? Forty-one-year-old me?' I note his expression, one of concern and confusion. 'I knew you'd think I'm mad.'

He holds his hands up defensively in surrender. 'I don't think you're mad, I just think that . . . well . . . what is more rational, that you . . . what? Have the power to go back in time and talk to teenage Ella . . .?' I try to interrupt with a *But*— 'Or . . .' he continues, 'that you've just had a massive shock, are hungover and have taken our conversation last night, an old mixed-up memory, and come up with this?'

I sigh, my shoulders sagging, my body sinking into the sofa. 'You're right.' I close my eyes briefly. 'I'm doing what I always do, fixating on something else rather than dealing with the problem at hand.' I open my eyes and trail Cole's focus to the cupboard where the whisky bottle is hiding.

He blinks and smiles back at me, dimples forming, dark brown eyes lighting up. 'So, what can I do to help?'

'Help me save my marriage? Maybe you could talk to him?'

'I think the last person Will Roberts wants to talk about relationships with is me.'

'What a fucking mess.' My phone rings, Dad's ringtone of 'Papa was a Rolling Stone' filling the room.

'Billster?'

I nod. 'What time is it?'

Cole glances at his watch. 'Half eleven.'

'Shit. I'd better get a move on, you know what a fuss they make on my birthday. God only knows what awaits me.'

'Well, Ells, I'm going to relieve you of my scintillating company while you get ready, and shall return this evening, whereby I shall cook the birthday girl her favourite dinner, American Hot à la Domino's, accompanied with a good dose of Christian Slater circa 1990 and a bottle of red grape flavour 20/20.'

'Do you know what? That sounds perfect, except for the bottle of 20/20. I can't believe we used to drink that stuff.'

'Diamond White?'

I feel my face blanch at the thought. Diamond White and me go way back, a friendship that often ended with me sleeping with my head on the toilet seat.

'Bottle of white?'

'Your wish, my lady . . .' he drops a kiss on my head, 'is my command.'

'Cole?' He shrugs on his jacket and turns to me. 'Do you think I can get him back? That I can fix our marriage?'

'I think he would be a fool to let you go.'

Chapter Fourteen

Then

May 2001

Ella and Will were in France, eight months into the tour. Will was now twenty. They had gigs for a month in Paris and so rather than staying in hotels with the rest of the band, they had rented a small dilapidated ground-floor flat. It was a short walk from the metro, pale blue plaster falling from the walls, the shutters barely hanging on their hinges, an old cast-iron bed that leant to and fro and screeched every time they tried to move, and which left them in fits of giggles. In the end, they'd dragged the mattress to the floor.

Will didn't ever think he had been as happy as he was in that apartment. But even so, there were still nights where he would wake up soaked in sweat, the taste of river water in the back of his throat. Ella would hold him, telling him he was OK, that he was safe, and he found that if he fell asleep in her arms, the nightmares would be kept at bay.

The tour had been running into trouble, though – Travis, the lead guitarist, had been turning up either drunk or high, his fingers clumsy. When Will had been briefed on how the tours would be run, he'd been told his job as a session guitarist was to blend into the background. He was there to fit in with the band as though he had always been there but not to take the limelight away from the original members and Will was happy with that: avoiding the limelight, playing his guitar and occasionally adding backing vocals suited him best.

But Travis's actions were becoming more and more erratic and so David told the band that until Travis straightened up, Will would be front of stage. The idea was originally met with resistance but after the first few nights, it was clear that it was the right move. The crowds began to grow, both men and women appreciating Will's talents. Travis didn't even bother turning up to some of the gigs. The band members were only loyal to their friend up to a point; they were not about to jeopardise their new contract with Red Records.

Ella bounded into the apartment, her face flushed, eyes bright, her art case hardly zipping up, paper exposed from the place where the zip could no longer contain its contents.

'Will!' She shouted his name. 'Will!' she repeated as he sprang from the iron chair on the balcony, his guitar leant to one side. He drew back the barely attached curtain as she ran, jumping into his arms, legs wrapping around him. 'You're never gonna guess what happened!'

'You were abducted by aliens?'

'Nope.'

'Been offered a place on a travelling circus as a fire-eater?'

'Better.' She kissed him.

'Better than fire-eating? Not possible.'

'I've got an offer to display my art in a gallery!'

He dropped Ella from his grip and followed her as she rushed back to her art case. Will grinned, lying down on the mattress while she started splaying out some of her pieces. Pride swelled up from his chest, his mouth lifting at the corners as she pushed her hair back from her face, eyes scanning the pages in front of her. The pieces mostly consisted of Will in unsuspecting poses, of places they had visited. Every picture of this collection held a reflection within it, a mirror, a glass window, a slice of water, with the reflection always holding pieces of England. 'She said she loved the juxtaposition between "the visitor and the native" and that if I could get enough material ready, she would love to show me in the spring! I wouldn't get paid or anything and it's only for a week, a "raw talent" exposé, to give artists outside education a chance to get a foot in the door. I doubt I will sell, and even if I did, it won't be much after the museum's commission and all that but, fuck, Will!' She climbed onto his lap, leaning her nose against his, 'I've always dreamed of having my own show, but I thought it would be, you know, as part of my degree, not here! We can come back to France in March, right?'

'We can. This is just the beginning for you, Ella.' He kissed her deeply. 'God, I love your mouth.' He pulled at her lower lip with his teeth.

Her hands lifted his shirt above his head, his fingers unbuttoning her shirt. 'Promise me, Will,' she breathed into his mouth. 'Promise me this is just the beginning for us.'

'I promise,' he said into her mouth as he lay back.

Will left Ella asleep on the mattress, her hair plaited to one side, her back exposed to him from beneath the low-slung sheets. The divots of her spine held his gaze; he replayed the way he had kissed them, each small indentation filled with her scent, her warmth.

'Tell me what you like,' he'd asked her, breathless as he lifted her and rolled her on her back. Ella's legs wrapped around him, her rib cage pushing against his own, his hands holding her hips. Their confidence in the bedroom was growing with every minute they spent together.

He scooped her hair back across her shoulder, the ink-blot birthmark a crashing wave today, and placed a kiss on the nape of her neck before leaving to have a meeting with David.

'Will!' David smiled, gesturing across the bistro table. Pastel-coloured town houses lined the street; a woman in a red blouse cycled past, the wheels juddering along the cobbles, her pug sitting in the front basket. A group of mid-teenaged boys jostled each other, compliments and teases fired in French but their actions easy to translate. David was sitting kerbside: suit jacket over a sage shirt, Ray-Bans; a cafetiere, fresh bread, small bowls of jams and butter.

Will crossed the street, the sun at the back of his neck, Ella's shampoo in his damp hair, an origami guitar in his back pocket.

'Hi, David.' Will shook his hand and pulled up a chair.

'Europe suits you.' David grinned from beneath his sunglasses as he poured them both strong coffee. 'I'm hearing great things, Will, great things.' Will nodded, unable to stop the smile spreading across his face.

'It's going well, I love it here.' Will looked up at the waitress and ordered a glass of orange juice.

'And the guys? They're treating you well?'

'Yeah, I mean, they have their reservations obviously, I haven't been with them for six years gigging, but yeah, they're good.'

'And Ella?' David reached for some bread, smoothing the butter across the fluffy white surface.

Will observed the pull of the delicate dough separating from the firm crust. There was something in his tone that made Will pause before responding. 'She's good, thanks.'

The waitress returned, handing Will his juice along with a napkin with her number written on. Will pretended not to see it, turning it over, the condensation from his glass smudging the numbers so that in half an hour, when he left the table, the number would be nothing but black marks without form.

The waitress, however, would think about Will for the rest

of the day, and when she recognised his face later that week on a poster, she would go to the concert and look up at the English man she wanted to take to bed. She would wait patiently for him to finish, apply a rich red to her lips and tousle her dark hair so it fell in glossy spirals. But Will wouldn't notice the waitress who had written her number on the back of the napkin waiting for him at the stage door; he would walk past her and she would watch him lift the girl with the mousy hair, with paint splattered on her bare legs that wrapped around him. And during the decades that followed, the waitress would think of him often; he would forever be the boy that every man she met would be measured against: a man who looked at his girlfriend as if nobody else existed.

'Remind me again, what is it that she does?' asked David.

'She's an artist,' Will replied. 'Actually, Intemporalité Gallery has just offered to show her work in the spring.' Artist was too small a word to describe the way she looked when she was standing in front of one of her pieces, one of Will's shirts hanging loosely above her thighs, paintbrush clamped between her teeth, beauty spot mingling with the dots of paint on her cheeks as though that mark had been put there to fit in with what her future held.

'Right, right. That's great! Good for Ella. And she still manages to come to all the gigs?' He smothered the bread with strawberry jam.

'That's right, she never misses one.' Will could hear the pride in his voice.

'Hmmmm.' David chewed on his bread thoughtfully. 'Well, the thing is, Will, I think it would be best if she didn't. Come to all of your gigs. I'm sure it must be getting boring for her, sitting listening to the same playlist over and over.'

'Um, no . . . she works all day on her art so she enjoys it.'

'Of course, of course. But the thing is, Will, Ella being there, well, it doesn't fit your brand.'

'My brand?'

'You know, good-looking lad, talented, the world at his feet.'

'I'm sorry, I don't follow.'

'You're bringing in the crowds, Will, and let's just say, it's not just your musical talents that are making the difference.'

'But Ella is—'

'I'm not saying Ella shouldn't be there, no, I'm not saying that at all. She left her life to come with you, that's right, isn't it?' Will ignored the tight knot in his stomach; he knew what Ella had given up to go with him. 'What I'm saying is that, it would be good, for the band, if you seemed . . . unattached.'

'Unattached? But I am attached.'

'Look, Will, this is a band. Bands have groupies, women and men who spend good money to see you play . . . imagine how much more they would pay if they thought that they had a chance with the talented guitarist from England. Do you think they would stop at just one gig? You've got a bright future ahead of you, don't throw it away on your first crush.' He swallowed down the rest of his coffee, stood and rested a hand on Will's shoulder. 'Think about it, Will, this could be your big break. Time to make a decision . . . if you're in, you have to be in one hundred per cent.'

Will walked the dusty pavements, the tall, brightly coloured, three-storey houses fanned out beside him like one of Ella's colour wheels: red-orange, yellow, yellow-green, blue, violet, each one with wrought-iron balconies, potted plants pouring over window boxes, the backstreet filled thick with life and vibrancy. David's words were stuck to Will like chewing gum on the bottom of a shoe; he stretched them out, feeling them lengthen and lose their elasticity. In the bakery window, elaborate displays of giant macarons beckoned him in. Will fumbled with the francs and centimes in his pocket, landing them on the glass counter with a clatter and an apology, buying coffee and lavender-coloured macarons for Ella's breakfast.

And by the time Will closed the door behind him and stepped into their apartment, he had left the remains of David's words on the kerb for someone else to step on.

Ella was still sleeping when he entered the room, her soft gasps of air disturbing the dust motes dancing in a silver pathway of light through the age-old shutters. Will placed the paper bag with her breakfast next to the mattress, quietly discarded his trainers and curved his body behind hers. She mumbled in her sleep, turning towards him, her arm at his waist, eyelids flickering, meeting his eyes with a sleepy gaze, her lips meeting his.

Every day that Ella woke up with Will, she held the moment in her palm; she cradled the sounds and smells, the feel of his skin against hers, the way he smiled at her. She pocketed the memories for the time that she knew would come. Because her time with Will was borrowed; she knew it, deep within her core. She could see the way women and men were drawn to him, women who were more attractive than her, more interesting . . . just more. She knew as she lay on that mattress that William Roberts believed he was in love with her, that he loved being with her, but she also knew that he needed her. Will needed Ella's strength, her support, her love, and with that, she had a strange sense of certainty that she was only a guest star in the screenplay of his lifetime . . . she would only have Will for a few chapters. Once he had discovered the man he still was, the man who could survive the guilt of his brother's death, he would realise that he had the rest of his life to find his equal. But, for now, he was all hers.

'Mmmm, you taste like oranges,' she mumbled against his mouth.

'I bought you breakfast.' He shuffled up and reached for the bag, letting it tap against her nose.

'What did I do to deserve you?'

'I have no idea . . . maybe you killed puppies in a former life?'

She batted him gently with her hand and reached over, pulling on one of Will's discarded T-shirts, peeking into the bag.

'Ooooh!' She took one out, balancing it carefully in her palm. 'It makes no sense to me, why everyone doesn't start the day with cake. Why save the best till last?' She took a bite, lilac dust falling onto his burgundy The Smiths T-shirt. She closed her eyes, focusing on the taste, her beauty spot folding beneath the curve of her cheek.

Later that night, Will lay back on the mattress, looking up at the plaster hanging in swirls from the ceiling like Christmas streamers as Ella laid her head on his chest. 'I can hear your heart beating. Thump. Bump. Thump. Bump.' She closed her eyes. 'I love you, Will.' Ella smiled, enjoying how the new words felt when she said them out loud, a laugh escaping her and running along Will's breastbone.

'Loving me is funny?' he asked, kissing the top of her head.

'No, but when I said it your heart went thump-bump-thump-bump like it was, I don't know . . . hyphenated?' Her finger ran up and down the xylophone of his ribs. 'I hope I always make your heart beat in hyphens.'

'I can't ever imagine my heart not speeding up when you're in bed beside me, not even when you've got false teeth and a purple rinse.'

And he meant it. He wanted the world to know: they were each other's beginning, middle and end.

Chapter Fifteen

Now

Ella

11th September 2022

The coat hangs across my shoulders like a friend or a lover: a small amount of pressure resting across my back, a comforting arm wrapped around my rib cage, a warm hand at the bottom of my spine guiding me forward. I tie the belt around me, my fingers slotting the material through the tortoiseshell buckle, my hand sliding across to the cool rutted surface of the brooch. I eye the mirror and step towards it tentatively, filling my lungs and lifting my chin: a battle stance. With relief, I can only smell the aftermath of coffee and toast, can only hear the clock ticking, a dog barking, the boiler igniting; there is no woodsmoke, no squeals and vibrations of fairground rides, no Fatboy Slim playing in the background. I examine my reflection, considering Cole's words and lining them up against my own experience. I know his is the more rational, the more realistic of the two, but I also know: I've seen this reflection before.

That morning, the morning that Will came over to my house for the first time, I had replayed the image I had seen, the fog, the figure of the woman, her desperation to be heard from behind an invisible barrier; I unfolded my unconscious mind out before me like a map. If – as I was led to believe – the woman who had seemed so real to me appeared not while I was conscious but passed out, I needed to analyse and decipher the image, pull it apart like the components of a dream. It was so easy to explain: a woman trapped – the stress of approaching exams and my inability to escape what was about to happen; the fog – my inability to see my future clearly if I didn't get the right grades to get into uni, what would happen if I didn't get in; the amber brooch – transference of the golden amber of the fire that I had been staring into just moments before I passed out. It could all be explained, all of it except that certainty: the certainty that there was a woman standing in front of me before I passed out, not after, not during – before, and no amount of analysing the facts had ever changed that feeling in the pit of my stomach. I lean in, pulling back the lines around my eyes, smoothing down the grooves around my mouth, my neck . . . the girl with the red plaits and the black eyeliner is hidden beneath a layer of pro-retinol and highlights. My phone rings, Will's face smiling up at me from the screen sobering me.

'Hi,' I clear my throat. 'Will, hi.'

'Happy birthday, Ella.'

'Thanks, and thank you for the flowers, they're beautiful.'

'You're welcome. I know Luigi is the enemy but . . .'

'No, it's, they're really nice.'

Silence.

'Are you OK?' he asks.

'Not really, you?'

'Not really.'

'Look, Will, we need to talk. Not today, I've got to brave The Walkers solo today, God help me, but soon?' I undo the belt, hold the phone between my shoulder and cheek and shrug off the coat.

'Ella, I think we need some time. To . . .'

'Well, do you know what, Will?' I drag my fingers through my hair. 'This isn't all about what you think is best.'

'I know, I'm sorry, it's just that—'

'You can either talk to me or sit in silence, but I'm coming to see you.'

'OK.' I can hear the smile in his voice, almost see him leaning against the wall, the look he would give me when I put up a ridiculous argument that I somehow make sound rational, like he's torn between being impressed, frustrated and finally resigned, a small smile chewing in the corner of his mouth.

'Will you tell them? The Walkers?' His voice breaks, a hairline fracture, easily recovered from.

'No. Not yet. I'll tell them you're ill. I don't want to worry them if this is just a, a . . . midlife crisis. And don't tell the kids either.'

'It's not a midlife crisis, Ella, you know that.'

'This time yesterday I didn't know my marriage was about to end, so what do I know? Look, let's not get into this now, I'm late.' I take a breath, knowing that telling him Cole was here last night would hurt him, but I carry on regardless. 'Cole was here last night and—'

'Of course he was.'

'What's that supposed to mean? You left me, Will, did you really think I wouldn't turn to my best friend?'

'I just . . . After everything that happened . . .' he sighs. 'But I guess it's no big surprise you would have called him. Cole Chapel, always there to pick up the pieces.'

'If you hadn't asked for a divorce, Will, there would be no pieces for him to pick up. Look—' I take a deep breath. 'I'm not getting into this now. I'll see you.' I hang up the phone, grab my car keys and head over to my parents'.

*

'Oh, my Jesus Christ.' I lower my head to look through my windscreen beneath the sun visor. It's one of those days that begins by letting you know that winter is on its way but seems to decide to hang on to summer for a while longer; the sun is bright as I indicate and follow the road to my childhood home. Attached to each lamp post are various laminated photographs of me throughout my childhood, as well as balloons bobbing up and down like, well, like balloons. As I round the corner, I'm met by a bouncy castle bloated with primary colour. Even taking into account all of this information, I still hold out the hope that this is for somebody else, that my pictures and the 'Happy Birthday Ella!' banner are actually for another Ella. Not this Ella, not me, not the Ella whose husband has just left her and who is contemplating whether she has finally lost her marbles.

I park and stare up at my old bedroom window, and for a second, I remember looking out from it, seeing Will that morning after the fair, so unsure of himself in a body that should have walked with confidence. I jump, a fog-horn sound screeching through the crack opening in my window.

'Fuck off, Kenny!' I yell. He responds by attaching his face to the outside of the driver window, dragging his nose downward: a piggy snout. Roddy opens the passenger side and discharges a Super Soaker, the water blasting my face and hair. 'Not in my car!' I fumble with the door handle and scramble from my seat, slamming the door behind me, my eyelashes dripping mascara. 'How old are you? Ten?'

Roddy ignores me and pumps the blaster, aiming it at me for a second round. 'Don't you dare! I mean it, Roddy.' I move towards the bonnet as he rounds towards the back of the car. 'Give me the gun!' I shout, chasing him, but by the time I get around to the back of the car I already know that I've lost. Because Kenny is waiting for me, a bucket of iced water at his belly, hidden from me by the car doors. The bucket is emptied over my head, ice landing between my cleavage, down my back, water running into my shoes.

My brothers then begin bellowing out the 'Happy Birthday' song while I stand, shoulders slumped, arms folded over my very alert nipples and shivering torso. I narrow my eyes and eyeball them both. 'You had better lock your doors, brothers,' I say with menace, which has them whooping and reeling with laughter.

My sister-in-law, Philippa, comes around the corner, her footsteps halting when she takes in the scene. 'Oh Roddy! You didn't!' Roddy's guffaws lose their enthusiasm as he meets his wife's steely glare. Kenny catches my eye, switching sibling allegiance as we both revel in Roddy being brought to heel by his wife. He drops the water pistol on the lawn and shuffles towards her, mumbling how it was Kenny's idea and how he only shot a water pistol. Seizing my chance, I grab the gun and aim it at his retreating back, being careful not to get Philippa; it's not just Roddy who she can bring to heel with an arctic glance. No doubt hearing the commotion, my parents emerge from the doorway. Just as my aim lands perfectly on the back of Roddy's head.

'Ella!' Mum screeches. 'Now is not the time for water pistols! Honestly! You're forty-one, not four!' Roddy turns and gives me a sly smirk from beneath his Joe Wicks locks.

'But—'

'Never mind, you can borrow one of my dresses . . . come here, my darling.' She opens her arms to bring me into a hug, but on seeing my saturated state, holds me in place by the shoulders. 'Happy birthday, Ella!'

'Thanks, Mum, and thanks for the . . . bouncy castle?'

'Oh, that's not for you, darling, that's to keep the kiddies entertained.'

'What kiddies?'

'Oh, you'll see! I've invited a few neighbours.'

I groan. My forty-first birthday is not one that needs a big celebration. I was hoping for a pork bap and a pint of beer, if I'm honest. 'I'd stay away from Brenda-from-thirty-two's coleslaw though . . . you remember Meghan and Harry's wedding day, don't you? Your father almost cracked the porcelain. He couldn't keep a thing inside for three days, everything ran out of him like lava and between you and me, I don't think the toilet bowl ever fully recovered.'

As if on cue, Dad arrives, wrapping a towel around my shoulders and bringing me into a hug. 'Happy birthday, Ella.'

'Thanks, Dad.'

'Roddy?' he asks.

I look up at him. 'Two-pronged attack.'

'Ah. I should have put two and two together when Kenny offered to fill up the bin with ice for the beers. I've got some Corona for Will.'

'Thanks, Dad, but, actually, Will can't make it.'

'Oh?' Mum questions, her eyebrow arching.

'Yes, he says to tell you he's really sorry. Stomach flu.'

'Oh dear. Rita, you know Rita? The lady who painted her garage with the—'

'Red glitter paint.' Dad and I join in, sharing a rueful smile.

'Yes, well, she's had a terrible case of D&V. Mind you, she looks fabulous. Lost over a stone. Right, well, Ella, let's get you into something dry and get you a drink, eh?' Mum smiles, her eyes narrowing across the lawn to where Philippa is giving Roddy a stern talking to. Whereas Will can do no wrong in my mother's eyes, Philippa can do no good. When Roddy first brought her home to meet us, we were all thrilled: she was pretty, polite, a little shy. But the longer they were together, the more confident she became and the quieter and more reserved Roddy was. He started working out all the time, his clothes names branded and expensive. Philippa had made a joke on her wedding day about knowing it wouldn't take long to whip Roddy into shape; we had all laughed nervously and Roddy had blushed. Kenny had whispered into my ear that if he ever fell for a woman like Philippa, I had his full consent to put his entire *Star Wars* toy collection on eBay and to burn his *Dungeons and Dragons* books. I had made him sign something to this effect on the back of a napkin; I still have it. But Kenny's quest for true love has so far proved fruitless. That never stops him dressing for success: Kenny always wears a shirt with a dicky bow, maintaining that when he meets his Guinevere, he wants to make sure he looks the part. I have tried to explain to him that wearing a dicky bow might in fact be the reason he hasn't landed a Guinevere, but he dismisses my protestations.

I lean into Dad's chest as we head back inside. My phone vibrates in my pocket and I pull it out. It's from Cole: *What do you fancy watching tonight?* Heathers *or* Pump up the Volume*?* My thumbs tap the latter.

Dad spots Cole's name. 'You're back in touch?'

'Um, yeah. He came over last night, actually.'

'While Will had stomach flu?'

'Yeah.' Dad turns towards me, his eyes scanning my face; I can feel myself blushing at the lie. Dad has always been able to tell when I'm bending the truth.

'And he's coming over again? Tonight?'

I nod. 'The house is quiet now that Jamie has gone and now seemed like a good idea to get back in touch with him. He's doing better.'

'It's a difficult thing, when your kids leave home.' He takes the towel from me as I kick off my pumps. 'It feels a little like someone has lifted anchor without telling you, and you find yourself unable to stop floating forward.'

'So how did *you* stop?'

'Oh, it was easy, your mother took hold of the wheel.' He smiles.

I rub my hair dry, pull Mum's brush through it and slide the hangers inside her wardrobe. I lean in, breathing in the smell of her; memories tumble over each other in the same way that the three of us would enter this room on Christmas morning. I remember crouching down amongst her shoes and dresses, all long and flowing but somehow managing to maintain a touch of chic – Mum has always been one step between a flower child and Coco Chanel. I reach for a plain black halterneck, normally worn with bangles-a-jangling, a bright patterned scarf and a kimono. The fabric slips from the hanger into my hands and I undress, pulling it over my frame. Whereas the dress flows loosely on her, it hugs all my curves.

'Ella?' she shouts from the bottom of the stairs. 'Are you coming down? I've got a surprise for you!'

Oh God. This does not bode well. I hurry to the window and twitch the curtain, my stomach landing by my knees. Outside on the lawn, watching a few brightly dressed pre-schoolers bouncing up and down, is my small group of friends from primary school. Why in holy hell would she think I'd want to see them? Rachael, Bailey, Tara and Kate – or The Girls as they referred to themselves back then. The Girls that ditched me the moment we graduated to year nine, when I started to get spots, had my braces fitted and when I had a particularly questionable incident with a trainee hairdresser – I wasn't cool enough to pull off a fringe an inch above my eyebrows. There was one last disastrous sleepover at Tara's house where I'd sat through 'Saturday Night' by

Whigfield twenty-nine times. Twenty-nine. That's a lot of the air getting hot. After that, I was happy to relinquish my membership to The Girls.

I reach for Mum's make-up bag, slick some lip gloss across my lips, bat my lashes against the mascara wand and brace myself for what is about to meet me below.

'Look who's here!' Mum waits beside the bouncy castle, holding out a glass of prosecco. I take it from her hand, and smile tightly at The Girls, a *Sex in the City*-style set.

'Hi!' I smile, pulling each one in turn into a cool-cheeked embrace.

'Happy birthday!' Each one smiles as if they hadn't slipped photos of celebrities with fringes and braces drawn-on into my locker.

'So lovely to see you!' I take another gulp of prosecco. Kenny halts at the corner of the lawn, swallowing a large piece of sausage roll, his cheeks colouring, as he takes in The Girls. Kenny wasn't the only one to have been affected by them, Tara in particular. I can still see the look on his face as he left for the year eleven disco to pick up Tara, an early prototype of The Dicky Bow already in situ. I never found out what actually happened, but I know Kenny came home an hour later, locked himself in his bedroom and never spoke about the disco again.

Mum, of course, doesn't know that any of this went on. The Girls are children of her oldest friends; how could we tell her that the friendships she had carefully cultivated since me and my brothers were little had ended in bullying and heartache? I look down at the neat row of miniature Adidas trainers beside the bouncy castle, my attention drawn to the small children bouncing up and down.

'Aren't they gorgeous?' I enthuse, I hope, convincingly. The Girls all smile in the direction of the yellow rubber, four pairs of primary-coloured socks suspended briefly before plummeting back down. They all agree that they are, and how clever they are for their ages, top of their class already. I stifle a smile by slipping the edge of the glass between my lips.

'And yours? You have two, isn't that right?' Tara smiles her veneers at me.

'Yes, Amber and Jamie, both at university now.'

'University! Goodness! I'd forgotten how you and Will gun-shotted down the aisle. Is he here?' she asks, looking around. My stomach clenches beneath my mum's dress.

'No, he's got stomach flu, unfortunately, but I'll be sure to tell him you were asking after him.'

'He's a teacher now, isn't he?' Rachael asks, as though it's a recent development.

'Yes.'

'Such a shame . . . Just imagine, Ella, if it wasn't for you, um, your circumstances, he'd be a millionaire now. Although, I never really liked The Knock, I'm more of a pop fan . . . He was so talented, though . . .'

'He still is.' I smile again, my cheeks beginning to ache. Behind them, I can see Mum having a frustrated conversation with Kenny. He looks over at The Girls, then back at Mum; then, defeated, he approaches us, his paunch sucked in, his beard wiped of stray pastry. He is taking care not to look at Tara.

'Can I get anyone a drink?' he asks in the same tone as you might use if you were calling up an ex to explain you had a mysterious rash.

'I'll have a sparkling water if you have it?' Tara flicks her hair off her shoulder, a stray tendril whipping Kenny's eye.

'We do,' he replies, his right eye clenched shut. 'Anyone else?'

Orders are placed and Kenny retreats, the weight of his task slumping his shoulders.

'So, what are you up to, Ella? Are you still working at that little florist in town?' Rachael asks, red hair catching the sun. Is it my imagination or are there more than one or two grey hairs weaving through the copper? I feel a momentary sense of triumph. So far, I don't have any.

I nod. 'Actually, I own it.'

'Oh! Wow, it must be a very . . . fulfilling job.'

'It is.'

'I do wonder how you working mothers do it.' The intonation sounds like a slur.

'Well, mine are a lot older now. But I do remember what a handful they can be at that age.' I smile, determined not to rise. 'I was lucky, though, I had a lot of help.'

I mean my parents and Will – the way he would still share the night-time feeds, even though he was working on his degree until gone midnight – but as is so often the case, I wish I could suck the words back in.

'That's *right*, Cole was around a lot back then, wasn't he? Before he, you know . . .' She knocks back an imaginary drink. 'It's all water under the bridge now, but . . .' she looks at the rest of The Girls as if looking for approval, 'I'll let you in on a secret.' She leans in. 'We all thought you might have been, well, having your cake and eating it.' She giggles, batting my arm to let me know she means no harm. 'Tara? Do you remember? We never did quite understand it, your strange little threesome.'

'Cole is just a friend. Always has been.'

Kenny returns with the drinks, a haze of recently applied aftershave mingling with his approach. He hands out the drinks, a raspberry floating in each flute.

'That's the alcohol-free.' He hands Tara the water.

'Not drinking, Tara?' I ask, changing the subject.

'No, I gave up. I went to a hypnotist and never looked back.'

'A hypnotist?'

'Oh, Ella, you must try one,' Bailey gushes. 'I've lost a stone since I started the sessions.' Close up her hair is a touch darker than is natural and noticeably thicker than it used to be. 'Not that I had any to lose, really, but after having Willy, I felt I needed that extra little push, you know?'

'Willy?'

She looks over at the little boy in blue trousers who is licking the side of the bouncy castle.

'Willy! Stop that!'

Willy doesn't stop that.

'You know, the hypnotist even helped me remember where I'd put the keys to the safe,' Bailey continues. 'I'd hunted high and low for them and couldn't find them. I mentioned that I had a memory like a sieve and told her about losing my keys and she offered to help retrieve my memories. Poof, ten minutes into the session and I could just see myself, walking across the kitchen, reaching up to Mother's antique teapot and hiding them inside. It was like magic!'

'So the hypnotist helped you remember?' I ask, my heart fluttering.

'Exactly! It was like watching a film. I never would have believed it if I hadn't gone through it myself.' Bailey scratched the back of her head with a shellac nail.

'So, hypothetically,' I suggest, 'a hypnotist could help retrieve your memories from, say, your teenage years?'

'Well, I suppose so. Gosh, I would love to go back and re-live those days,' she adds dreamily.

'Really? But what if . . . I don't know, you saw yourself being a complete bitch and ended up hating yourself afterwards? Imagine seeing yourself doing something so mean to a boy and thinking about poor little Willy going through the same thing?'

She lets out a high-pitched laugh. 'Oh, Ella, you're still our little weirdo!'

I scrunch up my nose and shrug my shoulders: you know me.

'I'd better mingle.' I drain the last of my drink. 'Oh, and do try the coleslaw from Brenda at number thirty-two, it's *divine*.'

It's dusk when Amira arrives. The air has turned cooler, the fairy lights hang from the fence posts and solar garden lights cast a soft amber glow around the garden; Van Morrison croons from Dad's 'stereo system' in the back garden where a group of Mum and Dad's friends have joined them around the rattan garden table. Their laughter and chatter rises and falls on the breeze. I smile. They have always hosted parties, always had a full circle of friends. Me and Will never really did the whole double date, group of friends thing. We would hold the occasional party or BBQ for his colleagues, but we were always happier when it was just the four of us.

I'm lying on my back on the bouncy castle, the prosecco giving reality a soft outline; my toes are cold as I focus on the stars starting to emerge like silver pins in black velvet.

'Sorry I'm late.' She kicks off her shoes and spacewalks towards me, my body lifting and sinking with the waterbed feel of her movements as she lies beside me.

'How you holding up, birthday girl?'

'Mum invited The Girls.'

'Fuck me.' Amira is well versed on my experience with The Girls.

'Yep. Kate is exactly the same, just repeats the ends of the rest of everyone's sentences but still somehow manages to sound and look superior. Tara is teetotal, Rachael is going grey, Bailey has either extensions or hair implants, I couldn't work out which, and has a hypnotist and a child with the same name as a penis.'

'Dick?'

'Willy.'

'Jesus.'

'Is that an aeroplane or a satellite?' I squint up, the stars looking more like running stitch than pin pricks now.

'Satellite.'

'They said something interesting, though. Bailey's hypnotist helped her find her keys. Isn't that amazing?'

'Well, it depends on where they were looking. If they were in the bottom of her bag then not really, no.'

'She found them in her *mind*.'

'How much have you had to drink? You're making fuck-all sense.'

'Bailey couldn't remember where she had put her keys and the hypnotist helped her recover her memories.'

'Oh-kay.'

'What if what I saw that night at the fair was real?'

'What night at the fair?'

'You know, the one I told you about, the night I got together with Will. The night the clocks went back. He walked me home after I made a tit of myself and passed out after Cole gave me neat bloody gin to drink. Remember? I told you I thought I saw a woman trying to talk to me.'

'Oh, hang on, the laaaady in reeeeeed!'

Amira belts out Chris de Burgh and I laugh as she rubs her face against mine, cheek to cheek. 'It was green, you plonker.'

'Same difference.'

'Not really, I don't reckon old Mr de Burgh would have got very far up the charts with that one.' My thoughts drift back to the subject in hand. 'What if it was real though?'

'What, that there was some weirdo hanging around a bunch of pissed-up teenagers, trying to talk to you?'

'No . . . it wasn't like she was *there*, there . . . it was like she was a messenger or something.'

'So, what, a fairy godmother?'

'No. This is going to sound mad, Amira, but I think it might have been me.'

'You?'

'Me. Like me now. She was wearing exactly the same outfit that I had for my birthday and when I looked in the mirror, I could see her, me, the woman who tried to talk to me. And she *really* wanted me to hear her.'

'What do you mean?'

'It was like what she was trying to say was important.'

'So what did she say?'

'I don't know. I can't remember.'

'Well, a fat lot of good that is.'

'What if it's real? What if, the night the clocks go back—'

'When do the clocks go back?'

'The last weekend in October.'

'Always?'

'Yes, always . . . how do you not know that?'

'Dunno.'

'Let's say it is real and that I *can* go back and tell my eighteen-year-old self something important.'

'Like what?'

'That's what I can't work out. I wouldn't change a thing, I don't think. I mean, I'd tell myself that pelvic floor exercises are way more important than the midwife makes out, and not to let my best friend convince me to have a tattoo on my arse-cheek on my thirtieth birthday.'

'Agreed, not my best idea.'

'Oh, and to not let Jamie loose with the Sharpies in my newly decorated lounge or to give Amber a home haircut when she's twelve . . . but other than that, what would be so important that I could risk telling myself something that could change my entire life?'

'You know how insane this sounds, right?'

'I know, but I know what I saw.'

'OK, for argument's sake, let's say that in, what, six weeks? seven? you are going to be able to go back and talk to yourself. Would you risk it? You could, what is it that Doc is always going on about in *Back to the Future*? You could be erased from existence!'

'That's if I mess with my parents' timeline.'

'But you'd be messing with Amber and Jamie's timeline, though, right? You pop back for a natter, accidentally mention that Will has asked you for a divorce and eighteen-year-old Ella thinks, fuck that, I'm not marrying him only to get dumped. I know, I'll go and shag Cole Chapel instead.'

'Why are you obsessed with shagging Cole Chapel? And ugh! It would be like shagging one of my brothers.'

'Hardly.'

'Right, so say you're right and I could mess up my whole timeline. Why would I risk it? It must be about saving my marriage because I wouldn't change anything in my past, but I do want to change my future.' I sit up. 'That must be it, it all makes sense!'

'Does it now? You haven't had any of Kenny's special mushroom soup, have you?'

'No, look. Getting the coat and scarf on the day after Will asks for a divorce, the fact that up until that point I wouldn't have changed a thing . . . what if this is, I don't know, fate or something?'

'So, you're telling me, that like something out of that programme with the hot Scot in kilts—'

'*Outlander*?'

'Yeah, that you're going to rock up at Dermont Arch on

the night the clocks go back and tell yourself . . . what exactly?'

'I don't know, don't you see? That's why I need to find a hypnotist. I have to find out what I said, I need to find out how to save my marriage.'

Chapter Sixteen

Then

July 2001

Applause filled the club. Palms against palms, fingers in mouths, voices catapulted back at the stage with three-hundred-strong whistles and cheers. The air was warm, laden with the violet haze of cigarette smoke, the after-smell of garlic and seafood mixing like the lights colouring Ella's face as she waited at the bar. Will's set was almost over and Ella was nursing a glass of water; she was recovering from a bout of food poisoning. She swallowed down another wave of nausea and concentrated on her sketchpad. The club used to be a church and beneath the modern décor, some of the original frescos remained. She stifled a yawn; it was almost midnight, but felt much later. Ella rotated her neck, took another sip of the water, clenched and unclenched her fists and picked the pencil back up.

On the stage, Will could feel the sweat accumulating along his spine beneath the black cotton of his T-shirt. As always, his eyes searched past the crowd, landing on Ella, who was bent over her sketchbook, her hair skimming the shoulder of a white shirt tied at the waist above her cut-offs.

'*Merci!*' The lead singer, Gus – face glistening with sweat, wooden beaded necklace above a pale-blue crew cut – took a deep sip from his water bottle while behind him the rest of the band continued to play the main riff repeatedly. The Knock were getting rave reviews, being dubbed as the next Blur, Gus the next Jarvis Cocker. Everything about the music industry, Will was discovering, was preceded by the words 'the next'.

Just at the side of the bar sat a group of men on a stag weekend. They had landed in this bar expecting dance music, strobes and a five a.m. finish and if they had arrived the next day, that is exactly what they would have found. But the band was too loud and the women were more interested in watching the stage than joining them for tequila shots.

The best-man-to-be, Jim (Jumbo, to his friends) noticed Ella at the bar. His eyes roamed over her tanned toned legs, supple and strong. It wouldn't have occurred to Jumbo to consider why her legs were so supple; he wouldn't know that they came from the long walks she and Will took whenever they could, so they could take in their surroundings, revelling in the adventure that they found themselves in. Jumbo wasn't thinking about the woman behind the skin, just what was on display. His focus licked the missing button at the top of her blouse and slid down to her cleavage, finding himself hard at the way she was licking her top lip while her hand flew over the paper.

Jumbo nudged his friend. 'Reckon I'd risk going bareback for that one, looks a bit like that Britney Spears bird,' he said. His friends all laughed; it was all just a bit of fun, no harm done.

'Really?' The groom looked over at Ella. She was nothing special, he concluded, pretty but plain and too Amazonian for his taste; he liked his women to be petite, almost elfin-like. 'Not my type, mate, but I reckon even you might be in with a shot.'

Jumbo knocked back his shot of tequila, clapped his hands together and headed for the bar.

Ella didn't notice the man standing behind her at first; she was looking over the crowd. The bar area was raised and she had a clear view of Will. She smiled, pride swelling in her chest as she watched him. With every venue, Will was becoming more confident. The tour should have ended by now, but instead, they had stayed in France; their popularity had grown quickly and so David had arranged more dates. Ella and Will were able to continue to rent the same apartment as last time and it was slowly starting to feel like home. Will laughed at something the drummer said as Gus introduced the next song. She watched the familiar twist of Will's fingers at the top of his guitar as he tuned it in, the way he held his plectrum between his teeth.

'Wow, that's really good.'

Ella jumped. A man was standing behind her, appraising her drawing over her shoulder. He was a little close for comfort; Ella could taste his aftershave at the back of her throat, smell the alcohol on his breath. But the bar was busy and Ella was polite. 'Thank you.'

The couple next to Ella paid for their drinks and moved away, and the man stepped forward and sat next to her, raising a hand at the boy behind the bar. 'Can I get you a drink? I'm Jim, but my friends call me Jumbo, on account of my . . . well, I'll leave the rest to your imagination.' He winked and ordered a bottle of Stella, turning to Ella for her order.

'I'm fine, thank you.' She returned her attention to her drawing and ignored the feeling of Jumbo's stares burning into her.

'The band are a bit shit, aren't they? Can't be doing with this indie crap. Give me some good techno any day.'

Ella kept her head down, letting her hair fall across her face as she continued to sketch, not wanting to get dragged into a conversation with a man whose opening line was a reference to the size of his penis.

'I didn't catch your name?' Not wanting to luck out just yet, Jumbo turned to Ella, making his intention to strike up a conversation unavoidable.

Ella sighed, her stomach churning, her head beginning to ache. 'Ella,' she replied. 'Sorry, but I really need to finish this.' She gestured at the drawing with her pencil. 'Enjoy the rest of your night.' She smiled politely and dipped her head.

Jumbo would look at his actions the next day through the haze of a hangover; he would think about his girlfriend and how he would feel if a man had behaved that way to her, and he would regret his next move. But here and now, his mates erupting into laughter behind him, Jumbo felt his embarrassment turning to anger at the girl next to him. Close up she looked nothing like Britney Spears; she was nothing special after all.

His hand reached out for her sketchbook, knocking over her water as he did. Ella jumped off her stool at the bar, the water seeping through her blouse, making it immediately transparent.

'Wow!' Jumbo leered, looking at her chest. 'You should make the most of your tits, love, I'd pay more money to see them than this crap.' He tore off a page and screwed it up, throwing it to the floor.

Ella crossed her hands across her chest. 'Give me that back,' she demanded as he flipped through the rest of her pictures, one of Will asleep, naked, catching his eye.

'I knew you were a goer when I first saw you.' His eyes roved over her body from her legs to her crotch, finally resting on her breasts. Ella shuddered under his gaze. She reached out a hand and snatched back the pad, reaching to the bar for the rest of her things.

Will had stopped playing. The band, confused, were looking in his direction, following his line of sight. Ripping off his guitar, he rushed from the stage, the other band members freestyling the arrangement, the bassist picking up some of Will's lead.

Will took the steps two at a time, almost losing his footing. His hands scrambled against the stage door, slamming his shoulder into it, the door throwing open. He began pushing his way through the crowd, but his progress was slowed by the mass of bodies. He felt like he was in one of his dreams, trying to swim against the tide, the dark shapes of the bodies dragging him back, an earring, a shoulder, a hip, a belt, a damp hand, sweat, perfume, aftershave, the bassline repeating, the drums occasionally hiccupping a break on the cymbal, his own soundtrack as he forced himself through the crowd: a glimpse of Ella's shirt, of her hair, of the man blocking her path, paper being ripped, the pad flying through the air. The last of the crowd parted and Will bounded up the steps to the bar.

Jumbo had discarded most of her drawings, throwing them up in the air, balling them and aiming them at his mates. Ella turned her back and began to walk away – she would go to the café next door and come back after Will finished – but Jumbo's meaty hand landed on her shoulder: the final straw.

'Take your hand off me!' She grabbed his hand, twisting it and turning to confront Jumbo face-on, shoving him backwards with her free hand. Losing his footing, Jumbo stumbled back, his backside crashing into a table, knocking drinks to the floor.

Will reached Ella's side as Jumbo gathered himself and stood back up just as the bouncer appeared.

'Time to go, pal,' the bouncer instructed, his French accent popping the world 'pal' out like a cork.

Jumbo spat on the floor. 'Didn't want to stay in this dive anyway.'

Will drew Ella to him, holding her face. She was pale, a sheen of perspiration along her top lip. 'Are you OK?'

'I'm fine, he was just drunk.'

Will pulled Ella into his chest, kissing the top of her head. Onstage, Gus was peering across, signalling to Will.

'I've got to go back, are you sure you're OK?' Will ran his finger along her jaw line, kissing her beauty spot.

Neither of them was paying any attention to Jumbo grabbing his stuff, his mates knocking back the rest of their drinks while the bouncer watched on. And as Will smiled back at Ella, he didn't see Jumbo's fist swinging around, didn't consider that blocking the punch of a drunken fool could break his hand, his wrist; he didn't realise that another jigsaw piece in their lives had formed.

Will didn't have the faintest idea that his hand would be put in a cast, that he would never again be able to play 'Eugene's Trick Bag', that his career as lead guitar would be over. Three years later, he would be sitting in a soft-play area – one eye on Amber flying down the slide, blonde pigtails above a denim pinafore, and a sleeping Jamie over his shoulder – and he would look up at the subtitles running along the news, announcing that The Knock had won a Grammy. He would see the future he could have had and the future he'd ended up with and wonder how his whole life had changed because of the actions of one drunk stranger.

But back in France, as the stag do were forcibly ejected from the bar, Will just knew that his hand was injured, that a screaming red-orange pain was pulsing behind his knuckles. He fought back the sting in his eyes: he would finish the set and then rest it on a bag of ice and be left with a nasty bruise tomorrow. Will knew that he needed to get back up onstage and that he wanted Ella with him. And so, while Jumbo was unceremoniously dumped onto the street outside, Will cradled his hand against his chest while holding Ella beneath his other arm. Together they made their way to the stage, the crowds parting now that they had seen some of what had happened. Will led Ella through the door, up the backstairs, kissing her and checking she was OK. He stepped back on stage, wincing as he threaded his hand through the guitar strap.

Gus, taking the discomfort Will was trying to hide, allowed Will a moment to compose himself. He turned back to the crowd, raised his hands, encouraging the crowd to join him in applauding the band. 'Before we leave you for the night, I'd like to take this opportunity to introduce you to the band.' A cheer rose up as Will tried to clasp the plectrum, but it fell through his fingers like melted butter. 'On bass guitar, Ben Hammond!' Ben played a deep thrumming riff. 'On drums, Olly Dean.' Olly's sticks crashed over the taut skin on the drums in a wave of sound. Gus turned towards Will: 'And our newest member of the band . . . Will Roberts!' A flush crept beneath Will's tanned face as the volume of cheers rose, the wolf-whistles adding to the crescendo. Gus grabbed the microphone and sang the last few bars of their most popular hit, Will positioning his left hand over the fret – even though he couldn't put any pressure on the neck – and plucked the string with his right hand. The cymbals crashed, lights flashed until the final song ended climactically. *'Bonne nuit!'*

Gus raised his hand to the crowd with a 'V'; the lights dimmed as the applause continued. Will took off his guitar, propped it up against the amp, and smiled back at the other band members, not ready yet to admit the truth to them. His hand was more damaged than he'd thought.

And he was right.

It was the last time Will Roberts ever played on a stage with The Knock.

Chapter Seventeen

Now

Ella

19th September 2022

I swallow down the rest of my coffee and glance at the gold plaque with the words 'Robin Jenkins – hypnotist' winking in the sun. I take a deep breath and push open the door. The reception area is similar to a dentist's and I walk to the desk, giving my name, sit myself down in the waiting area and open a magazine.

'Ella Roberts?'

I jolt, closing the magazine with a snap. Holding the door open to his office is a man in his mid-fifties, a welcoming smile, cardigan, and a look of kindness about him. I would expect him to have a hankie in his pocket and would wager it would smell of peppermints and clean laundry. I get up, stacking the magazine back on the small table in front of me. I look up at the man with the kind smile and brown loafers who will soon be nose-deep in my subconscious.

'Would you like tea? Coffee?' he asks from the doorway as I swerve past the magazine-laden table, knocking my shin in the process.

'Oh, tea would be lovely, thanks,' I squeak, trying not to hobble towards the room.

Inside it's nothing like I was anticipating, and I feel myself hesitate briefly on the threshold. The room I find myself – somewhat unexpectedly – inside is not unlike my parents' lounge. There is a desk at the back of the room, two recliners to my left, a rug beneath an oval coffee table separating them from the large brown sofa opposite, a patchwork throw hanging over the back, green cushions sinking into its corners. Behind the sofa, an overflowing bookcase, grandfather clock, landscape paintings, and beside it a lamp casting a sepia warmth against the grey clouds shooting rain at the large window opposite the door – its curtainless frame the only hint that this room does not sit inside a semi-detached house with a roast dinner cooking in the kitchen.

'You were expecting incense sticks, tie-dye and pocket watch?' he asks from the back of the room with a voice that implies a smile as he fills a teapot with hot water from the kettle.

'Actually, I was thinking white coat, clipboard . . . modern art,' I reply, taking off my coat and scarf and hanging them on the coat stand beside the door.

He chuckles as he carries a tray holding the teapot, two cups, a milk jug, sugar bowl and a plate of biscuits. I feel like I'm visiting my grandad.

'Take a seat, Ella.' He places the tray on the coffee table and sits himself in the recliner closest to me, a lectern next to it and on top a notepad. I hold my bag in my hands, my knuckles grasping it.

'Um, should I?' I look between the other recliner and the sofa.

'Sit wherever you feel the most comfortable.' He smiles at me over his half-moon glasses.

I move towards the sofa.

'Oh, and feel free to take off your shoes,' he adds, leaning forward, lifting the lid of the teapot, stirring the insides and clinking the edge twice with the spoon before pouring it into the waiting mugs.

'Oh, sorry, should I have left them at the door?'

He laughs, the sound like warm toffee. 'I just want you to feel as comfortable as possible. I encourage my clients to treat this room as they would if it were their own home, so if you usually sit with your feet tucked up on the sofa, I want you to feel that you can do that here.'

'Oh. Um. Cool.' I take off my shoes, grateful that I drove and didn't walk in my well-broken trainers that always leave my morning-fresh socks with the smell of wet dog. I do as he says, taking the right corner of the sofa and stretching my legs out.

He passes my tea and offers me a plate of digestives. 'The king and queen of dunkers,' he adds conspiratorially, as if this is a secret between the two of us. I take one, feeling at ease despite the strangeness of the situation. He settles himself back in his recliner, resting his cup on the arm while dunking his biscuit. Never being one to shy from a dunk, I copy his actions, gaining me a proud smile as he approves of my technique. I cast my eyes over the room, waiting for him to say something along the lines of your eyes are getting heavy, but I have finished my biscuit and he is reaching for another. The tick of the grandfather clock feels like it's getting louder, like when you accidentally sit on the TV controller. I'm starting to question if I made the right decision using a different hypnotist from The Girls, my main reason for coming here simply to avoid being speed-walked into their shellac-coated lives.

'So, Ella.' He wipes the crumbs from his corduroys and slurps his tea. 'You're here to recover some repressed memories?'

This is how I had explained things on the phone; I'd

thought it best not to go into the whole *I think I can travel through time* scenario.

I put my tea back on the table and tuck my feet beneath my bottom.

'Well, I, the thing is . . .' I let out a breath, making my lips vibrate in the same way that Jamie used to when he was pretending to ride a horse. 'You're going to think I'm bonkers.'

'I think we're all a little bonkers.' Again the smile, the warm toffee laugh.

'When I was eighteen, I was drunk and walked away from my friends. I was at the October Fair, have you ever been?'

'Wouldn't miss it. Used to take my kids and now I take my grandkids. Best toffee apples in Shropshire.'

'I know, right? Well, I was at the back of the grounds, by the Abbey?' He nods. 'And I saw this woman.' A shiver rolls over my skin, like a wave. 'She was standing on the other side of the archway. It was like she was trapped, like there was a barrier she wanted to get through and she was upset, frustrated, her mouth was moving like she was trying to tell me something.' I close my eyes briefly, trying to sharpen the image, but shake my head, meeting his eyes. 'And at the time, I know I could hear little snippets of her voice but I can't remember what she said, and, well, this is the part that is going to make you think I'm bonkers . . . I think she was, well, me. Like me now. Forty-one-year-old me.'

'What makes you think that?'

'She was wearing a green coat with an amber brooch and a red scarf.' I let him follow my gaze to the coat stand.

'You think the woman was you because you have the same outfit?' He doesn't say this question as if disbelieving my conclusion, more that he understands why I would think it was true.

'It's not just that, it's . . . it's the timing. My husband has just asked for a divorce and that outfit was a gift, I didn't choose it and . . . I can't help but think that if I was going to go and tell my past something to help me, it would be now.'

'You've never needed help before?'

'No. I mean, sure, but I wouldn't change anything. I love my life, my kids, my husband'. I reach for the cup, my hand shaking slightly. 'So . . .' I fix a smile in place, 'that's why I'm here. I want to find out what she . . .' I correct myself, 'what *I* said.'

'OK then.'

'OK? You don't think I'm crackers?'

'I make it my business never to think any idea isn't valid. People thought that Da Vinci was bonkers but everything he said turned out to be true, in a manner of speaking. I think the first thing we need to discuss is how this works. Forgive me if you've already been on the Google, a lot of my clients know almost as much as I do when they come for their first session.'

'No, not really, I've had a quick look, but that was more to make sure that you're not going to make me act like a chicken or become a vegan or anything.'

'Do you want to dance like a chicken and become a vegan?'

'No. I don't mind doing the birdy song after a few beers, but I draw the line at fake bacon.'

'You can get fake bacon?' His furry eyebrows furrow and then release like a broken spring. 'Is it called fake-on?'

I snort. 'Well if it isn't it should be. You can get vegan sausage rolls at Greggs too.'

He nods slowly, as if accepting a brave new world.

'I promise not to make you a vegan. In fact, the first thing you need to know is that throughout these sessions, you are the one in control. You will be aware of everything around you, you will be able to hear my voice, I will wake you up from the trance slowly, there will be no clicking of fingers bringing you back in the room and I won't be asking you to look into my eyes.'

'Noted. What made you want to be a hypnotist if you have no interest in making people flap imaginary wings or click your fingers at them?'

'Well, I was a therapist for twenty-five years but then my wife died.'

'Oh, I'm . . . I'm so very sorry.'

'Thank you. She was the strongest woman I've ever met, and then cancer got her.' I prop my elbow on the sofa and lean my hand against the heel of my palm, waiting for him to continue. 'I wasn't in a great place back then, I kept watching old home movies of her over and over again, until one night, the video tape broke. I fell apart, didn't want to carry on without her. So I started taking sleeping tablets, trying to force myself to dream about her, but then it occurred to me, I had years of memories stored up here.' He tapped his temple. 'So I went to a hypnotist, and she helped me recover old memories of our life together. I hate to think how I would have ended up without those sessions.

'You see, the thing is, Ella, that nobody forgets anything. You might say things like "I've forgotten his name" or "I've forgotten my phone number", but you haven't. All that is happening is that you haven't got access to that memory at that time. There is nothing mysterious about hypnosis, it's just a state of focused concentration.'

'A bit like Superman when he's trying to shoot his laser beams through his eyes?' I ask, squinting and focusing on the cup as though I can shatter it with a well-aimed red-hot beam.

He chuckles. 'The memory is a tricky beast that can change over time. Every time we access a memory it can alter; it doesn't always stay the same. That's why they no longer accept forensic hypnosis in court. Unless you discover some corroborating evidence to support your new-found memory, there is no way of knowing if what you remember is the truth.'

'So you're saying that what I remember might not be real?'

'Maybe, maybe not. You might have seen a woman in a green coat and red scarf that night, she may have been trying to talk to you, but your memory might have added the brooch detail, for example. Then again, we might access information that helps you remember more about that night, that helps confirm what you saw. The point I'm trying to make is that you can't use what we recover as proof that the memories are one hundred per cent accurate.'

'Understood. So how does it work?'

'Well, what I would like to do is talk some more about that night: what you could hear, smell, taste, anything that will help you access those memories. The conscious mind is linear: you remember things in order, breakfast, lunch, dinner, but time doesn't really exist in the unconscious mind, it's all tangled up and grouped together by emotion. So, what I would like to do is concentrate primarily on the emotions you were experiencing that night. I will ask you to be attentive to all your senses, I will ask you to describe images, sounds, feelings. The more you focus on every little detail, the more fully enhanced your memories.'

'Got it. So should I lie down? What's the plan of action?'

'Sorry, Ella, this is just the introductory session, so I can get a sense of how to approach your first hypnosis session.'

'Oh.'

My shoulders slump.

'But I have an opening next Thursday at four o'clock, if you want to get started then?'

'Yes! That would be great.'

'Your homework is to try and think about that night, not the event you want to recall, but the hours before it:

what you were wearing, what you had eaten, a song playing on the radio, a smell that will help you access those memories easily.'

'On it, boss.' I salute him and stand as he shakes his head at me like a favourite niece.

'See you soon, Ella.'

'I'll bring the bickies.' I grin but hesitate by the door, turning back to him. 'Robin?'

'Hmmm?' He smiles up at me over his glasses.

'Thank you, for today. For understanding.'

'My pleasure, Ella. See you soon.'

I open the front door, my eyes drawn to the space where Will's laptop bag should be resting. I take a deep breath and plaster on a smile, trying to ignore his absence as if it's not leaning back and stretching around the house, making itself comfortable. The smell of Will's post-work toast and marmite is replaced with the faint smell of tobacco and the sound of Liam Gallagher bellowing from the kitchen.

I discard my keys in the bowl by the door, kick off my shoes and hang my coat in the cupboard under the stairs. Cole is in the kitchen, Alexa blasting Oasis's 'Wonderwall' out of the speakers. The smell of garlic fills the air and I follow it, nose in the air like Scooby-doo. 'Ooh, what's for dinner?'

'For you, I'm cooking my speciality, Carbonara à la Cole.' He pours a glass of white wine for me, takes a sip of his own, then proffers a spoon. I blow on the sauce as he lifts it to my lips.

'Mmm, yum.' I swallow the food and sniff.

He gives himself a congratulatory, self-satisfied nod.

'Good day?' he asks, reaching into the fridge and pulling out a hunk of deli-fresh parmesan.

'Um, yes, kind of. I saw the hypnotist.'

Cole closes the fridge and turns his back on me, opening

and shutting cupboards. 'Cheese grater?' he asks over his shoulder. I open the correct cupboard and pass it to him. 'Thanks. How did it go?'

'Good. He was nice, he was a bit like Bernard Cribbins. It was just an introductory session, but he didn't laugh me out of the room for thinking I can time-travel so, you know, I'm taking that as a positive. The next session will be more interesting, I reckon.' Biting around my thumbnail, I watch Cole busying around the kitchen, grinding pepper into the pan. 'Do you think I should tell Will?'

'About the hypnosis or about me staying here?'

The night of my birthday, Cole had finished his pizza and then said he was going to call a taxi. But the idea of being in this house, alone, without Will, felt so close to the life I knew I would have to learn to live if I couldn't convince Will to come back, felt so raw, so real, that I'd asked Cole to stay. 'Um . . . the hypnosis. I don't think mentioning you being here would help matters.'

'It's not the first time I've been someone's dirty little secret and I'm sure it won't be the last.'

'You're not my dirty little secret.' I reach for the wine, glancing at the bottle. It's half empty but I'm fairly sure Cole is more than a glass down. 'It's just that I want to keep things between us simple. For the time being.' I pour myself a small glass. I'm under no illusions that Cole has been completely sober when he stays over – he's too much of an addict for that – but there are two different versions of Cole's alcoholism. There is Cole – the functioning alcoholic who will knock back a single shot in his morning coffee, grab a cereal bar, go for a run, laugh and joke, sink a bottle of wine like it's water, follow it up with a couple of shots and go to bed. Then there is the ugly, completely alcohol-dependent Cole, the Cole who will knock back three whiskies before he gets out of bed, who won't shower, who won't eat. Three-whisky

Cole doesn't stop; he carries on, losing days and weeks of his life, rolling through his friends and family like Miley Cyrus swinging on her wrecking ball, except – most of the time – he does wear more clothes. And I'll admit, there is part of me that thinks Cole staying here with me might be what he needs to turn the corner.

'And how *is* Will? Has he come to his senses?' Cole rubs the cheese aggressively against the grater.

'Not yet. But I'm seeing him tomorrow.'

Cole winces as he scrapes his knuckle. 'Shit.'

I grab some kitchen towel and lead him to the sink, running his hand under the tap. 'If I had a pound for every time I've patched you up, I'd be a millionaire.'

I reach up for the first-aid kit, pull out a plaster and tear off the wrapper with my teeth. Cole remains silent as I wrap the band around his finger. I lean towards him, sniffing like a bloodhound.

'You smell like perfume.'

He grins.

'Seriously?'

He laughs and raises his eyebrows at me. 'What? You thought I would be saving myself for you?'

'Ha, ha . . . very funny. So, who was she?'

'Ah, a gentleman should never kiss and tell.'

'Will you see her again?'

'Nah . . . She was a bit . . . savage.' He pulls down the neck of his shirt, revealing three scratches, as though he's spent the afternoon with Wolverine.

'Yikes.'

'And she kept calling me Poldark.'

I snort, drop his hand and sigh. 'So that is what I've got to look forward to if I can't convince him to stay? One-night stands with Wolverine?' I sigh. 'Am I mad for trying to make him change his mind? Should I just let him go?'

Cole pulls his hand away.

'He still loves me, Cole, I know he does.'

'So why is he asking for a divorce?'

'I don't know, it's like he wants me to see that it's over, but I don't. I don't see. Maybe he's right, maybe we just need a bit of space to think things through. Do you think he's having a mid-life crisis?'

'I don't know, Ells.' Cole returns to the cooker, lifting the spaghetti and draining it in the sink.

'Can we change the playlist? You know I can't stand Oasis.'

'I seriously don't get why you still think Blur are better.'

'Ah, well then, let me show you. Alexa! Play "To the End" by Blur.'

'It sounds like the beginning of *Tales of the Unexpected*!' Cole tips the pasta into the sauce.

'*Tales of the Unexpected*?' I burst out laughing. 'You're showing your age, old-timer!' He ignores me as I turn the volume up, swaying and singing loudly, hands fanned out beside my head. I take a deep breath and sing along with Damon about dirty words making me look dumb.

'And he always sounds out of tune!' Cole shouts above the music. I look at him purposefully as I echo the lyrics about him drinking too much and how we can hardly see straight any more. He turns off the heat, dimples forming as he crosses his arms and watches me hitting the higher notes, declaring that he and I collapsed in love; I fill my lungs, bellowing out the chorus, stating that it looked like we may have made it to the end.

Cole slow-claps as I bow theatrically. 'Thank you, thank you,' I say as though the kitchen is filled with my adoring fans.

Cole loads up the plates and I take them to the table as the song continues, Cole following with another bottle of wine.

I pick up my fork as Cole tucks in. Damon is continuing . . . it looks like we might have made it. The sounds of a fairground in the background of the song seem fitting somehow.

'What if we have, Cole?' I put the fork back down. 'What if me and Will have made it to the end?'

'Then you'll find a new beginning. Now eat up, before it gets cold.'

'Yes, Dad.'

He sticks out his tongue at me then shovels a forkful of spaghetti into his mouth, whistling up the last stragglers of pasta before shouting: 'Alexa! Play "Cigarettes and Alcohol" by Oasis!'

We spend the rest of the evening with a Blur versus Oasis battle, laughing and chatting. Cole drinks more than me but stops once the second bottle is finished; he doesn't go to the pub, doesn't suggest a nightcap.

Chapter Eighteen

Then

July 2001

The sun yawned, stretching lazily behind the row of pastel Parisian town houses. The baker, wide awake and ready for the day, tied his apron around his waist, covering his rounded tummy, and unfolded the wooden slatted chairs, placing them quietly beneath the red-and-white-striped awning. The smell of bread and pastry plaited with the cool morning air; it slipped between the cracks around windows, through shutters, the pumice walls a welcome pathway for the evocative, buttery smell to drift into rooms, some with couples wrapped in each other's arms, some with empty beds awaiting visitors already en route.

The sweet smell permeated through the small room with the mattress on the floor. Will had finally fallen asleep, his body folded into an uncomfortable position which allowed his hand to remain inside a bowl of ice, the plastic ice-cube bag now deflated and limp.

Ella's stomach clenched as the clear honey scent drenched her skin, seeping into her dreams. Saliva rushed into her mouth, waking her with a shock, her tanned bare feet scrambling from the mattress as she lifted up the toilet seat just in time for the remains of yesterday's meal to make a reappearance.

'You OK?' Will swallowed down the pain from his hand, holding it palm-side up in his other, noticing the swelling through gritty eyes and dawn light.

'I think I've still got food poisoning,' Ella managed to say just before her stomach heaved again. Her hand reached out, trying to close the door behind her, but Will ignored her protests and crouched down, rubbing her back with his free hand. In the harsh bathroom light, his other hand looked worse, the bruises purple, black, sage green. Ella retched again as Will's right hand rubbed up her spine, his fingers nimble, strong and slim. The hand that scaled the fret of his guitar hung beside him, monstrous, swollen, broken.

For the next two hours, Ella could barely move away from the toilet. Will didn't want to leave her but the small ice-cube tray in the top of their tiny fridge wasn't enough to help with the pain and swelling.

Will called David en route to the pharmacy, telling him the events of the night before, explaining that he needed an X-ray. David called back shortly after, an appointment at a local hospital made. He swallowed down painkillers and drank from a bottle of water before slipping the key into the door of the apartment.

Sun was streaming through the broken shutters, the doors to the balcony open, letting in the sound of traffic outside.

Ella had made it back to the bed, the sickness abated for the time being.

Will sat down on the mattress, her eyelids flickering open, an apologetic smile on her dry lips. She examined Will's face, his grey pallor, the way he was holding his hand.

She pulled herself up onto her elbow. 'Oh, Will, your hand.' Her eyes stung.

'It looks worse than it is, I've got an appointment for an X-ray tomorrow. How are you feeling?' He winced as he shifted his weight to face her.

'Like I've been tumble-dried.'

'I've always loved the way clothes feel after they're tumble dried, so soft and warm.' He rubbed her cheek with his nose.

'Oh God, don't get too close. I stink.'

'Do you want me to run you a bath? We've got time.' The large copper bath took about an hour to fill to normal household standards. 'There is no way I'm playing tonight.'

Ella stroked his face. 'Who will stand in?' Her voice was tentative.

'Travis. He's promised to be on his best behaviour, apparently.'

'He can be at his very best and he still wouldn't be a patch on you. Even with your ugly giant battered hand.'

He kissed her hair again, the painkillers making his words heavy.

'I'll run us a bath and make you a sling for your hand.'

'You know how to do that?'

'Yeah. I've lost count of the times Cole has broken his bones.'

'He always had to climb the highest, didn't he?'

'He'd love it here. You know, I don't think he's ever been any further than Birmingham. Did you know he'd never seen the sea until a couple of years ago?'

'Really?' Will's eyes were becoming heavy, his breathing deepening.

'Yep. He came with us on the May Day that the twins got chicken pox. I never caught it, Mum reckons I must have some kind of immunity.' She yawned. 'Dad and the twins stayed home so we had room in the car for Cole. It was that really hot weekend, do you remember?'

Will didn't reply. He barely remembered anything about that summer, just the absence of Jack.

'We went to Black Rock Sands in Wales,' she continued. 'You know, the one where you could drive onto the sand? Cole got out of the car and just *stood*, staring.'

Ella closed her eyes, picturing Cole's flushed face, his dark eyes bright, his hair curling and blowing away from his face, the freckles across his nose, the tops of his cheeks sunburnt from the day before. It was only a few months after Jack had died, when Ella had seen more of Cole than ever after his friendship with Will disintegrated.

'He had this look, like he was seeing something that he just couldn't understand or that he was trying to remember, something important. "It's so big," he said, and then I realised . . .' Ella yawned. 'He'd never seen it before.'

Will didn't hear this part of the story, though; he had slipped into a painkiller-rich dreamless sleep, where colours swelled and receded behind his eyelids. Perhaps if Will had heard, he would have understood why Cole had no idea of the risk he was taking when he swung out on the rope swing that day, how quickly the current would carry him away when that rope snapped. He'd never experienced the power of water before.

Chapter Nineteen

Now

Ella

20th September 2022

I wait for Will on the wall outside his school. After just over a week apart, he's agreed to meet me for dinner after work so we can talk about *things*. I glance over to the doors, inside sits the vending machine; I picture myself on my knees, arm trying to grab hold of the chocolate. I'm wearing my ripped jeans, and a grey T-shirt with the Sunnydale Class of 1999 T-shirt that Will bought me. 'I always thought I'd make a good Buffy,' I'd said a few weeks before, when we caught a re-run when flicking through the channels. Will always managed to remember little things like that.

I pull out my lip salve and run it across my lips just as Will appears. I shove it back in my too-tight jeans pocket, making me wiggle like I've got a bad bout of thrush. I swallow hard, my pulse quickening as Will strides through the door, blond hair flopping the same way it did when he was hunched over his guitar, same long legs that held us steady as my back leant against the cool tiled wall in Portugal when we first tried shower sex; perhaps shower sex with Will isn't the best thing to be thinking about right now. He waves with the same hand that held mine when he proposed, when he told me he had nothing to offer me but himself, like he was a consolation prize. I stand, my hands in my back pockets. He smiles when he sees me, then seems to correct himself.

'Hi,' I beam as we face each other, toe to toe. 'It's OK, Will, you can still smile at me, I won't call my solicitor.' My joke makes him wince and he gives his attention to adjusting his laptop bag on his shoulder. 'Too soon? Sorry, I'm still trying to negotiate divorce humour.'

'You look good, Ella.'

'Thanks, but let's face it, who doesn't look good in a Buffy T-shirt?'

He nods, his hand rubbing across his mouth. 'I booked us a table at Kilago. I thought, maybe, we could walk?' He frowns up at the gathering clouds, then back to me.

'Sounds great. I got the bus, figured we'd need a drink.'

'Oh, I'm not, I mean I've got the bike so . . .'

'No problem, I'm more than happy to drink for two!' *Oh, do shut up, Ella. Drink for two?*

We begin walking across the carpark. 'Jamie is settling in well, he's working hard,' Will begins.

I snort. 'Working hard at finding which bars sell the cheapest beer,' I counter.

Will's eyebrows furrow and I regret my words. Jamie always seems to have the need to impress, and Will always seems to have the need to be impressed.

'Have you spoken to Amber?' I ask, closing the gap of conversation. 'I worry she's working too many hours.'

Before he answers, the rain clouds split open. It's the type of rain that comes from nowhere; the sun is still shining somehow and yet our clothes are becoming soaked. 'Do you want to come on the bike?' Will shouts above the sounds of the rain hitting the tarmac. 'I know you don't like it, but it'll get us there faster?'

'OK!' I nod, deciding now is not the time to mention that

I have never said I don't like riding on the back of the bike; Will just stopped offering to take me. He unshoulders his laptop bag and holds it over my head as we run. He hands me the spare helmet; I'm surprised it's still there. Moments later, my legs hitched behind Will, we leave the shadow of the school.

We arrive ten minutes later, my whole body thrumming from the ride, from the feel of Will's back against my chest. It's been a long time since I've sat behind him.

My shirt is clinging to my skin as I climb off and hand him the helmet. I pull the material away from my skin as Will bends over the bike, attaching the helmets. I can't help but watch the muscles of his back moving beneath the blue of his shirt, the damp material drawing a line along his spine. He stands back upright, his hand pushing back his hair. I look away, letting my eyes focus across the street where the fairy-lighted bay trees are swaying against the elements. I'm trying to ignore the pull in the pit of my stomach but as I drag my focus from the restaurant and meet Will's eyes, I see my own reaction reflected back at me.

Up until about six months ago, our sex life was one of the cornerstones of our relationship. When you learn together, when you're as open about what you want and like, as Will and I were, when you have that attraction to each other that we have always had, it's hard for it not to become a way of communicating. It was like we sought each other out physically when we were too mentally drained to talk about things. That is why, when he started to distance himself physically, I knew something had changed, something was *about* to change. But as his hand reaches out and tucks a stray piece of hair behind my ear, I feel that all too familiar heat radiating between us. He swallows, drops his hand and steps back.

'I'm sorry, Ella.' He tears his hand through his hair, as

though he doesn't know what to do with himself. 'I . . . I can't do this.'

'What? Can't do what?' I ask, stepping forward, my hand reaching out to his arm.

'Be with you.' My hand drops. 'Not yet. I'm sorry, I thought I could do this.'

'Do what? Go out for dinner?'

'Yes, no, just be, I don't know . . . friends?'

'Friends?' The word clatters from my mouth, disbelief and shock pounding in my ears.

'We need more time, apart, to . . . figure things out,' he continues, as though trying to tell himself how he feels rather than me. A lorry passes us, spray landing along my bare arm, slashing up the leg of Will's trousers.

'You mean *you* need time to figure out things. *I* don't need to figure out anything. I love you, I want to be married to you, to grow old with you, and I get that you might not feel the same way any more but then you look at me like that and I think that you do still love me, so tell me, Will, what's going on? Because I feel like I'm losing my mind.'

He looks away but I reach for his cheek, turning him to me.

'Look at me, Will, let me help. Why do you want a divorce? Please, Will, just say it . . . because I thought we were happy. I know it's a big change, the kids leaving and us being just us again . . .' A young couple rush past us, hands held, hoods up; he watches them, a puzzled look on his face. 'That's it, isn't it? You don't want it just to be us, do you? That's what this is about?'

'No, it's . . . it's not just about what I want, Ella. Don't *you* wish we'd done things differently?'

'Don't turn this on me, Will! I want *you*. I've *always* wanted you.'

There are tears in his eyes and he rubs his hand across his face.

My voice is quiet when I ask him, 'Just tell me one thing. I need the truth, not what you think I need to hear, Will, the truth. Do you still love me?'

He nods his consent. 'Yes.' The word scrapes from his mouth, like it hurts him, like he's resigned to never being able to escape it. 'But . . . we should never have stayed together, we never had a choice, can't you see that? Don't you think it's time to face the truth?'

His words hang in the air, coated in years of regret and pain. My mouth goes dry and the rain stops as quickly as it started. The sun fights its way through the clouds, catching the raindrops falling from his eyelashes. My chest rises and falls as I process his words. Up until now he has never said it, never admitted that he wouldn't have chosen the life we have.

I breathe heavily, processing his words as Will looks away from me with tears in his eyes.

I place my hand on his chest.

Everything comes down to this.

He might be having a mid-life crisis, he might think that we don't belong together any more, but if he still loves me as much as I love him, then I'm going to fight for him, for us, regardless of what else is going on. And something *is* going on with Will; I just don't know what, yet.

'I love you,' I say, feeling his heartbeat beneath my palm. And there it is, the answer I need, the thump-bump-thump-bump. 'And you still love me in hyphens.'

'It's not enough,' he says but the words have lost their conviction; now they just sound like words that he has practised, words that sounded so certain the last time he spoke them just an echo, a faint imprint.

'Why? Why isn't love enough?'

'Because we're not happy, Ella.' He touches the side of my face. 'Don't you want to be free?'

I shake my head, trying to disperse the things he's saying,

that he wants freedom and a life without me, but I'm not ready to give him up. I know he loves me: I can feel it in the way he's touching my face, and he might not be telling me everything, but I can see the turmoil behind his eyes. I just need to remind him of the girl he fell in love with. No. Not the girl he fell in love with; he needs to fall in love with the woman I am.

I take a deep breath. 'You once gave me six weeks to decide to leave the life I had planned, my place at university, to follow *your* dreams, because you *knew* we belonged together.' I look up at him. 'Now I'm asking you to do the same. To give up *your* plans for me. I'll give you the space you need, we'll live separate lives, but give me the chance to prove to *you* that we belong together, that love *is* enough. Please, Will, just six weeks, until our anniversary, and if you still want a divorce then . . . I won't stand in your way.'

He pauses, his mouth open, ready to tell me no, tell me that it's over. But his mouth closes and his eyes search mine and I can see I've broken through the wall he is trying to build around himself.

'Don't say anything now. Just . . . take some time to think it over?'

He looks around the street, then gives me a small nod.

I breathe out a plume of relief. 'Thank you.'

I place my hand on his chest as a bus pulls up. I kiss his cheek and cross the road to the bus stop. And as I sit down, I watch him through the steamed-up window, still standing in the same spot. I put my hand against the glass as it pulls away; he raises his hand and then he is gone from my sight.

When I get home there is a text message from Cole, asking me if I still want him to come over. I text the affirmative and an hour later he arrives with an Indian takeaway and obligatory bag of booze, which we unload onto the kitchen table.

'So?' he asks as I dip a poppadom into a bowl of raita. 'How did it go?'

'Not great. We didn't even make it into the restaurant.'

'You had a row?' he asks, offering me his carton of madras. I shake my head.

'Not like you to turn down a madras?'

'Huh? Oh, I can't eat anything too hot any more, it gives me heartburn.'

'Since when?'

'Oh ages . . . Will always gets me a korma.'

'Sorry, I didn't know.'

'It's fine, I'm not that hungry.'

I forget sometimes that although Cole might know Ella Walker better than Will, he doesn't know Ella Roberts all that well any more.

'What happened, then?'

'He said he couldn't be around me yet. And then he tried to friend-zone me.'

Cole coughs on his food and takes a long draw on his lager.

'Friend-zone you?' he questions, now recovered.

'Yeah . . . but that was after he looked at me as though he was about to shag me.'

'Slightly too much information.'

'Sorry.' I reach for my glass of wine and take a sip.

'So what now?'

'Well . . .' I tear off a piece of naan bread. 'I've asked him to give us six weeks.'

'Six weeks? To what?' He forks rice into his mouth.

'To try.'

'Why six weeks?'

'That's-when-the-clocks-go-back,' I say quickly, filling my mouth with peshwari. My phone buzzes and I pick it up. 'It's Will!'

Did you know half the salt in the world is mined from the sea?

I laugh, glad that some things never change. **No, but thanks for the insight** ☺

Sorry about the whole friend thing . . .

'What's he say?' Cole asks, getting up for another beer, popping off the top and closing the bin lid.

'That he's sorry about the friend thing.' I don't explain how when Will is avoiding hurting my feelings or if he's nervous he spouts off random facts. 'What should I say?'

'Tell him you're having dinner with me; he'll be round like a shot.' Cole grins and begins rolling a cigarette.

My phone buzzes again.

So how do we do this?

We go on a date? I reply.

Cole steps out into the garden and lights up. I lean back and take another sip of wine. **Dinner?** I type, but I delete it. Will needs space. It has to be his decision. I try again and this time I press send. **You don't have to answer now, just promise me you'll think about it?**

It's all I've been thinking about . . . Well that and how I've managed to shrink all of my socks ☻

I laugh. Will has never got the hang of the tumble dryer and once Amber began buying her own clothes, Will was promptly banned from laundry duty. 🔒☻ **Night Will.**

Don't let the bed bugs bite.

Chapter Twenty

Then

Inside the apartment, Ella hunched over the toilet again.

'I'm so sorry, Will.' She sat back on her haunches. She'd been sick so many times since the early hours that she didn't understand how it was possible to have anything left inside.

'It's fine, I'll be in and out of the X-ray and back before we know it.'

Ella's eyes were drawn towards the window where the parp of a taxi was funnelled through the open shutters. 'Go, before you miss your appointment.'

Will kissed the top of her head, 'I'll be as quick as possible, I bet it's just a sprain. Love you.'

'Love you too.' Ella gave him a weak smile, her stomach churning again. She grabbed a glass of water and a small empty pudding bowl, made her way back to the mattress on the floor, and fell back to sleep.

Outside the door, a neighbour, Francine, waited with her baby girl balanced on her hip, gumming a frozen piece of celery. In Francine's hand was some crystallised ginger in a small glass jar. Francine had heard Ella's sickness through the door. She'd suffered from severe morning sickness with

Sabrine, her daughter, and sucking on ginger was the only thing that helped.

The knock at the door dragged Ella from sleep. As she stood and touched her hand to her face, she could feel the imprint of her pillow folding across her cheek. She heard a giggle from behind the door, a baby and a woman's voice: *'Bonjour?'*

Ella walked slowly towards the door, her limbs heavy, her eyes burning in their sockets.

'Ah! *Bonjour!'* The woman smiled broadly. Her dark hair twisted on top of her head; her daughter leant forward from her hip towards the open door.

'Bonjour,' Ella croaked.

'English?' The woman's face was open and friendly.

'Yes, hi.' Ella gave a wan smile.

Francine took in the girl standing at the door. She had seen the two neighbours walking hand in hand from a distance, an open display of love and mutual infatuation, and then, of course, there had been the sounds from behind the thin walls that gave her and her husband the giggles, both of them looking at each other, remembering the days they too could make love any time in the day. Of course, once Sabrine had arrived, the rhythm of their own lovemaking had found a different pattern. The girl looked pale, and so much younger than she had expected.

'I hear you . . .' She put a hand to her mouth and enacted something spewing from it. 'This help, when I sick with Sabrine.' She nodded at the little girl reaching for her mother's hair. 'For you. To help.' She passed the jar towards Ella.

'Oh.' Ella was blindsided by the conversation, the implications, the small girl looking up at her with wide eyes. 'Thank you.' Ella tilted the jar with the small amber cubes, rolling to the side, syrup sticking to the inside of the jar. 'I think I've eaten something bad.'

Francine placed her cold hand on Ella's and looked into her eyes, trying to read whether the young English girl knew what would have been plainly obvious to anyone who had heard the pattern of her sickness.

Ella had dismissed the idea of pregnancy. Morning sickness only happened in the morning, right? And she had been sick in the evening too. The afternoons seemed to be the only time when she would feel OK. She'd been eating too soon, that was all; she needed to give her stomach a complete rest. Ella was on the pill; she couldn't be pregnant.

Francine gave a kind smile, nodded at the young English girl with the wide brown eyes and full mouth, and stepped back.

'Thank you,' Ella repeated as the woman turned and walked away, closing the door behind her gently. Ella leant against the door, clutching the jar to her chest, her heart hammering in her rib cage. She stepped across the room in determined strides, rummaged inside the bottom of their wardrobe and pulled out her Filofax, her finger running along the dates, pausing as it landed on the day her period should have arrived. Three weeks ago.

Ella shook her head, turned the pages back and told herself to concentrate. That couldn't be right. It couldn't be. It just couldn't.

At the hospital, Will waited, his foot bouncing up and down.

Along the corridor, Doctor Ménard trod towards the good-looking English boy. He had a son around the same age; their whole lives ahead of them, he thought wistfully. Earlier in the day, the doctor had had to amputate the leg of a homeless man. Dr Ménard shook the image away; the news of three broken fingers and a fractured wrist was an easy piece of information to deliver in comparison. Still, as the boy looked up at him with hopeful eyes, Dr Ménard still felt a tug of remorse in the pit of his stomach. His medical care was courtesy of a record label in the UK: the boy was a guitarist – a successful one at that, if the level of insurance was any indication – and so this news would undoubtedly impact on his career. Such a shame, throwing away all that potential in a bar brawl. What a foolish way to behave. He could imagine a boy with those looks and a guitar would have had many opportunities ahead of him.

'William Roberts?'

'Will, um, hi, yes. Um, *oui*?'

Will swallowed hard, taking in the way the doctor with the Desperate Dan jawline was avoiding his eyes as he drew up a chair. It wasn't good news. Will knew that there was real damage to his hand. He had tried not to worry Ella, had tried to hide the way it felt like a nail was being struck between his knuckles when he tried to move it, how his wrist felt like it could snap at any time from the weight of his hand.

Dr Ménard sat beside Will. He always hated sitting on these chairs, the blue material somehow penetrating his trousers, making his skin itchy beneath the material. He opened the manilla folder and brought out his notes.

'I have the results of your X-ray. You have broken your fingers here, here and here, and your wrist is fractured here and here. I will send you over to have it put in a cast, follow the signs to . . .' He scribbled a French word that Will didn't recognise and passed him the scrap of paper. 'And then . . .' he smiled at Will with kind eyes, 'you rest, huh? You will still play guitar, but rest, rest, rest.'

'How long before I can play again?'

'I should think, five to six weeks until the cast comes off, then two, maybe three months' physiotherapy. All will be good.' Dr Ménard stood and squeezed Will's shoulder. 'No more fighting, huh?' He chuckled and strolled up the corridor, wondering if he had time to grab a quick bite to eat. If he hurried, he might even be able to grab something hot.

Will watched the doctor retreating, a tuneful whistle on his tongue. Six weeks. It was over. He wouldn't finish the end of this tour and wouldn't be fit to join The Knock in time to begin recording the album in the studio.

He followed the doctor's instructions until he found the sign with the corresponding word on his scrap of paper, his feet hitting the grey tiles as though nothing had changed. He waited for his name to be called, his heart beating slow and steady as he was led into a small room, as he smiled politely at the petite nurse, her hair grey and short, her glasses on the end of her nose.

She held his hand up and apologised as Will bit down on his lip; he tried not to cry out as the nurse pulled a nude-coloured sleeve over his fingers. Once his hand was covered, she unravelled a spool of cotton bandage and applied it over the sleeve before reaching for a bandage-like roll of plaster. With each layer the nurse added, Will replayed the events that had led to this, and as the nurse snipped at the plaster tape, with each layer of plaster his thoughts about his future continued to unravel.

Across the city, away from the loud horns and heavy traffic, Ella pushed open the door to the pharmacy, a bell above the door, a golden chime. She eyed the shelves, her hand deep in her pocket, fingers opening and closing the clasp of her purse: click, click, click, click, as she approached the pregnancy tests. Rows of rectangular boxes with women holding rounded tummies and smiling babies. Her fingers stilled over the clasp as she took a deep breath, her hand scraping the zip at the back of her pocket. She reached for a box, picking it up and balancing another on top. She took them to the counter, avoiding eye contact with the man behind as he folded over a brown paper bag, took the note from Ella's hand and gave her a receipt and a handful of change.

Half an hour later, Ella sat at the edge of the copper bath. Through the window, a slam of a car door, the click of heels, a coo of a pigeon, its feathers just catching the window pane as it launched into the air. Ella sucked on the crystallised ginger as she stared across the room. On the basin with the rusting taps and chipped porcelain, the white strip of plastic with two windows waited for her. Ella counted: fifty-eight, fifty-nine, sixty. Her hand gripped the side of the bath, knuckles white, the silver thumb ring Will had bought her last week clinking against the copper as she stood.

Six steps, that was all it was; six steps, one bare foot after another until they held her body close enough to see two stripes of pink. She could have painted them herself, the nib of her brush adding a touch of red to the white on her palette, a quick flick of her hand, two whooshes of bristle against paper: two lines, two words, two lives bound together; another jigsaw piece created.

A laugh escaped Ella's mouth and she clamped her hand over it, as if trying to contain the excitement, the unexpected thrill she was experiencing. She removed her hand from her lips and let it rest on her stomach. She spread her fingers, a star, while beneath her palm cells were dividing, burrowing into her, forming a new life.

Will rode the metro, the sound of the train squealing along the tracks merging with his memories of his hand being shattered, and with the conversation he'd just had with David – the payphone held in the crook of Will's neck, the coins clumsily positioned into the slot.

'I'm sorry, Will, but this changes everything. Red Records can't pay you if you can't work.'

'I know. I wouldn't expect them to.'

'Look, I don't want you to worry about the medical bills, that's all taken care of. And you'll be paid up until the end of the month. Let's talk again when you're healed, OK? When you're back in the UK?'

'I'll call Gus, and . . .'

'No need. I'll take care of all that. Keep in touch, Will.'

His legs carried him off the train, his eyes squinting as he rose from the station, blinking against the purples of the setting sun, the sky the colour of the lilac dust that he had kissed from Ella's mouth the day he told her he loved her. He tried to compose the words: how he was going to tell her that their great adventure, that she had sacrificed everything for, was over. That he had failed her, that her life would have been better if she had stayed, if he had been strong enough to let her go. He pictured the excitement on her face the day she had told him about the exhibition, questioned how she would feel when he told her that, yet again, he was going to have to ask her to change her plans because of him. Will knew Ella had mapped out their trips to the rest of Europe as a base for her collection. How could he tell her that they couldn't stay, that he would only be paid up until the end of the month?

A large brown dog barked from outside a small café, bringing Will's focus back to the street. The owner's face was mostly obscured by a newspaper, but there was something about the man's posture, the cross of his legs, that reminded Will of his father.

A feeling, like a sip of hot chocolate on a cold day, spread inside Will's chest: his inheritance. They could use that. They could still travel; he could support her, take her to where she wanted rather than her having to tag along to wherever he had to go. This was his chance to put things right, to make it up to her, to show her she hadn't made a mistake by following him.

The man took a small sip of his espresso, unaware of the young man with his arm in a navy-blue sling crossing the road.

Laughter tumbled from a window above, the rich smell of cassoulet rolling lazily along the road as Will's feet continued.

Ella was sat cross-legged on the mattress. As the door clicked into place behind Will, she looked up, her cheeks flushed, excitement making the browns of them almost golden.

Will's heart was pounding in his chest as he stepped towards her.

They both had so much to say and so said nothing.

Instead, Ella began to smile, the warmth from her expression warming his face as though he was facing the sun. He knelt down in front of her, a small laugh rising in her throat, his contagious but confused smile meeting hers.

'What's happening?' he asked. The room felt electric, the energy sparking beneath Ella's skin radiating it. She placed a white plastic wand in his hand.

'It's not food poisoning, Will.' She bit her lip as the lines in his forehead smoothed out, the realisation of what she was showing him hitting him. Suddenly he felt whole. For the first time since Jack's death, Will truly felt complete, like he had something to live for: his own family.

'We're having a baby?'

Will didn't know it, but those few words couldn't have been more perfect if he had spent years composing them – if he had written them down, scribbled them out, added beautiful adjectives or sweeping prose. 'We're having a baby?' was so immediate: there was no should we, could we, maybe, just fact.

'We're having a baby.'

And for the first time in their relationship, as those words fell from his lips without hesitation or concern, just love and conviction, Ella began to believe that she was the right woman for Will Roberts after all.

Chapter Twenty-One

Now

Ella

22nd September 2022

Work is busy. I'm quiet, barely listening to Amira's description of her tantric sex session with her husband while she clips a bunch of yellow roses on the counter beside the till. I spray some more window cleaner on the inside of the display window, vigorously rubbing the last smears from the bottom corner, and replace a silver basket of dried lavender.

'Hello! Earth to Ella!'

I pick up the cloth and window cleaner, stepping past our buckets, which are overflowing with autumnal colours: burnt-orange lilies, sunflowers, yellow and red roses, rich green ferns.

'Sorry, I was miles away.' I discard the cloth and cleaner on the shelf behind the counter, unwrapping a chocolate lime from the open bag beside Amira. 'Do you think I'm doing the right thing? Asking Will to give us another chance? To "date" me, as the youngsters say.' I tuck the sweet between my molars and inside cheek and lean my elbows on the wooden surface.

'Honestly?'

'Always,' I answer, the crystal coating of the lime knocking against my teeth as I speak.

'I don't think going on a few dates will fix whatever is going on, but . . .' She reaches across, pulls a length of red ribbon and snips the end, running it along the edge of her scissors to curl it. 'I think it will help you both find out what's broken.'

I crack open the sweet and warm chocolate runs along my tongue, mixing with the sharp taste of the lime. 'And what if we can't?' I ask, swallowing.

'Then you try tantric sex with Cole Chapel and spend the rest of your days languishing in red lingerie.'

I laugh. 'You do know he's a complete fuck-up, right?'

'Ah, he just needs to settle down with the love of a good woman.'

'He had the love of a good woman, he was with Jules for years and she was perfect for him but he still messed it up. Cole is not the type of guy you "settle down" with.'

'Then refer back to my previous suggestion.' She wraps the ribbon tightly around the stems of the roses. 'Red lingerie and tantric sex!'

My phone vibrates and I pull it out of my dungaree pocket, swiping the screen.

Yes.

'What is it? Why do you look like the cat who got the cream?' Amira leans over my shoulder.

'It's Will. He wants to try again.' I tap my reply.

Yes?

If you're sure, I mean really sure Ella.

'Are you? I mean, he's put you through hell over the last few weeks and—'

'He's the love of my life, Amira.'

'You sure about that?'

I look at her as if she's speaking Klingon. 'How can you ask me that?'

'It's just that Will is . . . OK . . .' She nods as if she has just discovered the secrets of eternal youth. 'You know in *The Avengers*?'

'What have *The Avengers* got to do with anything?'

'Bear with. OK, so we've got Thor.' She snips another length of ribbon. 'All buff and tanned and hair flicky, but then you've got Loki who is a bit damaged but fun and sexy and—'

'Are you comparing Will and Cole to Thor and Loki?'

'No! Um, not exactly.' She winks. 'But . . . I just imagine that if you shagged Thor, he'd be all sure of himself and checking his behind in the mirror while he was doing the deed, and you'd be like, oh my God, I need to cover up my stretch marks and stuff, but if you were shagging Loki, it would be more even, you know? You'd know that he's a bit damaged and he has that whole low self-esteem thing, but he's still all sparky and fun and eager to please.'

'You have thought about this way too much. And for your information, I'd choose Thor over Loki any day. *And* Will has never checked out his own arse or flicked his hair while we've been at it. So in answer to your question, yes. Of course I'm sure. Loki is *not* marriage material.'

'True, true.' She stares off into space, then grins at me. 'Although both of them at the same time could be fun!'

'Amira!'

She laughs a low dirty gurgle and begins writing on a gift card.

I squint against the sun coming through the window, my heart fluttering in my chest as I reread Will's message. My fingers begin to type the words that I had practised so many times in the summer of 1999 but never had the chance to say.

Will Roberts, will you go out with me?
Yes. Yes I will.

*

The house is dark when I get home. I call Cole's name, but as I flick on the lights in the kitchen there is a note. 'Gone out, I won't be late. C x'

I pick up the note. Anxiety twists its way across the last few weeks' memories like ivy: lying on the sofa talking until late into the night, cooking together, his eyes clear while we watched old films, him waking me up as I inevitably fell asleep on the sofa, me crying onto his chest when I woke and realised Will had gone. The ivy weaves through these images, wrapping itself around his smiling face, our laughter, smothering them with the stench of booze.

I wait up until half twelve but there is no sign of Cole. I toss and turn for hours, leaving him messages, asking him to let me know he's OK, finally drifting off to sleep in the early hours.

The sound of my phone ringing wakes me.

'Where the fuck are you?' Amira's voice is hissed into the receiver.

'Shit! Sorry! I've slept through my alarm.' I kick off my pjs, step into a clean pair of knickers and yank my T-shirt over my head.

'Well get your ass over here as soon as possible, we've got six bouquets due to be delivered by nine.' I roll some deodorant under my arm, and struggle into my dungarees. 'Are you ill?'

'Huh?' I ask, buckling them as I rush down the stairs. 'No, I'm just rushing around trying to get dressed.'

'Only I've never known you to sleep in.'

'Cole.'

'Oh I hear you, finally come to your senses, have you? Against the wall?'

'What? No! He was out on a bender and I was worried so didn't sleep very well.'

'Well, that's disappointing.'

'I know. I thought having him here might help him straighten out, you know?'

'No, I meant that it's disappointing you haven't had your way with him.'

'I'm hanging up now!' I say swiping the screen and forcing my feet into my boots.

I make the deliveries by the skin of my teeth and finish just in time to settle into position on Robin's sofa. I try to concentrate on being relaxed, but Cole hasn't returned my calls and I worry that he's gone. Cole's usual way of dealing with a bender is to disappear in a pit of self-hatred and I expect this one will be worse than usual. I give myself a mental shake and turn to Robin.

'Right. I'm ready.'

Robin chuckles, leans back in his chair and lifts his cup to his lips. I close my eyes and wait. But he stays silent. I open one eye, like Popeye. He continues to sip his tea. I clear my throat and give him another nod, in case he missed my previous 'I'm ready', and close my eyes again. My knickers are up my bum and I try not to fidget, trying to 'be present'. Jesus, that clock is loud, its sway of the pendulum is bloody deafening, tick, tock, tick, tock, it's a wonder Robin has any clients. Right. Focus. Breathe in, breathe out. My stomach rumbles loudly. I shift my buttocks, trying to unleash the cotton.

'Comfortable?' Robin asks. I can hear humour in his voice. I Popeye again and he raises his eyebrow at me.

'Not really, no.' I sit back up, my head taking a moment to catch up with my movement, and let out a long breath. 'Have I failed?'

He takes a sip of his tea, then places his cup on the saucer. 'It's quite hard to go into a trance state when you come in the room like a hurricane, Ella.'

'Oh. Right. Sorry.'

'You don't need to apologise. But let's just . . . take a minute, shall we?'

'Should I . . .' I pull the cuffs of my jumper over my hands, 'lie back down?'

'Were you comfortable lying down?'

'Not really,' I admit.

'How do you lie on the sofa when you watch the TV?'

'Like this.' I lie on my right side, my legs curved beneath me.

'Better?'

I fidget a bit, and discreetly pull the fabric out of my bum. 'Much better.'

'Right, then, you remember what we talked about during your last session? That you will be completely aware of my voice and of your surroundings?'

'Roger that,' I say.

'You can close your eyes now.' He smiles kindly. 'And let your breathing become deeper. Listen to your breath filling your lungs and exhaling from your body.'

I breathe in and hold my breath for ten seconds before breathing out. 'Like this? I did this when I was in labour. Sorry. Right.'

I take a few more breaths.

'That's it. You're doing brilliantly, Ella. Just let yourself listen to my voice. You don't have to concentrate on anything, your body will be in complete control.'

I can feel myself resisting his words. *This isn't going to work. What was I thinking?*

'The muscles in and around your eyes are beginning to relax as you continue breathing, in . . . and out . . . no need to concentrate on anything else other than the sounds of my voice and the rise and fall of your breathing.'

It's not going to work but I may as well enjoy ten minutes of rest where someone else is doing all the thinking.

'There is nothing important for your conscious mind to think about. Nothing important except to let your mind rest. It's nothing you have to do, it's just like dreaming . . .'

This is so nice. God, I hope I don't fart or snore.

'You are responding brilliantly, without noticing it, you have already altered your breathing.'

Have . . . I?

The thought is slow; I almost can't be bothered to think it.

'You are breathing without needing to focus, and you are already revealing signs that you are beginning to drift into a hypnotic trance. Ella, you can really enjoy relaxing now, and your subconscious mind will listen to everything I say. It's less important for you to consciously listen to my voice, because you will hear me . . . even if I whisper.'

I breathe in. And. Out . . . In . . . and . . . out.

'You are continuing to drift into a more detached state as you let your mind travel back to the last Saturday in October, 1999. You will begin to have feelings, sensations . . . it's easy, there is no hard work involved. Just keep listening to the sound of my voice.

'Let your mind drift back to earlier that day, think about the events before you left your house. Picture yourself inside your home on that Saturday. What was eighteen-year-old Ella up to that day?'

'I'm sitting on my bed, flicking through *NME*.' My voice is slow, heavy; it's hard work making my lips move. 'I'm wearing red tights beneath a denim skirt, and there is an open CD case on my bed. It's *Showbiz* by Muse. "Sunburn" is playing on the stereo.'

'What time is it, Ella?'

'It's almost lunch time. I can hear Mum's electric knife downstairs, she is slicing through the fresh bread she always bought to go with the homemade soup. We always have soup for lunch on Saturdays. I can hear my brothers playing Monopoly.' I smile.

'I would like you to picture yourself at the top of your stairs, can you do that?'

'Mmhmmmm.'

'OK, Ella. I want you to pay attention as you take your first step. I'm going to count down with you. Ready? Ten.'

I take a step, feeling the thick carpet beneath my toes. Mark Goodier is counting down the chart on the radio playing in the kitchen. It's last week's chart; Mum always recorded it on tape.

'Nine. Concentrate on the feeling of descent as you take the next step downwards.'

I take another step.

'You're sinking into a deeper sense of trance now, Ella . . . Eight.'

There is a hole in the toe of my tights; a car flashes outside the porch door.

'Seven.'

My hand rests on the banister; there is a chip in the white gloss from where I hit Roddy with my hairbrush.

'Six. You're entering the second state of trance now, Ella. Five.'

The sounds from the TV are coming from the lounge, and I can smell the soup bubbling on the hob.

'Four.'

Another step.

'Three.'

The news on the radio.

'Two. Last step now, Ella. I want you to go wherever it feels natural. One . . . can you describe where you are?'

'I'm in the kitchen.'

I speak the words, but they feel far away. Mum stands in front of me; her hair is darker than it is now, and she has a fringe. I'd forgotten about the fringe. There are two foil OXO wrappers on the kitchen side. Mum slices the rest of the loaf. She always bought it from the baker's in town on Saturday morning.

'Mum is stirring the soup. She's telling me it's all in the splash of cream and a handful of rice.'

She kisses me on the cheek as I lean over the pan; she taps her nose. 'Family secret.'

'Can you move from the kitchen now, Ella? To about an hour before you leave for the fair.'

I leave the kitchen, the light from the window in the door begins to fade, the colours changing from midday, my shadow lengthening along the laminate flooring as sunset steps into night like a stop-motion film. I open the door to the lounge and sit down.

'Where are you now?'

'In the lounge. We're watching the lottery being drawn and eating egg sandwiches. Cole is on the sofa next to me; he always came round on a Saturday night for egg sandwiches. He looks nice, his hair smells of apples. Kenny is picking out bits of cress and putting them into Roddy's hair.'

'Anything else? Anything specific to that Saturday in particular?'

My body is relaxed but I know I'm not under hypnosis. I could open my eyes right now if I wanted, but I don't want to. 'The phone is ringing. It's Granny Grunt.'

I can hear the rattle of the bottle-green wall-mounted phone, feel the cold spiral of the cord on the phone as I twist it around my fingers, hear Granny's voice: 'Ella, love, remind your mother to put the clocks back.'

'She's ringing to remind us to put the clocks back.'

'Moving forward in time now, Ella . . . you have arrived at the fair, can you describe it?'

Colours flash as the lounge fades, the feel of the phone in

my hand switching to the warmth of my red gloves, the flashes from the TV replaced with fireworks booming overhead.

'It's so loud, I can feel the explosions in my chest. Cole is laughing at the way I crouch with every boom, as though one of them is going to land on me.'

Cole links his arm through mine. We're late. Cole wants a go on the hook-a-duck and leads me to the stall.

'Where are you, Ella?'

'I'm next to the hook-a-duck stand. People are squealing on the octopus ride, but I want to get to the Abbey, I want to see Will, even though he doesn't know I exist. I'm a bit drunk, we've been drinking from a bottle of gin.'

As I say these words a cool feeling spreads through my body. I'm aware that I'm talking like my teenage self, my drunk teenage self, but I'm too relaxed to mind.

'You've made your way to the back of the fair now, Ella . . .'

'Me and Cole are sitting on a log, close to the fire. I feel a bit sick, and I'm finding it hard to concentrate. I'm trying not to look at Will Roberts but I can't stop. I'm watching the way he is nodding when his friend talks to him, he has this smile, not a smile but an almost smile. Will is looking at me across the fire but Cole is talking to me.'

'What is Cole saying?'

'I can't . . . I don't remember, I can't hear him. Something about a star. I'm not listening to him, what he is saying. I'm thinking about Will, I don't like how Lisa is moving closer to him.'

'Turning your attention back to Cole, Ella, I want you to try and see that conversation, that lost memory. Bring back the moment where Cole is talking to you. I want you to picture your missing memories as presents, gift-wrapped . . . make them bright and colourful, there are ribbons and bows but they're a strange shape, all angles and wrapping paper.

Sellotape is stopping you from getting your nail under a corner, but you're curious about what is inside. You can't force the present open, though, or it may break, you need to open up the wrapping carefully.'

I pick around the edge of my memory. Beside me is Cole: his arms are moving as he talks; I try to hear what he is talking about but around the bottom of his face is brown paper.

'I'm going to take you a little deeper, Ella. Your breathing is slowing down, your legs feel heavier, the deep black sky is closer to you, the stars shining down, the light from them making you notice things you haven't seen before. Tell me what you can see now?'

'Cole's leg is bouncing up and down while he's talking.' I say the words but it is an effort, my lips feel heavy. 'He's nervous.'

I reach over, the warmth from the fire against my right cheek as I run my finger beneath the tape over Cole's mouth. I catch the edge of it with my nail.

'I'm wearing a friendship bracelet, green and burgundy embroidery thread,' I say through my gluey lips. My attention is pulled away from Cole as my finger keeps picking. 'Will is looking over at me, like he wants to say something.' I feel the friction of Robin's sofa against my cheek.

Am I shaking my head? That's not right. I remember Will never looked at me that night; he was too busy snogging Lisa.

'Can you pull the paper away, Ella?' I return my attention to Cole: his hand has reached for the gin while I was distracted. I feel the end of my nail grip the paper, and I pinch the end of it, and tear it away, gently. I can feel it rough against the inside of my palm.

'We're the same, you and me,' I repeat. I want to clarify to Robin that this is Cole talking, but I'm too tired. 'We're the same, you and me. We aren't the star.' I hesitate, the words thick and cloying inside my mouth. I follow Cole's gaze when he stares over at Will. 'We just get trapped by its gravity.'

'OK, Ella, the sky is lifting away, the light from the stars softer. You can feel the breeze on your face, it's making you more alert.'

'Wait,' sleepy Ella says.

'Your legs are starting to lose their heaviness. I'm going to count down from five and you're going to become more aware of this room. Five.'

'Wait,' I begin to say, but the light of the fire is losing its form; the pictures that feel so real are fading, as though I'm watching the scene on a cinema screen and the camera is pulling back.

'You're becoming more alert, your breathing less shallow. Four.' The images of myself and Cole, of Will looking at me across the fire, recede further.

'Three.'

The sound of the grandfather clock in the room is becoming louder, my mind bringing me back into the present.

'Your eyelids are becoming lighter. Two.'

'And you're almost awake now, feeling calm and well rested.'

'One.'

My eyes open, Robin's room coming into focus.

I feel like I've just had an afternoon nap in the sun. My mouth is dry.

'Tea?' Robin asks softly, pouring me a cup before I can answer. I begin to sit up, wiping the corner of my mouth, embarrassed that it appears that I've been drooling. I pull myself upright, reaching out and taking the cup. 'How do you feel?'

'Relaxed?' I offer up a smile and take a grateful sip. 'How did I do?' I ask.

'You can listen for yourself if you'd like?' He nods towards the phone resting on the lectern. I'd forgotten that he had mentioned that the sessions would be recorded. 'I'll email it later to you if you want to listen?'

'Oh, um . . . yes, please. We didn't get to the archway, though?'

'I thought it best if we really examine the moments before the event, as the event you're talking about is quite complex. There might be a conversation going on around you that would explain why you think that this happened.'

'*Think* this has happened?' I give him a wry smile. 'So you don't believe me.'

'I believe that you believe it.' He launches his smile again, the 'favourite granddad' smile.

'So that's why you wanted me to listen to Cole?'

He nods. 'I think there are clues around you that made you think that what you saw was real.'

I take another sip of tea, my mind fumbling through the session. 'I get what you mean about your mind making up memories, though.'

'How so?'

'I know Will didn't look over at me like that, that night. Will Roberts didn't know I was alive until he found me bleeding on the floor and went all Will Roberts.'

'All Will Roberts?'

'Will is . . . Will saves people. I mean, it's not like he goes out of his way to find a damsel in distress or anything, but he's the guy you want around if the Zombies attack, you know what I mean?'

Robin tilts his head, as though he's trying to work something out; it unsettles me a little.

I change the subject. 'Why did you ask me to imagine my lost memories as a present? It was a bit creepy really, Cole's mouth was covered in parcel tape.'

Robin leans forward and offers me a digestive. I shake my

head, declining. 'It just tricks your mind into wanting to see inside the memories, making it curious.'

'What other tricks have you got up your sleeve?'

'Well, like I've said before, time isn't really happening in the unconscious mind but if you can access one memory by being in the same emotional state as you were at the time, you can get to the others. It makes the images run smoothly, like you've wiped Vaseline from the lens.'

'Like starting the evening being relaxed at home with my parents on a Saturday night?'

He grins, like one of the mischievous kids that can get away with murder.

'That was exactly what it felt like, I could see it all so clearly.'

There is a gentle knock at the door.

'Sorry to interrupt, your next appointment is here.'

'Thanks, Sally,' he replies as I drain my cup and stand, looping my bag over my shoulder. 'Same time next week?'

'Oh, I was hoping to get an earlier appointment if I can? I'm kind of on a tight timeline.'

'How so?'

'I . . .' I don't know why I hesitate, why I don't say I need to find out how to save my marriage and I only have just over a month to do it. 'I'm just impatient.' I smile.

'Have a word with Sally, see if she can get you in earlier. I think there is a cancellation on Monday.'

'OK, and thanks, Robin. I've really enjoyed this afternoon.'

As I leave the room, a text from Will appears.

Did you know my mum has taken up salsa lessons?

I smile as I walk down the stairs and out onto the street. Gwen has come on so far since I first met her. She used to be like this porcelain doll that I was afraid I would break if I sneezed too loud. But two decades, a lot of therapy and the right medication, and boom. Salsa dancing.

No!

And that she watches re-runs of Columbo every. Single. Night. 🕷

Who can blame her? Columbo is hot. Maybe she has a Columbo lookalike dancing partner? And he searches her for clues?

I've just been sick in my mouth. ‼️

I laugh as I cross the carpark and climb into my car.

So I've been thinking about . . . stuff.

Stuff?

Yeah. Some types of turtles can breathe through their bottoms. 🐢

😵 **Bye Will**

I let myself in, flicking on the lights. I hear movement above me in the spare room, so Cole is up. I brace myself as I head up the stairs, readying myself for his promises and excuses. 'Cole?' I knock and push the door open gently. The room smells of vomit, of sweat, but as I brace myself for the hit of alcohol there is none.

'Hey,' he says, leaning over and retching into the toilet in the en suite. I rush over, sit next to him, my hand on his back; there is a tattoo of a kingfisher on his left shoulder blade that I haven't seen before. His bare skin is clammy beneath my hands. He retches again but there is nothing left in his stomach, it seems.

'All done?' I ask gently.

I notice he's packed his things: his holdall is open, his clothes folded inside. He reaches for a tissue and wipes his mouth.

I get up. 'I'll get you some fresh water.'

'I can do it, Ells, you don't have to . . .'

'I know I don't have to.'

I return with a fresh glass of water. Cole's body is shaking as he tries to zip up the bag.

I place my hand on his. 'Going somewhere?' I ask.

He quirks a smile beneath his pale skin. 'Trying to, just for a couple of days until this passes.'

'How long?' I ask him, gently. 'Since you've had a drink?'

'Sixteen hours, give or take.' His voice is raw, like it's been sandpapered.

'Why don't you lie down? You can go when you feel a bit better?'

'It's now or never.' His fingers pull the zip. 'You don't want to be around for the next bit, Ells, trust me.'

'And what if I do? Want to be around for the next bit?'

'You don't.' He says it with a certainty that grates.

'Do you know what?' My voice clambers from behind the lump in my throat, escaping around its edges. 'I'm getting pretty fed up of men telling me what I do and don't want.' I slide the glass onto the bedside cabinet.

Cole sits on the bed, defeated. 'I don't want you to see me like this.' He reaches for the water and takes tentative sips.

'And I don't want to let you go through this alone. Please, Cole.' I reach for his hand. 'Let me help you through this? You don't have to be alone. I'm right here.'

'Will won't like it,' he says, replacing the glass.

'Will isn't here. It's just you and me, just how it used to be.' He lies back on the bed, his arm across his eyes; I lie on the bed next to him, my hand reaching for his, holding it firmly. 'I thought you were going out?' I ask gently.

'I was, then I just knew if I walked into that pub, I wouldn't be able to walk back out and I didn't want to be that person any more.' He drops his arm from his face and turns to me. 'You've got enough on your plate at the moment . . . you need a friend that you can depend on, not one that gets shit-faced and passes out somewhere close to your door. So, I went to a meeting . . . and then I went for a walk.'

'I thought you'd stopped going to them?'

'I had. But . . .' His body shivers, his eyes brimming. 'It's time, Ells, it's just time.'

'Tell me what you need me to do.' He clenches his jaw, leaving small indentations along the bone.

'I need you to be strong for me.' He meets my eyes. 'Because I won't have the strength.'

'I'm not going anywhere.'

And I don't. I cancel my appointment with Robin, and I call Amira and tell her I can't come in for a few days. I don't leave Cole when he sweats so much that the bed sheets are soaked, when he wets the bed, when he hallucinates Jack standing in the room, when he sobs in my arms, when he tries to leave, when his legs buckle beneath him. I stay by his side, running him a bath and helping him in, even though he pleads with me, telling me he can do it himself, covering himself with his hand until the embarrassment is pushed away by the tremors and pain in his stomach and he lets me help him into the water, eventually allowing me to wash him like he's a child. I shampoo his hair while he sits hugging his knees, the tremors chattering his teeth.

By the end of the third day, I wake to see my friend asleep, the bed still.

I rise, rotating away the crick in my neck from the tub chair where I've spent the last few nights. I drop my hand against his forehead, relief sweeping over me when I feel his temperature is stable.

I've read pages of online advice and from what I can gather, he's through the worst of the detox stages, but this is where the hard work starts.

'Just so you know . . .' Cole begins to speak, his voice steady but scratchy. 'That was not a true representation of my manhood. It was very cold and the boy hasn't been getting his regular exercise.' He grins, his eye opening with a wince.

'You're disgusting.' But I'm smiling. 'How're you feeling?' I place my hand on his forehead again.

'Like I'm an alcoholic who hasn't had a drink?'

'Fabulous. We're right on track then. Do you think you can eat?'

'Not sure.'

'Cup of tea?'

'Sounds like heaven. Ells?'

'Hmmmm?' I hesitate at the door.

'Thank you.'

'You're welcome.'

I yawn as I flick on the kettle, rotating my neck. My phone vibrates with a message from Will.

So . . . Dinner?

I'd love that.

Next Saturday?

It's a date x

PART TWO

THE MIDDLE

Chapter Twenty-Two

Then

September 2001

Cole twisted the wrench from beneath the chassis. On the radio, Destiny's Child's 'Bootylicious' played. His legs ached. He had started running before work, finding his feet hammering against the road a welcome release from his long hours working in the garage. Most days he started at eight in the morning and didn't leave until eight at night. He didn't mind: it kept him busy, kept him away from the one-night stands and late nights that had become a habit over the last year since Ella and Will left. Cole was fast becoming one of the more experienced mechanics, getting a reputation for being hardworking, quick to learn and with a great sense of humour, making him one of the lads.

'Chapel!' Vince shouted from behind his desk, the office door propped open with a Marilyn Monroe statue, mid air-up-the-skirt pose.

'Yeah?' Cole blew a piece of hair out of his eyes. He needed to get it cut.

'Someone to see you!'

'Shit,' Cole muttered under his breath. He'd had a few of his one-nighters turning up lately, asking if he fancied a drink, a coffee, lunch; they were always 'just passing'. His arm ached beneath his new tattoo, a Celtic ring around his right bicep, as he screwed the final bolt into place and stepped out from the pit.

He squinted, the sunlight fragmenting around her like a child's drawing of the sun.

Ella waited beside the shutter with a smile, swinging a plastic bag.

Cole made fast work of crossing the garage, scooping her into his arms, swinging her around, as she laughed. 'Put me down!' she managed to squeal between her laughter. 'Cole, you're filthy and I'm wearing white!'

'That's exactly what the girl I was with last night said,' he replied, while the industrial park blurred around them like the inside of a kaleidoscope, the colour of her hair, her sweet smell, the cars parked in the background. The colours were all suddenly brought into sharp focus as Cole's momentary joy was shaken by her bony frame, the purple shadows beneath her eyes, the pale pallor despite the tan.

'When did you get back?' he asked, his eyes scanning the sharp lines of her cheekbones, the cracked lips still visible beneath the layer of bramble berry lipstick.

'Yesterday. I thought I'd surprise you!' she shielded her eyes, looking away from the concern in his. 'We could sit by the canal? I brought your favourite.' She dangled the bag at him; he opened it and peered inside, taking in the brown bread, the snags of cress wilting inside the clingfilm.

'You peeled eggs?'

'As if.' She shuddered and Cole beamed, Ella's gesture so familiar to him. 'Momma Walker made them.'

'And that is why I shall marry her when Billy kicks the bucket.'

'You're disgusting.'

'So you keep telling me.' He pulled her into a hug, resting his chin on her scalp. 'It's so good to see you.' Then he released her and shouted over his shoulder, 'Be back in an hour, Vince!' Cole unzipped his overall, pulling it free of his favourite jeans, the pair with a Chinese dragon running up the left side of his leg, and hung it on the peg.

'Bit early for a lunch break, isn't it?' Vince replied.

'It's lunch time somewhere in the world.'

'Smart arse. Grab me a Chelsea bun on your way back, will ya?'

'You sure, old man? I thought you were watching your cholesterol!'

'You're still on probation you know, Chapel.'

Vince Harlow had been working out of this garage since he was fifteen and in all that time, he hadn't felt about one of his lads the way he felt about Cole. There was something about the boy that was special, that made him want to look out for him. God knew, no one else was going to. It made his heart sing to see the pretty girl waiting for him – Ella, she'd said her name was. The name was familiar to him. Cole always talked about a girl called Ella; a mate, Cole so very often said, as if the more times he uttered the words, the truer it would sound, but Vince knew true love when he saw it. He had seen lads like Cole before, sowing their oats and not settling down, but as he watched Chapel cross that floor, the look on his face told him all he needed to know. That girl was more than a mate, and the girls who frequently called for Cole didn't stand a chance. That lad was head over heels for the girl in the white dress with black boots and a wide smile.

'You know you'd be lost without me!' Cole winked at Ella, grinning.

'Lads like you are a penny a pound. I could replace your skinny behind by the end of the day.'

'Yeah, yeah.' Cole wrapped his arm around her tiny shoulders, pulling her towards him as they walked along the street. They turned off the road and followed the canal path, barges lying lazily one behind another. They approached a bench, a pigeon pecking a torn-off piece of chip paper beside it. Cole clapped his hands, shooing it away. They sat down. Trees lined the canal, rich green leaves brushing the beginnings of autumn back, hiding away the brittle brown leaves, like grey hair at the temples.

Cole offered her a bite of his sandwich; she shook her head as if he was offering her poison, taking a sip of water from an Evian bottle instead.

'Hungover?' She didn't reply, just smiled, shaking her head and taking another sip of water, the swallowing action only magnifying her protruding collarbone. 'How's Will's hand?'

Ella blinked.

'Momma Walker filled me in on the fight. I was surprised . . . the great Will Roberts in a bar fight? It sounds more like something I'd do.' He took another bite, grinning while he chewed.

'It wasn't like that. Will just defended himself, he didn't even throw a punch, which is a shame really, the guy was a twat.' Ella looked out over the canal. 'He's good, all things considered. And, you know, Mum and Dad are fussing and doing everything they can to make him welcome. I think he kind of loves it, the routines, having his place in the family. Dad's got him helping with his jigsaws and Mum is, well, Mum. He was sorting out buttons into shades of blue when I left.'

'He's not staying at his own house?' Cole swallowed down the rest of the sandwich with difficulty.

'No. We wanted to stay together and he's in a lot of pain; he didn't want to worry Gwen. She's at a tricky stage with her meds and sticking to a routine helps her. He tries to hide it, the pain, but you can see how uncomfortable he is . . . but you know Will, he never complains.' She twisted the lid back on the bottle. 'Not like you.' She nudged him with her shoulder as they sat. 'Remember the time you got the splinter when we tried to build our den? It was like I was performing open heart surgery without anaesthetic when I took the tweezers to your pinky.'

'It was a big bastard splinter.'

'It was tiny!'

They were quiet for a moment. Cole watched a kingfisher darting across the canal, the blues and greens catching the light as it hovered above the water.

He would think of that bird often in time to come, how in the time it took for him to notice it, to the time it flew away, how his whole world was shattered.

'So,' Cole began, 'what's next? You wait for Will's hand to recover, then go back?'

'That's a bit of a long story.'

Cole tracked the bird as it dipped into the water, droplets of blues and greens hitting the brown water like jewels falling from a broken necklace.

'Actually, it's not that long, I don't know why I said that. I'm pregnant, Cole.'

Cole burst out laughing.

When Cole looked back at his reaction, he would never quite understand why he'd laughed, when he felt like his life was slipping away, like everything that had been upright and stable and solid was beginning to disintegrate. During those few seconds, he was suddenly aware of his thoughts, images that he hadn't consciously acknowledged, one by one falling from his grasp, shattering on the floor: Ella beginning to tire of Will, realising that Will with all his good looks and talent wasn't her equal, wasn't her match, that he wasn't like them. Them. Ella and Cole were a them. Cole wanted Will to finally let her go, let her get on with her life; he wanted Will to be strong enough to see that he didn't need her any more, that he would be OK without her. Cole would watch them part ways, a hug, tears in their eyes as they agreed that they had some wonderful memories but yes, they just weren't right for each other. They would wish each other well and Ella would tell Cole that she was sad but it was for the best; Will would tell Cole that Ella had been there when he needed her most but that now he was stronger, he could carry on without her. He would sling his guitar case on his shoulder and hug them both as he set sail to pastures new, the world at his feet. And Cole would wait: he would wait until the time was right to tell her how he felt and she would look into his eyes and see that he was the one, he was the other half of her, he had always been her other half.

But a baby with Will?

These thoughts wrapped around him, snagging on every scenario like barbed wire on a rabbit's fur, and no matter which way he turned, he couldn't escape; a short laugh caught in the back of his throat.

'I'm serious, Cole.' She put a hand on his arm; it was cold, like ice, despite the warmth from the sun. 'We're going to have a baby.'

She smiled then, his friend, the love of his life, her whole face lighting up, her free hand and gaze landing on her stomach.

Cole swallowed the acid in his throat, trying to stop his face from displaying the utter horror that he was feeling as he imagined a small baby inside her, inside Ella. Then the horror was replaced with anger at Will. How could he have done this to her, hadn't he taken enough?

'Wow,' Cole's mouth replied, his tone somehow calm, a flat surface. The twisting and turning had stopped: it was futile; he was caught by the barbs, stationary, bleeding, accepting. 'Wow,' he repeated. 'How, I mean not, um, how . . .' He shook his head, trying to eradicate that line of thought, of Ella look-ing deeply into Will's eyes in the way he had hoped she would one day look at him. The way he imagined the women he slept with had Ella's eyes, that it was Ella's voice gasping out his name, Ella lying curled up in his arms, naked and satiated. He cleared his throat. 'When?'

'I'm due in March. A spring baby.'

Baby. With fingers and toes and a face made up of Ella and Will, a living, breathing, inescapable reminder that they were a they. It would never be them.

'And, there is more . . .' She sat up and pulled a silver chain from around her neck, hanging in its centre, a ring, a small opal on a silver band. 'Will asked me to marry him.'

'Wow,' Cole said. He tried to find other words but it felt like his skin was being ripped apart.

'The ring did fit,' she rushed on, 'but I've lost a lot of weight because of the morning sickness.' Cole shook his head, trying to focus, trying to ignore the pain.

'Are you . . . I mean, that's a lot, Ells, marriage? Are you ready for that?'

'What do you mean?'

Her face was confused, as though there would be no ques-tion at all about her decision, as if marrying Will Roberts and getting pregnant was perfectly normal, that she had sat and written down life goals to achieve by the time she was twenty and ticked them off one by one. Find boyfriend? Tick. Travel Europe? Tick. Have a baby? Tick. Get married? Tick. It was as if she hadn't ever talked to him about her dreams of becoming an artist, having her own gallery, her own collec-tion. As if she hadn't sat with him, their feet dangling over the edge of Pooh bridge, throwing twigs and racing them against each other and talking about how the light hit the water, wondering if it would look and feel the same in different places, how she wanted to paint it so others could see what she saw.

Cole considered the ring, holding it between his fingers, his mouth uttering appropriate words like *It's beautiful, Ells, it's perfect*, while trying not to show the thoughts behind his eyes; it was so like Will to propose, to be the hero, to pick up the pieces. Making all the decisions. Again.

'But what about uni?' He dropped the ring, watching it wink at him as it nestled back inside her cleavage. 'Your show?'

Your dreams! he wanted to shout. *Your life!*

'I'm not going to uni. We're going to go back to Europe next year for a few months . . .'

'With a baby?' He had to almost cough up the word, like a hairball.

'With the baby.' She frowned. 'I thought you would be happy for me.'

'I am!' He pulled her to him, involuntarily keeping his lower torso away from the bump. 'I am, it's just a shock, that's all.'

Ella sat with Cole's arm around her as she told him about France, the bar, her sickness, Will's proposal.

It was only an hour's lunch break but when Cole returned to work and threw down the Chelsea bun, he told Vince that he had a migraine and then headed straight to the nearest bar, where he ordered a pint of bitter and two whisky chasers.

The TV in the corner of the room was switched to the news, and Cole, along with the other five members of the room, became united as they watched the news unfolding in America, as United Airlines Flight 175 crashed into the Twin Towers.

Later that night, Cole would take a woman to bed. He wouldn't remember her name the next morning, but he would remember crying in her arms.

The woman, Beth, would cry with Cole too; she would be thinking about the man in her arms, how she could do with a man who was so emotionally available, who felt the devastation of people half-way across the world so acutely.

She would meet Cole again, in another bar, another time. He would have aged, but he would still be handsome, still full of mischief at first glance, full of life. But when he bumped into her on the way to the men's room, and apologised without a glimmer of recognition of that night, Beth would be glad that he'd never returned her calls, that she'd given up passing by the garage, that she'd married her husband, who, as she returned to the bar, would hold out her coat and ask her if she was ready to go.

Chapter Twenty-Three

Now

Ella

1st October 2022

I attach the silver hoops to my ears as I step into my bedroom with my dressing gown wrapped around me.

'What. The Fuck. Is. This?' Amira sits up, dreadlocks clattering together, secretary glasses pushed further up her nose as she reaches over and holds my underwear like a dirty sock.

'It's a body suit.' I pick it up and twang the nude fabric like a catapult. 'You know, to suck in all my wobbly bits, the dress is a bit clingy.' I nod over to where the red dress is hanging on the wardrobe door.

'Ella, you're going on a date with the man who has seen you naked almost every day for a quarter of a century. Do you really think he won't know what is going on under your dress? Do you think Jessica Rabbit wears . . .' she snatches the body suit back, 'that?'

'She's a cartoon character, so no.'

'Ella, you have a figure women dream of, big boobs, tiny waist, legs up to your armpits.'

'Figure like a truck driver, more like,' I grumble.

She slides off the bed, rummaging in my underwear

drawer, pulling out a pair of high-waisted black lace Brazilians from Marks and Sparks.

'Just tell me, if Will makes a move . . .' I raise my eyebrows at her, 'or *you* make a move, what do you think is going to be sexier? Your softer bits on show and these bad boys? Or him trying to pull you out of that thing, tugging away like a, a backwards sausage?'

'A backwards sausage?'

'You know what I mean, like the sausage meat being forced into its skin. But in reverse. And there is nothing sexy about a sausage skin. Although I suppose that depends on the sausage.' She winks.

'I told you. I'm going to set rules, no sex.'

'Yeah well, no sex doesn't mean there has to be no foreplay.' I groan, turning the body suit left and right; it probably would take some manipulating to roll it down, so at least this would help me to stick to the rules. I'm fairly sure Will trying to yank this off wouldn't be the most romantic of beginnings.

'Ells?' I hear Cole take the stairs two at a time.

'Ah! Just the man!' Amira catapults from the bed as I pull my dressing gown tighter, Velcro rollers bobbing up and down on my scalp.

'Do NOT come in, I'm not dressed!' I shriek as the door opens a crack.

'Mr Chapel. In your opinion. What would you find more sexy? This?' Amira pinches the body suit between thumb and index finger and swings it through the gap in the doorway for inspection before throwing it at me. 'Or . . .' she reaches over to the bed, swinging the black lace on her fingers, 'these?'

'Ignore her!' I shout, tightening the towelling belt of my dressing gown and snatching the lace from her hands, poking my head around the door jamb.

'The black.' Cole grins, dimples, twinkling eyes: an adult Peter Pan.

'I was just letting you know that I'm going back to my flat for the night.'

'Oh! You don't have to, I doubt we will be coming back here, all things considered.'

Cole raises an eyebrow at me, his mouth twitching. 'If you go for the black lace you might.' He winks at me and rushes down the stairs. I follow him out, standing at the top of the landing as he grabs his leather jacket from the banister, worry tugging me down the stairs.

'Will you be OK?'

'I can't stay here for ever, and it's just one night. I'm going to a meeting first, then the gym.'

'Do you have enough Percy Pigs?'

'I have.'

'Look, I know things are weird, with Will, and, well . . . just ring me, OK? If you feel like you can't do it. Call me.' Cole looks away, tapping his pockets for his things. I reach out and hold his arm. 'Hey.' My voice is soft, serious. 'Promise me you'll call if it's too hard or, or . . . I'll cancel my date and you will be solely responsible for the destruction of my marriage.' I fold my arms, challenging him with a raise of the eyebrow.

'I'll be fine, Ells. But yes, I promise. Now go and wake Will up from whatever coma he's in and show him what he's missing.' He leans forward, kissing me on the cheek, the bristles of his stubble catching me along my jaw line.

'Amira!' he yells up the stairs.

'Yeah?'

'I'm at home alone tonight, so if you come to your senses and decide to leave that husband of yours, give me a call.'

'Ha! You should be so lucky, Chapel,' Amira shouts from

my bedroom. 'That ship has sailed! You were never really my type! Too much hair!'

'Could have fooled me.' He winks, laughing.

'Get out, you creep.' I bat him away as he ducks from my hand and closes the door behind him. I swallow down my concern and return to the bedroom.

'So tell me the plan again!' Amira asks as I snatch the pair of knickers and head back into the en suite, wriggling out of the dressing gown.

'I'm taking him out for dinner,' I shout bending over and stepping into the underwear. 'Where I will stun him with my beauty and scintillating company.' I pull on my bra, Amira's hand appearing through the door, the red dress flirting on its hanger. 'And then over the next few weeks we're going to date. I thought I'd take him to the shop on one of them.'

I smooth the dress over my hips, and smile into the mirror. Will always liked me in red. Amira looks up from the bed as I step back into the room.

'Wow.'

'Thank you.' I head towards the wardrobe and pick out my shoes, red thin straps across my toes, kitten heels not hooker ones.

'Not wow to the dress,' she corrects half-groaning. 'Although, wow. I mean why are you taking him to "the shop"?'

'He's never really seen me at work.'

'What are you talking about? Will has been in the shop hundreds of times, he helped decorate it!'

'That's not what I mean. He's never just watched me. When I do my thing.'

'Huh?'

'Look. When Will comes to the shop, it's always because

he's dropping me off some lunch, or picking up the kids, or I've asked him to help me carry stuff in, or . . . or stop the tap from dripping or fix the light—'

'You know that makes you sound like a rubbish example of a strong woman?' She flutters her eyelashes and coos like a southern belle. 'I need a big strong mayne to help me carry the boxes and I'm too feeble-minded to tackle the likes of eeelectriciiidee.'

'Shut your face. It has nothing to do with not being a strong woman, it's to do with the fact I'm crap with anything technical.'

'Or plumbing?'

'Piss off. What I mean is he's never been there when I'm on my own, you know, like when it's just me and my music and . . .'

'If you say my art I'm going to bat you around the head with these bloomers.'

'All I'm saying is I want to show him how much I love it, the process. I always get the feeling that Will thinks I settled for floristry rather than choosing it. And if I'm right and we belong together, which I *am*, I want him to see me. To fall back in love with me, all of me. Not just the end of the day me, the loading the washing machine me, the ordering a weekend takeaway me, does that make sense?'

She scans my face, something like pride there, and clears her throat. 'OK, but if you end up shagging on my desk, make sure you disinfect afterwards.'

'Agreed.'

I fidget with the bottle of wine, rearranging the breadbasket until Will strides through the restaurant doors, hesitating beside the waitress as she asks if he has a booking. He glances past the booths with velvet patterns and brass lighting until his eyes land on me, the grooves around his mouth deepening, his hand held high, his body leaning forward, telling the waitress that he can see me. His long legs weave through the tables, his hand rubbing his chin, wedding ring catching the light, that well-worn smile chewed in the corner of his mouth, eyes drawn towards me. His hair is damp, his skin freshly shaved, and as he leans down to kiss me on the cheek I'm bathed in the warmth from his skin, the deep fresh sea-salt and rosemary smell of him.

'Sorry,' he apologises, sitting opposite, taking a sip from the red wine I've already poured. 'The taxi was late.' His eyes meet mine as he takes in my appearance. I can feel the pull of attraction from across the table and I'm floored again by the pain of his words, of the weight of what it will mean if my plan to convince him that we should stay together fails. I will never want a man as much as I want Will Roberts.

'You look beautiful, Ella.' His voice always manages to carry such weight; spoken by anyone else and it wouldn't sound the same. It's the same effect that he had when we were younger, that hidden depth that made The Girls write poetry about him, that was the cause of many a shimmering red gel-penned heart shape.

'Oh, this old thing?' I flick my hair away from my shoulder and give him a wry smile; he will know how long I'll have taken to get ready, the pain of watching me manipulate it into curlers, the asthmatic application of hairspray. I have a flash of memory, of the last time I wore a dress like this, the feel of his hands brushing back my hair, the feel of his lips against the bare skin of my shoulder, his finger tracing the shape of my birthmark.

I bring myself back. 'So do you. Obviously.' I laugh nervously. The lines in his forehead draw together at my compliment. 'God, this is weird, isn't it? I feel like we're on a first date. We never really had a first date though, did we?

Breakfast with The Walkers wasn't the pinnacle of romance, was it?' I rush on, picking up my glass and raising it in a toast. 'To new first dates?' My tone rises at the end of the sentence; I don't mean it to but there it is. I suppose I need clarification that Will is still on board with this plan, that he wants it to work, that he's not about to tell me again that we need space. But he clinks his glass against mine.

'To first dates.'

I take a sip, the base of the glass scraping as it lands back on the table. 'I have some rules.'

'Rules?' Will laughs, taking another sip of wine and leaning back against the purple velvet of the seat. I pull out a piece of paper from my handbag and unfold it, ironing out the veins of wear crisscrossed beneath my writing. The red nail polish on my thumb is already chipped.

'Number one.' I look up at him through my lashes. 'We can talk about the kids for five minutes, no more.'

His mouth opens and closes and I hold up a finger to silence him. He props his chin on his elbow.

'I am on a mission to make you fall in love with me again, and I'm not going to do that talking about the same things.'

Will begins to speak. 'I don't need—'

'Rule number two,' I interrupt, my eyes pleading: *Let me do this, don't tell me how it won't work, not yet.* He reaches over and pours a glass of water from the carafe. I brace myself before saying, 'No sex.'

It comes out louder than I intended and we gain the attention of the couple slurping tagliatelle across the aisle. They look like one of Grandma Grunt's novelty cruet sets, both squat, grey-haired, shiny faces. Will cough-laughs.

'I mean it, Will. We always just shag when things get tricky and we can't fix whatever this . . .' I waft the air around us like I'm in a Febreze advert, 'is by boning on the kitchen counter. Sorry,' I add to the woman opposite; it's clear I'm putting her off her carbonara. I lean forward, speaking a little more quietly. 'Heavy petting and kissing *is* allowed, however.'

'Good to know.' Will's mouth twitches. 'Do I get a say in these rules?'

'Sure, fill your boots.' Beneath the table, my ankle rotates; the red strap rubs against the bridge of my foot.

'OK.' He links his fingers and stretches his hands outwards. 'We take it in turns to decide on the venues for our dates.'

'Why, what's wrong with this one? Has it got a bad hygiene rating or something?' I eye the breadsticks warily.

'I don't know. They're done for though if it does.' He gives a subtle nod to where the tagliatelle is splattering up Mrs Salt and Mr Pepper's chops and chins. I snort and he smiles at me: it's open, there is no hidden agenda, just pure, wholesome Will Roberts. I reach for his hand, letting my fingers lie on top of his. He looks down, his fingers relinquishing beneath my weight, his hand entwining my fingers in his.

He lifts my hand a fraction, then places it back down. The gesture is familiar; I expect his lips to graze my knuckles but he pauses the action, breaking the familiarity. 'Hand-kissing is also considered acceptable on our dates,' I add gently. His gaze runs from the tip of my index finger, along my palm towards the silver chain around my wrist, and I'm suddenly back in France and nineteen. We've just woken up and he has brought my arm around him.

'I love how your wrists smell.'

'My wrists?'

'They smell of your skin and your hair and sleep. Of you.'

'Wrist-smelling,' I begin, trying to lighten the atmosphere, 'is forbidden, though. Weirdo,' I add, swallowing hard.

He laughs, releases my hand, and reaches for the menu.

'How about one of the rules is we have to order for each other?' he asks, a mischievous glint in his eye.

'But . . .' I begin.

'If I'm banned from your wrists . . .'

'Unless we're heavy-petting, in which case I may permit it.'

'Noted.' His eyebrow arches with a tilt of the head before continuing. 'Then you're banned from burgers.'

'What? No! I chose here because they do a Hawaiian with a pineapple ring and I've never had one on a burger!' I have long been on the hunt for the perfect burger. I always intend to order something new but nine out of ten times, I go for a burger.

Will holds out his hands, a take it or leave it gesture.

'Fine. But you have to have pudding for a starter.' I sit back with a smug smile.

'But . . .'

'Them's the rules.'

'Does cheese and biscuits count?'

'Nope. It has to be something rich and gooey.'

'Then you have to have something involving seafood.'

I scrunch up my nose.

'Those are my terms. Take it or leave it.'

'Fine. Rule number three, or is it five now you've added the whole venue and ordering thing?' I start counting on my fingers, chewing my bottom lip as I concentrate, my eyeline drawn to the gold coin in the corner of the table, the table number of nineteen engraved in it. Will is watching me; I catch him off guard, that familiar love in his eyes, and once again, 'I want a divorce' ricochets through me, five syllables pinching and scraping at my skin. 'Anyway, rule number . . . whatever it is, is we are not allowed to talk about work, or family or . . . Cole,' I add as an afterthought. 'Or if we need to, we can have five passes, so if, say, I desperately want to tell you something about work, I'll use one of my passes.'

I reach for a breadstick, snapping it and sending shards of stick all over the wooden table.

'Then what are we supposed to talk about?'

I usher the stray stick beneath the table and look up. 'That's what we need to find out. We need to see why we fell in love in the first place, Will, don't you see? We need to see us. Not everyone else,'

'That makes sense.' His head dips back into the menu; burgundy leather and golden embossed olive branch replace his eyes.

'Can I ask you a question?' I unfold my napkin and refold it.

'As long as it's not about our children, our family, work, or . . . what was the other one?' He tilts the menu forward.

'Cole.'

'Cole.' The menu replaces his face again. 'What about seafood risotto?'

'Oooh, fish and rice, as if asking for a divorce wasn't torture enough. Sorry.' I pick up the napkin again, rolling it up in a sausage.

'So what's the question?' he asks, closing the menu with a worryingly satisfied air.

'You know the night I passed out at the bonfire? The night you walked me home?'

He signals to the waitress that we're ready to order, his manner somehow friendly, apologetic, confident. 'I do.'

'Were you looking at me?' I stop fidgeting with the napkin and take a sip of wine. I always fancy red wine but the first glass always seems to taste like Ribena straight from the bottle without adding any water.

'What do you mean?'

'When I was sitting across from you, before that girl snogged your face off in front of me. Had you been looking at me?'

'Of course. Who else would I be looking at?'

'Well, Lisa for one.'

'Huh. I'd forgotten her name was Lisa.'

'Because, when I remember that night, I didn't think you knew I existed. Not really. Not in any other way than as Cole's friend.'

'Bong. That's one of your points used.'

'That doesn't count! I wasn't talking about Cole, I was mentioning he was there in passing.'

'Still counts.'

The waitress arrives at our sides, a notebook in hand, a ready smile flashing in Will's direction even though I'm guessing he's old enough to be her father.

'Hi.'

'Hi,' she responds, dropping a hip and turning in.

'We'll have the lemon sole with minted new potatoes and the Hawaiian burger, no tomato sauce and extra onion rings, please.'

'But first,' I interrupt, 'can we have two death-by-chocolate sundaes, please? As a starter?'

'You want desserts first?' she asks, confused. I cock my head at Will.

'Yes, um, yes we would,' he replies, with a disbelieving shake of the head.

I grin, clapping my hands and rubbing them together.

'Anything to drink?'

'Chardonnay?' he asks me, manoeuvring his head so he can see me past the pencil-skirt.

I lean my head to the side and nod with a grin, tipping the rest of my glass in his as she shimmies off, giving a quick flash of a smile over her shoulder. 'Thank you,' I smirk.

'What for? The burger is for me.' He grins.

'I've been thinking a lot, about our past and that night.

Tell me what you remember,' I say softly. 'It's important to me.'

'I remember you had your hair in plaits, that you were smoking and drinking gin and I wanted to take it from you, I could see you were drinking too much, too fast and I was worried.' He grabs a fistful of hair at the back of his head and releases it. 'And I wanted so much to talk to you, but I didn't know how to or what I would say. But you were talking to . . .' I sit upright and wait for him to use a point but he pauses and corrects, 'someone else all night and I thought that I would never be able to get you away from that person.'

I swallow hard and thank the waitress as she returns with my white wine, asking Will again if there is anything she can get for him.

He waits until she leaves before continuing. 'I couldn't take my eyes off you all night, Ella.'

'Really?' I ask, my surprise catching on the words like a rough nail on a piece of clothing. Tears are in my eyes and I feel ridiculous. I wipe them away.

'Why are you surprised? I've told you the way I felt about you back then. My whole birthmark-stalking in the canteen.' He reaches for my hand and runs his thumb over my knuckles.

I shake my head dismissively and laugh lightly. 'I suppose that, for me, I always think of our relationship starting that night . . . it's hard for me to imagine you feeling the same way as I felt about you before you had to pick me up off the floor and I went all damsel in distress.'

'You have never been a damsel in distress, Ella. You saved me, remember?'

I'm about to reply when the waitress appears with two goldfish-style bowls, each one filled to the brim with cream and all things chocolate.

'There you go, two death-by-chocolates.'

Will's eyes widen. 'I think I may have been over ambitious ordering the extra onion rings.' He bends his head over the dessert, picking up his spoon and clinking it against mine. 'OK, let's do this.'

Chapter Twenty-Four

Then

December 2001

At least ten years of dirt and grime obscured the view of the narrow garden. Over the last decade, the fir trees had been edging closer and closer to the small patch of lawn, like a game of grandmother's footsteps. The whole house was tired. It had been so long that it had felt new energy; the light from the smiles of the young couple's faces seemed to burn into the beams, smooth over the tired walls and soothe the creaks and cracks of the staircase's spine.

Ella leant forward towards the window, her bump skirting the edge of the kitchen counter. She knew that this house didn't make sense. One half of it was beautiful, the beams strong and confident, the tiles surrounding the fireplace ornate enough to demand attention, but subtle enough to not shout for it: a blushing debutante in the corner of the room. The other half of the house was forced, like an ugly sister trying to make the glass slipper fit: seventies décor, carpets sick with too many rich colours, age-old deep-fryer fat clinging to the fibres, beige kitchen tiles, avocado bathroom. But as Ella roamed beneath the cobwebs, she could feel the house opening up, its walls stretching, the old bones and joints flexing, the back walls straightening, welcoming them home. She turned and met Will's eyes, and she knew he felt it too. They were home.

'It's a fixer-upper, that's for sure . . .' the estate agent brushed off the dust on his navy trousers, 'but it's got great character. Original beams, cellar, open fireplace.'

Will and Ella had been married for a little over a month, renting a small flat in the middle of town. Will had returned to Music Maestro, working full-time and giving extra music lessons in the evenings, while Ella worked at the checkout in a local supermarket.

He joined her at the window, his arm wrapped around her thickening waist; he didn't let anyone see the wince of pain as he did this. He hadn't told Ella that he could no longer play for hours on end without painkillers: he didn't want to worry her; she had enough on her plate. She was regaining some of the weight in her face, the softness beginning to return to the sharp angles and pale skin that had seemed to be stretched across her cheek and jaw bones. Will had felt helpless, watching her day after day battling in a constant state of dehydration and nausea, watching her try to stay upright so she could begin working on her collection, only to have to nap after an hour.

'There is no upwards chain,' the estate agent continued, rolling something sticky and greasy between his thumb and index finger while trying to still encourage the young couple. Personally, he wouldn't touch this property with a barge pole; it had been on the market for almost ten months and although he could see the potential, it needed a lot of work. The couple would be wiser to go for the nice compact semi-detached property he had shown them earlier in the week. But *Changing Rooms* had a lot to blame for younger couples making the wrong decisions; they looked at bad décor and saw themselves as the next Laurence Llewelyn-Bowen, throwing a quick lick of paint, some fancy material and *ta da*, an upgraded house within a week. 'And it has so much potential, fresh paint, a modern twist . . .' But then he observed the look passing between the couple and grinned, already calculating his commission. This was a done deal.

He was right. And another piece of the jigsaw slotted into place.

The couple moved into the house a month later, but Ella's pregnancy would continue to be difficult and soon she would have to stop working at the supermarket.

And when Amber was born prematurely, with a small hole in her heart, the little nest egg left over from Will's inheritance would dwindle away on travel expenses to and from the hospital. House renovations and Will's physiotherapy appointments would be pushed back on their list of priorities.

Amber would be three months old when, exhausted and bewildered, the three finally spent their first night in that house together as a family.

They had no idea that those three months would be the easiest.

Chapter Twenty-Five

Now

Ella

2nd October 2022

There is something illicit about being inside a garage after dark. The artificial flicker of the strip light reflects through the windshield of a red Nissan Micra raised up on the ramp, its bumper half removed. Overalls hang on the pegs, oil-stained fingerprints smear the handles of tools discarded across the floor: an identikit of Cole's team of mechanics. I breathe in the petrol mixed with school-lunch-sandwich-wrapper smell, evoking memories of watching Cole as he worked, of Jamie and Amber wearing their own overalls, Cole teaching them the names of engine parts: Amber, her face serious as she listened, as though a test would be given at the end of the day; Jamie sitting behind a steering wheel, eyes wide as he commentated on his own imaginary circuit around a race course. Cole is due back at work next week and he's asked me to help him 'get ready'.

'You ready?' I ask, my hand on his shoulder, the soft fleece of his jumper warm and firm beneath my fingers. He hesitates on the threshold to his office briefly and makes his way across the room, orange desk light flickering before it finds purchase, illuminating the coffee-stained desk splayed with receipts. Behind the desk are posters of car engines and adverts for high-performance oil, Britney gazing down, blonde hair swinging just above her bare abdomen above Pocahontas shorts.

'Britney? Still?' I ask with a sardonic smile.

'Ours is a love that you could never understand, Ells.' He rolls up the sleeves of his jumper, the tattoo of ivy twisting around the scar along his cephalic vein. 'Let's get this over with. Are you ready?' he asks, the muscle along his jaw corrugated with tension.

'I was boooorn ready.' I try to lighten the mood by throwing a few warm-up punches, like I'm about to walk up to a boxing ring with 'Eye of the Tiger' playing in the background.

Cole shakes his head, but I've raised a small smile. The top drawer of his desk slides open, a quarter bottle of Glenfiddich retrieved. He holds it up to the light. 'Do you know how much I want to twist the top off this right now?'

'I can do this for you if it's too difficult, Cole, just tell me where they are and you can wait outside.'

'No, it's OK.' He tilts the amber liquid behind the label. 'So long, my friend, it's been fun.' He rests his head against the bottle before passing it to me; I immediately hide it inside a black bin bag. The filing cabinet reveals an almost full bottle this time, another one into the bag. There is another in his old gym bag. I hesitate as Cole heads towards the toilet.

'This won't be my finest hour,' he says. There is a quarter bottle hidden in the toilet cistern.

'I'm proud of you,' I say, as he switches off the lights and draws down the shutter, fixing the padlock in place.

The industrial estate is quiet, the main road punctuated by streetlights and the constant rush of traffic on the dual carriageway in the distance.

'Oh, just wait for the pièce de résistance,' he says, meeting my eyes briefly, before swinging his car keys around his finger. I follow him to his car, a red TR7 that he keeps restoring year after year. 'Let's see how proud this makes you.' The door creaks as he bends, opening the glove compartment. Inside is an empty bottle, just an inch swilling around the bottom. Beneath the seat is another, vodka this time.

'Fancied a change?' I ask. I'm attempting humour again, but my stomach is tight, my mouth dry.

'Nope. I swiped it after a one nighter . . . I don't even remember her name, don't remember meeting her or going back to her place. I just woke up, naked, with a hicky on my chest, so you know, she must have been one classy lady. I swiped this on the way out while she was still asleep.'

'Jesus.'

'Yup. Still proud of me?' I try to arrange my expression so it's impassive, so he doesn't see the . . . what exactly? Alarm? Disgust? Concern? I'm not sure what he sees when he meets my eyes but he looks away, his fingers scratching a clump of dark hair at the back of his head. 'I drank out of this still half-cut from the night before while I was driving. I could have hit your car, or Jamie's, Amber's, Will's . . .'

'Drunk you is a tosser.'

He nods. 'Drunk me doesn't give a shit that he's a tosser, he's just looking for the next drink.' Cole turns his back on me, crouching through the doors, running his hand between the seats, the inside of the doors, the boot; it was almost clear except for a miniature bottle of gin. 'I have no idea where this came from.'

I take it from his hand, adding it with a clink to the black sack as he locks the car doors. We walk towards the back of the garage, where my Murray Mint-filled glove compartment and Yankee Candle-fragranced car waits.

'Cole?' My thoughts have run back to the hicky-giving

woman as the security light blazes across the tarmac. 'When was the last time you had an STD check?'

'Charming. We've established that I'm a drunk tosser and you want to throw herpes into the conversation? Talk about kicking a man when he's down.'

'I'm serious, Cole, you could have all sorts of . . .' I waft my hand in his groin area, 'stuff going on.'

'Thank you for your concern, but I am as clean as a whistle, thank you very much. And, well . . . you've been up close and personal with Cole junior, did you see anything wrong?' Heat rises up my neck and into my cheeks. A rumble of laughter catches me off-guard as Cole smirks, walking backwards as he dips his head, trying to examine my face. 'Are you blushing?'

'No.'

'Yes you are!'

'Shut up.'

'See anything you like?' he enquires, mischievous.

'No I did not. Now piss off or I'll wallop you with my Santa sack.' I stop beside the skip, bend down and tie a knot in the top of the bag, preparing to throw it into the skip, but he places a hand on my arm, squeezing my forearm. The light-hearted teasing is replaced with sincerity. 'Not there.'

'Really? They'll be smashed . . .'

'Didn't put me off last time.' He holds out his hand, the glow of a security light shining on a pale silver scar along his palm.

'Oh.'

'Just take it somewhere I don't know about, OK?'

'OK.' Cole walks me to my car, the lights flashing twice while the central locking works its magic. I put the bag in the boot and pull him into a hug. 'Is there anything else I can do?'

'Can you . . . not ask me how I'm doing?' I look up at him,

questioning. 'I'll be using all of my energy to not drink, having to use some of that energy to convince you I'm not thinking about it every spare minute of the day won't help. Because I will, Ella. I might be walking and talking and eating and watching the telly and going to work, but I will be thinking about it every single minute. For the next few months at least. This is all me, Ella, there is nothing you can say or do that will stop me having a drink if I want one, it all comes down to me.'

I swallow down the lump in my throat. 'Of course.' My voice wobbles and I clear my throat. 'I shall be completely self-involved and not give another thought to how my best friend is going through hell.'

'You could never be self-involved, even if you tried your very best. Just don't ask, because, believe me, there is nobody going to be more worried that I'm going to fuck up than me.'

'Under one condition. You tell me when you're struggling, if you think you're going to drink, just tell me, alright? You don't need to do this alone.'

'I can't promise you that, but I'll try . . .'

Chapter Twenty-Six

Then

January 2003

Amber Roberts, chubby arms and legs below a dandelion fluff of blonde hair, bounced up and down and rocked on her knees. She was taking on the task of getting from her spot on the navy lounge carpet to where her mother was sitting still on the sofa. A gurgle escaped her mouth, a clear line of dribble hanging from her chin. A rectangle of light from the window was drawn onto the carpet, like a pathway.

Ella sat staring at the plastic in her hand, shell-shocked. How could she be pregnant again? She was taking the mini-pill; she was still breastfeeding Amber. She looked down to where Amber rocked again, her hand reaching forward before she plonked heavily down with a determined thud, her right knee nudging onwards. On the TV, the theme tune to the *Tweenies* was singing into the room: characters with giant yellow heads and spotty trousers were asking if Ella was ready to play with them; it was time to come and play with the *Tweenies*.

The fire hissed and spat in the grate. The joy of having a real fire had already lost its appeal, the beauty of it already diminished, encapsulated by the fire-guard fortress.

It would have been so much easier to be able to flick a

switch and have heat, but the central heating system had stopped working shortly after they moved in and so Ella and Will were saving up for a new one. In the meantime, they were making do with showers instead of baths and open fires, a fan heater in the bedroom and a Calor Gas burner in the kitchen.

The phone rang, and Ella stood, still holding the plastic receiver. 'Hello?'

In Wolverhampton, a forty-five-minute commute away, Will slotted money into the telephone box. His phone had run out of credit and he'd forgotten to buy a top-up card. He raised a hand at the group of friends from his teaching degree course. They were going to the pub, but Will was behind with his assignment and needed to stay for another few hours in the library. He loved being home with his daughter, with Ella, but he just couldn't get any work done once he was there. It would be different once he was qualified, once he got a teaching job: he would be home all of the school holidays, so Ella could get back to painting; he would be there in the mornings, be there in the evening to cook dinner.

Will wasn't aware yet that his teaching hours would be longer than the school day, that most evenings he wouldn't get home until after the kids had eaten, that he would have to leave before they left for school, that Ella would get barely any time to paint over the next ten years because Will's wage wouldn't cover the loan they'd take to replace the central heating, to take care of the damp in the cellar, to have a new kitchen fitted.

But as the coins smacked against the inside of the phone box with a clatter, Will still thought that getting a degree was the hard part. 'Hi.' Will closed his eyes and pictured Ella standing in their newly decorated lounge, the first room that they had managed to renovate since buying the house.

'How's your day been?'

'OK, she almost crawled today. What time are you coming home? I thought we'd have jacket potatoes, beans and cheese? Make a change from beans on toast?'

Will closed his eyes briefly. When they had more money, he never wanted to eat another baked bean in his life. 'Sounds good, but you go on ahead and eat before I get back, I'm going to be late.'

Ella looked down at Amber, who had slumped back onto her behind, her bottom lip beginning to dip, a cry breathed in, her blue eyes filling. Ella held the phone in the crook of her neck and bent down, hoisting Amber on to her hip while simultaneously reaching for a dummy, managing to get it into her mouth before a full-blown crying session began. 'Again? Will, it's the third day this week and they've forecast snow later.'

'It's not due until later tonight, I'll just be a couple of hours tops.' Will wanted nothing more than to go home, but he knew the minute he stepped through the door, all he would want to do is play with his daughter, spend time with Ella, let her rest while he heated up the beans, listen to her as she told him about her day, hold her while she fell asleep just ten minutes into whatever film they were attempting to watch. But he had to get this work done; he had to pass this degree. 'I'll get home as quickly as I can. It's the referencing, it's taking for ever, and I need to hand in the books at the end of the week.'

Coming down the campus steps, a girl from Will's course, Adeline, slowed her pace and watched where inside the phone box, Will Roberts leant his forehead against the glass door. There was one thing that made being stuck in that stuffy room better and that was sitting across from Will Roberts. He had a habit of tapping his hand against the top of his thigh when he was concentrating, a brown watch strap, tanned wrists, blond hair, long elegant fingers that she had pictured running along her thigh. Adeline took in the long legs, the broad shoulders, head dipped in conversation, and let a slow smile spread across her face. She tucked her long red hair behind her ears and told her friends that she'd catch them later.

'You know he's married, right?' Tianna her roommate said, shaking her head.

'I know,' Adeline grinned, flashing her straight teeth.

'And he's got a kid?'

'I'm not looking for anything serious, just a bit of fun.' Adeline winked and Tianna laughed.

'You're a nightmare! Don't do anything I wouldn't do!'

Adeline dropped to her knee by the side of the telephone box, a pretence of tying her shoelace.

In the phone box, Will continued to reassure Ella. 'I'll head back to the library now. I'll try and be back for bath time.'

'You won't make it, she's missed her nap and she's getting grizzly.'

Will tapped his head against the glass again, frustration and fatigue all there in that one tap, that one touch of cold glass against the line of worry between his eyebrows. 'Give her a kiss from me. I'll get back as soon as I can. I love you.'

'Love you too.'

Ella placed the plastic test on the windowsill, two strong blue lines gloating up at her —*Ta-da! Guess what?* — and burst into tears.

Will slid the telephone back into its cradle, his hand resting on the black plastic. He pulled up the collars of his coat, cold January air biting down. Every morning, Will listened to the weather forecast with a growing sense of dread as every day the country slipped further into a 'cold snap'. His heart would sink: their electricity meter was already eating up twenty pounds a week and the coal bill was getting higher and higher each month. He knew that Ella had asked for help from the Walkers and he shouldn't mind; it was ridiculous, this macho sense of not being able to provide for his family, but it was there, nevertheless. He pushed the heavy door open with his shoulder, forcing the rusting hinge in the top corner to open like the blades of a pair of scissors. Beside the telephone box, Will saw a girl with red hair crouched down, emptying the contents of her bag.

'Damn!' she said under her breath. 'Where is it?' The girl continued to empty her bag onto the pavement. The wind whistled between the buildings piled up high either side, sloping towards them, lifting her red hair around her head.

Will recognised the girl from his course, Adele? Abigail? The wind snatched hold of a loose ten-pound note from her bag, running away from them, mocking and taunting like a school bully holding a love letter aloft. Will sprinted after it, slamming his boot on top of Charles Darwin's face, his thumb pinching the paper between the hummingbird and the ten-pound logo, holding it firmly as the wind tried to wrench it from his grip.

Adeline looked up, drinking in Will's easy stride, the way his jeans clung to his backside as he bent down to grab her escaping beer money. She chewed on her bottom lip, her face landing somewhere between surprise and relief.

Will held the note and returned to the steps.

'Thank you!' the girl breathed, hand clutched dramatically to her chest. 'That's my beer money for the week!' She took the note from Will's outstretched hand, letting her thumb and middle fingers run along his skin, feeling a callus on his index finger.

She had freckles smattered across her cheeks, and feline green eyes; she looked like a superhero Will thought absently as she slipped the note into the back pocket of her apple-bottom jeans. 'I can't find my library pass,' she explained, pulling a stray lock of hair from her mouth before bending back down and rushing her belongings back into her bag. 'And I really need to pick up the books on my reading list so I can get the last part of my paper done before the end of this week. I was hoping I'd be able to crack on today, I can't make it in tomorrow and Friday is cutting it fine, you know?' She pulled her bottom lip with an incisor.

Adeline watched Will's eyes flicker towards her mouth; she smiled up him, just the right balance of coy-yet-interested that she had perfected.

The girl's red hair reminded Will of Ella, of the day she leant out of the window, looking down at him. He pictured her back in their lounge hanging up the phone, picking up Amber and carrying her into the kitchen and boiling the kettle ready for a bath in the sink, the gas heater glowing orange in the room as Ella pinched Amber's toes, making her giggle as she sang 'This Little Piggy Went to Market'. He could feel the motorway stretching between them, the air freezing along the way, a barrier from here and there.

He could work while Ella slept.

'You can use mine if you want?' Will found himself saying, the decision made, lifting his mouth, lighting his eyes from within. 'I mean . . .' he grinned, doing up the toggles of his duffel coat, 'as long as you don't leave the country or anything?' It felt like fate, meeting this girl. Reminding him of what was important.

'Oh, how about I take the book out and we grab a coffee somewhere and work together?'

'A coffee sounds great . . .'

'I know a little place around the corner,' Adeline began. Will Roberts was a slam dunk, easily caught. She looked at his hands as he helped her put the last of her things in her bag: a copy of *Bridget Jones*, a pack of gum, a pencil case; she couldn't wait to see what he could do with those fingers.

Adeline replayed her morning, pleased for once that her underwear had still been damp from the washing machine and that she'd had to resort to her Friday night emerald-green thong and matching bra.

'. . . but I have to get home.'

The end of the sentence came like the crack of an ankle against a misplaced chair; she had thought this was a done deal. They stood, the things now safely back in her bag. She felt confusion flickering across her features. Couldn't he see what she was offering him?

Will opened his wallet and drew out his library pass, offering it to her with a flourish, like a get-out-of-jail card in the centre of a Monopoly board. 'You can get it back to me by Friday?' he asked with a smile.

'Oh, yeah, but are you sure? I don't want to put you out, and the coffee shop is only a few minutes away. My treat, for being my knight in shining armour?'

Will looked down to where her hand rested on his forearm – it felt alien, the weight too heavy, the nails too long – and resisted the urge to shake it off. Instead, he took a step back, her hand falling away like a leaf at the end of autumn.

'Oh no need, honestly.' His cheeks took on a pink glow, his hand raking through his hair as he avoided eye contact. 'You've done me a favour.' He dragged his eyes back, rocking on his heels and raising his other hand in an awkward farewell. 'See you.'

Will turned on his heels, already digging out his keys. If he hurried, Amber would still hold that baby oil warmth from the bath, her hair only just drying into the soft down that curled up like a question mark from her scalp.

'See you, and thanks!' Adeline shouted at his back as he walked away, bag on his shoulder, hands dug deep into his pockets, head down against the wind.

'Well, shit.' Adeline considered if she was off her game as she turned over the laminated card, the edges rough and beginning to separate from months of wear and tear from the inside of Will's pocket. She brought Will's photo close. He even looked good on that; hers made her look like she'd just had a rectal examination. The wind bit into her cheeks and sleet began to fall as she reluctantly fastened the clasp on her bag, turning over Will's card. Sandwiched into the back of the plastic holder was a photo hidden inside. On it, Will was holding a baby and looking into the camera with such love that she was filled with relief; it had nothing to do with her game. That man was head over heels for the person behind the camera.

Chapter Twenty-Seven

Now

Ella

5th October 2022

I stop chopping onions, wipe my hand and swipe the screen to accept Will's video call.

'Hello, you.' I grin at Will's face on my screen as he sits on the steps outside of school.

'Hi,' he smiles back at me. 'Thank you for the gift, it was really thoughtful, Ella.'

'You're welcome.'

I'd seen it in the front of a music shop, a leather-bound notebook filled with blank chord diagrams and a place for writing down fret numbers. I'd had his initials embossed on the front and inside I'd left him an origami peony. I was going to give it him on our next date, but patience has never been my thing, so I dropped it off at his school on the way to the dentist this morning.

'The kids in the class thought it was my birthday.'

'What did you tell them?'

'The truth, that it was a gift from my wife. They think you must be having an affair, by the way, because apparently when Ruby Finch's dad had an affair, he kept buying her mum presents.'

'Uh-oh. Busted. It's Mr Davis from number thirty-two. What can I say? I can't resist his dandruff, it's like it's snowing every time I kiss him.' I exhale a dramatic sigh. 'He's just magical.'

'Ah, well then, maybe I should bow out, what with such strong competition.' There is a heavy pause for a moment before he continues. 'And thank you for the flower. It's been a while since you've done that.'

'Tell me about it, it took me four tries and it's still a bit wonky.'

'It's perfect. Shit, that's the bell, sorry, got to go. I'll see you Friday?'

'You will.'

'Bye.'

'Bye, Will.'

I throw another stick in the incinerating bin and step closer, wafting the smoke towards me with a cough.

'What are you doing?' Cole asks, stepping into the garden, licking the edge of the cigarette paper and closing it around the tobacco, engine oil beneath his fingernails.

'I've got my appointment with Robin so I'm trying to get myself in the zone.'

'That explains the burnt onions in the kitchen and all the . . .' he gestures up and down with his hand, 'denim. I didn't think you were still going to go ahead with that. What with your whole dating-your-husband plan.'

'That's *why* I need to see Robin, to get Will back.'

'I don't understand why you think the key to getting your husband back is by discovering the secrets of some mystical conversation that you think you *time-travelled* to have.'

'Because I know, deep down, that she was trying to tell

me something important. It's only three weeks away, what else would it be about?'

'Lottery numbers?'

I ignore him. He flicks the lid of the Zippo, the end of his cigarette glowing amber.

'Hah! Perfect!' I say. 'Come here.'

'Oh-kay.'

'Now blow smoke at me.' I close my eyes.

'What?'

My eyes flash open. 'I need to feel and smell like the night of the fair before my session with Robin. So, come on, blow your disgusting habit all over me.' He takes a deep drag of his cigarette.

'Closer, come on, Cole, it needs to cling to my hair.' I hold out a plait.

Cole puts his bare arm around me; he's wearing a T-shirt, despite the bite of autumn in the air. The absence of the smell of alcohol on him feels stronger than when it was present. Instead, beneath the peppery sandalwood scent of his deodorant, I'm hit with pure Cole: his skin after we spent hours in the sun climbing trees and playing pooh sticks, the curve of his neck as I cried into it when Will dumped me the first time. The dark chest hair skirting beneath his collarbone rises as he takes a breath in and exhales just above my left ear, sending goosebumps running up my neck. 'Ugh, Cole! Not in my ear!' I rub my arms. 'You've given me goosebumps!'

'You're not the first.' His dimples sink as I shove him away and roll my eyes at him.

'Just . . . oh, never mind.' I take it out of his hand, lift the filter to my lips and inhale a deep intake of smoke.

Cole crosses his arms, an amused look as the nicotine hits the back of my throat, the same expression as he'd had the first time I tried smoking, when I was sixteen.

I cough. 'God, I can't believe I used to do this.'

His hand slips over mine as he tries to take it back from me.

'Hold on, just one more, I need to have that taste in my mouth.' I blow out the smoke, feeling the head rush that I used to enjoy so much. 'Can you think of anything else from that night?'

'You were wearing Charlie Red.'

'I was! How do you remember that?'

He shrugs his shoulders and crushes the roll-up beneath his boot.

'I think I might still have some in one of the boxes in the attic.'

I rush into the house, pull down the ladder, poking my head up into the cool dark space above, the torch light from my phone bouncing along the rafters, spotlighting the outsides of the many cardboard boxes that we haven't unpacked since moving in. I hold my phone between my teeth and clamber into darkness, finding myself between boxes of Christmas decorations and clutter from the old house: old guitars that Will intended on restoring to their former glory, Amber's first bike, Jamie's skateboard. I shift a couple of boxes: old photo albums, a whole box filled with Jamie's and Amber's school books. Dust billows out, making me sneeze.

'You OK up there?' Cole shouts from the bottom of the ladder.

'Yeah, can you wait there? I think . . . hah! Yes!' I bend over, scanning the words scrawled on the sides of boxes, grabbing the box with Amber's neat writing on: Mum and Dad when they were young!

I shift the other boxes until I have the right one and I pass it down to Cole, his fingers brushing mine as I lower it into his hands and climb down the ladder, wiping a cobweb from my cheek.

'God, my mouth tastes disgusting. I can't remember cigs tasting so gross.'

'You always chewed green Orbit when you smoked.'

'Did I?' I carry the box into the kitchen and dig out a knife, puncturing the Sellotape. I rummage between mix tapes, photographs, my first CD, Will's old Stereophonics T-shirt, and there at the bottom of the box is my old ruck-sack from school. I rummage around the insides, pull out an unopened packet of green Orbit, at which Cole raises his eyebrows with a smug look, a round tub of clementine-flavoured lip gloss, some broken pencils, an origami frog and a bottle of Charlie Red. 'Jackpot!' I open the bottle, taking a quick whiff. 'Jesus, was it always this strong?'

I shove the open bottle under Cole's nose, which he immediately pinches. 'Get that away from me, I have night-mares of my clothes stinking of that stuff.'

'Pfft. You're one to talk, you reeked of CK one.' I nudge him good-naturedly, reaching for a photo of me and Will, a clichéd strip of photobooth shots: the top one we're nose to nose, the second I'm kissing his cheek, the third is of us laughing, in the last one we're pulling faces at the screen. 'This was the day we went to get our passport photos, nei-ther of us knew how to work the machine so we did this together as a trial run.'

Cole gets up from the table and reaches into the cup-board, a packet of Percy Pigs ripped open and two shoved into his mouth. 'I need the sugar,' he says, mouth full in answer to my curious look. 'Does he know I'm staying here yet?'

'Not officially. But I'll tell him soon.'

'Maybe I should move out?'

'Are you ready?'

'Not, really . . . no.'

'Then you're staying here. Right then! I'd better get going. I'm going back to the future!'

'Well, no, you're not, you're going back to the past.'

'Shut up and eat your pigs.'

He grabs a handful and shoves them in, his cheeks bulging.

Robin's door opens and I stand with a smile. 'Nice plaits,' Robin greets me as I plonk myself on the sofa.

'Thanks, thought I'd rock the Ella Walker circa 1999 look, and . . . ta-da!' I pull out the bottle of perfume. 'Thought I'd have a quick sniff before, you know . . .' I put on a slow hypnotist voice, 'I start to feel very sleepy.'

'Everything OK?'

'Yeah, sorry for cancelling. My friend Cole was having a bit of a rough time.'

'And he's better now?'

I hesitate, picturing the moments when Cole's mask slips, when I see him rotating his Zippo lighter over and over, when he chain-smokes, when he comes back from a meeting and doesn't want to talk. I take a deep breath. 'He's an alcoholic. Recovering alcoholic.' I correct. 'And he's staying with me while Will and I have some space.' Robin smiles his favourite grandfather smile and adjusts his glasses. 'Look what else I found.' I reach into the bag, my fingers circling the lip gloss. I wiggle it at him. 'It's the one I was wearing that night. Do you think you can get food poisoning from old lip gloss?'

'I don't know. But if you cancel your next appointment, I'll know why.'

I stare at the greasy glob at the end of my index finger, shrug my shoulders and run it along the bottom of my lip, smacking my lips together. 'In for a penny.' I tighten the lid and replace it in my bag, retrieve the perfume, twist open the silver lid, my thumb landing beside the red 'Charlie' scrolled across the front of the bottle. I spray it liberally and apologise to Robin as he coughs behind his hand. I lie back, cross my hands across my stomach, assuming a mummy-in-a-sarcophagus pose. I turn to Robin. 'Do you think we can, you know, skip to the good bit today?'

'We can't just jump in, Ella, your mind has deliberately kept this information from you for a reason.'

'What do you mean?'

'Well, our memories are clever things. People who have had a traumatic experience, for example, are protected from that memory, our mind suppresses it. If I take you straight into that part of the brain that for some reason is trying to protect you, the less chance we have of opening it up. Your mind needs to know that when we start unwrapping those memories, it is safe to reveal them to you. Your mind needs to trust us, this process, it needs to feel safe. Does that make sense?'

'You think there is something bad being hidden?'

'It's possible, but then again it might just be something that made you feel uncomfortable. What we don't want to do is scare your memories away. So I think I would like to take you back to your entrance point again, the Saturday afternoon.'

It doesn't take long for me to be soothed by Robin's voice. This time, there is no fighting it: I'm already at the bottom of the stairs, answering the phone to Grandma Grunt, remembering to turn the clocks back, walking to the fair, watching Cole eating a hotdog, sitting down on the log, the rich smells and sounds from before even more vivid. This time I can hear the dried paper scrunch of the leaves in the trees, the sound of Cole's zip as he takes off his jacket, the conversations around the fire clearer, the girl telling Will that they should start a band. My memory of this is confused, though:

Will had been so interested in everything she was saying, but now, as the smell of woodsmoke burns in the back of my throat and I take a deep drag of a cigarette, the smoke hitting me as I watch them, Will keeps looking over at me, like he's distracted.

'I want you to turn to Cole again, Ella, replay the conversation we talked about last time.'

I turn to Cole. I can feel cool air around the back of my neck, but the side of my face feels hot from the fire. 'He needs to tell me something. Something important.'

I look into young Cole's face; he licks his bottom lip, but I can feel the pull of Will looking at me. I turn back to Will; the reflection of the light from the fire is flickering across his face, his focus switching from me to Cole and back again.

'What is Cole saying, Ella?' Robin's voice interrupts and I see him. I see Robin standing leaning against the bark of a tree; he's holding a clipboard.

I turn my attention back to Cole. 'He's telling me we're the same.'

'How do you feel when he says this, Ella?'

'Confused. I don't know what he is talking about, I'm distracted. The girl sitting next to Will has moved forward, she is on his knee. She . . . she's kissing him and I feel like I might die.'

In my trance I can feel myself inwardly wincing at the dramatics of eighteen-year-old Ella.

'I'm drinking the gin, and it tastes disgusting, it burns my throat, but I take another swig anyway. Oh, God. Her hand is in Will's hair. I can see the gap between the top of her jeans and her jumper. Will's fingers are on her skin. I need to get up, I'm too hot. Cole wants to come with me, but I don't want him to . . . I need to walk, I feel sick. *I said I'm fine, Cole.*'

I think I've just said that out loud in Robin's office.

My feet are walking unsteadily away. The air cools and darkens like soot, the mud beneath my feet muffling my steps while the trees wrap themselves around me protectively. A flap of wings above echoes amongst the branches, drawing my attention; I stumble on a piece of bark, but I carry on walking along the pathway through the trees. I've run through this forest so many times on Sunday afternoons that I don't have to concentrate on where I'm going. The forest around me stretches, a guard of honour towards the Abbey. I'm crying.

'What did you think was going to happen, Ella?' my voice hiccups around the office. 'That Will Roberts would notice you? Don't be so stupid. As if . . . as if that would happen.'

Ahead, I see Robin and his clipboard; he's waiting just by the archway. 'You're safe, Ella, I'm right here.'

But as I approach the archway, a fog whistles in, the mist following me through the guard of honour settling around me, and my feet stop. This isn't what happened: I didn't stop. I carried on walking.

'I can't move,' I say to the Robin in the forest, to the Robin in the office. 'My feet are stuck.'

The mud is holding them in place. I try to pick them up, but they remain trapped. Behind me, a dragging sound: I turn my head over my shoulder; a bramble weaves across the forest floor, a snake with a ropy body, thorns hissing along the dirt; it's moving faster and faster; I try to pull my feet up, but I can't get them out; the bramble is almost here.

'I can't get out!' My heart fights against the bones of my rib cage. 'Robin!' I look up, but he's disappeared. 'Robin!' The bramble wraps around my feet.

'I'm here, Ella, I'm going to bring you out of your trance in five . . .'

The thorns are biting into my skin, the length of the bramble's ropy spine wrapping around and around my shins.

'Four . . . you're beginning to become more aware of your surroundings here in my office, my voice is louder.'

'The brambles are around my knees, Robin.' They continue to bind me; my arms are now pinioned to my torso.

'The sun is streaming in through the window of my office, Ella, you can feel it on your face. Three.'

The night sky above me begins to turn blue, the brambles hissing and retracting as though the sunlight burns. All at once, the brambles fall away, sliding away into the shadows, the sun breaks through the forest canopy and my feet are free.

'Two.'

I look up to the sky, white clouds rushing past.

'One.'

My body feels light as my eyes open. I sit bolt upright. 'What the fuck was that?'

Robin looks up at me. 'I don't know. But I think it's a sure sign that your subconscious is trying to stop you from getting back those memories.'

'Why?'

'I don't know, but I think it's time that you consider whether you really want to know what happened that night. It might not be something you want to hear.'

'I don't need to consider it. I need to know, Robin.'

He nods slowly. 'I have a cancellation tomorrow, if you're sure?'

'I am.'

'OK, but if you change your mind, just give us a bell.'

'I won't, but thanks, Robin.'

I pass Cole a spoon, lift the lid from the Ben & Jerry's, pulling the grey chenille throw over our feet. We're watching

The Lake House. Cole gestures at the screen with his spoon. 'This has so many plot holes.'

'Shush. Keanu Reeves can do no wrong in my eyes.'

'I've never noticed how flawed this is before.'

'You're normally drunk though, so . . .'

'Ouch.'

'Sorry.'

'Do you know what I keep noticing? How much booze is everywhere. I mean, look, poor old Sandra has had a bad day at work, glass of wine . . . advert break, Disaronno, Keanu at a bar, beer in hand . . . it's just relentless. It's a wonder we're not all raging alcoholics really. See, it's not my fault I'm a complete fuckup, it's society, I've been subliminally fed this all my life. And now I know that fact, I'm cured! Hurrah!'

I nudge him with my foot; he holds on to my toes and gives me the smile that says he knows I know he's talking utter bollocks.

'Do you know one of the hardest things? The thing I'm dreading?' I shake my head. 'Explaining why I'm not drinking. Alcohol is the only drug that we have to defend not taking. Can you imagine how different it would be if I was a heroin addict instead? Friends asking why I'm not shooting up, feeling awkward because I'm not joining in? And yet, for me, ordering a pint at the bar would be the same as rolling up my sleeves and tapping a needle. I'm worried that they'll all see me differently, that I'll become the outsider for not joining in, that I won't be *fun* any more.'

'I've never looked at it like that before. You're right, though, the first thing anyone would say at a party if I ordered a soft drink would be, "How come you're not drinking? Can you not get a taxi?"' We return our attention to the TV. 'And you *are* still fun.'

He grins over at me as my phone lights up.

'It's Amber. Would you mind . . .'

'Pretending I'm Harry Potter?'

'Huh?'

'I'll be in my room, making no noise and pretending I don't exist?' Cole shakes his head at my confusion; I'd forgotten what a Potterhead he was. 'I'll go upstairs, but do not press play until my return. I've only found five plot holes so far and I'm hoping to hit double digits.'

I wait until he leaves the room and swipe the screen. Amber yawns and tightens a top knot of blonde hair. 'Sorry, hi, Mum.'

'Hi, how was your day?'

'Long. I've been awake for almost twenty-eight hours and to be honest I think I might be starting to hallucinate. Where's Dad?'

'He's, at the . . . kebab shop.'

'Now?'

'Yeah, I had a craving.'

'Ugh, if you had seen the state of the colonoscopy that I've been in today, you would be reaching for a kale smoothy instead.'

'There is nothing on this earth that would make me reach for a kale smoothy.'

'So what are you up to?'

She zips up her hoody and reaches for a can of Diet Coke; her blue eyes, the exact same shape and colour of Will's, meet mine.

Seeing a hypnotist about my past memories, trying to rekindle your father's love for me and watching my best friend go through detox. The actual words that come out are: 'I'm thinking of taking your father out on a surprise date.' She pulls the ring pull, the hiss of release echoing into my lounge.

'Aw that's cute! What's brought that on?' She takes a slurp from the can.

'Oh you know, I thought I'd spice things up a bit. We went out for dinner last week. I'm planning on doing something spontaneous.'

'Planning kind of takes the spontaneity out of it, don't you think?' She gives me a wry smile.

'Smart arse.' She opens a bag of nuts; whereas mine would be dry-roasted, hers look like they are mixed with dried fruit.

'Hardly. Jam got the brains, I've just got a . . .' she puts on a nasally voice, which means she's imitating one of the doctors at the hospital she volunteers at, 'good work ethic'. She chomps on her healthy nuts venomously and takes another swig of Coke. 'Just think, if you'd had a third child, you might have got one with brains and a good work ethic.'

'Or neither. And you have brains, Amber, you're going to be a bloody doctor!' Amber has always put herself down, always compared herself to her brother. Everything academically came so easily to Jamie. Amber had to work that much harder at everything, but she still managed to get straight As and has always been the more ambitious of the two. Whereas she was a fan of lists and organisation, the only time Jam would write a list was if it was to Santa.

'I'm not a doctor yet. Sometimes I think I'd have been better going into teaching instead; at least as a teacher you don't get vomited on most days.'

'That's not how your dad tells it.'

'True.' She yawns again. 'Why don't you take him to an open mic night? You know, relive your *glory* days?'

'An open mic night?

'Yeah. Have a look online, I bet there's one close by. I'd better go.' She glances at her watch. 'Six hours until my next shift.'

'OK, I'll get back to *The Lake House*.'

'Ah, that explains why Dad has gone to fetch you a kebab.

That film has so many plot holes I don't know how you can watch it.'

'Two words. Keanu Reeves.'

'Fair enough. Have fun on your date, oh and tell Dad thanks for reading over my notes.'

'Will do. Love you.'

'Love you too.'

I shout Cole down, and he appears with a half-eaten bag of Percy Pigs. 'How's my goddaughter?'

'Tired. Beautiful. Clever.'

'Pig?' He slumps back on the sofa and pushes the packet at me.

'No thanks, I'm good.'

He shrugs his shoulders and hits play on the controller, his jaw working as he shoves in pig after pig, after pig. Cole's foot is rotating over and over again and it's only moments before his tobacco tin is opened and he excuses himself for a smoke.

'Want some company?' I shout at his retreating back. He hesitates, turning to meet my eyes, and the pain and battle meet me full on. His eyes fill and he nods. I sit on the back step as he lights up. I talk about my conversation with Amber, I talk about Jam, we talk about the news, we talk about my session with Robin and my upcoming date with Will. We talk and talk.

But it feels like we don't say a word.

And when I hear the door unlock at three in the morning and I go downstairs to find Cole smoking and drinking a black coffee, I continue our conversation as if I'd just popped to the loo. The thread leads us to a conversation about *Buffy the Vampire Slayer*: we have a difference of opinion about the musical episode and so we re-watch it, and because we've watched that episode, we decide we may as well watch the next one. I stay awake until I hear his breathing slow; I tuck myself at the other end of the sofa and listen to the sounds of early morning outside the window, and when Cole's work alarm goes off, when he takes a shower, I make us both a coffee, and we both pretend that the absence of alcohol hasn't been banging against the windows, scraping its fingers across the glass, hammering its fists and demanding to be let in.

Chapter Twenty-Eight

Then

January 2003

In the corner shop, Cole handed over the change from his pocket and added the packet of Milky Bar buttons to the plastic bag already containing a bottle of white wine, the ring of the bell above the door pealing behind him. He tightened the scarf around his neck; sleet was beginning to fall as he dug his chin into his chest, making fast work of the half-mile walk to Ella and Will's house.

His knock on the door sank into the quiet. No answer. He trod past the weeds sprouting between the paving-slab cracks, around the side of the house to the lounge window, tapping gently on the pane in case Amber was sleeping. The curtain was drawn aside, Ella's tired eyes meeting his. He held his hand up in salute as the curtain fell back into place, the sound of the key chain being drawn back following moments later.

'Hi.' Ella yawned, her hair greasy and pulled into a ponytail, her skin sallow. Amber sat on her hip with a candy-cane-striped teething ring held fiercely between her gums, a long thread of drool going unnoticed against the grey of one of Will's old sweatshirts. Cole grinned up, swinging his plastic bag at her.

'I've brought provisions!' Amber's feet bounced up against Ella's leggings, her body jerking, using her mother's skin like a trampoline; the ring clattered onto the floor with a squeal of delight from Amber as she recognised her godfather. Ella sighed and offered her daughter to Cole.

'Come here, Bamber!' Cole exclaimed, his original nickname of Amber Bamber filed down and shaped until it found its place. He held her familiar weight, the love for his goddaughter filling his chest like helium. No one had been more surprised than Cole at the all-consuming love he held for Ella and Will's daughter. He had turned up at their doorstep, an 'It's a girl!' balloon impaled on a stick in his hand, a badly wrapped pink rabbit – later named Blancmange – clutched in a Mothercare bag, his body braced for fake joy, for false sentiments about how beautiful she was, when everyone knew that all babies resembled old men.

But when he'd leant in to kiss Ella on the cheek, there, head to foot in a beige and lemon sleepsuit, was the most perfect baby he'd ever seen. There had been none of the jealousy he was expecting as he processed this fact, because of course Will Roberts would have a perfect daughter; instead there was a sense of recognition, of kindred spirits: Cole and Amber were on the outside of the couple.

Ella's slippered feet flapped against the floorboards still waiting to be sanded as she headed towards the kitchen. Cole stamped the frost from his feet, a ricochet of giggles as he marched on the spot, lifting Amber high up into the air, with every movement making her squeal in delight.

'Close the door, will you!' Ella's voice, tired and impatient, fired from the kitchen. Cole grimaced at Amber conspiratorially as she giggled again.

'Ugh-oh, are we in trouble again?' he asked her, and she gurgled in reply. 'Thought so. Watch and learn, Bamber, watch and learn.' He kissed the top of her head, following the sounds from the kitchen.

'Tea?'

'I'll make it.' Cole went to hand Amber back to her mum.

'No, you keep her, my arm feels like it's going to drop off. Will is stuck at uni *again* and she was supposed to have a nap but she's refusing to go down.'

'Well, maybe she wants to stay up and paaaarty like it's 1999?' Cole belted out the Prince classic, dancing Amber around the kitchen. It took him a moment to register Ella's shoulders heaving.

'Hey, what's wrong?'

Ella shook her head, covering her face with her hands. Cole secured Amber in her highchair, reaching for the packet of white chocolate buttons from his bag and emptying some out onto the plastic, Amber's fingers immediately manipulating them into her mouth. He returned to Ella, drawing her into his chest as she let out great heaving sobs.

'What is it? What's wrong?' He pulled back from her, smoothing the stray hair from her face, wiping the tears from beneath her eyes. She opened her mouth to speak, but clamped her lips together, wrapping her arms back around him and hanging on to the fabric of his shirt with her fists. Cole stroked her hair, making shush noises as Amber focused on the sweets and concentrated on the task at hand with the concentration of the surgeon that she would one day become.

The tears started to subside, Ella spent and blotchy.

'Why don't you go and have a bath? Take some time to yourself, eh?'

'I can't, the heating's broken.'

'A shower, then? I'll give Amber her bath in the kitchen sink.'

'But . . .'

'Ella, I've watched you bath her a dozen times. I'll put cold water in before I add the hot from the kettle, I'll check the water in the sink with my elbow and get the towel on the heater, OK? Now go.'

Cole released his friend, turning her by the shoulders and walking her conga-style to the bottom of the stairs, worry lying heavily in his stomach as he watched her climb the stairs.

Amber was falling asleep in Cole's arms when Ella came back into the lounge, her hair wet and smelling of citrus, a thick dressing gown wrapped around her.

'Sorry,' he whispered. 'I didn't know if I should let her sleep?'

'You don't need to apologise, remember?' Ella smiled sadly; the words felt like they came from a lifetime ago. She bent down and kissed the top of her daughter's head, taking her from Cole's arms and laying her down in the travel cot that served as a playpen. Ella remained quiet as she added a log to the fire, the old, disgruntled embers hissing and spitting. Then she sank onto the sofa, feet lifted onto Cole's lap.

'Want to talk?' Cole asked quietly.

Ella shook her head and tilted it back, closing her eyes, but the two blue lines shouted from behind her lids. She bit her lip, her incisor drawing blood from her mouth. She didn't know why she was reacting this way. She should be happy; what was there not to be happy about? She had a home, a husband she loved, a beautiful daughter, now healthy and happy and yet . . . now there was this.

'I'm pregnant.' She let the words fall from her mouth; like the snow beginning to fall outside, they drifted down, melting on impact, and if Cole hadn't have caught them, she could have pretended that they didn't exist, but she knew the words would keep falling, and she was terrified they would bury her.

'Pregnant?' Cole questioned.

Her eyelids flickered open, a tear falling from her eye. She nodded. Ella knew that to everyone else, she would smile as she said the words – what kind of mother wouldn't? She thought back to the last time she had found out she was pregnant, sitting in that apartment across the Channel, and for a moment she felt a flush of jealousy towards her former self. To the girl who had no idea what was coming, to the girl who would spend months with constant nausea, who would endure a rushed and traumatic labour, her daughter ripped from her body and encased in an incubator, of months not knowing if her baby would live or die. She was jealous of that girl, that Ella, who thought she would be a good mother, who expected to bond with her child the moment she was placed in her arms. She didn't expect to feel like she was swimming against a tide of muddy waters, grasping for a way to crawl up the river bank where above her, Stepford women sat on checked picnic blankets with gurgling babies, the sun beaming down on their happiness, a magic thread glittering like spun silver, connecting their offspring to their heart; that magical thread that mothers are supposed to be born with.

The heat from the fire and her dressing gown was making Ella queasy and she shifted, taking it off, busying herself so she didn't have to look at Cole. The cool draught was welcome on her skin as she tucked her feet up beneath her old navy maternity nightie.

'Pregnant?' Cole repeated, watching Ella's every move. He had seen the destruction Amber's pregnancy had wreaked on his friend. He saw the things others didn't: he saw the days when Ella would be staring off to a fixed point visible to only her, the days when he could see the exhaustion, the blank canvas stretched over her skin, happiness and contentment painted over it with thick careful strokes when people came to visit. He had often wondered over the past year if even Will saw how thickly she applied the paint to cover up the cracks. But then there were days when he saw her with Amber, when he watched them as a family, and he could see that she was still happy, despite everything; she was living a different kind of happy. However, as he watched his friend, the grey pallor already returning to her face despite the flush of heat from the fire, her cheeks already beginning to sink, a knot formed inside his chest. She met his eyes and crumbled; his brave, funny, strong friend, the girl who always found beauty in everything, fell apart right in front of him. He brought her into his arms, her body on his lap, her arms holding tightly around his neck.

Cole wanted to pick her up, to carry her away, to slam the door behind them. He could see himself doing it, rising from the sofa, opening the door and carrying her to his house, throwing their things into cases, calling a taxi, holding her hand as they ran to catch a flight, their future playing out like a romantic comedy. But his montage paused as Amber stirred in her cot, her white-blonde curls turning towards him, her pink dummy pulsing in her mouth, her fists clenched at either side of her head. Instead, he saw the answer to his problems, the fantasy that he couldn't help but play out, because Cole would often imagine Will wasn't part of the picture any more. Behind closed eyes, Cole would sometimes see Ella opening a door on an illicit affair, Will begging for forgiveness, Ella telling him she couldn't and that their relationship was over. But now, Cole replayed his darkest fantasy, the one with Ella opening the front door, a policewoman standing there: it's bad news, the policewoman might say, or I'm afraid there has been an accident; Will was killed instantly, there was nothing anyone could do.

Guilt and self-loathing filled Cole.

He was dirt; he wouldn't ever deserve Ella.

Will killed the engine of his bike at the top of their road and pushed it the last few yards up the street; if Amber was already asleep, he didn't want to disturb her. Snow had begun to fall like lemon sherbet in the orange light spilling out onto the pavement. He walked around to the kitchen door at the side of the house, slipping in his key, turning it gingerly, wincing as the handle creaked. He could smell Amber's baby shampoo, see the detritus of her bath, her towel over the airer, the last few inches of her milk remaining in the bottle.

He pushed open the door to the lounge gently, expecting to see Ella curled up on the sofa, but instead, what greeted him was his wife half-dressed: wet hair, her arms around Cole's neck, his head burrowed into hers, eyes closed, as she uttered the words, 'How am I going to tell Will? How am I going to tell him I'm pregnant?' The regret in her voice, the image in front, hit Will full force in the chest, like he'd been thrown against the wall, the air knocked from his lungs. Thoughts tumbled over in his mind as he tried to make sense of what he could see.

'Pregnant?' Will repeated, the sound of his own voice startling him as much as the couple tangled up on the sofa.

'Will?'

Ella unwrapped herself from Cole's embrace, embarrassed. Cole glanced away, straightening himself as Ella stepped towards her husband, a smile fixed in place.

'Surprise?' she laughed.

Her reaction upended Will for a moment. The guilt he had heard was gone – there was only lightness, flippancy, almost excitement in her tone.

Will's focus was drawn to Ella, to Cole, then back again.

It was a moment, less than the time it takes for the clock hands on the wall to graze the passing of a second, but it was there. He could feel the emotions written on his face: hurt, distrust, the acceptance of a fate that he had almost been expecting. Ella and Cole, Cole and Ella.

A laugh exploded from Ella's throat. 'You didn't think . . .' She pointed to herself, her finger almost limp with the effort of moving it from her to Cole then back again. She laughed again, almost hysterically. 'Me and Cole?' Her hands landed on her knees, her body bent over laughing, a hand clamping over her mouth as she straightened and Amber stirred. 'Oh, Will.' She touched his cheek. 'Your face!'

She turned to look at Cole as he shook his head, his gesture indulgent, a roll of the eyes, a 'what is he like?' expression joining in with her humour.

'Ugh! That would be like me shagging Roddy or worse, Kenny! Jesus! What a thought!' She landed a kiss on Will's cheek, her hands cupping his face, a gentle kiss on his lips. 'I know we didn't plan this, but Amber is going to have a brother or sister.'

Will had no words at that moment; everything he wanted to say was bottlenecked in his throat. Instead, he pulled her into his chest, wrapped his arms around her, holding her tightly.

Over her head, Will and Cole's gazes locked. Ella hadn't seen the hurt that had flickered in Cole's eyes as she compared him to her brothers. But Will had. She might have thought that the idea of her and Cole as anything more than friends was utterly preposterous, but the expression on Cole's face, the one that was replaced so quickly that a blink would have erased it, told a different story.

For the first time, Will saw that not only did Cole believe there could be something more than friendship between him and Ella, but that, somehow, he believed it was inevitable.

And over the next few months and years, during the days when Will would be stuck at work and Cole was at his home playing with his children, when his son reached for Cole rather than Will, he replayed that look, and that small kernel of doubt would grow and feed until one day, Will Roberts would begin to believe that there was a real possibility that Cole Chapel would eventually take his family away from him.

Chapter Twenty-Nine

Now

Ella

6th October 2022

Robin's sofa gives beneath me, the familiar feel of cord, the soft lighting and homely smell of the room easing my sleep-deprived eyes. My night staying up with Cole is making my actions slow and clumsy.

He rolls up his brown cardigan, apple cheeks shining as though he's buffed them after a vigorous Imperial Leather lathering. He leans back in his seat. 'I thought you might change your mind, that our last session might have scared you off!' He chuckles as if he's just delivered the punch line to a knock-knock joke rather than referring to being trapped in a nightmare. 'Now, are you sure you want to proceed? Because I've been reading up on how to get you to flap your wings like a chicken if you'd prefer?'

I laugh politely. 'Will it happen again?' I ask, the feeling of the thorns digging into my skin making me scratch the back of my calf.

'Well, I've been thinking about that, and rather than trying to skip past walking through the woods, it's better that I give you the tools to hack through the brambles. That is if you're certain you want to go ahead?'

'What, like visualisation and stuff?' I yawn.

He holds his finger up in the air as though there is a light bulb above his head. 'Better!' From beneath his chair a plastic Tesco bag swings forward. Inside, are well-used yellow gardening gloves and a pair of green-handled secateurs. I look down at the gloves and back at him, questioning. 'Put them on! I want you to be able to feel them when you go back under, be able to root you to the present if you'll excuse the pun.' His shoulders rise and fall, an excited, pleased-with-himself shrug.

I can't help but smile as I slip my fingers inside them, the rough material catching on my wedding ring. I reach out for the secateurs. 'What if I stab myself with these?' I enact Stephen Kinging myself in the eye-socket, before opening and closing them a few times at a distance.

'Oh, I won't let you hold them while you're under!' He rolls his eyes, taking them from me. 'I just wanted you to be able to have a good fresh image of them, hear the . . .' he snip-snips the blades, 'sounds and be able to imagine the weight of them in your hands.'

'Rightio. Should I keep these bad boys on?' I ask, holding my hands up in a 'Freeze! You're under arrest!' gesture.

'No, but have a good look at them, have a sniff.'

'A sniff?'

'A sniff! Smell is a powerful route to the subconscious.'

I bring them gingerly towards my nostrils and give them a quick snort; they smell like rubber and feet.

'When you're in the trance, you should be able to smell them, it'll help.'

I have a few more snorts.

'I think this should be enough,' I say, scrunching up my nose, taking them off and passing them over. 'Let's get cracking, shall we?' I get straight into position, curled up on my side, my eyelids ready and waiting to close. I yawn again as Robin arranges the gloves and secateurs on the table in front of us and pops a Murray Mint in his mouth.

'Rough night?' Robin asks, sucking with determination, eyebrows drawn together above his glasses.

'*Buffy* marathon.'

His bushy eyebrows shoot up. 'A naked marathon?'

I snort. 'No! A *Buffy the Vampire* marathon. Cole was having a tough night.'

'Oh. Oh I see. I thought for a minute, that you were . . .' He shakes his head, seeming to clear the thought.

'Running in the buff? Nope. Not even a glimmer of a nipple.' His apple cheeks burn beneath his glasses. 'Sorry, Robin, I didn't mean to embarrass you with nipple talk. I have no filter when I'm tired. I'm sure the last thing you want to be picturing is me running in the buff, boobs a-swinging, buttocks wobbling like a pair of pink blancmanges, stretchmarks as far as the eye can see.' Robin swallows his mint with difficulty. 'You don't hear of blancmange much any more, do you? Sorry. I don't suppose you want to hear about my stretchmarks and sagging boobs. Shall we get started?'

'Yes. Um, yes. Let's.'

It doesn't take long to find myself in the woods, Robin's syrup-smooth voice guiding me forward.

The night sounds echo around me; there is a disturbance of the ground under my boots, hidden insects sent scurrying away as I continue to step forward. Ahead, a branch stretches away from the trunk like a child trying to escape its mother's grasp. I reach out; the cool, gnarled surface gives way to the pressure of my fingers. I scrape past, the branches creaking and complaining like gossiping women in a market square. A torch-like beam casts down from the moon, highlighting the end of the pathway, the Abbey low-lit in stripes of bluegrey: pathways from the moon to the ground. Around me, the rich, dank smell of earth mixes with woodsmoke, with the scent of cigarettes in my hair. The residue of gin on my breath leaves my mouth in small puffs of air.

'Tell me what you can see, Ella.'

'I can see the path ahead, the archway. It's cold, colder here than it was. The moon is bright and I can see shadows on the ground.'

Just as I say these words, along the forest floor, the hiss of the brambles scratch across the dirt. I turn my head, watching them snake towards me, the whip and thrash faster than last time, and within moments I can feel the scratch against the denim of my jeans. 'The brambles,' I say, my voice snagging like the barbs in my shins.

'OK, Ella, I want you to slow your breathing further. You feel calm, you're in control. In two three, out two three.' In the woods I see the blue air leave my mouth slowly, feel it filling my lungs. 'That's it, Ella. I want you to reach into your pockets, inside your jeans is a pair of gardening gloves.'

I concentrate on my breathing, try to remind myself that this isn't real, that there never were any brambles that night. I force my cold hands into my jeans, clutching the yellow material and fumbling with them, forcing my hands inside them. The brambles are now up to my knees, I can hear them hissing, the thick stems creaking like the bow of a ship.

'OK, I've got them on.'

'Good, now reach inside your back pocket, you'll find the secateurs.'

I do as he says, clutching them in my shaking hands. 'That's it, Ella, now start to trim those brambles away, pull at them with your gloves, they can't hurt you.'

I sink the blades into the tough flesh; a squeal like the caw of a thousand crows ricochets around the forest. I reach for the final piece around my knees, contracting my grip around its sinewy throat in my fist. I throw it to the floor, from where it hisses along the bracken, retracting into the darkness, the shadows swallowing it whole.

'They've gone,' I say, breathless. I bend over, my hands on my knees as I recover.

'That's good, Ella, you're doing really well. Can you see the path to the Abbey now?'

I nod and begin the familiar walk, the crunch beneath my feet echoing between the trees; a cloud passes by the moon, dulling the sharp edges of the light like a finger along a charcoal outline.

The scene in front of me is much more familiar; it's the same as that night in 1999. I stop walking, taking in the arch ahead. But, although my feet are stationary, in a rush of movement my body is being drawn forward like I'm on a high-speed travelator, my surroundings tearing past my peripheral vision as my body is propelled onwards. I hold my hands up either side to protect myself from crashing into the stone of the Abbey. I brace for impact, but my movement comes to an abrupt halt, my palms a metre away from the archway.

I blink, my vision obscured, until through the soft edges, a glimpse of green, of red.

'She's here, Robin. I'm here.'

'Good. Let yourself feel nervous, Ella, let yourself be curious, just as you did that night.'

My breath comes out in fast puffs; my hands remain held up, still bracing myself for contact, but I'm stationary. In front of me, the fog is dissipating and tiny glimpses of the woman the other side are filtering through.

'Hello?' I say, just as I did that night. I feel my mouth moving slowly in the office, but here, amongst the fog, it reverberates deep within my chest. As the word leaves my lips the air separates around my breath, parting like a curtain on opening night, clearing the archway. 'I can see her.'

'OK, Ella, you're doing good. I want you to listen to the sound of my voice. I'm going to take you deeper into the trance now. You don't need to do anything, I'll do all the hard work, you just wait where you are and I'll do the rest. I'm going to count down from five to zero and you will feel your body becoming more present in the forest, like you're adjusting the tuning on an old TV dial. Five.'

In the forest a cloud disperses from in front of the moon, the light shining brightly, like a spotlight on a stage.

'Four. You are filled with a deep sense of calm, the ground is soft beneath your feet, the air around you comforting like a blanket. Three. I want you to lift your hand and wipe away the fog, just like you would against a steamed-up mirror.'

My arm feels heavy as I lift it. The fog is still, like a sheet of ice, but with a smooth arch of my hand, one smooth motion, it scatters around me, tiny droplets fall to the floor, the sound like hail against a window.

'That's good, Ella. Two.'

My forty-one-year-old reflection stares back at me, but it's not how I remember: now it's like looking in a mirror, the arch framing it in the same way as the sea glass frames the one at home. The reflection has tears in her eyes; she, I, am scared, worried, urgent.

'One. You're deeply relaxed now, Ella.'

The reflection begins to speak, her mouth opening, words clambering from her mouth, hitting the barrier, only fragments slipping through.

'She's trying to speak to me, but I can't hear her.'

'Ella, I want you to cover your ears, I want you to feel the sound around you dampen. My voice will be the only thing you can hear, all sounds from the forest will be muted, OK?'

I do as he says, still watching my older self talking, her fists clenched either side of her face like she wants to break through.

'And in a moment, very slowly and carefully, you are going to move your hands and the sound will come back, just like taking off a pair of headphones. OK? Three. Your fingers feel a little looser around your ears. Two. Your hands are moving away. And one. All of the sound is returned. What can you hear?'

'I can hear her but it's like a phone with a bad reception, she keeps breaking up. I think she's asking if I can hear her. I'm nodding, I think I nodded that night. My head feels heavy.'

She looks relieved; she's seems to be calming herself. '. . . *at's good*,' she's saying.

I want to ask her why she is here, but that's not what happened.

She bites her lip and closes her eyes. I can see from her actions that she is trying not to rush into something. It's the way I've always handled situations when I'm angry or upset, when I need a second to process the thoughts: a close of the eyes, a deep breath in counting to five and exhaling slowly. It's strange watching my reflection performing this action. She smiles and ice runs through my veins because I know that smile, I created it: she is hiding something. It's the expression I used when I told Jamie having a filling wouldn't really hurt, the expression I would arrange when I was pregnant with Jamie, when Will would come home and I would tell him that I'd had a lovely day, when in fact all I had done was sit and stare at the wall.

My reflection seems to have an idea. She holds up a finger, an 'Ah!' expression.

'. . . *ake . . . rek . . . ast*,' my older self says.

What? I want to shout.

I hold my hands out, a sorry, I don't understand.

She shakes her head: '*No . . . can't . . . tell you . . . soon.*' She looks behind her, biting her lip and fighting back tears.

I want to scream, *Just tell me!* But in the forest, I remain standing still.

'*Robin.*'

'You're doing really well, Ella, continue to repeat everything she says back to me.'

'*Watch out . . . number seven . . . yellow.*'

'OK, Ella, I'm going to bring you away from the Abbey now. In five. You're stepping backwards, the mist is softening everything around you, you feel soothed by my voice. Four.'

No, wait! I try to say to Robin, but my lips feel closed, sandwiched together; I'm not sure the words have got out.

My reflection is fading but as my body drifts backwards, I think I see her hand on her heart, tapping in hyphens.

'The sounds in the forest are dulling, you can hear the clock in my office. Three.' I try to fight against Robin's words, try to lift my hands and grasp at the fog, but they won't move, they're too heavy. 'The sun is breaking through the clouds, you can feel the light from the office on your eyelids, which are beginning to open. Two.'

The forest sinks back as I hear water filling the radiator in the office, the rush of a tap in the room next door, the sound of a bus splashing through puddles outside the window.

'One.'

My eyelids flicker open and Robin is leaning forward, offering me a glass of water.

'Holy crap,' I gasp, sitting up and swallowing the water.

'How are you feeling?'

'Weird.' I gulp down some more water. 'What do you think she was saying? Did I repeat it?'

'You did. I think it might be something to do with cake and breakfast? Does that make any sense to you?'

I freeze, taking the glass away from my lips slowly and replacing it on the table. 'I eat cake for breakfast.'

'Since when?'

'Since . . . since the day after the fair, before Will came round. Is that what you meant? Before? When you said I needed something to corroborate my memories, to see if they're real? She even said your name.'

'Or it could just be something your conscious mind already knows about yourself?'

'True. What do you think she meant about a yellow number seven?'

'No idea.'

I thank Robin, book my next appointment and head out of the door. There is a voicemail from Will waiting for me.

'Hi Ella, it's, um, Will . . . obviously.' He clears his throat. 'I just wanted to check that you're still free tomorrow? That you still want to . . . go ahead?' I can hear the sounds of the school behind his voice, the chatter of teenagers rushing to lessons, a door being slammed shut. It's as though it's me being persuaded to go out with him rather than the other way around and again I wonder what is going on with him, why he feels that I need to be persuaded to go out with him. 'If you want to cancel, I just wanted to say that I would understand . . . all things considered. Anyway, I've got to go, year seven violin, pray for me. I, um, bye. Bye.' I bash out a text wishing him luck with the strangled cats and confirm that I'm still on if he is. He replies a second later: 'I am. See you tomorrow.'

It's raining and I reach into my bag, grabbing an umbrella as I make my way along the street, past a café with the owner scraping the chairs back beneath the canopy. Still battling with the clasp, I swerve around a woman walking with headphones and a determined stride. I stop walking and stand outside a bookshop while I try to force the catch of the umbrella just as a bus whooshes past me, the wheels dipping into a pot-hole, sending dirty water up the left side of my body. It saturates my hair, the side of my face and my favourite yellow suede boots.

'Thank you!' I yell, spinning around at the retreating vehicle, throwing up my hands in frustration. My heart beats loudly in my chest as I glance down at my yellow boots, then read the number on the back of the bus: seven.

I freeze, my heart hammering against my ribs as I hear my own voice: *Watch out . . . number seven . . . yellow.*

Holy, holy, hell.

I wait for Will, butterflies in my stomach, the flyer to the open mic session later held tightly in my hand as I sit at the bar and order a soda and lime. I'm trying to cut back for Cole, solidarity and all that. I feel more nervous than when we met for dinner; I'm still not sure if an open mic night is the right thing to do. The memory of my session with Robin surrounds me: she was – *I* was – scared, trying to tell myself something I don't want to hear. What if all of this is for nothing? What if nothing we do on these dates will make a difference and he will still want a divorce?

'Hi.' Will's voice behind me makes me jump. I have been focusing on the main door but he has arrived from behind.

'Hi! Hi!' I repeat, nerves making me loud and repetitive, and European for some reason, I note, as I kiss him on both cheeks. 'Can I get you a drink? I'm driving, so fizzy lime for me!' *Why oh why am I shouting and acting like a complete arse? This is Will, for God's sake. Just Will.*

'Thanks, I'll have a Coke, I'm driving too.'

'Ha! There we go then! We're already on the same wave-length! Samesies!'

Samesies? Oh Sweet Lord above. I close my eyes briefly, trying to regain some control, then smile at the barman. 'Coke, please. Oh!' I turn to Will. 'Full sugar or diet? Not that you need to diet,' I correct myself, landing a hand on his arm. 'You look great, slim, not that you're skinny or, or . . .'

'Diet would be great.' Will pushes his lips together, a grin barely hidden away.

'Grrreat! Like the Frosties tiger!'

Oh holy fuck. What am I talking about?

I clear my throat. 'Oh and some pork scratchings if you have them?' I add, smiling at Will just to confirm to him that I do *not* think he needs to go on a diet.

'Any flavour?'

'Oh, um, pork, please.'

'Riiight, well they're all pork-flavoured, what with them being pork scratchings.'

'Oh yes, ha, yes, yes. Um . . . whichever flavour you recommend.'

He plants a packet in front of me.

'THANKS!' I shout. *Why am I shouting?*

We take our drinks and I follow Will to the back of the room, slopping my lime soda on my white top along the way, leaving me looking like I have a radioactive belly button. Perfect. I sit opposite him, opening the packet, sending pork flying across the table.

'Sorry! Sorry!' I scoop the remaining snacks into the bag.

Will's hand reaches out, stilling me. 'Relax, Ella.' He smiles softly and I swallow.

'Sorry, I'm just nervous, even more than last time. Weird, isn't it?'

He nods. 'I changed my top three times,' he says, pulling the collar of his grey shirt.

I grin broadly. 'Really?' I ask, ridiculously happy tears pricking my eyes. 'Oh, God, I was hoping to make it back home before I started to cry!' I tuck my forefinger under my eye, running the tears away.

'You said we're going somewhere different?' Will asks,

pushing his finger against an ice cube. I try to focus on it bobbing up and down, but my eye appears to be on fire.

'We are!' I push forward the flyer quickly, returning my finger to my eye socket.

'Are you OK?' Will asks, looking up, a frown of concern.

'Yes! Yeeees.' I nod reassuringly while water streams from my socket. 'I think I've got something in my eye, shit. It hurts quite a lot actually.' My eyelid starts twitching and batting like a butterfly's wings. 'I'll be fine!' I squeeze my eye shut while reaching blindly in my bag for a tissue. 'I thought we could go to an open mic? This one is only around the corner and I thought it would be fun? Fuck.' My eye is burning behind the tissue. 'What is in those pork scratchings? Bleach?'

Will reaches for the packet and turns it towards him. 'Almost. Ghost chilli.'

'Ghost chilli?!' I shriek. 'Why? WHY?' I pull out another ream of tissues, forcing them against my eyelids.

'Maybe you should wash it out?'

'Good idea. GRRReat idea, oh there I go again with the Tony the Tiger impression!' I laugh hysterically, bumping my leg against the table as I fumble my way to the ladies, where I rush to the sink and run the tap at full pelt.

Perfect, Ella, just wonderful. I cup my hand beneath the tap, blasting my eye and face with water until the burning has mostly subsided. When I take the tissue away, my eyelid is so swollen it's practically shut. *Fabulous. I look like I've been in the ring with Rocky.* I shake my head at my reflection and rummage in my bag. There at the bottom is an old packet of antihistamines, left over from the summer. I down two, look at my reflection and knock an extra one back. That should sort it out.

Well done, Ella, this is exactly the way to win back the love of your life.

I straighten my shoulders, shake my hair out, take a deep breath and return to the table.

'Jesus!' Will's eyes widen. 'Should we get you to A&E?' He stands, his hand lifting my chin, examining my face. I pull away gently.

'It's fine, honestly, looks worse than it is.'

'Are you sure, because it looks . . .'

'Awful, yes. I know.'

I sit back down, trying to fix a smile in place, carrying on as if I don't look like I've been attacked by a swarm of bees. 'I've looked online and this club sounds like great fun. People of all ages go to the open mic, wannabe comedians, singers, poets . . . I thought you might want to have a go?'

'What? Me?' Will asks, as if I've just suggested that he puts a pair of knickers on his head and runs around the pub shouting *I'm a Pelican, watch me fly*.

'Yes, you. I thought it would be nice, Amber suggested it actually.'

His eyebrows shoot up in concern.

'Oh, don't worry, I just said we were trying to go on more dates. They have loads of instruments there apparently. They even have castanets, I can be your backing percussion!' I shake imaginary coffee beans.

'That's a maraca.' He imitates me, a smile playing at his mouth. Then he opens and shuts his hands like a crab. 'That's a castanet.'

'Oh. Well, whatever. I shall be your accompaniment.'

'But your eye . . .'

'My eye will be fine. Come on, Will, it'll be fun, like old times.'

I smile and he rubs the back of his head. 'I'll go and watch, but I'm not getting onstage.'

'That's OK, I bet you change your mind once we get there though!' I clink my glass against his. 'Cheers!'

By the time we get to the club, the antihistamines have begun to take effect and I feel a bottle of wine in.

The club is intimate, dark, a bar running the length of the wall, a small stage at the foot of the room. An aisle of space splits the four-deep row of chairs, half full of spectators holding beer and wine, scribbling in notebooks, closing eyes, savouring the sounds or falling asleep – it's hard to tell, my closed eye is blotting out a portion of the room.

On the stage there is a young woman, a cello between her legs, a low sombre tune vibrating through the room. 'Ooh, she's good,' I whisper out of the corner of my mouth to Will, who nods in agreement as we take our seats. A koala of a man approaches, small, furry, fuzzy sideburns and tiny eyes. He offers a clipboard to us and scurries away to the back of the room.

I raise my shoulders and eyebrows at Will, all excitement in contrast to his expression, which is . . . less enthusiastic. I scan the paper with my one eye, and begin to fill it in. Name: Ella Roberts. Talent: Yes. Performing: Black Velvet. I grin and pass it on to Will, who whispers back.

'You're not serious?'

I frown. 'I am, it'll be fun!'

'Ella, it's not karaoke, these places can be brutal.'

'Oh. Maybe *you* should perform instead, then?'

'I, um, no, I . . .'

'But you're so good, Will.'

'Not any more.'

'You are. OK, so you're not in The Knock, but you could still kick her ass.' I nod at the weird Kate Bush-like movements going on behind the cello.

'Shhhhh!'

A Robert Smith with acne hisses at me from in front. I stick my tongue out at him as he turns his head back to the stage. I pass the clipboard to Will and concentrate on Kate gyrating against the cello, her movements making me wonder if she has one of those vibrating bullet things that I saw at an Ann Summers party a few years back. Amira almost collapsed in Asda when she took hers out for a daytrip.

The koala returns, taking the clipboard like a little furry ninja, and scampers back down the aisle before I can see if Will has written anything.

After Kate and her cello exit the stage, spotty Robert Smith, who is introduced as Bruce, takes hold of the microphone stand. Will and I both clamp our lips together, sharing the humour as his poem about toenails (a metaphor for the government, apparently) is spat viciously from his mouth. There is one particular moment, describing the pain of the jagged in-grower, that almost has us turning blue as we try not to laugh out loud. Once done – with the removal of a festering nail – Will and I clap heartily.

'Up next, Ella Roberts and "Black Velvet".' My face falls: the bottle-of-wine sensation from the antihistamines has waned and I now feel the difference between karaoke when drunk and, God forbid, karaoke when sober. 'Um, I . . .' The faces of the spectators turn to me and my Rocky busted eye. 'Sorry! I've had a change of heart. Ha! Um, next act please!'

Bruce is by my side in a flash. 'Nerves aren't real, they're a state of mind forced on us by the weight of society's expectations. Free yourself from that burden.'

'Right. Oh, but I'm not very good.'

'Who is to say what is good? For years the establishment has hounded us with labels and expectations, it's time to throw off those shackles.'

'It is?'

Bruce stands clapping, the rest of the clientele clapping along: some with gusto at the prospect of me throwing off the shackles of 'the establishment'; others, feeling my embarrassment.

'Right, then, OK. I'll just . . .' I begin to whisper to Will. 'If I do this, Will Roberts, you had better get up there after me,' I instruct, stepping towards the stage as Will tries to hide his smirk with his hand.

I turn to face the crowd; a squeal of feedback winces through the audience as I adjust the height of the stand. The light is bright in my one eye. From nowhere, the ninja koala appears, telling me he has the backing track ready. Bloody Spotify. The music begins and I clear my throat, the sultry guitar starting as I squint into the crowd. Will is leaning back in his seat; he gives me a thumbs up as I begin singing about Mississippi amid a dry spell. I mumble a bit, then remember the line about momma's baby being in the heart of every schoolgirl, and then try to eke out a few words in between the humming and la-la's as I fill in the blanks. I don't know the rest of the words and so mumble a bit more, then bellow out, 'Blaaaaaaack Veeeeeellvet and that slow southern Styyyyyyle, some religious-thingy that will brrrrring you to your kneeeeeeees! Blacck velvet if you pleeeeeeeeease.'

I carry on, ignoring the flinches from the crowd as I try to hit a high note, and the woman in front trying to discreetly put her finger in her ear. The claps are half-hearted, embarrassed, and trickle out by the time my eye and flaming cheeks have sat down.

'And if one Roberts isn't enough,' says the koala, widening his little eyes, 'we now have Will. Um, Will Roberts, everyone.' He claps and I can feel eyes turn towards him as he stands. I smile up, pride glistening from my one open eye. I watch him retrieve a guitar from the side of the stage and tune it. Hah. Watch this. I lean back and fold my arms with self-satisfaction.

'It's been a while, so sorry in advance,' he says.

My throat is dry as I watch him begin. He favours finger-picking now, but as the opening bars of 'Blackbird' by the

Beatles begin, warmth floods through me as the boy I fell in love with opens up on the stage. He casts a spell on the room as he plays; his voice is steady and calm and still holds a slight break when he hits the chorus. He passes the guitar back to whoops and hearty applause, and by the time he returns to my side, he's smiling broadly.

We spend the next few hours chatting about the acts, about songs that they played, about politics and interesting articles in the newspaper.

'How's your mum?' I ask, grimacing as I take a sip of the virgin mojito that tastes like the water from a pot of new potatoes.

Will smiles. 'She's good. It's nice to, you know, spend some proper time with her.'

'Have you told her . . . about us?'

Will hesitates. 'Yeah, yeah I have.'

'Oh,' I say, surprised.

'I know, right?' Will shakes his head.

'Does it . . . help? Talking to her?'

'It does. And she's got a wicked sense of humour, I'd forgotten that.'

The bar begins to close up around us and so we shrug on our coats and grab hot chocolates on the way back to the carpark.

The night is cool and I'm shivering in my light jacket as we stand awkwardly beside my car.

'Thank you, Ella.' Will tucks his hands in his pockets.

'Thank *you*! It was wonderful to see you play onstage again. And sorry again, for the whole "Black Velvet" thing. And the eye. And the shouting.'

He leans in and hesitates beside my cheek before kissing it softly. 'You'd better get going, you're shivering.' He rubs the outside of my arms like I'm one of the kids.

'Right, yes, don't want to get sore nipples.'

He laughs then, loudly, and I grin back.

'See you next week?'

'Next week sounds good.'

'OK. Bye then.'

'Bye.'

I yank the door handle but the car is locked and so I set off the alarm. I open my bag and root around for the keys, the flashes of light pouncing on the contents of my bag. I yank them out, waving them around. Will's hand closes over mine, calm, warm, firm. He takes the keys and blip-blips the alarm off, passing them back to me.

'Night, Ella.'

'Night, Will.'

Chapter Thirty

Then

Summer 2004

The sun shone; it smiled and winked from the blue sky, reverent, boastful, rich with the promise of a day outside, of BBQs and ice creams with sticky cones and eager hands.

Inside the house, Cole aeroplaned the pureed apple into Jamie's mouth while Ella wrestled Amber into her trainers. Since turning two, Amber had changed from a mild-mannered blonde angel into a miniature Horsewoman of the Apocalypse. She was always on the go, she didn't sleep, was easily bored and was always trying to escape her mother. Will had started a placement at a junior school, even though he wanted to teach music at secondary level; this was the closest one taking applicants, but it was an hour's drive away, which meant he was leaving at seven and not getting back until six at best, by which time Ella was exhausted and barely had the energy to hold a conversation.

Today, they were going to the park. Cole had persuaded Ella to venture out. He wasn't sure whether it was the thought of taking both children out on her own that was the problem or going out full stop, but Ella was either in this house or her parents'. But the weather was bright and he had the whole day off work and so had arrived early, ready to help get the kids sorted.

'Amber, keep still for Mummy, OK?'

From the dining-table chair, Amber stared at her mother, a stand-off. 'No like it.'

'I know, sweetheart, but you like the park, don't you?'

'Daddy come.'

'Daddy is at work, but Daddy come on Saturday?'

'No, Daddy come.'

'Uncle Cole can come, though, won't that be fun?'

Amber scowled at Cole; Will's blue eyes bored into him beneath blonde pigtails. Cole looked away. Amber's attachment to him had waned once Jamie had been born and he often found her looking at him as if he was an intruder. Jamie, on the other hand, was all for Cole.

Jamie grinned up, two teeth popping up from his bottom gum, his apple-pureed hand reaching for the purple spoon. Cole swiped the spoon away just in time and scraped the rest of the apple from the blue plastic bowl, making a 'neeeeeeeeaaaaaaawwwwwwwwwwwmmmmmmmm' noise as he expertly landed it into Jamie's mouth.

'Right, dude, you're done.' Cole unbuckled the belt holding him in place and swung him around the kitchen as Jamie chuckled. Cole pulled his nose towards Jamie's bottom area, giving a grimace. 'Again?' he asked Jamie as the baby hiccupped. 'You, young man, will owe me many, many beers when you come of age. Changing bag?' Cole asked as Ella swung her body round, clamping Amber's leg between hers and forcing her shoe on.

'On the bed,' Ella puffed out through puce cheeks. Cole took Jamie upstairs, pushing open the bedroom door.

Cole scanned the room for the changing bag, Jamie tugging onto Cole's curls. He told himself to ignore the dark brown circles inside the tea cup beside Will's side of the bed;

it wasn't his business if Will didn't take his dirty cup out. He told himself it was nothing to do with him that the laundry was overflowing in the corner, and bit down his anger at Will for not helping Ella more.

'Your dad, mate . . .' Cole said quietly to Jamie, reaching for the changing mat from the corner of the room and laying it on top of the unmade bed, 'needs to pull his finger out.' Cole made a pop noise, making Jamie giggle.

He unpopped Jamie's buttons, held his ankles in one hand, discarded and replaced the nappy with a clean one and tied the bag of the nappy sack. He refilled the changing bag with a few spares from the bag of Huggies in the corner of the room and carried Jamie back downstairs to where Amber was standing in the middle of the kitchen, fists clenched beside her hips, screaming at the top of her lungs.

Ella sat, her chest rising and falling and her face red and sweaty as though she had just run a marathon, but her face was blank. Outside the window, rain clouds had gathered; the sun had slithered away, regretful, embarrassed at getting hopes up. The rain coughed from the clouds apologetically: *I know I'm not supposed to be here today but here I am, sorry about that.*

The class Will had been given were year five, and the thirty-five nine-year-olds were running circles around him. He wouldn't normally be given his own class yet, but Will was on a quick-start course where he was given the opportunity to teach and do his degree simultaneously. It had seemed like a good idea at the time. The class was loud, and the memory stick Will had saved his lesson plans on had corrupted, so he was attempting to follow a lesson written by a different teacher while trying to remind himself of the properties of a 3D shape. The teaching assistant was doing her best to support him, reminding the children of the class rules, but they had smelt his fear and were feeding on him.

The bell for break was due to go in just five minutes and Will was counting down the seconds when the class would be let out onto the playground, but as he asked a boy with ruddy cheeks and the features of a man rather than a nine-year-old to please stop twanging the ruler against the desk, rain began sliding down the windows. Two words that he hated to hear were already ringing in his ears: wet play.

The head, Mrs Simpson, as she was known to the kids, knocked on the door and walked in, the class immediately hushing, the ruler twanger a picture of obedience and serenity.

'Just to let you know that it will be wet play today. Mr Roberts, if I could borrow you during break? Miss Jackson, if you wouldn't mind covering the class? You can have a late break once Mr Roberts returns?' She nodded her agreement and Will tried not to be offended by the sympathetic look she gave him when he left the class.

Five minutes later, Will knocked on Julie Simpson's office and stepped inside. She held aloft a finger, finishing her call.

Will hovered by the door, not knowing whether to sit or stand.

'Please, take a seat.' She gestured to the bucket chair and Will sank into it with a sense of defeat.

'So how are you finding 5J?'

'Good, fine, I mean there are a few characters but I'm finding my feet.'

'Right, right.' She tented her fingers together. 'Only I've noticed the noise level is quite high?'

'Yes, it's quite a chatty class but I'm making headway.'

'Can I offer some advice, Will?'

'Please do.' He nodded encouragingly, almost with a sigh. He knew he needed the help.

'I've been in this job for almost thirty years and I've worked with many, many teachers, both those new to the job like you and others who have been in education for years, and when you've had that amount of experience, you get a nose.'

'A nose?'

'For who has what it takes and who doesn't.'

'Oh. Right.'

'And do you know the main difference between the two?'

Will shook his head slowly.

'It's simple really. The ones that succeed are the ones who want to be a teacher. Who choose to do this job, not do this job because they don't know what they want. You were a guitarist?'

'Yes. But I had an injury so . . .' Will let his voice trail off.

'You thought you'd teach instead?'

Will winced. 'Something like that.'

'Look, I'm not here to tell you what to do with your career, Will, but I have a responsibility to the parents of those children and I can't in all good conscience allow you to continue your placement here unless you start to control the class. Every time I look into that room you seem like a rabbit caught in the headlights.'

The sound of rushing water surged in Will's ears; the room blurred around the edge; the desk that had felt so close moments ago stretched far away. The words Julie continued to speak ran into one another. It had been a while since this had happened, since he had been thrown back into the river. He blinked, once, twice, the desk returning, the words finding clarity.

'Take the rest of the day, Will. Emily Jackson will cover class. Have a break, mull over what I've said here, and if you decide that teaching is what you want to do, not what you *need* to do, then come and see me in the morning before class and I'll go through a few methods to help you control them.'

She smiled and for a second, Will imagined it was Sue

Walker standing in front of him, asking him to take care of her daughter, telling him she was precious and that she couldn't have wished for a better husband for her only daughter.

Ella pinched the bridge of her nose and watched the trail of raindrops drawing snakes and ladders against the window, dropping her hand to the edge of the sink.

'Park! Park! Park!' Amber shouted from behind her as Ella's knuckles grew white and began to ache from her grip.

'Uncle Cole can take you to the park.' Cole's voice came to her rescue, eager to please. 'But it's a special park, a secret indoors park.'

Ella turned, watching Amber eyeing him suspiciously, her eyes narrowed.

'Come on, let me show you, but you have to be a good girl, because only good girls go to the park *inside*.'

Cole shifted Jamie on his hip, glancing up to Ella for permission; she gave him a *sure, what the hell* shrug of her shoulders.

'Right then! We're going to the park, park, park, you can come too, too, too!'

He pointed to Ella; a reluctant smile returned as she shook her head at his ridiculous plan.

'And guess what else, Bamber?' Cole continued, eyes twinkling from one of Ella's children to the other. 'There is a party at this special park, hear that, little man? A party!' He swung Jamie around, Jamie's laugh cascading over them like mist from a waterfall.

Amber put her hands on her hips, still holding on to her fury but relinquishing a little. 'Party?' She lowered her guard, her furious appearance replaced with guarded speculation.

'With music and a tent and a bouncy slide.'

'Cole, don't . . .' Ella folded her arms with a *please don't promise her stuff you can't deliver* expression.

'What? You've never been to the secret park either? What do you say, Bamber? Shall we let Mummy come to the secret park?'

'Mummy you come?' Her voice rose, the scowl replaced with hopeful eyes and a hand outstretched, opening and closing.

Ella's throat tightened at her daughter's expression, that need for attention from her mother.

'Mummy would love to come!' Ella took two steps towards her daughter, reaching out and taking Amber's warm hand in hers. 'Lead the way, Uncle Cole.'

'Oh, you can't go to this special park without a pearl.'

'A pearl?' Ella asked, raising her eyebrow.

'A special blue pearl. I bet if you look upstairs you might be able to find some.' Cole tilted his head, trying to convey to Ella that he was referring to the bath oil pearls in the bathroom. It took Ella a moment before his meaning dawned on her. 'It might take you a little while to find them, though, they're very rare.'

'We find them!' Amber nodded with determination.

'Good girl. I'll wait here for you, and don't forget one for me! How many blue pearls will you need to find? Can you count them?' Cole pointed to himself: 'One.' Then to Ella: 'Two.' He tickled Jamie: 'Three, and there is one more person, I think, who else needs a special pearl?'

'Bamber!' Amber grinned, pointing to herself.

'Oh yeah! One, two, three, four!'

Cole passed Jamie to his mother. 'I think it should take about ten minutes to find the magic pearls.' He signalled to the lounge, leaning in and whispering to Ella, 'Can you throw down a sheet?'

Ella nodded and departed with her children, trying to replicate the excitement that Cole had managed to convey.

Chapter Thirty-One

Now

Ella

13th October 2022

I've battled the brambles, my feet stepping over their corpses as I approach the archway. I brace myself for the feeling of motion sickness as once again, I'm propelled forward, an elastic band buried deep in my solar plexus dragging me towards the archway, my hair fanning back from my face, the sky, the branches, the lights of the moon all rushing outside my vision until I stop again, hand braced for an impact that never hits.

This time, my reflection is clearer.

'What can you see, Ella?' Robin asks.

'I can see her, me.' My voice is thick syrup. 'Her hair is the same length as mine is now, perhaps a touch longer but not much. Above my right eye is a scratch and raised bump, a fifty-pence-piece-sized bruise.' I can feel that I'm trying to lift my hand to touch my forehead, but my body remains leaded.

'Ella? Can you hear me?' The wind in the forest wraps around her words, making them lift and fall on the breeze like one of the ochre leaves beneath my boots. I want to ask her why she is here, but I have to remind myself I'm not

there; I don't have the power to change the events, just see them as I did then.

'Her voice is clearer. She's asking me if I can hear her.'

I nod. She looks pleased . . . no, not pleased, relieved. She says, *'That's good,'* so maybe I did that on the actual night.

She repeats the smile that I recognise, the smile that I know is hiding something. She lifts her finger again, the *aha, I have an idea!* movement. *'Have cake . . . breakfast.'*

That's it? I want to ask her. I can feel my teenage self almost roll her eyes. *I go back in time to tell my younger self to have cake for breakfast?*

'I can't . . . and tell . . . everything. It would . . . too soon. Ask Robin, I can't scare you . . . never remember.'

She's fighting back tears, even though she is trying to smile, trying to make the next sentence sound like fun.

'Watch out for seven . . . bus. Yellow.' She pauses.

I want to tell her that I believe her, about the bus, that this happened. I want to ask her why she is scared.

'Other people. Just . . . on each other. God . . . so young . . . beautiful Ella, I wish . . . could see how beautiful you are.'

'Ella, I'm going to bring you out in five. OK, Ella, you're going to take a careful step back now. Four . . .'

Robin is looking at me with a concerned look when I open my eyes, the expression of a grandfather picking up his granddaughter after she has fallen off her bike after trying to ride it without stabilisers for the first time.

'What?' I ask, sitting up. 'What is that face?' I point and draw a wiggly line in front of him.

'What face?' He corrects himself but his new smile is guarded briefly before it's replaced, the Werther's Original comfort back in situ. 'It's just my face.'

'Nooooo. *That's* your face.' I wiggle the line in front of

him again. 'You had a worried face. So come on, fess up. What is it?'

He gets up and fetches the biscuit tin, offering it to me and taking a digestive for himself. He chews thoughtfully, then gives himself a nod, almost in permission, and sits back down. 'Well, I think your subconscious is trying to protect you. From learning something that could potentially have a big impact on you.'

'But I cut down the brambles.'

'You did, but . . . OK. Let's for a second say that in a few weeks, you go to the October Fair and at two in the morning, when the clocks go back, you stand in the exact spot that you believe that woman—'

'Me.'

'. . . the woman you believe to be you stands and the world goes topsy turvy and you are able to tell yourself something very important. Let's say this information is difficult or upsetting. The first thing your conscious mind is going to do is protect you.'

'By hiding the memories?'

'Exactly. I've been thinking about you and how I would feel if I was given the chance to go back. To tell myself what was going to happen to my wife when we were just falling in love. The implications of that information at such a young age could be catastrophic. To have to make a choice to carry on as I was, courting her, falling in love with a woman who I knew was going to die in such a painful way? I think that would be too much of a shock for me to take in. I'd never have remembered it, my brain would have shut that information down quick smart. So, for argument's sake, let's say it did happen to me . . . I might, instead, tell myself something easier to access, something to introduce me to new information without scaring my conscious mind away. Do you understand?'

I nod, processing his words.

'Do you think that's what she meant? She knew that you would tell me to go easy? To only tell me little bits at a time?'

'Perhaps. But, Ella, I'm going to be honest with you. I don't think that you have the ability to time-travel; I don't think you saw your older self when you were eighteen. I think that you have had a shock, your husband has asked you for a divorce that you don't want, your children have both left home, your friend is struggling with his addiction and it is these circumstances that have led you down this path. It's natural for you to be thinking about the past, about the things you could have done differently. I think this is your brain's way of coping with the change and helping you understand how to deal with it.'

'You think I'm bonkers.'

'I don't think you're bonkers. In fact, I think this is one of the most complex and interesting cases I've had as a hypnotist and as a therapist. I think you are on a journey of self-discovery, Ella. I think that deep down you already have the answers to why Will asked you for a divorce and what led you both to this stage, and more importantly, what you need to do to fix it.'

He hands me a tissue; I hadn't realised I was crying.

His voice softens. 'You've already told me yourself that you wouldn't change the past. I think this is about you asking yourself the questions you already have the answers to.'

'It's a bit creepy, isn't it? Can I rewind it?' Cole reaches across the sofa for my phone, sliding the cursor back to the beginning where Robin's voice begins: *Ella Roberts, memory regression, session five*. He then moves it further along until my voice begins: Heavy, sleepy.

I clutch my cup in my hand and watch him over the rim. 'Sure.'

'Right, so this bit.' He pauses me recounting where she tells me to have cake for breakfast.

'When did you start having cake for breakfast?' he asks, dipping into the bag of sweets, taking out a strawberry lace, tipping his head back and letting it wiggle into his open mouth.

'The day Will came round, the night after the fair . . . I had cake. For breakfast. I'm pretty sure that was the first time.' I nod, picturing myself unwrapping the cake, holding the pink fondant in my hands, thinking how lovely it was and wondering why we only have the prettiest food when we're already full, like it's something to be forced down rather than savoured. How, if anything, we should savour the dessert first, the food with the brightest colours, the most beautiful finish. 'I thought it was because I was hungover that I wanted the sugar. I remember grabbing a French Fancy out of the cupboard. I'd snuck it up into my room just before I opened the blinds. Before I saw Will—'

'Stalking you?'

'Checking I was OK.'

'Probably just a coincidence?'

'It could be. I mean, it's not as though I'd never raided the cupboards for junk food before breakfast before. But Jesus, Cole, what if somewhere in my subconscious I had heard everything she said. What if it's real? What if I *really do* go back in time and talk to myself? Fuck me.'

'That's very forward of you and to be honest I'm not sure I'm in the mood.' Cole winks and I kick him.

'Ouch!' he rubs his thigh. 'What does, what's his name, Robin think?'

'That I'm bonkers. That this is all about my subconscious helping me find answers about why Will asked for a divorce, which is stupid, because I already know that, don't I?'

'You do?'

'Oh come on, and you don't?'

'What do you mean?'

'You know as well as I did that Will settled for me. I wouldn't have even been on his radar if Jack hadn't have died, if my family weren't there when his wasn't, if I hadn't got pregnant.'

Cole's face creases with concern. 'Ells . . .'

'It's fine, I've always known. I'm not blind, I just thought that we'd got past that, somewhere along the way, you know? That he loved me anyway. And we're good together, and these last few weeks, it's like I can see that he still feels it too, you know? The Thing.'

'The thing?'

'Not the thing in little letters, the feeling, you know, The Thing, when you know you've found your person, like the way you felt about Jules.'

'Thanks for opening that old wound.'

'Sorry. But you know what I mean though, right? About The Thing?'

'Yeah. I do.' He turns his attention back to the paper bag, pulling out a white chocolate Jazzie.

'Maybe I'm just imagining it? Maybe it was just me that felt The Thing and oh, I don't know, Cole, maybe I should just let him go? Once and for all, stop trying to hold on to a man that should never have been mine in the first place.'

'So is that what you think you might tell yourself? That you should never have got married?'

'No, God no. No. I don't know what I would say. Enjoy your time together because he'll dump you when you're old and past it?'

'You're not old and past it, not that old, anyway.'

I ignore him and continue. 'Not to mention the whole messing with my own timeline stuff that Doctor Who is always banging on about. I mean seriously, Cole, what could be so important that I would risk losing the life I've had? My life with the love of my life, my two incredible kids . . . you're right and so is Robin. It's madness to even think it could happen. But she did warn me about the bus.'

'I know but come on, the number seven passes every twenty minutes, it stands to reason you would get splashed by it at some point.'

I lean forward, hit play and we listen on.

'So what's this bit about?' Cole asks, rolling a cigarette between his fingers, his tongue licking the tip of the paper in a neat line.

'Well, Robin says that he thinks that if I was going to tell myself something bad then my mind would hide it. So if it is real, if I can go back, I, as in younger me, would have a better chance of remembering it if I told myself something easy to digest first, you know, like building blocks, one bit of information at a time, so when I get to the top it won't feel so scary. But then again, he agrees with you, that I'm trying to convince myself of something that didn't happen, he thinks my subconscious is trying to lead me on a journey of self-discovery.'

Cole hits play again, my voice repeating her words. 'It's dead creepy, your voice changes when you repeat what she says, have you noticed? It's sounds like you have a sore throat.'

'I know, right?'

We listen to the rest of the recording and finish the bag of sweets.

'So, what's next? Where is your next big date?' Cole asks me as he scrunches up the paper bag and aims it at the bin, landing it first time.

'I've invited Will to the florist's tomorrow night.'

'The florist's?' Cole stands with his cigarette between his fingers.

'I need Will to fall back in love with me . . . not who I was but the woman I am now. I want him to see how much I love my job.'

I flick the lights on and shrug out of my coat. The lime green of the far wall blinks into focus, the flagstones shining brightly below the Victorian chandelier hanging down in the middle of the room. Around the edges are silver buckets flowing over with a rainbow of colour and texture. Opposite the counter, a bookcase filled with locally made scented candles in pastel tins, bath bombs, hand creams and bespoke cards – Amira's idea of competing with Moonpig.

'We're not supposed to talk about work, but it's OK to go to work?' Will is smiling as he takes off his jacket.

'I wanted to share something with you. Come with me.'

I lead him into the back. The strip light buzzes above the bench table; vases line the shelves at the back; cellophane in all colours is rolled along the wall, scissors, ribbons, tools all scattered at various points on the surface.

I wrap an apron around myself, looking at him over my shoulder. 'Take a seat.'

He sits on a stool in the corner of the room as I begin pulling out my tools and laying them out on the work bench. I pull my hair up with a piece of ribbon, snipping from the reel with a pair of scissors. I click on the speakers and Ella Fitzgerald begins singing about summertime and the living being easy, saxophones crooning along.

'Do you remember when I would paint and try and explain why I was choosing a specific colour?'

'I remember. That's why you love painting water, it uses all the happy colours.'

I grin at him, pleased that he could remember something I'd said so many years ago. 'I can't believe you remember that.'

'You told me how colours were more about a feeling, a message, a gift from you to the viewer.'

I nod, taken aback a little at the way he says these words; I bite my lower lip and nod. It's as though he's memorised them.

'It was never about the colour for me, but about the way the colour made me feel. Paint a bedroom dark red and it feels heavy and close and warm. Paint it the blue of a spring sky and the same room will feel open and fresh. It's exactly the same when I make a bouquet.' I smile up at him. 'This is still art, Will.'

The groove between Will's eyes relaxes a little, his eyebrows lifting. I begin pulling on my gloves and reaching for a length of cellophane, unrolling it across the surface.

'It can be as personal or as impersonal as I want it to be. That's why I always ask the buyer something about the person that I'm delivering to, why they're sending the flowers.' I smile up at him. 'When I was writing our rules, I was thinking about all the things we never talk about and it occurred to me that this is one. It's the biggest part of my life besides you and the kids and I never really talked about it and every time I tried, you always had this sad look, like you were disappointed that I chose to become a florist, that I should have been doing something else. So I stopped trying.'

'I'm sorry.' His words are sincere; they land firmly, unwavering, unquestionable. 'I never meant to make you feel like that. I just thought that, well, you never chose this, did you?' He looks around the room, the groove deepening again. 'You took the job with Amira to help pay the bills. A job Cole set up. I wanted more for you.'

'More than doing something I love?'

'I guess I was waiting for you to start painting again, but after Jamie, you just stopped. It was like you'd lost part of what makes you *you*. I felt guilty that I'd taken that from you.'

I step towards him, taking his hands in mine. 'You didn't take anything from me, Will, you gave me *everything*.' My voice wavers as I say this. 'Right!' I shake my head and grin. 'Let me show you what I mean. Excuse me.' I swallow as my hip leans against his thigh as I reach around his frame for the bucket, stretching my hands towards the white anemones and taking two long stems. I step back, the heat from where our legs touched still radiating. 'What do you think this is?'

He pushes his lips together, one eye closing with a grimace, knowing he will get the answer wrong. 'A daisy?' he guesses.

I laugh in response, rolling my eyes as he elaborates.

'A BIG daisy?'

'They're anemones. They always remind me of you on our wedding day, ivory white petal like your shirt, dark black interior like the cufflinks we bought from that car boot sale we went to, do you remember? The day we went on a day trip to Lake Vyrnwy? The car wouldn't start and we spent two hours wandering around every boot, trying to kill time while we waited to be towed.'

'I remember. The tow guy talked about pork chops and different herbs to add to the marinade. It was like listening to Bubba talking about his shrimp in *Forrest Gump*.'

'Ha! I'd forgotten that! What was his name? Harold? Henry?'

'Herbert.'

'That's it! Herby Herbert!' We laugh.

I return to the bench, trimming the stems and laying them flat, humming along as I walk to the back of the room. The clipping of my heels sounds alien, a strange contrast to the thud of the boots that normally hit these tiles. I chose this yellow dress for tonight. I can't really remember thinking about what I would wear to feel good about my appearance until we started dating again . . . I wonder when I stopped doing that, stopped dressing to feel nice. I dip into another basket. 'This is a spine flower.' I hold it carefully, the baby pink of the flowers clumped closely together like a ready-made posy. 'Up until 1999, our year, it was thought to be extinct, but it was found in a field in San Fernando Valley.' I lean forward and his shirt brushes against my bare arm; I smile up at him, his blue eyes dark in this light. I drag my focus back to the flower. 'It's still very rare, I had to make a deal with the devil to get these.' I return to the bench, ignoring the flush of my skin as I turn my back to him, snipping its tough stem. 'Excuse me,' I apologise again as I edge towards the buckets behind him; he jumps the stool to the right as I reach over for another flower. Will's hand lands on my waist to steady me, making me pause my movement; I close my eyes, swallowing down the attraction that runs along my hip at his touch. I pull back, lifting the flower to him, holding it beneath his nose, long green stems, clutches of delicate lavender-coloured flowers at hand-span intervals.

His eyebrows raise in recognition. 'What is that? I recognise the smell.'

'Lavender Japanese sweet peas. It's the lavender you recognise, we had it in our garden.'

'Do you know what that makes me think of? The slide.'

'Oh, God,' I laugh, bringing it beneath my nose. 'How many days did it take to put up?'

'Six, and we still had loads of pieces left over.'

I lay the flower down onto the paper. 'Could you pass me two more?' I ask, blowing a stray piece of hair from my eyelashes. Will adds the stems to the bench, looping his little finger beneath my hair, tucking it behind my ear, my breath catching with the heat of his rib cage against my back. I lean away, slightly turning to look at him over my shoulder. Our mouths are so close; I'm breathing in as he exhales; our eyes meet before he looks away. I sidestep him, feeling the blush rise in my cheeks. 'Now this one . . .' I change my tone so it is light and brisk, like I'm a curator giving a tour of a museum, 'has a very distinctive smell. Close your eyes, tell me what it makes you think of?'

He obliges, as I hold it beneath his nose. 'It smells like lemon and something like a herb . . . Rosemary?' He opens his eyes.

'It smells like you,' I say, touching his nose with the end of the sprig before moving back. 'Back in a min.' I leave him and return to the main room of the shop, taking a large handful of pink peonies. 'Now, here is a test for you, do you recognise these?'

'Of course. You had them in your wedding bouquet.'

'Very good! You get a gold star.'

I continue reaching for different flowers, one the colour of the walls in our Paris apartment, roses from our first garden.

'Each flower paints a picture, a story. These are my colour palette.' I gesture to the buckets and drawers surrounding us. 'I never stopped painting pictures, Will. Watch.'

I turn up the volume, letting Van Morrison's 'Brown Eyed Girl' fill the room. I can feel Will's gaze on my hands as I prune and cut the stems, bending them to my design. Tension blooms around my neck as I bend over, humming to the music, my body swaying in time as I lose myself in the process, just as I did when I would paint on the beach. I sing along, 'Sha-la-la-la-la-la-la-tee-da.' I add more lilac, more rose, trim back the white baby's breath, add some pale green eucalyptus until the spray is how I want it. The play list switches to 'Fix You' by Coldplay as I plait sprigs of rosemary around the base and pull a ribbon around the stems, holding them in place. The song ends as I finish.

'There.' I hold it like a bride and take aisle steps towards him. 'For you. A portrait of us.'

He takes the bouquet from my hands. 'It's beautiful.'

'And wouldn't you be mad not to fight for something this beautiful?'

'I would.' He places the bouquet down on the bench gently, and stands, reaching up and pulling the ribbon free from my hair, catching it as it falls in his hand, and then slowly, as if waiting for my consent, he brings his mouth down on mine.

Chapter Thirty-Two

Then

Summer 2004

Ella had spent fifteen minutes upstairs searching for the elusive magic pearls, her heart filling with the way Amber was looking up at her as she took on the role of adventurer. She narrated, she changed her voice, she unrolled an old shopping list from a discarded handbag and pretended it was a treasure map. This was the mum she'd always thought she would be – she'd just never imagined it would take so much energy to pretend that it was all natural. She didn't want to be the mother whose daughter looked at her like it was Christmas morning just because she was being fun for once: it shouldn't be like this; this should be normal behaviour for her children to see, not abnormal.

When they returned downstairs, Cole was standing with one hand behind him, a guard to the magic wonderland behind the door to the lounge.

'Good afternoon.' He dipped an imaginary bowler hat. 'Do you have a magic pearl?'

Amber nodded, her small blonde pigtails bobbing with the action, opening her hand and passing him three of the pearls.

'Thank you, madam, and yours?'

'Me keep mine.'

'Very well. You may enter.'

He swung open the door and let them pass.

In the short amount of time that it had taken Ella to perform a fake treasure hunt, he had transformed the room, the sofa cushions in a square on the floor, an ironing board tilted from the back of the sofa in a mock slide, a plastic mini bowling area, a colouring-in station, and in the corner, a tent held up with duct tape to the wall, slanting down to where it was tucked beneath a dining chair, fairy lights taken from the dried flowers in the vase at the corner of the room.

On the stereo, 'She Will be Loved' by Maroon 5 sang out, Jamie's body immediately jerking and bobbing in time to the music. Ever since he was born, Jamie had had music in his blood, only sleeping when music was playing, his body never still at the sound of a radio jingle, an advert, the ice-cream van.

Ella placed Jamie on the floor, where he immediately began crawling towards the slide, Amber's mouth open in a wide 'o' as she made her way to the crayons and colouring book.

Cole swiped Jamie from the floor, holding him on the slide and whooshing him down. Amber wandered over to the square of sofa cushions and began bouncing on them, her very own bouncy castle. She bounced three times – 'Mummy! Mummy! Mummy!' – then crashed to her bottom. Ella clapped and knelt beside her daughter, holding her hands while she pulled herself up.

Ella met Cole's eyes, mouthing a thank you, tears pricking behind her eyes; he acknowledged her thanks with a gentle inclination of the head. Cole aimed Jamie towards them like an aeroplane complete with neeeeaaaaaaw noises, bouncing him up and down beside his sister.

Ricky Martin's Livin' 'La Vida Loca' began on the stereo,

Cole's face lighting up as he stood, mimicking Ricky with a couple of hip flicks before unzipping his hoody, swinging it around his head as he took it off and pretended to dance in the rain, pointing at Ella as he sang about taking away his crazy life, like a bullet to the brain. Jamie rocked backwards and forwards on his hands and knees while Amber danced along, flapping her arms, trying to copy Cole's wiggles and hip flicks as they continued living la vida loca, Cole's pelvis rotating like Patrick Swayze's.

'More, Uncle Cole!' Amber shouted as the song finished. He returned to the stereo and clicked on another Cole karaoke classic and the opening bars to Britney Spears' 'Hit Me Baby One More Time' began. Cole rolled up his top into a makeshift bikini, revealing a tanned and toned stomach, a line of dark hair towards the belt holding up his jeans. Cole fluttered his eyelashes singing: 'babe-eh, babe-eh,' as Ella held her palms over her face in embarrassment, her hands falling away in laughter as Cole continued, his voice hopping up an octave as he sang Britney's words. He held out his hand, pulling Ella up, singing about how he wasn't supposed to know . . . that something wasn't right and how he should have let her, 'go-oo-oh-oh'.

Ella laughed as he took her hand and twirled her around and continued singing, asking her to show him, 'how you one-ed tooooo be,' raising his voice as he sang, 'baaaay-bay, 'coz I neeeeed to know, now, what we gah-hat'. Cole bent and scooped Jamie up, resting him on his hip, which continued to lift and drop in time to the music as he sang about how his 'lone-li-ness' was killing him, finally holding Jamie's fist against his jaw while singing, 'Hit me Baby One More Time'.

Spent, the four of them collapsed onto the cushions laughing, their breath fast, their chests lifting and crashing in a post-Britney haze.

While the adults were still catching their breath, Jamie made a beeline for the tent, Amber rushing after her brother. Ella and Cole followed the children, laughter still in their lungs as Cole rolled his top back down. Ella tried to avoid looking at his bare skin, embarrassed at the close proximity to his tanned washboard stomach, the sheer maleness of the dark hairs on his chest. She elbowed him gently as he yanked down the last of his top.

'Been working out?'

Distracted by straightening his clothing, Cole was caught off-guard. Looking down at her, confusion and surprise were quickly replaced by a wink, the cocky lad from the pub covering for that brief moment of vulnerability. 'Checking me out, Ella Walker?'

She rolled her eyes, suddenly conscious of her caesarean scar and left-over Jamie weight. 'I'd better, um, get Jamie's milk.' She ducked out of the room briefly and grabbed Jamie's bottle; it was almost time for his nap. When she returned, Cole was holding the entrance to the tent to one side. Inside, cushions, books, and teddies were slotted around the edges, keeping the reality of daylight out and the magical hue inside.

'Fairies!' Amber looked up at the lights.

They sank down onto the cushions; Amber picked up a story book and placed it on Cole's lap. Ella settled herself, securing Jamie on her lap and plugging his bottle into his mouth.

'Story!' Amber demanded, reaching for a chocolate finger and settling herself against Cole's knees.

The book was *Cinderella*, thick cardboard pages with bright garish pictures. 'Once upon a time,' he began, 'there was a beautiful princess called Ella-Dora. She was the most beautiful princess in the whole world.' Ella leant over to see the pages, suspiciously shaking her head at him as he made up the words. Cole didn't look up at Ella as he spoke; he kept his focus on the make-believe words. 'She was brave and funny and the most special princess in all the land.'

'Princess!' Amber declared, pointing to the picture.

'That's right! But one day, an eeeeevil queen cast a spell on the beautiful princess, making a heavy black cloud hang over her.' Cole tapped to a white cloud on the page.

'Big cloud!' Amber repeated.

'The princess tried to run away from it, but it followed her everywhere and even when the sun shone, the cloud lay over her head.

'Now, our brave princess thought she could defeat the cloud all by herself, she tried to run away, but it followed her everywhere, she climbed a ladder to paint the cloud silver instead, but the paint washed away, she tried to blow it away by huffing and puffing like one of the little pigs. Can you blow the cloud away, Bamber?'

Amber filled her soft cheeks with air at the same time as Cole, and after three they both blew hard.

'But look, the cloud was still there.' Cole turned the page, pointing to a cloud in the sky. 'It just wouldn't move.'

Ella avoided Cole's gaze, instead concentrating on Jamie's hand opening and closing against the bottle, his eyelids beginning to grow heavy as his toes curled, one foot bare, the sock lost somewhere in the lounge.

'The princess even tried cutting it up with scissors, but the cloud just grew again.' He turned the page.

'Princess sad.' Amber looked at the page where Cinderella sat next to the fire grate in her rags.

'She *was* sad, very sad, and even though she had everything she wanted, a beautiful castle, a handsome prince, the princess couldn't get rid of the cloud. Until one day, a ruggedly handsome knight came charging into her castle.'

Ella shifted her arm, Jamie's nine-month-old weight lying heavily against her.

Amber climbed onto Cole's knee, pointing to the prince from the story. 'Who he?'

'Sir, um, Shag-a-lot.' Ella gave Cole a warning look, as Amber began sucking her thumb, her body leaning into Cole.

'I mean his name was, Sir, Sir . . .'

'Sir Not-so-subtle-a-lot?' Ella intervened.

'No-oh.' Cole looked up at Ella's questioning eyebrow. 'It was actually Sir Friend-a-lot.' He matched her raised eyebrows with an air of self-satisfaction and returned his attention to the story, shifting slightly as Amber burrowed against him, yawning around her thumb. 'Now, the knight had been on a great quest and had heard the wicked witch retelling her story of how she had cursed Princess Ella-Dora and how the only way to break the spell was if the princess asked for help. The witch laughed when she said this, because Princess Ella-Dora was known for being brave, fearless and stubborn.'

'What stubborn?' Amber yawned.

'Stubborn means when someone refuses to change even though everyone around them can show them a way to help,' Cole explained, looking straight into Ella's brown eyes.

Ella returned her gaze to her now sleeping son, extracting the bottle from between his lips. 'So how did the princess get away from the cloud?' she asked quietly.

'She asked Sir Friend-a-lot for help. And her friend fetched his own ladder to lean against hers, and he found another pair of scissors to cut away the cloud. They blew as hard as they could together and after a lot of work, the cloud broke in two and eventually fell apart. Rain fell from the cloud and the princess and the knight danced and danced in the rain.'

'Then what happened?'

'The sun came out.' Cole grinned at her. 'And you know

what happens when it's rained and the sun comes out? It makes a rainbow.'

Amber's breathing had become slow without them noticing, her eyes closing, her hand twirling in her hair as she drifted off.

'Let me help, Ells.' Cole said, his voice soft.

Ella found the act of keeping everything inside too much to bear: it ripped free. Just like the rain in the story, it fell from her, her words in small drops at first.

'When I found out I was pregnant, I was so happy, Cole, I felt all this love for our baby, even when I was so ill that I didn't think I would survive her being born. But the moment I looked at her tiny body in the incubator, and later when I was finally allowed to hold her, do you know what I felt?' Ella wiped away a tear and met Cole's eyes. 'Nothing. I just felt hollow. What kind of mother doesn't love their own child?'

'It's not your fault, Ells, it was a traumatic time.'

'It was, but Will loved her, it was on his face the moment he looked at her.'

'It wasn't until she was five months old that I felt it, that love, that imaginary thread that holds them to you. I love my children, Cole, but my life begins and ends in exhaustion, and do you know the worst part?' Ella's voice was frayed and threadbare. 'I'm so afraid that Will is going to find out that I'm not the girl he fell in love with, that I pretend to be her, every single day. Every day I act like this is everything I ever wanted, and it is, it really is, I love my kids and I love this stupid house, but I feel like I'm living through someone else's eyes, does that make sense? And trying to pretend that it's all I ever wanted is exhausting.'

Cole reached over and held her hand tightly.

'I feel like I've lost me, the girl I was.'

'You're still here, Ells, you're just a bit bruised.'

She smiled gratefully, taking a deep breath. 'And I feel guilty every single day, because the only time I ever feel anything like my old self . . . is, is when you're here.'

'I'm not going anywhere.'

Ella wiped the tears away with the heel of her hand. 'Thank you, Cole. For today. For everything. I would be so lost without you in my life.'

'My pleasure . . . where else would your knight in shining armour be?'

Cole kissed the top of Amber's head, Ella's daughter's hand relaxing, a blue iridescent bath pearl rolling free of her palm and running beneath the sheet, out into the real world that surrounded the tent. It rolled along the newly reclaimed floorboards, past Jamie's blue-and-red-striped sock, a scrunched-up page from a colouring book, a lidless red felt-tip pen. On it rolled, the surface catching the lights so its pearlescent surface changed from blue to green to silver; on it went until it hit Will's polished black shoe and another jigsaw piece of their lives slotted into place.

The shoes in question had been immobile for some time, unable to move, to step their owner away from the conversation being held inside a sepia-lighted tent, where his daughter slept in the arms of another man, as his wife told that man that she only ever felt alive when he was in their home. Will bent down and picked the pearl up, rolling it in his palm.

The shoes shifted; they trod out of the room, their soles soft, apologetic, awkward as they took their owner from the house with hushed tones along the pathway. They crunched their grip against the path, witnessed the zebra flashes of a crossing, lifted against the scrape of a step. They tapped on the black-and-white tiles beneath a counter, before negotiating a steady footway, the shoes finally sliding beneath a table, crossing over themselves beneath black socks rubbing against suit trousers.

Behind the counter worked Bess. She prided herself on being hard-working and attentive to customers, and as she wiped down the counter her attention was drawn to the handsome man with the flop of blond hair, his broad shoulders hunched, his hand stirring and restirring his coffee. There was little, Bess had found, that couldn't be cured by a piece of coffee cake, made to her grandmother's recipe. She took out a slab, looking over to the man again, plated them both a slice, and made a pot of tea. Bess's son had taken his own life ten years before, God rest his soul. She'd vowed at his graveside that she would make his death mean something, and so every weekend she worked at the Samaritans, and in her day-to-day life she always made time for people who were alone.

'You look like you could do with a bit of sugar,' she suggested, sliding the cake in front of the man. He looked up at her, sapphire-blue eyes surrounded by thick lashes, heartache and loss only just visible beneath all the beauty; he reminded her of a lost child in a carnival.

Will looked up to the woman at his table, her hair dyed the colour of a new penny, backcombed and framing her face like a halo. 'Thank you.' He heard his voice: brittle.

'Mind if I join you?' she asked.

Will didn't want company, but he was always polite and so smiled as best as he could.

'I'm Bess.' She stretched out her hand to him.

'Will.'

'So, Will, what brings you to my little café on a Tuesday afternoon? Now don't say my cake because I know you've never tried it.'

Will didn't think about the words that stabbed into the soft warm air; they just erupted without warning, without fanfare.

'I think my wife is in love with another man. I think she's

always been in love with another man. She just doesn't know it.'

Behind them, the door bell alerted Bess to another customer.

'In my experience, Will, marriage is a marathon not a sprint. There are often hurdles in the way, but if you really want to get to the finish line, sometimes you just have to go around those hurdles until you're strong enough to jump over them.'

'What if I'm never strong enough?'

'Well, if you put in the right training and you still can't jump over them . . . that is when you'll know you're in the wrong race.' She got up and rested a hand on Will's shoulder, giving it a gentle squeeze as she moved away. Will looked up in thanks, contemplating her words.

But because Will loved Ella and his family so much, he would hide this conversation away; he would seal it inside a box, smooth Sellotape over the seam and bury it: his own dirty secret. And over the next few months, as he got Ella the help she needed, that box would become old, squashed, faded with age, sinking under the weight of everything that happened afterwards. Yet even so, as Ella began to improve, as she laughed again, as she unfolded like a sunflower towards the sun, Will could still feel them, the words that sat hibernating, waiting for the moment when the box would spring open, when the words and the feelings they encapsulated would devour everything in their path.

Chapter Thirty-Three

Now

Ella

15th October 2022

'Where do you want these?' Cole shouts from behind a stacked box of deliveries. I look up from behind the counter as I double-check the address on my notepad.

'Oh, in the back please.'

He heads there as the bell above the door rings. My husband walks in, watery sun framing him, white jumper, faded grey jeans, sunglasses. He takes the glasses off and steps into the florist's.

'Hey,' I grin, glad that I tried the new foundation that promises a youthful glow, and that I declined the left-over kebab meat drenched in garlic mayo that Cole had offered me last night. He is working through a list of takeaways that he has never tried sober. Not surprisingly, he is slightly disappointed by them.

'Hi.' He hesitates at the threshold, as if he's considering reversing back out. 'I, um . . . I thought you might feel like a ride?'

'A ride?' I arch my eyebrow.

'On the bike. A ride on the bike,' he corrects, blushing.

'There is an exhibition at the gallery in town and I wondered if you might like to go? I thought Amira does Saturday afternoon?' He looks as though he expects my friend to appear.

'Oh. She does, um, usually but . . .'

'Ells? Did you want these putting in the van?'

Like a shutter being drawn down, Will's expression closes as Cole appears, his face obscured by a gift basket.

'She does normally,' I say, my sentence rushing in, my focus batting from Cole to Will and back again, 'but she's got a wedding in Ireland and so I said I'd work and . . .' The words come out panicked and over-explanatory. Cole lowers the basket, catching sight of Will in the doorway. 'Cole offered to help out, so . . .'

'Hi, Will.'

'Cole.' Will nods once, the action abrupt. 'It's fine.' His hand is already reaching for the door. 'I was just . . . passing and . . .' I can sense him cringing as he uses the *I was just passing* line. 'And thought it might be . . . I'll . . .'

'It sounds lovely, I would love to come!' I jump in, already walking around the counter towards Will; I don't want him to leave. 'I have a few deliveries first and I was closing at one anyway.'

'Oh, I . . .'

Cole shifts, grabbing the keys from the van, hugging the basket to his chest. 'I'll pop this in the van, then I'll get going.'

'Oh, right yes, thank you, Cole, for helping out.' My words sound formal and false, even to my own ears.

Will steps aside, Cole hovering briefly at the door. 'It's good to see you, Will.'

Unexpected tears prick my eyes. I can hear how sincere those words are, and I hope Will can too.

'Yeah. Um, you too.'

Cole lets himself out and lets the silence in.

'So!' I clap my hands, trying to inject sound into the vacuum. 'How about you come with me?'

Will's focus slides from the space outside that belongs to Cole and back to me, the lightness he held when he walked in already dissipated.

'You've never been and if you're a good boy, I'll even let you knock the doors.'

He smiles back but it doesn't reach his eyes. I can almost feel the excuse that Will has lying on his tongue.

'He's sober,' I intervene, before he has a chance to make his excuses and leave. 'Has been for a few weeks actually.'

'Right.'

'Oh shit! Does that count as one of my points used?' I slap my head with my hand.

'Hmmm?' Will asks, distracted.

'Never mind. Look, I would really like to go to the exhibition and I would also really love you to come with me while I deliver these flowers.' I loop my arms around Will's neck and he makes a small noise as I run my nose against his. I go to kiss him, but he pulls back; it's only a fraction of movement but it stings, the progress we had made last night seemingly reset. I step back and try not to let the hurt show.

'Can I drive?' he says, teasing, finding his way to fixing that millimetre of movement.

'Not on your life.'

By the time we pull up at the first address, the mood between us has lightened, but I can still sense the issue of Cole; it's sitting in the back of the van like a kid asking if they're there yet.

'Come on, you.' I grin, unbuckling my seatbelt.

'I'm good, I'll wait here,' Will replies, his hand tapping his thigh.

'Oh no you won't. I want to show you why I have the best job in the world. It's not always about the art, you know.

Now, this is a bunch of flowers for a seventy-year-old whose daughter lives in Kenya. I had the email and the daughter, Saira, says that her mum isn't going anywhere or doing anything as she's got a bad foot, so this will be a good one to get you started. I've thrown in some extras too, some bath salts and stuff.'

'Free of charge?'

'Yeah, I mean they're no big expense and Saira says her mum's had a tough year with her foot and her house was burgled a while back too. Saira's a charity worker; she gives out old glasses to third-world countries and helps deprived areas. I've signed up to their newsletter and I've put it up on the noticeboard in the shop in case any of my other customers have any old glasses hanging around.'

Will is smiling at me, the light back in his eyes.

'What?'

'Just . . . you. Always trying to make the world a brighter place.'

'And there I was thinking I was the one doing the wooing.'

'Wooing?'

'Never mind, come on, the curtains are twitching.'

I slam the doors at the back of the van and pass the flowers to Will. The house is set among a row of similar-style bungalows, all with neat square lawns and white PVC doors.

'Oh no, I'm not doing it, I don't know what to say!' Will panics, trying to pass them back, but I duck away.

'You just say "Delivery for Mrs Omondi" and pass them over. It's the best part of the job, you'll see what I mean. Now go. I'll wait here.' I gesture at the van.

Will clears his throat, opens the small gate and takes long strides, clearing his throat again as he approaches and knocks the door. From the pathway, I bounce on the balls of my feet, stretching up to tiptoe so I can see his face when the door is opened.

As the door swings open I watch my husband, see his nerves, the awkwardness that has never suited the body he has been given. Mrs Omondi reaches out her hands to receive the bouquet and I watch as her excitement and joy overflow towards Will. I see him catch it, throw a small laugh as he leans in just a fraction as she reads the card. He stands there, talking, before turning on his heel with a wave as Mrs Omondi closes the door behind him. He's grinning as he approaches me. I lean against the van, self-satisfied and smug.

'Now do you get it?' I ask him.

'Now I get it,' he replies, resting his hand either side of me, our bodies a breath apart. 'Why have you never told me?' His voice is deep, soft.

'I've told you how much I love my job a million times.' The words are supposed to be exasperated, flippant, but instead I find myself swallowing hard. 'We need to get to the next address,' I say, looking up at him. He steps back, allowing me to return to the driver's side. Across the bonnet I can feel him watching me; I catch him as I open my door and stick out my tongue, and he laughs as he joins me inside the van.

There are two more deliveries and by the third one, Will has really found his stride, knocking on the door confidently, smiling broadly at the man with two dogs yapping at his feet, a bouquet for the birth of his son.

Will practically jogs up the path of the last delivery, a congratulations-on-your-new-job arrangement in yellows, reds and oranges. A woman in head-to-toe lycra and a swinging ponytail opens the door. I laugh as he returns to the van.

'What?'

'Well, which do you think she was more excited to see? The flowers or you on her doorstep?'

'The flowers, obviously.' The line forms between his eyebrows.

'You sure?' I laugh.

'I'm sure! She was telling me about how long she's been looking for a job and how excited she is to be starting. Look!' He roots in his pocket and pulls out a card. 'She even gave me her card in case I need a website designer.'

I snort. 'Oh, Will, you are so clueless.'

'What? I might need a website designer.'

I chew my lip, stifling a laugh, and turn the key, the tractor-like diesel engine sparking into life. 'So, we're done for the day, shall we go and pick up the bike?'

'Yeah, I mean sure. You've probably got lots on and I don't want to hold you up.'

'Huh? I do recall someone offering me a ride?'

He looks to his watch. 'I don't think we've got time to get to the museum before it closes.'

'So . . . let's go somewhere else?'

'Shall we drive? I know you don't like the bike . . .'

'Why do you think I don't like the bike?'

'I, well . . .' He rubs the lines of his forehead, turning to me, letting out a sigh clipped with a laugh. 'I don't really know.'

'I love the bike, Will, I always have.'

'So why did you stop coming with me?'

'Because you stopped asking.'

My legs are burning as I take Will's hand and let him pull me to the top of the hill. The sun is setting, the air cold in my lungs despite the burning in my throat and cheeks. Below us, the town, the steeple of the church, are like the props of a child's railway, the kidney shape of the pool like a cut-out of blue felt; the cotton wool clouds could be attached by crazy glue.

'It's beautiful,' I say. I lean my head against the top of his arm, pointing ahead of me. 'What is that pool?'

He laughs. 'It's a lake.'

'Ah. You'll be relieved to know my spatial awareness remains unchanged in your absence.'

'What else?'

'Hmmm?'

'What else has stayed the same since I left?'

I stand in front of him, holding his hands in mine. 'The way I feel about you.' He leans his head against mine. 'Have you changed? Have you changed the way you feel about me?' He closes his eyes, I watch his Adam's apple rise and fall. 'Do you still want a divorce, Will?'

'I never wanted a divorce.'

'But that's what you said: "I want a divorce".'

'No, I said I *think* we should get a divorce. Not the same.'

I replay the conversation. Maybe Robin is right about our memories; is this another example of how my mind can change them?

'Do you still think love isn't enough?' I ask.

'I don't know.'

I lean into him again, feel the sound of his heart against my cheek as we watch the sun set.

It's dark when we return, my legs stiff as I climb off the bike and hand Will the helmet. Inside the lights are still off; Cole isn't home.

'Do you want to come in?' I ask. He hesitates.

'I don't think that's a good idea,' he answers, his eyes drawn up to our bedroom window.

'Oh, OK. Well . . . thank you for today, I've loved it.'

'Thank you for taking me to work,' he grins. 'I can see why you love it so much. I wish I'd known that . . . before.'

'Well, you are quite the delivery man, so any time you fancy a ride along, feel free to give me a call.' We both laugh nervously. Tears sting briefly, my body filled with sadness at the thought of saying goodbye to him again. Instead I lean in and kiss his cheek. 'See you.'

'See you,' he replies, and I turn on my heel, rummage in my handbag and dig out my keys, letting myself into my family home without a family. I'm groaning as I take off my shoes, padding through the hall, flicking on lights and reaching for the post. In the kitchen, a note from Cole: 'Me and Percy are staying home. Hope your date went well! C x'.

The light from inside the fridge gestures to the contents like an air hostess on a plane: to the right we have some left-over ham that needs throwing out and to the left, a selection of low-fat yogurts and a packet of bacon; if you pull down the freezer compartment with a sharp tug you will see half a box of fishfingers and two Tupperware containers with dubious left-overs. I close it, flick on the kettle and then flick it back off at a knock on the door.

I open the door to see Will on the step.

'When?' he says. My mouth dries, my heart knocking against my chest as I wait for him to finish the sentence, hoping that he is about to say the words that I'm so desperate for him to speak. 'When?' he repeats, softly, tears in his eyes. 'You said, "See you . . .", and I was wondering when.'

Then we are together, mouths and hands, stairs and jackets, buckles and shirts, skin against skin, and once again I am his and he is mine.

Chapter Thirty-Four

Then

Summer 2004

'So, you've discovered that teaching *is* what you want?' Julie Simpson asked, smiling at Will from over her desk. She took off her glasses, letting them dangle around her neck on a red string. 'You've really come into your own, Will, I'm pleased for you.'

'Thank you. I got there in the end.'

'5J are going to really miss you, and your guitar, although I think Mr Green will be relieved. I'm not sure he approved of your musical methods for teaching English.'

'Ah, he came round eventually.' Will grinned.

'Will, I hope you don't mind, but I've mentioned you to an old colleague, the head over at Wilmlow Secondary School?'

Will looked up, surprised. The school was only a stone's throw from their home.

'There is an opening at the Music department at the end of term. I know you have found your feet here, but you said that you're aiming for a secondary position?'

'I am, yes, that would be . . . wow, thank you. I'm hoping the older kids will have grown out of friendship bracelets.' He held up his arm, pulling back the cuff of his shirt, where six bracelets stretched around his wrist. Julie laughed softly.

'I'll give the head over there a call and let them know you're interested. I'll give you a glowing reference, of course.'

'Thank you, for everything.'

'My pleasure. You're going to be missed here, Will, and if you do change your mind and decide secondary isn't for you, remember us, won't you?'

They both stand, her hand outstretched.

'Like I said, I can always tell when a teacher has got it, and you have it in spades. Good luck, Will.'

'Thank you.'

Will threw his keys on the table, along with a bunch of flowers, following the claps and whoops from the lounge. He took a deep breath and tried not to feel the familiar irritation at Cole's voice.

'That's it! Good boy! Good boy!' Ella's and Cole's voices: mixing and encouraging.

'You can do it, Jam, come on!'

'Yaaaaaaay!' Both voices cheered as Will stepped into the lounge, a smile fixed as he took in the event that he'd missed by seconds.

'Will!' Ella beamed up, her face flushed with pleasure and pride.

Amber was being spun around in Cole's hands. 'Isn't your brother a clever boy!' he enthused.

'Jam's just taken his first steps!' She nuzzled into her son's neck as Will joined him.

Will took Jamie from Ella and lifted him up, his hands somehow awkward around his son's waist, his voice clipped and more pronounced, as if he was trying to put on a show, trying to convince the spectators that he was right for the role.

'You little superstar!' Will encouraged, but Jamie's lip had begun to wobble, his feet kicking as his body squirmed in Will's arms.

Cole could see the tension around Will: he could see it the moment he walked past him; it was in the sideways glance, the set of his jaw. Cole stood, knowing it was time for him to leave and give them some space. He ruffled Amber's hair as he reached for his jacket on the back of the sofa.

'Right, I'm off, there is a pint with my name on it.' He leant towards Jamie, wiggling his dimpled clenched fist. 'Well done, little man.'

Jamie wasn't aware of social niceties, of family loyalty; he only understood what he wanted, and he wanted it immediately. He wanted the fun man to hold him – his Daddy's fingers were hurting him – and so he reached his arms out towards Cole, his body shifting, feet kicking.

Jamie didn't like that he wasn't being passed over to the man with the long dark hair, the one who came with chocolate and pulled funny faces. His mummy wasn't fixing it; she was too busy tickling Bamber. And so Jamie took a deep breath and opened his mouth, letting out a howl.

Cole looked away, saving Will the embarrassment as his friend tried to placate his son. He tried not to feel a glow of pride as Jamie continued to cry, reaching and twisting towards Cole; instead he focused on patting his pockets, checking that he had everything. Ella had her back to him as she adjusted the bobble in Amber's hair and Cole tried to squash the thoughts running through his mind, the wish that she had turned at that moment, that she had seen how her son wanted him more than his own father, a small victory in a lost battle. Ella was becoming less dependent on him, and that was good: he was pleased she was getting better, that Will was there to help her more, that things were becoming easier for her. It was the natural order of things; it was how it should be.

'Later, Ells.' He leant in and wiggled Amber's foot. 'Later, Bamber.'

'Bye, Uncle Cole!'

The door closed and Will felt the walls of his home close around him, blocking out the people who didn't belong here. His wife smiled at him, then pulled a funny frown at her son, taking him from Will's hands, cooing in his ears. 'What's all this fuss, eh? What's all this noise about? Let's show Daddy what a clever boy you are!'

But Jamie had had enough and instead sat on his bottom and scowled across the room to where the daddy man had sat down and where Bamber was crawling onto his knee.

The following week, Will sat at a table in the corner of the bar, very much aware that he had come straight from an interview with his sharply ironed creases along his white shirt. As Cole walked in, Will took in his dark, curly hair – still jaw-length, tucked behind one ear, the same style as when he was fourteen – black denim jeans, band T-shirt; his broad dimpled smile met with the people in the pub with cheerful greetings, inside jokes, comments on the latest news. Cole raised a hand at Will as he chatted with the girl behind the bar, her hands already pouring his pint. Cole belonged inside these walls, like the scuffed edge of the beer mat rotating in Will's hand.

'Hey,' Cole greeted, a sip already taken from his pint, the foam wiped on the back of his hand as he sat opposite his old friend.

'Hi, thanks for coming.'

Cole shrugged, taking another sip, looking around the bar, a hand held aloft as another regular came in.

'So . . .' Cole leant back against the arc of the mahogany chair, 'what do you think of the job?'

'Good, I think I'm in with a good chance, my old head is giving me a reference so that'll help. It's only a five-minute walk from our house.'

'Oh, I didn't mean . . . but that's great, Will, I'm pleased for you.' Cole slurped his beer, almost halving it. 'Ella and the kids will be pleased.'

Will nodded, his eyes fixed on the rotation of the beer mat between his fingers.

'Secondary?'

Will nodded. 'It's where I feel like I can make the biggest difference. What did you think I was talking about?'

'Ella's job, at the florist's?'

'Oh, yeah, right.' Will peeled back part of the beer mat; it ripped at the corner, so he began picking at the top layer of paper.

'Yeah, when I hooked up with Amira . . .' Cole leant in, winking, 'she mentioned that she had a job going and you know how desperate Ella's been to have one so I thought why not get those two talking, you know?'

Will nodded. He didn't know; he didn't know any of it.

'She'll enjoy it, getting back out there, meeting people, being creative.'

'Yeah, it's good . . . thanks, Cole, it's . . . yeah. It'll be good.'

'And Momma Walker can't wait to have the kids more.'

Will's head continued to nod, like he was agreeing with every single syllable that Cole uttered.

'And I said I'd have them on a Wednesday.'

'That won't be necessary,' Will replied, reaching for his drink, letting the taste smooth the edges of his words.

'It's no bother.' Cole drained the rest of his drink, tilted the glass towards Will's. 'Another?' He was already rising from his seat.

'No, thanks, I'm good.'

Cole laughed at the bar, a conversation passing between the regulars as they all looked up at the TV in the corner, wincing and chuckling at a comedy show.

Cole returned, a packet of dry-roasted peanuts clamped between his straight teeth. 'Cheers.'

He ripped open the bag, his attention still on the TV in the corner of the room. He winced again, returning his focus to Will.

Cole sobered, reading the tension around Will, the set of his shoulders, the words that he could almost see being rehearsed behind his eyes.

'I need you to stop, Cole.' Will's words landed like a slap on the table surface: they were firm, hollow; they stung against Cole's skin. 'I need you to step back, from Ella, from my children, my home.'

Cole took a sip of his drink, trying to extinguish the heat crawling across his skin. He grinned, letting out a small laugh, rolling his eyes and slurping again. 'This is because Jam reached for me the other day, isn't it?'

Will ignored him, searching his mind for the words he had practised over and over. 'I saved *your* life, Cole.'

Cole clenched his teeth together.

'I lost my brother and saved *you* and I have never asked for *anything* in return.'

Cole began flicking the edge of his glass, his focus on the amber liquid inside, on the peal of nail against glass.

'But I'm asking you now. You need to find your own wife, your own kids, your own home. It's time to let her go, Cole. She chose me.'

Cole's eyes flicked up at this; he reacted, defensively – the cocky bloke at the bar, holding his hands up in surrender. 'Whoa, I don't know what you think is going on, mate, but you've got the wrong end of the stick.' He laughed, took another long pull of beer, grinning and laughing again as he put the glass down with a thud. '"She chose me?"' he mimicked, chuckling. 'Of course she chose you, Will.' He shook his head, as if Will was talking utter nonsense. 'Look, whatever this is about, don't worry. Me and Ells are mates. That's it. End of. But if you think me being around so much is causing you problems then no bother, man, I've just been helping out. They're great kids, Ells is a mate and, well, sorry, if I've been overstepping, it was never my intention.' He knocked the drink back. 'We good?' Then he scraped back his chair and grabbed his jacket, shrugging it on and tucking his hair behind his ear.

And for almost two decades, Cole would keep the truth locked inside his chest. He would never utter it to another soul; he had swallowed the key and it would sit inside him corroding, releasing tiny bits of poison into his blood stream for years. Until one afternoon, the key would slip into the lock and all his secrets would come pouring out; but Cole wouldn't remember the words he had spoken. He would remember a broken window, blood pouring down nineteen-year-old Jamie's face; he would remember Ella holding Jamie, but he wouldn't remember a word of what was said.

But Will? He would remember every word. He would examine each and every one, and they would plague his thoughts for months, until one day, when his son left home, Will Roberts would finally have the guts to do what he should have done years ago: give his wife the freedom to choose her future.

However, here in the bar, Will drained his drink, leant back in his chair and said, 'Yeah. We're good.'

'Good. Look, I've got a . . . a thing . . .' Cole explained.

'Yeah, I've got to get going anyway so . . .'

'Later.' Cole avoided Will's eyes as he turned and left, waving a salute to the bar, the door swinging behind him, a new jigsaw piece fixed in place.

Cole walked to the end of the street. He walked through the door of the Spar at the end of the road, bought a litre of whisky and two packets of tobacco, climbed onto the bus and went home.

It would be two days before Cole surfaced from his flat in time to drop off Susan Walker's birthday present. He would be polite when he called around to the house: he would stay for a cup of tea, he would play with the kids for ten minutes and then he would leave. He didn't give Ella a kiss on the cheek; he didn't stay for longer than half an hour. When he left and Ella asked Will what he thought was wrong with Cole, Will would shrug his shoulders and say that he had no idea. And when Cole came around for a BBQ three weeks later with Jules, Ella would squeeze his arm, telling him how pleased she was for him that he'd found his match.

And Jules *was* special; they had fun; Cole would think that maybe this was as close to love without Ella as he could get. But for Jules, fifteen years would be a long time to play second fiddle to the two real loves of Cole Chapel's life.

And as she slammed the door behind her for the last time, leaving an unconscious boyfriend asleep on the lounge floor, she would wonder which Cole Chapel loved more . . . Ella Roberts or alcohol.

PART THREE
THE END

Chapter Thirty-Five

Now

Ella

16th October 2022

'I've missed your smell,' I say, breathing in Will's chest, my finger running up and down his rib cage, closing my eyes and savouring everything that I have in this moment. Will shifts and I prop myself up, my hair falling across his collarbone, reaching my mouth up to his, the kiss long and deep as he rolls me onto my back and runs his thumb along my mouth.

'God, this mouth. You're so beautiful, Ella.' He looks down at me, his hands holding mine above my head, running his fingers down the inside of my arm. 'I love you more than I ever thought it was possible to love anyone.' We begin again, the dance of two bodies meant to fit, to hold, to be together.

'Ells?' The door below slams shut and Will freezes. 'Ells? You in?'

Will pulls back. Pain covers his face, a wave that skims his features, that pulls his body apart from mine.

'Wait, Will, it's not what you think, he's been staying here, he's . . .'

Will gets off the bed, reaching for his jeans, which lie tangled on the floor.

I hold the sheet around me, shuffling forward trying to reach for him, but he's already standing. 'Will, hold on, let me explain. He's sober, Will. I've been helping him recover, he's been staying here while he gets better.'

Will turns and looks at me. I expect anger, but he's calm. He drags fingers through his hair. 'I can't do this again, Ella.' He bends down and pulls his jumper over his head.

'What do you mean?'

'This. You, me, *him*. I can't do it.'

'I know that he's fucked up in the past, Will, but it's different this time.'

'Really? And why do you think that is? Why do you think I said we should get a divorce?'

'Because—'

He raises an eyebrow.

'Because you settled for me! I've always known that, Will, I mean, come on! Why do you think people look at us the way they do, the way they have always done? Do you think I didn't know why you asked me to come with you to Europe? You were scared, Will, you were so scared to be on your own. If Jack hadn't have died, if you hadn't needed me to hold you up, you would have never asked me. And you knew it too, didn't you? That's why you tried to break up with me when David offered you the job.'

I pull the sheet around me and stand in front of him, placing my hand on his heart.

'When I felt your heart beat, every time it sped up when I said, "I love you," it was guilt that made it quicken, wasn't it?'

He shakes his head.

'It's not your fault, Will.' I keep my hand there. 'I did this to you, I convinced myself that you loved me the way I loved you, but I knew. I've always known.'

'You're wrong, Ella.'

'Am I?'

He nods.

'Then why ask me for a divorce?'

'Because I wanted to give you a choice.'

'I don't understand.'

'I think you do. You've been lying to yourself for *years*, Ella. It's always been him. I just don't think you ever wanted to admit it, even to yourself.'

'Cole? Don't be ridiculous!'

'You have always seen the beauty in the world, you've always wanted to make the world a better place, your alarm is Mr Blue Sky, for God's sake! You surround yourself with colour. What do you think your world would look like if you admitted to me, to your kids, that hidden beneath all of that light, you really love someone else? It's not in you, Ella, to cause me pain, to hurt the kids, to step away from the blue skies and—'

'You're not making any sense. And even if I did, Cole wouldn't want me! We're like brother and sister; he doesn't feel like that about me. Is that really what you think? What you've been thinking all our lives? Jesus, this is crazy, Will!'

'Is it?'

'Yes!'

'Ask him. Ask Cole how he really feels about you.'

'I don't need to! I know how Cole feels about me!' I turn my back on him, suddenly angry. I reach for my clothes, while behind me Will's breathing slows.

'Ella,' he says softly. 'Think about it. He's always been there for you, hasn't he? Always there to pick up the pieces. Cole Chapel, who could ask for a better *friend*? Have you never asked yourself why he's never settled down? Why he's never had kids?'

I pull a jumper over my head, wrapping my arms around myself and turning to face him.

His expression is pained, sad, like he's telling me that Santa isn't real, like he doesn't want to burst the illusion.

'Because he's Cole, he's a free spirit, he can barely look after himself, let alone a family.'

'He looked after you, though? When Amber was a baby? When I was doing my degree?'

'That's different. Do you know what, Will? If you don't want to be with me, then fine, but don't try and blame this on some fictional affair!'

'Let me ask you . . . When did he get sober?'

'What's that got to do with anything?'

'It's got *everything* to do with it. When? Before or after I asked you for a divorce?'

I hesitate. 'After, but that doesn't mean anything!'

'It means *everything*! He's been waiting for you to wake up and see what is so *painfully* clear to everyone else but you! Don't you see?'

'No. No. I don't. Right! Let's ask him, shall we? He's right downstairs, let me show you how ridiculous this is!' I scrape my hair into a ponytail, as though I'm going for a jog, and wrench open the door, rushing down the stairs with Will following slowly.

In the kitchen, Cole sits, a coffee in front of him. He looks up as I storm into the room, his eyes looking past me to Will; he looks away. I stand in the threshold, breathless. And everything that I thought was true, everything about my relationship with Cole, falls away in that one look. That one look that tells me Cole has heard every word that has just been spoken.

'Tell her,' Will says.

I turn to him, then back to Cole.

'For once, Cole, just tell her the fucking truth. Tell her what you said to me when you came here so drunk that my son ended up in an ambulance.'

I stand there. No words come; I just watch them, these two men who I have known all my life and who suddenly feel like strangers. 'Cole?' The word comes out but it's like a ghost: there is no edge, no structure, just an impression – an echo of a person I'd thought was real. 'Tell him it's not true.'

'I . . . I can't.'

I find my feet moving backwards as he stands, his hand reaching towards me.

'Ells, wait, I . . .'

My head is shaking. The walls lean in, changing the prospect of the room; I feel small, like I'm at the edge of a narrowing hallway.

Will turns to me. I look up at him, my head still shaking. 'I'll leave you two alone. I'm sure there is lots to discuss.'

I watch him walk down the hall. He pauses at the threshold, turning his head towards me, a small nod and a sad smile telling me to be brave, as though he's saying goodbye.

Cole is pacing the room when I return. He stops, his hands wringing; he tucks his hair behind his ears, then hides his hands deep in his pockets. He takes a beat and gives himself a small nod. 'OK. OK, right. Ells?'

I blink up at him. He pulls out a chair for me. I look down at it; everything in this room feels alien. I look back at him.

'This isn't how I . . . how I've imagined having this conversation, but if it has to be now, well then.' He clears his throat and takes my hands in his. 'I'm sorry, Ells, really, I am . . . I don't remember what I said to Will that day, but I was wasted and, well, it doesn't matter now.' He takes a deep breath. 'I love you, Ells, I'm *in* love with you. God . . .' he lets out a small laugh, 'you don't know how long I've waited to tell you that.'

I stay focused on his knuckles, small scars from fights he can't remember. 'How long?' I ask, my voice quiet. I drag my eyes up to his; mine feel dry, parched, burnt, but his are filled with light, with excitement, and I see the boy from my childhood looking at me.

'Since we were kids, since you fell from the tree and broke your arm. You were so brave, Ells, and I knew it, in here.' He bangs his fist against his chest. 'It was like until that moment, I had been struggling to breathe and then, with that one look you gave me, when you looked up and asked me to pick you up, I felt like I could breathe again, it was like a puncture, this rush of life and air in my lungs.'

I remember that day. I was twelve. He was thirteen.

'You really didn't know?' he asks, tilting his head, trying to read me.

I shake my head. 'Why didn't you say anything?'

'I was a coward, scared if I told you, you would laugh, that you wouldn't want me around.'

'We were kids then, Cole. Why didn't you tell me later, before Will?'

'I tried, that night at the fair. But I hadn't noticed before, the way you felt about Will, and then I saw the way you looked at him and I knew it wasn't the right time. So I waited. I'll be honest, I didn't think I'd have to wait so long.' He laughs again, but the sparkle in his eyes has started to dim.

'So you've lied to me my whole life?' I say, and he winces like I've slapped him.

'No, I never lied, Ells, I just didn't . . . I couldn't . . .'

'Do you know what you've done?' I take my hands from his. 'You've taken all of my memories of us, all of my love for my friend, and you've lit a torch to it all. You've burnt it all to the ground.'

'Ells, no, that's not . . .'

'I need you to go.'

'Ells, let's talk, let's . . .'

'No. Cole. Just leave.'

He moves towards me, his hand on my arm, and I snatch it back.

'Get. OUT!' I pick up his tin from the table and throw it at him. 'Can't you see what this means? Our whole marriage Will hasn't been able to see how much I love him because you've been in the fucking way! You've been there the whole time, like . . . like poison, drip-feeding him with doubt until he finally gave up! Jesus, that night you came round, the night I called you to tell you he'd left me, no wonder you were so eager to help me through. My *selfless* friend. Tell me, Cole, how long were you going to wait until you made a move? Christ, you moved in the next fucking day!'

'I'm still your friend. I'm still me, nothing's changed.'

'*Everything* has changed.'

'Ells . . .'

'Just go, Cole.'

The door closes behind him, behind us, behind everything that I had thought was real.

Chapter Thirty-Six

Then

Years had flown by, the jigsaw puzzle of Ella and Will's lives now a collage of birthdays, Christmases, infant and junior school plays, promotions; arguments and laughter lines; college and house moves; Cole's face appearing sporadically depending on his alcoholism and sobriety.

It was Valentine's Day 2022, almost seven months before Will would ask Ella for a divorce. While Jamie helped Ella at the shop, Will hung multi-coloured Christmas lights up around the kitchen, preparing his Valentine's gift.

The warm smell of burnt sugar surrounded a plate of slightly wonky toffee apples, sitting on the kitchen side next to a candy-floss machine that Will was terrified of. He climbed the stepladder and pinned up the posters of fairground rides around the kitchen extension; he had stacked up the wood outside ready for a small bonfire, fireworks and hotdogs later.

Valentine's Day was the busiest day of the year for Ella and she had been in the shop since the early hours, but Will had got up before her alarm, bringing her a selection of iced pastries and coffee as they opened their gifts to each other. Ella had bought Will a watch with their initials engraved on the back and he had given her a pair of rose quartz earrings with a matching pendant. But this, *this*, he smiled as he climbed back down the ladder, was her real present. Will was re-creating their anniversary night at the fair in their own home. Jamie was in on it all, and would be making himself scarce later on in the evening, telling Will the last thing he wanted to hear was his parents' fireworks going off.

Outside, as Ella and Jamie drove to the last delivery of the day, a tin can tripped and fell against the kerb. The owner had slurped the dregs of it, crushed it and thrown it down the road. A strong gust of wind kicked it further along the path, and it rolled left and right, unable to keep its bearing until it found itself cornered, rattling against the drainpipe at the back of Will and Ella's house.

Will flicked on the Christmas lights so that they pulsed around the room and looked at the wind picking up, hoping that it wasn't going to be too blustery for a bonfire. A rattling sound from outside drew his attention and he opened the back door, bending down to release the can from where it had become ensnared in the wisteria.

On the ground lay Cole, his dark curls across his face, his body a semi-colon: a separate part of Will and Ella's life, existing on its own, but part of their story nonetheless.

'Jesus Christ.' Will knelt beside him, reaching out his hand and shaking him. He leant in, placing his head close to Cole's; stale breath escaped in a series of slow exclamations. Relief and anger roiled in Will's chest as he cupped Cole under the arms and tried to pull him up. 'Wake up! Cole! Cole? Wake up!'

Cole tried to speak, but his words were incoherent as he rolled over, vomiting. Will waited, making sure that Cole remained on his side.

'You done?' Will asked, the concern and irritation merging into one jaw-clenched question.

Cole shifted himself, trying to stand; he failed and slammed into the wall. Will gritted his teeth and led Cole through the pitched-roof end of the kitchen, helping him onto the sofa and fetching a bowl.

'Here.' But Cole was already unconscious again. Will landed the bowl on the floor next to him, contemplating what to do. Will was no expert, but he would guess that this was more than a day bender: Cole stank, urine and alcohol surrounding him.

He was almost right. Cole had been drinking for over forty-eight hours: he was unaware of the day, the week, the month; sleep only came in small pockets of relief when his body could no longer cope without it. As Cole Chapel lay on the sofa in Ella's house, his dreams were a series of sounds: the slam of a door, Will's hard stare, this house.

As Cole's body evacuated more of the last week's drink, Will managed to get the bowl beneath his chin just in time. Then Cole slipped back into sleep. Will rinsed out the bowl, poured Cole a glass of water and returned to him, debating whether or not to call for an ambulance.

'Where's Ells?' Cole asked, the 's' like a snake, elongated, hard to control as it slithered from his tongue.

'Out, but she'll be back soon. You need to be gone. I don't want her to see you like this.'

Cole laughed, a low noise that dripped from his mouth. 'You'd like that, wouldn't you?' The words came, thick and heavy, saturated in regret. 'For me to be gone.'

Will didn't respond as he stood over Cole, the man whose life he'd saved at the cost of his brother's.

Cole was not aware that his words were forming, spitting from his mouth, his unconscious and conscious mind tangled around each other. He was there, he wasn't there: a vampire's reflection.

'You ruined her.'

'That's enough, Cole,' Will warned, his voice penetrating Cole's conscious mind as his eyes opened. A rush of adrenaline pulled Cole up, like a flash of electricity along his spine.

Cole leant back, a smirk in the corner of his mouth. 'And you know it, don't you?'

'I'm calling you a taxi before you or I say something we'll regret.'

'You destroyed her life. You, Will fucking Roberts, who could have had any woman he wanted, chose the one that I loved. What was it, Will? Did you want to punish me for Jack? Is that why you took her from me?'

Will flinched, his jaw tightening.

Cole let out a low laugh.

'You're drunk.'

'I am!' Cole threw open his arms in declaration, the adrenaline pumped through his system snapping him into sobriety, Will's reaction to his words his own shot from an epi-pen. Cole continued, and although his words were blurred around the edges, even though he couldn't control the gaps between them, he could find the ones he needed. 'I am drunk, I *am* a drunk. But you made me. I'm your life's biggest achievement. You shaped me into the man I became when you took her from me, when you tricked her into believing *you* were the right man for her. And then you destroyed her dreams, you knocked her up, you took everything that she could have been and folded her into a life that she should never have been in. She was mine, Will, she loved *me*, but you made sure she couldn't see that, didn't you?'

'I'm calling you a taxi,' Will repeated.

Will left Cole's side and he struggled to his feet, walking over to the painting on the wall, his own breathing and footsteps dampened, like his head was underwater, his hands slow and indistinct as they reached out, touching the lines of paint as Will walked back into the room.

'Don't touch that.' Will's voice was firm.

Cole sneered at him over his shoulder. 'Look at her, look at who she was.' Cole hovered his palm over the canvas but then removed his hand, gesturing to the rest of the kitchen, stumbling towards Will. 'And look at what you tried to turn her into.'

'Get your shit and get out.' Will's voice was dangerous, low, shaking.

Cole smirked at Will. 'Make me.'

'What, are you twelve?'

'Come on, Will, you know you've always wanted to take a pop at me, here's your chance.' Cole's hands pushed against Will's chest.

Will took hold of his wrists, holding them either side of Cole's head firmly. 'I hate to break it to you, but I don't really give you much thought, Cole, except how to help you get on with your own life instead of syphoning from ours like a leech. You're a fucking parasite.'

'Will!' Ella shouted from behind, Jamie at her shoulder, wide-eyed, taking in the lights, the fairground posters and the two men in front of her.

Cole's surroundings closed in on him. He shook his head, the room suddenly becoming bright, the sickly-sweet smell of toffee, the sound of the rain and wind outside crystal-glass clear, the flashing lights, blue, then red, then orange. Will dropped Cole's hands as something like cold water ran through Cole's veins, a warning in his gut, a surge of the regret yet to come.

Cole would try to capture those words spoken under-water in the weeks and months that followed; he would wake with the fear of what he had said, what he had done. It would eat him from inside as he tried to both force and bury the memory of what happened next.

The shock of reality, of Ella in front of him, of Jamie

looking at him with confusion, hit Cole and he stumbled back as Will's hands released him. His shoulder blades and the base of his spine hit the wall, his body leaning to the right, the adrenaline-fuelled clarity running away like the last of the water from a shower; it dripped from his nerve endings, swirling down the plug, leaving him naked. Cole tried to correct himself, moving away from the wall, trying to hold still for a moment, but the momentum of his movement hadn't given his brain time to rebalance and so as he tried to remain upright, he found himself veering off to the right.

Jamie moved quickly, four strides across the room as he tried to stop Cole from falling.

Cole's fingers gripped onto Jamie but the momentum of an inebriated full-grown man was a hard beast to tame, and in the fraction of time that it took for Ella and Will to react, to move forward, to try to stop the two men falling, the damage was already done.

Colours from the glass doors exploded, and a new jigsaw piece, filled with yellow, orange, greens, emerged. The glass thrown around the two bodies that fell through, strewing around them both: a rainbow scattered around their bodies as they landed on the hard ground outside. A shriek leapt from Ella's mouth, as she took in the glass shards on the floor, Cole's body and Jamie's facing away from each other, blood pouring from a gash in Jamie's head, Cole's body seemingly unharmed.

'Jamie!' Ella grasped at her son as he sat up, her eyes searching his face, blood running into his eye socket, filling it; she had never seen so much blood.

Will was on the phone, calling for an ambulance with one hand, grabbing a tea towel with the other. He stepped out over the broken pane, the glass crunching beneath his feet as he passed it to Ella while she tried to control the bleeding with her hands.

'Are you hurt anywhere else? Jamie? Anywhere else?' She looked over his body, leaning over his shoulder and trying to see the back of his head.

'I'm fine, it's fine, I just feel a bit dizzy. It's just a cut, Mum, it's fine.' He flinched as she removed the towel briefly where blood was pulsing from a gash in his forehead.

'The ambulance is on its way.' Will knelt in front of Jamie, taking over Ella's hand, putting the pressure of the towel against Jamie's head as the wind and rain mixed the blood against his son's face.

'Is Uncle Cole OK?' Jamie asked.

Beside them, Cole groaned.

Ella stepped over to him. 'Cole? Cole! Are you hurt?' She pushed back his hair, turning him gently, her fingers around his collar, her hands pushing back his jacket, trying to find the source of the blood on the floor. 'You're OK, you're OK, the ambulance is on its way. Talk to me, Cole, are you hurt?' He held up his arm, blood running from around his cuff. She ripped off her scarf and wrapped it around the gash. 'You need to stay awake, Cole, do you hear me? Cole?'

Cole had begun to cry, softly at first, the words 'I'm sorry,' coming over and over. She shifted his body upwards, his back against her front. 'You're OK.' She rocked him like he was a child. 'You're alright, everything is going to be OK.'

She turned back to her son, the blood seeping and spreading fast across the white of the towel. Will's arm was around him, holding onto the towel with his other hand. Ella fought back the tears as she met Will's gaze, expecting to see her own concern reflected back at her, but Will's stare wasn't filled with concern, it was something else. Will looked tired, broken, and something that Ella couldn't understand: defeated.

She looked away, continuing to rock Cole, who was sobbing in her arms as the wind carried the screech of sirens.

Cole was stretchered into the back of the ambulance, while the other paramedic worked on Jamie's cut, Ella holding her son's hand while the paramedic asked Will questions about Cole, asking for any information that Will could give them.

'He's an alcoholic.'

'Any idea how long for?'

'I don't know, I mean years, but I've never seen him this bad.'

'Who is his next of kin?'

Will looked over at his wife, smiling up at the paramedic who was placing gauze over the cut and was reassuring them both that he just needed a couple of stitches and then he'd be right as rain.

'His mother, she lives down south, I don't have a contact number, so I suppose my wife would be next.' Will's voice was robotic as he gave Ella's details.

'Thank you, we'll get him checked out. His stomach may have to be pumped, but if you give the hospital a call . . .' The rest of the sentence was lost on Will, who was stepping into the ambulance as another paramedic worked on Cole, a drip being adjusted from behind.

Cole blinked, scanning Will's face.

Will leant in, his words almost a breath. 'Don't come here again, Cole. We're done. You don't visit, you don't call. Stay away from my family.'

'Do you want to follow in your car?' the paramedic asked.

'No.' Will cleared his throat. 'No, thank you. That won't be necessary.'

But as much as Will wanted to believe that this was the last they would have to do with Cole Chapel, as much as he wanted to believe that Ella would see him for what he was, Cole's words would haunt him. They would be there when he tried to sleep, they would be there when Ella replaced the photo of them all together after he threw it away, they would be there until, seven months later, he would ask Ella for a divorce, when he finally decided it was time for her to make a choice.

He just hoped and prayed that she would choose him.

Chapter Thirty-Seven

Now

Ella

16th October 2022

I pour gravy onto the side of my plate, even though I have no appetite for a Sunday roast at my parents' after the morning I've just had.

'Did you know?'

Mum and Dad exchange shifty glances as my brothers fidget uncomfortably, although that could also be due to the quest for the most severe wedgy that has just caused Roddy to pluck his Calvin Kleins from his arse.

'Jesus! Did everyone know except me?' I land my cutlery back down.

'Love,' Mum begins, glancing at Dad before continuing. He meets my eyes before shovelling in a mouthful of mash. 'We all thought you knew. I mean, I love the boy, but subtlety has never been his strong point.'

'Really?' I fork the chicken, turning it over before looking around the table. 'How long have you known?' They all find somewhere else to focus. 'Kenny?' I ask, my cutlery resting again on the side of the plate, hoping that my brother has been as oblivious to this fact as he is to his belief that the bow tie and his full chubby James Bond ensemble will get him the next Miss Moneypenny.

'Since you were kids?' he says, filling his mouth with food.

'Kids?' I say, my voice quiet.

'You never thought it was odd the way he would be here all the time? How he never really had a girlfriend?' Roddy intervenes as Kenny fills his already brimming mouth with a slurp of red wine.

'Ha!' I laugh, triumphant. 'He had loads of girlfriends!'

'No he didn't!' Mum scoffs, shaking her head.

'He did! There was Natali, Priya, Meghan, Katy,' I begin ticking them off on my fingers. 'Cole had more girlfriends in year ten than Kenny's had in his whole life!'

Kenny's brow furrows at my insult, then he shrugs his shoulders: fair point.

'Ella! There is no need to be mean to your brother!' Mum scowls, shaking her head at my bad behaviour.

'Sorry, but it's the truth. Roddy?'

He shrugs, helping himself to extra roast potatoes, the empty carbs speaking his response.

'How did I not know?' I whine.

'We thought you did!' Mum reaches for the pepper, grinding it ferociously across her plate. 'And to be honest, until Will asked you to go with him to Europe, we all . . . well, we all thought it would be a done deal.'

'A done deal?' My voice is verging on hilarity.

'That you and Cole . . . that you would get together.' She spoons her food, a gentle nod that it now has the right amount of seasoning.

'Get together?' I gasp.

'In the end,' she confirms, after swallowing demurely. 'We were a bit worried about it actually, given Cole's . . . issues.'

'The end?'

I seem to have lost the ability to do anything other than repeat things.

'Why? Why would you think that?' I fill my glass with water, taking a long sip, my hand shaking.

'Oh, Ella, because you were always so happy when you were together. You and Cole have always been two peas in a pod, you even looked like a couple. Whereas you and Will . . .'

'Me and Will what?'

'Nothing.' She turns her plate, inspecting how it lies like she's laying out a banquet for the queen.

'No, go on, what? It's just that Will is so . . .? So out of my league?'

'No, that's not what I meant. Look, you and Cole would have dirty knees and scrapes.' She adjusts the plate again. 'You both made mud pies and chased each other around with a worm dangling from your fingers and, well, it's just that Will has never been a worm-dangler, has he?'

'No, and that's exactly the point! I don't want to have a worm-dangler for a husband, I want the man I fell in love with who is kind and quiet and considerate and who always, *always* puts me first. I have no idea why any of you would think I would want Cole that way. He's my friend, he has always just been my friend.'

'You must see why he stayed around though, Ella?'

'Yes! He stayed around because he's Cole. He's never wanted anything other than to be knee-deep in engine oil, booze and women. He's my *friend*.'

'Oh, my sweet girl. You've never been good at reading between the lines, have you? It always said that on your school reports, do you remember, Bill? No matter how much we read with you, your teachers would always say you needed to work on your . . . what was that word?'

'Inference,' Dad mumbles, still avoiding my eyes.

'Inference! That's it!'

'Are you saying I led him on?'

'No,' she says, making it sound exactly as if she had just said yes. 'Well, not led him on *exactly*.'

'Exactly?'

'Well, you have to admit, Ella, you did give him mixed signals.'

'I have never given him mixed signals. I love Will, I have always loved Will.'

'Oh we know that, love, of course we know that, but there have been times when you've . . . relied on Cole.'

'Relied on him?'

'What your mother means . . .' Dad gives Mum a warning glance that tells her she needs to rein it in a bit, 'is that you tend to turn to Cole when things get rough.'

'Exactly!' Mum's hand lands on Dad's, giving it a squeeze. 'And you have to admit, when the kids were young, you relied on him an awful lot, what with Will being so busy and . . . we did wonder if, well, if you were . . . closer than just friends?'

'You thought I was having an affair? Mother! I had post-natal depression. Cole was the only one who understood, who could help.'

'*I* could have helped, *we* could have helped, but you didn't want us, you wanted Cole.'

'Because I was ashamed! How could I come to you, you of all people? You who makes Yorkshire puddings from scratch, Mum.' I stab a yorkie to emphasise my point. 'From scratch! I can barely mix some instant gravy.'

The room is filled with uncomfortable silence as my mind works, processing all the words that have landed in the middle of the table, sitting there waiting to be consumed, masked by the sounds of a normal Sunday lunch at the Walker house: the radio in the kitchen, the scrape of cutlery against china.

'Oh, God. You're right, aren't you?' I break the silence.

'I've led him on. I've let him believe that, and . . . and . . fuck.'

'Ella!' Mum chastises.

'Sorry, but fuck. Will has watched me do it. He's been right there the whole time, thinking that I have feelings for Cole.'

Mum raises her eyebrows in an *I told you so* expression.

'So what are you going to do?' Dad asks gently, reaching for the water jug and refilling his glass.

'I don't know. The funny thing is, my instant reaction is to call Cole.' I laugh dryly. 'That's why Will asked for a divorce, isn't it? Because he thinks I've always been in love with Cole?'

'Will knew what he was getting into, Ella.' Mum's face softens. 'He's a smart man, he knows you loved him. I just believe he thinks that you loved Cole too. Maybe it just got too much.'

'Too much?'

'Competing?'

'Competing?'

'Stop repeating everything I say! You sound like a parrot.'

'Sorry. But there was never any competition. Will is the love of my life.'

'But does he know that?'

I pause. Does he?

'Does Cole?' Roddy interjects, his words seeming to shock him as much as the rest of the table. Roddy is never one to weigh in on sensitive subjects.

I meet his eyes, blinking. 'I don't know.'

'Look, why don't I get the Risk board out and we can have a game?' Roddy suggests. Kenny's eyes widen as he nods at our brother, appraising his actions and concurring that that would be a perfect plan. 'Take your mind off things for a couple of hours?' Roddy continues. 'You'll feel better after. Give you time to let things settle for a bit before you do anything *rash*. And tomorrow, you can figure out what to do?'

I exhale loudly. 'Fine.' Kenny grins, pushing back his plate and rubbing his belly. 'But I'm yellow, and no fixing the cards, Kenny! I mean it!'

Dawn is still far off as I hold my cup of coffee, photo albums laid out in front of me. There in technicoloured glory is the evidence that everyone could see except me. I reach for a photo of the five of us. It was Amber's sixth birthday and we'd all gone to the zoo; Jules had come too, she's the one behind the camera. Jamie was on Cole's shoulders, Amber holding Will's hand as he looked over at us, a smile fixed in place that didn't quite reach his eyes, me in the middle laughing at something Cole said. Did Jules know? Was she trying to show me what was so blatantly obvious? The gap between us, me closer to Cole than Will, a metaphorical and literal elephant in the background. We hadn't seen much of Cole back then: once he met Jules, his visits to our house had lessened. I was working with Amira, Will was settled in his job; life was just getting on.

But after Vince died and left the garage to Cole, he started drinking more. A mixture of grief and the pressure of running the business, I suppose. And then, when Jules left and Cole returned to his old ways – a series of one-night stands, his nights out beginning earlier and earlier – we didn't see him as much.

I move that photo and reach for another. Me and Will this time, a rare date night, me looking adoringly at my handsome husband, his arm tightly around mine, looking into my eyes, pride in his smile, the River Severn gurgling behind us, the sun just beginning to set. I put the two photos together side by side: the difference in Will is astounding when Cole isn't in the picture. I let out a hollow laugh, the sound echoing against the walls of my empty lounge.

I did this. I did this to them both.

I know what I have to do.

The next morning, I open the door to see Cole standing there. I've cleaned the house, changed four times, finally settling on a white blouse and jeans. He's in his usual attire: open checked shirt, white vest beneath, triangle of chest hair just visible, his hair washed, leather jacket.

'Hi,' I say, exhaling deeply, relief that he's sober and nerves vying for my attention. 'Come in,' I say, opening the door and walking ahead of him.

'Tea?' I ask as though everything is normal.

'Um, yeah, that would be great.'

'It's supposed to brighten up later,' I begin, inwardly groaning.

'So they say,' he replies, taking off his jacket and hanging it over the back of a chair.

'Biscuit?' I ask, my back turned. 'I think we have some of those chocolate-chip digestives somewhere in here. I begin opening and closing doors on the hunt. 'Ah-ha!' I clasp the packet and wiggle it in his direction. He smiles back politely. 'Shall we go in the lounge?'

We assume our positions on the sofa but I sit cross-legged; he glances towards my feet, hesitating briefly before sitting down.

'So . . .' I begin.

'So . . .' He smiles at me, a hand through his hair.

'So . . .' I say again, both of us laughing nervously, 'I guess we have some things to talk about?'

'We do,' he confirms, dimples sinking, eyes wary.

'I didn't know, Cole.' He tilts his head and leans back against the corner of the sofa. 'I had no idea.'

He nods contemplatively. 'I know, I think, but there was a time where I thought that . . . that maybe you did? When the kids were young?'

I shake my head slowly. 'Do you think that Will thought that too? That I had feelings for you?'

He nods.

'How long? How long have you known that Will thought that there was . . . more to us than just friends?'

'Since before you got together, I think. I think he always knew.'

'Right. Right.' I reach for a biscuit for something to do with my hands but leave it on the plate. 'And you've talked about it? You and Will?'

'No, not as such.'

'Not as such? You're going to have to give me more than that, Cole. I'm trying to put the pieces of my life together here.' I laugh, nerves making me edgy.

'He asked me to step back. From you, the kids.'

'When?'

'Well, Jam was just a toddler so . . . 2004.'

'2004?! Before you met Jules?'

He hesitates before nodding.

'But you loved Jules, she broke your heart.'

He exhales, meeting my eyes, and with that one look I know.

'Ah. You never loved her?'

He shook his head. 'I liked her, I liked her a lot, and there was a time that I thought it would work and, well, it made things . . . easier, for Will, for me to still be around you and the kids.'

'You used her?'

'No. I did have feelings for her, really I did. We had a good time, me and Jules, but she . . . well I guess she knew.'

'Knew what exactly?'

'That she would never be you. She wanted more than I could give her, Ells, she wanted kids, to settle down, but she wanted me to want it too, and I just couldn't. I already had a family.'

'No you didn't, Cole.'

'I loved your kids as much as I could love my own. Do you remember how Jam would reach for me instead of Will? How Bamber would fall asleep if I rocked her? They might not be my kids, Ells, but I love them like they are.'

'I'm sorry. I'm sorry I did this to you.'

'What do you mean?'

'Stole your life. Stopped you from meeting someone else.'

Cole fidgets in his seat. 'I never wanted anyone else.'

'But you should have.' I turn my body, reaching for his hands, wrapping mine around his. 'You should have found someone else, Cole.'

He shakes his head, his mouth opening about to speak, his dark curls falling over his eyes as I rush on.

'I love you.' I say the words, hot in my mouth, my eyes filming over with tears.

He looks up at me, dark eyelashes already glistening.

'But as a friend. No more.'

'It's just come as a shock, that's all.' He sniffs, lifting his chin. I release his hands as he reaches up, one hand at the back of my neck, drawing my forehead to his. 'Just give me a chance, Ells. Let me prove to you that I can be good enough for you, that we can be more. Please.' He rubs his nose against mine.

'I can't,' I say, my voice wobbling, unsure for a moment.

'Try,' he whispers.

His lips are soft as they meet mine, warm, tentative. I hesitate. I have considered this over the last couple of days, what it might feel like to let him kiss me, have tried to picture us as more than friends to see how and if it would fit, because until this moment there has been that tiny doubt in the back of my mind that I've been wrong, that maybe I have felt more for Cole than just friendship. But as the tip of his tongue searches out mine, a jolt of electricity bolts through me, from the pit of my stomach to the tips of my hands.

'Stop,' I say, my hands against his chest. The fire inside burns, but it's not the fire he wants from me; the fire that is burning through me is pure, clear, primal: wrong.

We're still so close that we're breathing in each other's air. His hand is still in my hair, one hand at the side of my face, his dark eyes searching mine.

'Stop,' I say again slowly.

He pulls back. 'Sorry,' he says. 'It's too soon, I've just wanted to do that for so long.' He smiles: that smile that women have fallen for so many times.

'It's not too soon, Cole.' He frowns. 'It's too late. It's Will, Cole. It's always been and always will be Will.'

He moves back, my words both landing and missing their target, confusion and denial falling across his face; he shakes his head, dragging his fingers through his hair.

'I'm sorry, Cole.' I reach out to take his hand again, but he moves it back, getting up from the sofa. 'I'm sorry that I let you believe we could be anything more.'

'I have to go,' he says, unfolding from the sofa, backing out of the room, grabbing his jacket from the kitchen.

'Wait, Cole, don't go like this. We can still be friends, we just need to work out how to move past this.'

'Don't you see?' He turns to me. 'We have *never* been just friends. I don't know *how* to be just your friend,' he says. 'And I don't know how to live without you.'

'You don't have to live without me. We just need time.'

'We've run out of time.' He stops still then, pulls me against him, his chin on my head as he holds me, his words falling into my ears. 'It looks like we may have made it . . . to the end.'

I sniff. 'Have you just quoted Blur?'

He kisses the top of my head, 'Goodbye, Ells.' And releases me.

'Cole, wait!' I follow him through the hall. 'Don't do this, don't throw everything we have away!'

But my words slam against the closed door.

Chapter Thirty-Eight

Then

April 2022

Ella sat staring at the newly double-glazed door. The air in the room was weighted with the aftermath of Susan's phone call. 'Mum said he was sober, he took her some flowers round for Easter.' Ella's words were quiet.

Will tried to calm his anger and spoke slowly and carefully. 'I don't care, Ella, I don't want him near my kids again.' Ella winced at the anger in Will's words. Will stood, clearing the detritus of Easter-egg paper and left-over breakfast dishes.

'But . . . he just needs help. Will. We can help him.' Will slammed the door to the dishwasher and turned to face her.

'Don't you think we've given him enough? Haven't *I* given him enough?' Ella flinched as Will sighed and dragged his hands through his hair, sitting back down at the table. 'What if it had been worse? What if Jamie had been really hurt, Ella? Do you think I could forgive myself if it happened again? If Cole's actions took another part of my family away? Could *you*?'

'He wouldn't—'

'But he did! I don't know how you can't see it.'

'He's my friend, I owe it to him—'

'You don't owe him anything!'

'Don't I, Will? *Don't* I? Do you really think I would have survived without him when the kids were little?'

Will leant back in the chair.

'Sorry, I didn't mean—'

'Look, I know it's not fair, and I wish things could be different, but I'm asking you, please . . .' he reached forward and held her hand against his mouth, 'please don't bring him back into our lives, because he *always* takes more than he gives, and I'm scared, Ella, I'm terrified that if we forgive him, if we give him one more chance, then someone else that I love will get *really* hurt.' He closed his eyes. 'I'm begging you, Ella.' He kissed her knuckles. 'Let him go. Let him get on with his own life.'

Ella looked at her husband, her emotions churning in her stomach as the emotion behind his words sank in. He was right. Enough was enough. 'OK.'

Will opened his eyes, tears filling them as he breathed out a sigh of relief. 'Thank you.'

Orange lights from the road sweeper reflected behind the bar, blinking back from the optics as Cole ordered a whisky. He was only going to have one, to take the edge off.

The barwoman, Jody, filled the glass, giving her co-worker an eyeroll, both throwing worried glances back at the man on the bar stool. They were all too aware of where one glass would lead. It was such a shame, the unspoken conversation passed between them, such a good-looking man, so funny and full of life, such a waste to dampen that part of him with glass after glass.

Cole sat, images of broken coloured glass, Jamie's face bleeding, Ella holding him, telling him it would be OK, then Will's voice, sharp, unwavering, clear: *Don't come here again, Cole. We're done. You don't visit, you don't call. Stay away from my family.*

He tipped the glass to the left, to the right, then knocked it back. But he didn't order another. Instead, he went home, poured another glass from his bottle, then tipped the rest down the sink. Cole had tried to detox outside hospital before and knew that he wasn't strong enough to go through it, that by the third day he would give up and walk to the nearest off-licence, that when he caved he would spiral into a pit of self-hatred. What he needed to do was cut back; he needed to ease himself off slowly, but he wouldn't survive it on his own.

He picked up his phone, scrolling down for her number, dialling.

Ella indicated and pulled up outside Cole's flat, waiting for him, the hit of booze filling her car as he climbed in beside her. She left the engine running, the blowers keeping the steam away from the rain-splattered windows, the indicator light flashing in the windows of the downstairs flat.

'Thanks for coming,' he said, his damp hair falling across his face.

Ella nodded, tasting the words that she needed to speak, rusty and tarnished nails on her tongue.

'I wanted to say sorry. I know we said we never needed to, but I think in the circumstances it needs to be said.'

She turned to him, the nails sharp as they forced themselves out of her mouth. 'Do you know what for?'

Cole pushed his hair back, his dark eyes almost black. 'No, not really.'

'Then why bother?'

'Is Jam OK?'

'He's fine. The scar is healing.'

'Scar?'

'I can't do this any more, Cole. You need to get some help.'

'That's what I needed to say. I'm going to try, Ells, I'm going to stop, but it's going to take time.'

She nodded, looking back out through the window. Ahead, the traffic lights were changing from amber to red.

'Good, I'm glad.' She turned back to him, searching his face. 'But I can't be here for you, not this time. I made a promise, to Will. I can't be around you any more, Cole, not after last time, do you understand?'

'He's told you not to see me?'

'No. He asked me.'

'He has no right to ask that of you.'

'He has every right! Can you imagine how hard it must have been for him having you always around? He tolerated our relationship because he knows what you mean to me, but even Will isn't a saint, Cole, everyone has their breaking point.'

'Don't do this, not now, please, Ells. I know I fucked up, I know I . . .'

'Do you remember any of it?'

Cole looks dead ahead, trying to grasp at the wisps of fog-like memories of that afternoon, but there is nothing there for him to hold on to. He shakes his head slowly. 'I just remember the glass, Jam bleeding, you holding me, waking up in the hospital.'

Ella sighed; she'd been hoping for more.

Cole pulled out a roll-up, opened the window, lit the end and blew smoke out into the rain.

'I can't ever go through that again, Cole. I never want to have to choose between tending my bleeding son and you ever again, do you understand?'

'You won't.' The rain landed on the end of his cigarette, extinguishing it. Cole flicked it to the kerb and closed the window. 'I'm going to get sober, I promise.'

Ella swallowed down the hurt. 'We've danced this dance

before. You're drunk *now*, Cole, I can't trust a thing you say. It's time for me to put my family first.'

'I can do it. I'll do it for you, I'll go to AA, I'll—'

'That's just it. You need to do it for yourself, Cole, not for me, not for anyone else, you need to do it for yourself. Do you know I've had to lie to him tonight to come here? You've made me a liar, Cole. I can't see you any more.'

'Don't tell me it's over, Ells. I can't do this without you.'

Ella turned to him, her hand on the side of his cheek, the graze of stubble beneath her palm so familiar. 'Yes you can,' she said firmly. 'I have to go.'

'Ells? Please, I—'

'Will's waiting for me.' She cut his words off, feeling her resolve leaking from her with every moment she spent with him. 'Good luck, Cole.'

Cole's hand grappled with the handle of the door; he fumbled until the door fell open and he pulled himself out. He hesitated, leaning back in, resisting the urge to reach out and wipe the tears falling from Ella's face.

'I am sorry, Ells,' Cole said.

'I know. Goodbye, Cole.'

The next day, Will twisted the screw further into the wall, securing the new mirror. The new plain glass doors reflected in the corner as Will took a step backwards. She had chosen this mirror, surrounded by sea glass, to reflect the painting opposite. Will pushed back the image of Cole's fingers on the painting, the words he'd said: *And look at what you tried to turn her into.* Then Ella, holding him, rocking him back and forth, telling him he would be OK. Jamie had sat beside her and yet her arms had been around Cole.

'That looks nice,' Ella said from behind, wrapping her arms around his waist, but her arms felt too tight, too forced.

358

He moved away from her, not seeing the look on her face as she followed his movements across the room.

'Is everything OK, Will?'

'Yeah, I've just got a lot on with work.'

'I thought we could cook something nice together?'

'I can't, I've got to nip into school, I've not finished my marking.'

'Can't that wait?'

'Sorry, no.'

'Oh, right. We could get a takeaway when you get back?'

'No, no, you and Jamie go ahead. I'll grab something when I get in.'

As Will drove away from his house, he rewound the events of the last few months, when he thought that it was all going to be OK, when he believed that he and Ella had moved on now that Cole was out of the picture. But he'd heard the call last night; he'd heard Ella tiptoeing down the stairs, heard the gentle tone of her voice as she talked, as she arranged to meet him.

He hadn't reacted when she said she was nipping out to Amira's; he pretended to be asleep when she climbed back into bed and tried to ignore the faint smell of cigarettes in her hair. And even then, even as he attempted to rationalise Ella's actions, he hated himself when he checked her phone while she was in the shower the next morning: the recent call log, Cole's name like a smirk, gloating up at him.

It was then that he knew there would be no end to it. Cole had lain in a puddle of blood and urine, he had hurt their son and yet, there she was, Ella Roberts, still rushing to Cole's side. And even though she knew that her husband had said enough was enough, even though he had begged her not to see him, she was still willing to risk everything for Cole Chapel.

And the worst part was that Will knew that it was partly

his own fault, that he hadn't been there when she needed him most and that Cole had been. It hurt him more than she would ever know that she had needed to turn to Cole for emotional support rather than her own husband, but he couldn't go on blaming himself, and he couldn't go on like this.

He didn't have a choice; he had to let her go.

It just hurt too much to be the third wheel in his own marriage: he couldn't live like that any longer, no matter how much he loved her.

Chapter Thirty-Nine

Now

Ella

19th October 2022

I hesitate outside Robin's office, listening to Will's voice on my voicemail: 'Hi Ella, I know we need to talk but . . . I just . . . look, I need some space and, I think you do too . . . OK? I've got to go. Bye.' It's the fourth time I've listened to his response to my calls. I haven't told him about Cole yet; that is a conversation that needs to be held face to face. I step inside, leaving Will's message in my pocket.

Robin's office wraps its arms around me as I sink into the sofa, accepting a cup of tea gratefully.

'Thanks.' I blow over the rim.

'Everything OK?'

'Yes, fine, *fine*.'

'You seem a bit . . .' His face pulls, an expression as though I've said something particularly cringeworthy at a dinner party.

I laugh, shaking my head. 'I don't know where to start really, I've just discovered that my best friend has been in love with me for years, and that my husband thinks I reciprocate my friend's feelings and probably have for our entire marriage, and doesn't want to talk to me about it yet.'

'And how do you feel about that?'

'Sad? But most of all I feel angry.'

'How so?'

I put the cup down on the table and tuck my feet beneath me. 'Because Cole lied to me, and Will hid the truth, and now I'm left with all these memories that I have to readjust, you know? Like everything I thought I knew was all wrong. And I'm wondering, if this . . .' I point to him and then back to myself, 'has all been about my subconscious trying to tell me what everyone else could already see. I'm such an idiot.'

'You're not an idiot, Ella, there were just things in the way that stopped you from seeing the truth. When we first met, I got the impression that you never felt good enough for Will, am I right?'

'Well, yes, I mean you only have to look at us together to see that.'

'So is it possible that that is why you couldn't see what was in front of you? That your own insecurities were blocking you?'

'I'm not following.'

'In our first session, Cole was trying to tell you something and yet you couldn't hear him because you were looking at Will. Is it possible that your own insecurities about your relationship with Will are the reason you couldn't hear the truth? I'm going to pop on my therapist head for a minute if that's OK with you?'

'Sure, fill your boots.'

'Why is it that you have never felt good enough for Will? I don't want you to focus on the cosmetics of you as a couple, what else?'

'Well, I've always known that I loved him more than he loves me.'

'Why?'

'I . . . I don't know, I mean he says all the right things,

and physically there has never been a problem . . . I suppose I've just always had this sense that he's never really given me all of him, like there was a part of him that has been holding back. But me? I gave my whole body, my bones, my blood, my soul, everything I have I gave to Will, but I guess I've never really felt that I had all of him. Does that make sense?'

'It does, but let me ask you, how could he give you all of him if he believed that deep down you were in love with someone else? Is it possible that he was trying to protect himself?'

'From what?'

'From losing you.'

I blink.

'Right, back to the day job, that is if you still want to go ahead?'

I nod, still contemplating his words.

Robin takes me back to the fire. The scene is set, the burnt orange feel of that night now so clear in my memory.

I look across the fire. Will is watching me, his gaze steady, a small smile in my direction, a jolt in my stomach as I take in the obvious attraction he feels for me, something I had never registered before.

'OK, Ella, can you repeat what it is that Cole is saying?'

'We're the same, you and me,' my voice repeats. 'We aren't the star.' He glances over at Will. 'We just get trapped by its gravity.'

I tune my attention to my friend: I see the look in his eyes, the pure love and adoration there, the words he's saying so hard for him to say, but the meaning is crystal clear.

'Ella, I need to tell you something—'

I open my mouth to tell him to stop, to tell him that I don't feel the same way, but of course the words don't come. Instead, I look across the fire; I see Lisa on Will's lap.

I find myself moving away: the greys and whites of the

moonlit sky, the crunch of the brambles beneath my feet, the audience of trees, the branches pulling back the curtains to the archway ahead, my forty-one-year-old self waiting patiently.

I stand in front of her, the image clearer still; I register the small bump and bruise on her right temple as she pushes her hair back, but this time I'm not apprehensive: I'm ready.

We go through the same patches of conversation as before, but there are more fragments; she talks for a much longer period of time, but I still can't grasp the words. They come in snippets:

'There is so much . . . you won't remember . . . ' she shakes her head, '. . . but I . . . will . . . don't have much time.' She wipes a tear away from her face.

'Here . . . knows? Will . . . knows . . . trust me, I'm standing here . . . please try to remember that, Ella . . . enough.'

She puts her hand up and I reach up, reflecting her actions. I can't feel her; the air is cold and resists my movement like two magnets repelling each other. She smiles, and I see myself when I watch Will play, when I see the kids do well: complete and utter pride. Her hand drops and her stature changes.

The smile falls. She swallows hard, controlling herself, her expression becoming upset, torn, the tell-tale twitch of her lip as she tries to stop herself from crying.

'There is something . . . need to tell you . . . something is going to happen . . .'

The wind picks up; the lost signal of the phone returns, my pulse quickening. She continues talking, her mouth urgent, her posture changing, her hands moving quickly in front of her, gestures that I recognise as panic, as urgent. My heart is hammering in my chest, fear of what she is trying to say filming a layer of sweat above my lip. She wipes away tears from her cheek.

'*You have to believe this.*' She pinches the brooch. '*Remember this, you know this happened.*'

The sound dims again. I can feel myself moving against the sofa: I'm agitated, scared; I can feel the ridge along the sofa cushion in Robin's office.

'Ella, you're becoming distressed, so I'm going to bring you back now. You need to remember that you're safe. Five. Listen to the sound of my voice.'

'No,' I try to say but the noise is a blur.

'*Vase,*' she continues like a flash of inspiration. '*You're going to smash it . . . way out . . . this is real.*'

'What?'

'Four. You're feeling relaxed, calm, you can hear the sound of the clock in the room. Three.'

'What vase?' I ask, but her image is further away, my feet back on the travelator, dragging me backwards.

'Two. Your eyelids are flickering, you are becoming more aware of your surroundings, you can hear the tick of the clock.'

'One.'

I blink, the room coming into focus. Robin's face is close; his hand is on my wrist.

'Are you OK, Ella? You have been quite distraught. Can you sit up? I need you to breathe deeply, in, one, two, three, out, one, two, three. That's it, good girl.'

My whole body is shaking, like I have the flu.

'She was trying to tell me something, warn me about something. I need to go back.' I lie back down.

'I'm sorry, Ella, your pulse rate was very, very fast and you're clearly very shaken . . .'

'No, Robin, you have to take me back. Something is going to happen and she's scared. I need to know, put me back under.'

'I'm sorry, Ella, I can't in all good conscience . . . I worry I'd be risking your health.'

'Please, Robin, I have to know.'

'Let's just take a moment. Here, have some water.'

'I don't want any water,' I say, snapping. I see the grand-fatherly concern fall across his face. 'I'm sorry.'

'It's OK. Look, let's take a moment, let's process what has just happened. And remember this is just your subconscious trying to tell you something.' I calm down a little, slowing my breathing, feeling the cold water sliding down my throat.

I lean my head back against the sofa. 'It feels so real.'

'Do you remember what we talked about in the very first session? About how you can't trust everything you see under hypnosis, that the mind can make false memories?'

I nod, keeping my eyes closed, replaying her face, the panic and anxiety distorting her features. 'This is just your brain protecting you from something important. Your rela-tionships between Cole and Will are at a very difficult stage, I believe that you're just very scared about what is about to happen. No matter how carefully you handle the situation, from what you have told me, you're going to break some-one's heart. Your mind knows this, that's all.'

'I'm not so sure it is just that, though.' I let out a slow breath. 'I don't know, maybe you're right and it is all in my head.'

'The brain is a powerful thing.' He leans forward, his hands knotted. 'Can I get you something to eat? For the shock? Toffee?'

My laugh turns into a groan. 'Sorry, Robin, for . . . well, for all this drama.'

'I love a bit of a drama. My next patient has been trying to give up smoking for three years now but she still keeps com-ing back despite the fact that she never lets herself go under.'

'How do you know?'

'I just do, her breathing never slows.'

'Maybe she doesn't trust you? You are a pretty dodgy character.' I smile at him and he chuckles. 'So what next?'

'I would love to be able to recommend that we continue with your sessions, but, Ella, I must advise you that I wouldn't feel comfortable with that, given how distressed you were in your last trance. It wouldn't be ethical of me to carry on when I feel your health, both mental and physical, are at risk.'

'So, is this goodbye?' I ask, a lump forming in my throat.

'How about we don't say goodbye? Let's leave it as see you later?'

I smile at the synergy of the phrase.

We both stand and Robin holds out his hand.

'Oh, come here, you daft bugger.' I pull him into a hug, his warm cardigan soft beneath my chin. I pull back, tears in my eyes. Robin has been so much of my life over the past weeks that saying goodbye feels harder than I expect it to. I laugh at the tears in my eyes as he hands me a hanky.

'It's been a pleasure knowing you, Ella, and don't forget, if you ever fancy becoming vegan, I'm your man.'

'Thank you again, Robin, for everything.'

'You're welcome. And good luck. Will and Cole are both lucky to have had you in their lives. You deserve every happiness, Ella.'

I close the door behind me. Sally waits expectantly at the desk, her pen poised over the diary. She's just visible from behind a huge bouquet of flowers. I eye the yellow vase, feeling my heart rate pick up. The words *the vase* echo in my mind, sending a chill up my spine.

'Special occasion?' I ask.

'Oh, yes . . . it's my sixtieth today. These are from my sister, gorgeous, aren't they?'

'Oh, happy birthday! Yes, they are, gladioli are favourites of mine.'

'Same time next week?' She clicks the top of her pen where it hovers over the diary.

'No, um, my time here with Robin is over.'

'Oh! That's such a shame. We look forward to your visits, Ella, you're like a ray of sunshine, the office always feels a little brighter when you visit.'

'Really?'

'Yes! It's that smile, you could brighten the darkest of days with that!'

'Oh well, thank you, I hope you enjoy the rest of your birthday.'

'I will. Good luck, Ella.'

'You too.'

I hitch my bag on my shoulder, making sure not to step anywhere near the vase, backing away from it like Scooby-doo would from a ghost, and turn to go. I feel the contact my bag makes before the sound shatters into the office. I'm too late to stop the inevitable: in my care not to knock over the bouquet, my bag has instead caught a glass vase on the shelf behind me, fake lavender remains ridged amongst the shards of glass. My throat goes dry as I crouch down; heat rushes in my veins, my heart powering hard against my ribs. I'm vaguely aware of my apologies as Sally appears with a dust pan and brush, muttering that worse things happen at sea, saying how she had been meaning to throw this old thing out for ages anyway. I make my apologies again and leave the office, my feet running down the narrow staircase until I'm out onto the street, the number seven bus passing by.

'You know how mad you sound, right?' Amira drags the stand with handmade cards through the door and locks it behind her. I roll a piece of twine between my fingers as I lean against the counter. 'That because you knocked over a vase, you can time-travel?'

'I'm aware of that but, Amira, it can't be coincidence! It happened exactly as she said!'

'You sound like the Oracle in *The Matrix* . . . hey! That's probably where you got that from! Your subconscious is just tapping on your Keanu knowledge . . . isn't that what happens? He knocks over the vase as he leaves the room, and she says something like, what will fry your noodle is whether he would have knocked it over if she hadn't said it?'

'Huh. Maybe,' I sigh. 'Maybe you're right.'

On the radio, the newscaster is describing how red balloons across the UK have been released to raise money for research into heart conditions. I wonder if Amber has released one.

'And even if it's not your mind riffing on Keanu scenarios, who's to say that wouldn't have happened anyway?'

I sigh. 'Well, I can't.'

'Look, I know it might feel like these are all signs.' She waves jazz hands either side of her head, then reaches for a length of lemon ribbon, wrapping it back around the spool as she crosses the room towards me. 'But honestly, it's hardly a once in a lifetime thing that she's predicting, is it? The number seven passes all the time, of course you're going to get blasted eventually.'

'But I would never have knocked over that vase if she hadn't told me to, I was trying to stay away from the other one.'

'But you might have knocked it over anyway! It doesn't mean that you can time-travel just because you knocked over a vase. You own a florist's, Ella, do you really think that over the course of the next few years you won't knock over a vase or two?'

I sigh and pick at the edge of my pocket. 'You're right.'

'What's going on, Ella?' Amira comes to my side, unknotting her pinny.

'Cole kissed me.'

Amira throws up her hands in hallelujah.

'And?'

'And nothing. It was . . .'

'Mind-blowing? Erotic beyond all measure, made your girl parts quiver like jellyfish?'

'No! It was . . . empty.'

'Empty? What you mean? He didn't, you know . . .' she sticks out her pierced tongue and wiggles it about, 'slip you the tongue?'

'You're gross, and well, yes he did, but . . .' I raise my eyebrows to acknowledge that she is off the mark. 'It's not that, it just wasn't Will, there wasn't that THING, you know?'

She nods, leaning her back against the counter with an air of disappointment. 'How did he take it?'

'Not great, if I'm honest, and he's not returning my calls, so I'm worried he's gone on a bender.'

'So what now?'

'Now I tell Will everything.'

The bench is cold beneath my jeans and I wrap my scarf closer around my neck. It's Sunday; the clocks will go back next weekend. The past few days on my own have given me time to think, to process everything that has happened. I've walked through my time together with Will, looking at all the hidden cracks that were never visible to me before, replacing my own insecurities with Will's, watching our life through his eyes . . . and Cole's.

The park still holds its familiar Sunday-afternoon feel and shape from years before: time has made the edges a little fuller, the elm trees around the perimeter are taller and swollen with age, and the lime-fresh green paint of twenty years ago is now faded and cracked, but the path we walked along as teens remains the same – the same corners, the same bumps along the way. Will's figure rounds the corner, his hands deep in his pockets, his broad shoulders dipped, hair hidden by a black woollen hat.

'Hi.'

'Thanks for coming,' I say. He gives me a guarded smile and sits beside me.

I expect my voice to hold the nerves that have jittered beneath my skin over the last few weeks, the crushing feeling of embarrassment as I've tried to show Will how much *fun* I can be, how *beautiful* I am, how big a *mistake* he's been making by throwing it all away. But as I begin, there is none of that: my voice is steady and strong. I'm not here to convince him of anything, I'm here to tell him the truth.

'There are some things I need to say, Will, and whether you believe them or not is up to you, but they're the truth.'

Will nods, looking straight ahead. A gust of wind lifts a swirl of orange leaves, a mini tornado dancing in front of us like fire.

'I never knew that Cole was in love with me, Will.'

He turns his head, the wind making his cheeks pink, his eyes bright; his blue eyes briefly meet mine before returning their focus back on the leaves.

I reach out and turn his face back to me. There is so much pain in his eyes that my mouth goes dry: how could I have been so blind to the pain he had hidden for so long? 'But I can see it now, I can see everything so clearly.' I shake my head, clearing the fog that has been shrouding our lives together. 'I can't believe I was so blind.'

He looks down at his hands.

'But you have to believe me when I say that I don't feel the same way.'

He looks up at this, hope and surprise taking my breath away.

'He kissed me, Will.'

Will swallows hard, a small nod of acceptance with the action.

'And do you know what I felt?' I duck my head so he has

to look at me while I speak. 'Nothing.' I reach out and cup his face. 'I felt. Nothing. *You* are the man I want, you are the man I've *always* been in love with.'

Will leans his forehead against mine. 'Are you sure?' A film of tears glistens over his eyes, edging towards his eyelashes. 'I mean really sure, Ella? Because I don't think I can take it again if you're not.'

'I am.' I wipe a tear from beneath his eye. 'And I can prove it. Walk with me.'

We stand and I take Will's hand in mine. He focuses on our hands linked together; there is a glimmer of a smile but the crease between his eyebrows remains. He needs convincing of the truth. I almost laugh at how wrong we have both had it, all these years: there I was thinking I loved him more than he loved me, and the whole time, he was worried I didn't love him enough. I lead the way, heading to the back of the park, both of us silent, happy to just be us. Autumn folds around us, arms slipped into warm jackets, amber glowing street lamps firing up along the path, the smell of damp earth and log-burning smoke rising into the atmosphere from the houses surrounding the park. Red wellies kick up leaves, scarves are pulled closer around collarbones, fingers are covered by gloves as the temperature begins to drop. We follow the route we've taken so many times before, Jamie on Will's shoulders, Amber swinging a leg and a wing between us, but there are also the memories of a different man holding Amber's hand, another man running through the wood with Jamie's arms outstretched, making aeroplane noises. A thick sadness fills me as the memories jostle side by side: two men, two fathers, not the woman, her two children and her childhood friend at all. To me, it has always been so obvious that Cole wasn't my husband, but I look back at these memories now through a different lens, through the eyes of a woman on her daily jog, an octogenarian walking his golden lab, parents of other children from the school, and see what they have seen, see what Will has watched for years.

I lead Will towards the wood at the back of the field that still holds the Autumn Fair. Off in the distance, pallet wood is beginning to be stacked in time for the fair next week.

'You remember the night of the fair?' I begin as I hold back a branch and let Will step through. Beneath his feet the crack and snap of twigs, above the gentle whistle of wind, weaves through the timber. 'What I thought I saw?'

'The woman?'

'Mmmhmm.' Our feet continue along the path.

'Did I tell you what she looked like?' I watch my brown boots walk along freely, no hiss of brambles coming to stop my progress.

'She was old, tall, had a blue coat on?'

'Green, she had a green coat on and she wasn't *that* old,' I say, a smile in my voice meeting the curious look in Will's eyes. Ahead of us, the Abbey comes into view. It's not as ethereal as in my hypnosis sessions; there is moss growing over the arch, giving it a softer hue. I let go of Will's hand and walk towards the archway, resting my hand against it and turning back to Will.

'You see the thing is, Will . . . I think it was me.' His eyebrows rise, his head tilting. 'Here that night. Forty-one-year-old me, in a green coat and red scarf.' Will steps closer to me, leaning his shoulder against the brick. 'I know what it sounds like, but I've been seeing a hypnotist and . . .'

'A hypnotist?' Will asks.

'His name's Robin and I've been trying to recover the memories from that night.'

'Why?'

'Because this is the exact coat she was wearing.' I pull on the lapel. 'This was the scarf, and this . . .' I circle the brooch. 'She was wearing this. Don't you see? These were all gifts for my birthday, Will, the day after you asked me for a divorce and my whole world turned upside down.' He nods slowly, his face trying hard to remain impassive. 'And there are things she said that have happened.' I tell him about the vase, the bus, the feeling in my gut that I'm right. 'You think I've lost the plot, huh?' I bite my bottom lip.

'No . . .' he says the word slowly, 'but it's a lot to take in. So, what else did you say?'

'I don't know, I haven't been able to access all the memories yet. But that's why I've brought you here: I want to show you that I would never have changed anything. This happens next weekend, the night the clocks go back.' I take a step towards him. 'I want you to know that I wouldn't change a thing, Will. I don't want to go back and tell my younger self to marry Cole bloody Chapel, I don't want to tell her to not follow you to Europe, I don't want to warn her that she'll get pregnant, because then I wouldn't have Amber. I need you to see that I will always choose you. I will always choose us. It's always been us.'

He rests a hand against my cheek. 'Next week? You could go back and stop it all from happening? You really believe it, don't you?'

'Yup. I think. I mean . . . maybe? But it doesn't matter if it is or isn't real. The point is I'm not going. Come home, Will. Let's have our last date next Saturday.' I pause for a moment, 'Do you remember when we tried to have our anniversary dinner, the night Amber and Jamie had that stomach bug?'

'Ah, the beef bourguignon that ruined the casserole dish and the cremated roast potatoes?'

'That's the one . . . do you remember what we did?'

'How could I forget, the midnight feast to end all feasts.' He grins.

I laugh at the memory. Once they had finally gone to sleep, we had thrown away the remnants of our meal, raided the cupboards and eaten the prawns for our starter followed by cheese toasties and a chocolate tart out of the tin and a tub of ice cream.

'How about we have another midnight feast? Come over . . . just before twelve?'

'Midnight?' he questions as he considers my request before quirking a smile.

'Yeah, it'll be . . . fun, romantic, different to our normal dates. I'll cook us dinner and you'll see. The night I have the chance to go back and tell myself what I know now, as the clock turns past two on Sunday morning, I shall be drinking wine with the man I love. I want you to be with me in the hours that lead up to my . . .' I invert my fingers into speech marks, '"second chance". I want you to watch the hours pass by, to see that I don't want or need it. I want to prove to you that I would and will always choose you.' He chews the corner of his mouth, that incisor pulling at the flesh as he processes my words. 'But . . .' I take a deep breath. 'And here's the kicker. I will go back if *you* want me to.' I place my hand on his chest, feeling his heartbeat quicken.

'What? I don't understand.'

'If you want me to go back and tell young Ella to warn you about the fight, I will. I'll tell her to make sure you don't play that night. And then . . . then I'll tell her that once Jamie is born, you start sleeping around or, or do something horrible so I have to leave you . . . ooh! I could tell her that you give me herpes or . . . syphilis! Anyway, what I'm trying to say is you have a chance here . . . you could have an entirely different life. Your hand wouldn't get broken . . . who knows? You might still be with The Knock, living in a mansion, have thousands of adoring fans.' I grin and wiggle my eyebrows at him to lighten the mood before I waver.

'You would do that?'

I nod. 'I would do anything to make you happy, Will

Roberts, even if it means not having the life I love, with the man I love. But if you want me to do this, you need to be sure. Anything I say could change *everything*. Potentially. If young Ella remembers, I mean, I didn't the first time round so this is all probably speculation anyway, but . . .'

'Why would you think I'd want you to do that?' He holds my face in his hands, smooths my hair back, searching every part of my face with his eyes as if he's trying to drink me in.

'You could have everything, Will.' I fight back the tears. 'You could have the life you should have had, not a life with someone . . .' I gesture up and down at my body, 'like me.'

'*You* are everything I ever wanted, Ella.' He kisses my forehead, my cheeks, my eyelids, my lips, a kiss that fills my body with want and need. 'Just you.'

Chapter Forty

Then

17th October 2022

Cole walked from Ella's house, the feel of her lips still burning against his own. He knew it was the end of his relationship with Ella, and as he left her house, pain had ripped through him so viciously that he had found it hard to breathe. He replayed how she had looked, the utter certainty he could see in her eyes as she told him it would always be Will. With every word she spoke, he could feel it being hammered deeper into his chest, through the bone of his ribs, through the soft tissue of his heart; the pain was so visceral that he didn't know if he would be able to survive the puncture wound.

There was only one way Cole Chapel knew how to numb that pain.

But as he'd walked towards the off-licence, something had stopped him from opening the door, an emotion he couldn't yet place. It was as though from the puncture wound in his heart, something had begun to leak around the edges; it had released something, like a gust of cold air inside his body, an emotion that he couldn't identify. Cole's thoughts had followed their usual path of self-hatred, the voice in his head that told him he didn't deserve love, that his very existence had always been a problem. But as that strange sensation, that emotion like the remnants of a dream just moments after waking, began to grow, instead of the white-hot pain of regret and hate he was used to, a faint glimmer of buttery-warm hope began to fill him; after all, if he was the problem, wasn't he also the cure?

Cole now sat nursing a cold cup of coffee. 'Livin' La Vida Loca' played on a radio behind the counter and Cole thought back to that day when he had made the inside fair, how happy he had been making Ella laugh, the way she had looked at him as he rolled his top back down, that glimmer of hope as he asked if she was checking him out. The windows were steamed up, rain sliding down, as the deep rumbling of an engine vibrated through the glass as the bus idled at the stop.

He'd been sitting in the café for over an hour; the coffee in front of him had been replaced and although a slice of coffee cake had been planted in front of him at some point, Cole barely registered it.

Cole spun his white sobriety coin in front of him. Soon he would receive his one month sober coin; to a non-alcoholic might sound like nothing, but to him, a month without a drink might as well have been a year. Thoughts rolled through his head, a boulder gathering speed with each rotation of the coin, picking up more and more as his thoughts collided with each other. He was becoming aware that he had spent his life as a prisoner, held by the shackles of guilt for being alive when Jack was dead, handcuffed by his love for Ella . . . his body held behind invisible bars for his whole life. He had tried to find ways to ease the pain of those restraints with one-night stands, with Jules, with alcohol, but it was always still there when he woke, his skin rubbed raw from regret the next morning.

Cole Chapel had been condemned from the minute he

suggested dangling on the rope swing over a river with a power that he didn't understand.

Outside the window, a woman with a buggy climbed off the bus, a baby boy at her hip, a blonde girl clutching onto her mother's hand, looking wide-eyed as she was guided into the warmth and shelter of the café. Cole looked away, and drew the outline of his white chip among the steam of the window before wiping it away with his hand. A ball knocked against his boot, and he glanced down, reaching to pick it up. He caught the little girl's eye and she buried back into her mother's coat. Cole leant over the aisle. 'Excuse me?'

The woman, pretty, harassed and with a dry cough met his eyes. 'Oh, thank you!' She smiled gratefully and passed it back into her daughter's hand. 'Hold it tight, now.' She yanked her coat free as Cole smiled back, blowing a damp ringlet of hair away from her face. 'Do you have kids?'

'No, no.'

'Good decision.' She laughed. 'I haven't slept more than two hours in one go for two years.'

'Ah, I'm sure it's all worth it though.' Cole pulled a face at the baby boy juggling up and down on her hip, making him giggle.

The woman observed the good-looking man's playful and relaxed nature with her children. She watched his brown eyes twinkle beneath their red-rimmed edges, the easy manner with which he tucked his jaw-length curls behind his ears. He was exactly her type: before she'd met Leo, she had always been a sucker for the tall dark and dangerous ones. She glanced down to where a smattering of chest hair was visible above the curve of the vest beneath his checked shirt, and swallowed down a long-forgotten rush of lust.

'You're good with kids.' She smiled, shifting into the seat. 'Never been tempted?'

'Just never met the right woman, I guess.' Cole cleared his

throat and pocketed his coin, but not before she'd registered it. Her uncle had been an alcoholic and she noticed the token with a tug in her heart. She hoped he stayed on the road to recovery.

Bess approached the table: a cup of tea and toast, glass of milk and cookie for the little girl. The woman was now distracted with her children and Cole stood, said his goodbyes, and stepped out onto the path, where the rain fell from the sky. He tilted his head, looking up into the grey clouds, as a lightning bolt split the sky in two. Cole stayed where he was, opening his arms, the water covering his body, washing away the dirt of the past. He opened his eyes, and time stilled around him: the cars on the roads slowing to a crawl, the rain hesitant so he could watch each drop falling, feeling the splash of each one against his skin. He opened his mouth and let the rain fall into it; water dripped from his skin, into his shirt, his curls heavy with the weight of it as Cole felt the change: freedom.

As the rain continued to fall, in his chest Cole felt the grind of a key turning inside a lock, could hear the groan and creak of it, feel the ridges click, the springs and pins released, as somewhere inside a door swung open. He imagined pushing the door wider, and felt his feet stepping over the threshold.

Cole opened his eyes, and time settled back into its usual rhythm; the cars continued along the road and his footsteps continued along the path. Behind him, his feelings for Ella began to fall away, each layer of emotion dripping from his skin, sharp pain replaced by the cool water, a lightness of touch as he stepped forward.

Ella's truth had set him free.

Gravel sprayed up around Cole's tyres as he peered through his windscreen at the grand Victorian building in front of him. It looked like a luxury hotel from a Groupon voucher.

If only they did rehab on Groupon, he thought, as the steering wheel passed through his grip; his stay was going to take up most of his savings, but it was worth it.

Cole knew he was standing on the edge of recovery: without Ella to keep him stable and with her loss so close to his thoughts, this was the only way. He had made a choice, one that he had never made before. He wanted to live. He wanted his own family, his own happy ever after, and now, for the first time in his life, he felt like he could have it.

And so, as Cole Chapel opened the door and smiled, giving his name and condition to the receptionist and requesting voluntary rehabilitation, he knew that this was a new beginning for him, that finally he could begin to forgive himself.

Cole followed her along the corridor and was led into a small room where he was breathalysed, where he unleashed his cheeky grin to the nurse, and felt a warm sense of achievement when his reading was zero, when he sat down on the bed in the room that would be his home for the weeks that followed.

And even though, at that moment, Cole believed he would stay in the rehab clinic for as long as it took for him to recover properly, that room would be home to another tenant before the year was out.

Chapter Forty-One

Now

Ella

Saturday 29th October – The Night the Clocks go Back

I head past the shelves overflowing with all things Hallow-
een, make my way to the freezer section, grabbing a tub of
chocolate ice cream and stand in the queue behind a little
girl dressed as Cruella de Vil and a father with a green face
in a Frankenstein outfit. At half-five, the Co-op is busy, a
last minute dash for Saturday night wine and snacks for
early trick or treaters. My phone flashes with Will's face, a
message from him that makes my heart flutter. I laugh at my
reaction: this is how I used to feel when I was a teenager,
that mix of nerves and excitement when I would see him
waiting outside school for me, the way my stomach would
flip when he looked across the crowd at me as he played.
Ridiculous, given I'm forty-one and this is my husband of
over two decades, but there they are: butterflies.

**Do you need me to pick up anything for dinner?
Wine? Flux-Capacitor? Plutonium?'**

Not unless I need it?

I bite the skin around my French-manicured thumb and
watch the three dots running along the blue box.

It's not too late, you could wake up tomorrow living

in a chateau in France with your art curator husband and your work in the Louvre.

And you could wake up tomorrow with thousands of adoring fans.

But without you.

No need for a Flux Capacitor or Plutonium. I could go for a Chardonnay though?

Pork scratchings? ☺

No thanks, I'd like to be able to see tonight. See you later?

I-love-you.

I smile like a teenaged girl, twirling my hair for good measure.

I-love-you too.

I adjust the white-gold eternity rings in the grey velvet box, letting my index finger run along Will's band before leaning in and kissing the metal. I know it's a little sentimental and naff, but tonight is the start of the rest of our lives, the time when we have freely chosen to be together, not because of an accidental pregnancy, not because we needed someone to lean on, but because we love each other wholly and uncon-ditionally. *Oh, God, please don't let me sound part of the cast from* Four Weddings and a Funeral *when I give it him*. I reach for the silver paper and wrap the box carefully, adding a whirl of silver ribbon.

I step into my La Perla lingerie, a bit of an expense but if there is one night that allows for all-out red undies it's the night you ask your husband to spend the rest of his life with you. I reach for the hanger, the orange-silk dress floating over my arms and sliding over my skin. I spray my wrists with a new perfume called 'New Beginnings', giving my wrist a quick sniff. It's different to my usual citrus-fresh choice: it has something smoky about it, which feels right for the occasion; I'm going full-on optimistic symbolism tonight.

I sit on the edge of my bed, glance at the clock, which reads 11:24, and take a deep breath, dialling Cole's number.

'Hi, this is Cole. I'm not here at the moment, I've moved on to pastures new, but if you need to get in touch urgently, please contact Britney Spears, she has all my forwarding details.'

I allow a wry smile and clear my throat. 'Hi, it's me, Ella. I . . . I wanted to say that I hope you're doing OK. I popped into the garage when I saw the For Sale sign, the lads said that you've moved down south? I, I hope you're doing well. Tonight's the night I'm supposed to go . . .' I put on my best Doc Brown impression, '*back to the future*! but I'm not. But then, I think you always knew that deep down, didn't you? Anyway, I'd better go. Take care, Cole . . . and for what it's worth I am sor—' But my voice is cut off.

The sale of the garage is being handled by solicitors, apparently, and I can understand him needing a clean break, from here, from us, me . . . but still my stomach clenches at the thought of losing him. I smooth my hands over the orange material over my knees. But it's time: time for us to all start living our best lives. Jesus Christ, I'm going to have to stay away from Instagram for a while; I'm starting to sound like a walking talking Insta-post.

I look around the bedroom, at the candles burning, at the bed ready to be used, and smile.

Downstairs, I finish laying the table, fidgeting with napkins and wiping wine glasses as the minute hands slide towards midnight. I run the tap and take a long drink of water; I'm tempted to open the wine but I want to be completely sober when I give him the rings. I want to remember everything about Will when he answers me after I ask him to be my forever, I want to taste every word he says and

384

drink in every expression so I can finally believe that I am his forever as much as he is mine.

I go to the loo, double-check my make-up and return to the table. I turn my watch towards me; ten minutes late doesn't mean anything. I turn the volume up on the speakers, then turn it back down. I slice the cheese ready for the toasties, sprinkle dill over the prawns and turn the bottle in the cooler.

I'll wait until half past and then I'll ring him. He's probably waiting for a taxi; he wouldn't be able to fit all his stuff on the bike.

'Will, hi. It's no bother if you're running late. Give me a ring when you get this if there's a problem with getting a taxi or anything. Um, I can pick you up if you need a lift? You're probably at the door now!' I laugh and swallow down the worry that has started to rise in my throat. 'Call me when you get this? Bye.'

I begin pacing the room, looking up at the clock, my watch, pulling back the curtain and looking out onto the security-lit drive.

But there is no sign of Will.

And when the clock reads one, he still hasn't arrived.

Chapter Forty-Two

Then

As Ella closed up the florist's, humming to herself as she planned the midnight feast later that night, and while Cole lay on his bed in the small room inside Severn Oaks reading his first novel for a decade, Will sat on his mother's sofa, a letter drooping in his hand.

He re-read the letter again, the typeset of the paper headed with Severn Oaks Rehabilitation Centre, Cole's writing beneath.

Dear Will,

I know I'm the last person on earth that you want to hear from right now, and truth be told, if I was in your position, I would probably have already screwed this in a ball and thrown it in the bin. But on the off chance that you're still reading this, I wanted to ask you a favour (I'm almost certain you've chucked this in the bin now!). Still reading? You're a better man than I am, but then again, you always have been.

As you will have gathered from the rather fetching paper, I am in rehab – voluntarily, not that it matters, not really.

As part of my recovery, I want to apologise for my actions to those people I have hurt the most. And of all the people I have wronged, you are top of the list. Congrats.

I understand if you don't want to see my face ever again, but I want you to know that I'm sober, that I'm moving down south, not far from Mum. I'm going to start afresh . . . I've already got my eye on a small garage, not far from the sea.

I really hope that in time we will be able to put the past firmly behind us and who knows, maybe one day you could all come and visit? But I'll leave that in your hands. I'm done with trying to force my way into your life, I want my own.

I have open visitation . . . this is a private clinic and I'm here voluntarily so if you can face listening to me apologising for all the shit I've caused you, you can come any time, day or night. I'm about an hour away, but I understand if this is the last time we speak.

I don't think I ever said thank you for saving my life, Will, so even if I don't get to say sorry, at least I can say that.

Thank you. It's time for me to start living the life you gave me.

Cole

Will folded the letter back into the envelope and tapped it against his thigh. He swallowed down the heat at the back of his throat.

'Everything alright, darling?' Gwendoline sat opposite him with a groan, her paper-thin hands rubbing her knees, reminding her that she must learn to stretch before her dance class.

'Yeah.' Will held up the envelope. 'It's from Cole. He wants to see me, face to face. To apologise.'

'Ah. And how do you feel about that?'

'I don't know. Part of me wants to hear him out, but then I think of Jamie and Ella and . . .'

'Would it be difficult for you? To hear him out?'

'Not really. I . . .' Will exhaled loudly and leant back. 'I kind of owe it to him, but then I think about Jack and Jamie and—'

'Why do you think you owe him? I would have thought that Cole owes you?' Gwendoline folded her hands in her lap, concern etching her face.

Will paused, taking a deep breath. 'He was always there. Cole. In the days when I couldn't be. If I had been there more when the kids were little, when Ella needed me, then he wouldn't have been in our lives so much, and Ella wouldn't have turned to him when she should have turned to me. And I think that's when things changed, when he thought that he was the one she needed, that *they* needed. Does that make sense? It was *my* fault he never got on with his own life. But then I think about everything he has done and I want to screw this letter up and let him stew. I don't want to go and listen to him try to explain . . . to *forgive* him. Am I being an asshole?'

'You're not an asshole.'

Will laughed lightly at that. His mum never swore.

'You're just being stubborn. You always were. Do you remember when you and Jack used to play I spy?'

Will looked up at his mother; he still couldn't get used to her speaking about Jack as if it came naturally to her. It had taken ten years and a lot of therapy for her to get to where she was now. 'You would never give up. Jack would get bored and offer you a clue, but you always told him you didn't want it and you would persist and persist. And there was the game that lasted over two days, do you remember? We watched you becoming more and more frustrated and eventually Jack shouted it out because he was so fed up with playing it.'

The memory tugged a smile onto Will's face.

'Do you remember what it was?

'Phantom.'

'You should have been furious that Jack had spelt it wrong and that it started with a "p" not an "f", but instead, you told him it was a brilliant clue. You never were one for spite, even if you did go straight outside and kick the football as hard as you could.'

Will laughed lightly at that.

'He's in rehab, you said? Cole?'

Will nodded, rotating the envelope on his knee.

'You've already won, William, but maybe you could let him have the last word? You'll only end up regretting it if you don't. Now . . .' Gwendoline rose from the chair and rested her hand on her son's hair. 'Let me get you a nice cup of tea.'

'That would be lovely, thanks, Mum.'

'I'll make us some nice sandwiches too. I've got a lovely piece of ham in the fridge.'

Will checked the route and figured he could finish packing his bags, see Cole and be back in plenty of time for dinner at midnight. He liked the idea of turning the page on Cole Chapel before he started his new chapter with Ella.

The journey had taken longer than Will had hoped, roadworks and slow traffic hindering his progress, and as he parked his bike and followed the steps up to Severn Oaks, he glanced at his watch – 9:26 – and wondered if it would be too late for visitation. Will gave Cole's name, and was asked to sign a disclosure form against carrying any contraband, before being led to a community room: white walls; loud TV in the corner of the room; round tables and plastic chairs. Cole was laughing across the table at a woman, his curls tucked behind one ear, his body angled towards her, chair set away from the table. Cole had always been like that, Will observed, always making the person he was talking to feel like the most special person in the room, his body language open and friendly.

Of course, Will didn't know that Cole's opponent was a recovering methamphetamine addict and had been for most of her life. He saw the missing teeth, the sallow skin clinging to her cheekbones, the brittle grey hair held in a ponytail, and placed her at around her late sixties, whereas in fact, Helena was forty-eight. She came from a middle-class family in Cheshire and had never been diagnosed with bipolar until her first stint in rehab ten years before.

Cole laughed and spread a winning hand of cards out on the table before leaning back on his chair, hands clasped behind his head, legs stretched out beneath the table.

'Read 'em and weep, gorgeous, you owe me pudding!'

'Ah, shit . . . best out of three?' Helena winked in his direction, enjoying seeing Cole in high spirits today. Yesterday had been a tough one for the lad: he had opened up in group about his guilt over the death of his friend's brother, how he had never felt that he deserved to be alive, and then also the guilt of being in love with a married woman, how he had always been battling two addictions, the booze and his love for the woman who would never want him the same way as he wanted her. Helena recalled his words: 'And now I'm left with myself and if I'm stuck with this asshole for the rest of my life, I'd better make sure he's good company.' The group had laughed as Cole smiled and picked at the frayed denim in the knee-hole of his jeans; the counsellor thanked him for his honesty and moved on to the next patient, but in that sentence, Helena could sense a change in him. Sometimes the best recovery comes from the ability to see yourself and all your faults and accept them, but most importantly to find a way to forgive yourself.

'Oh, go on then,' Cole replied. Helena grinned at him.

Cole swooped up the cards and began shuffling, his eyes lifting from the table and looking up towards the doorway.

'Sorry, Hel, I've got a visitor. I'll tell you what, how about we put the pudding on ice until the next round, eh?'

Helena looked over to the good-looking man and wondered what business he had with Cole: there was no family resemblance, but anyone could see that there was a weight to their relationship . . . ah, the husband, she concluded. She watched Cole's flippant manner and easy smile tighten, his hands shaking slightly as he gathered the cards, watched the whites of his knuckles as he tucked the chair under and made his way across the room.

Will's throat was dry. He didn't know what to say to the man walking towards him, the man who had kissed his wife, who had been responsible for the death of his brother; if it was forgiveness Cole wanted, he wasn't sure he could give it.

'Thanks for coming,' Cole said, his hand landing on the edge of a plastic chair.

Will nodded once and cleared his throat. 'I got your letter.'

'So it would seem.' Cole chipped away a piece of white gloss from the edge of the chair with his nail. 'Walk?'

'Um, yeah, sorry for coming so late, I, I wasn't sure if they'd let me see you?'

'Oh it's a pretty cool place really . . . the staff, well they understand that late nights can be hardest for us, too much time and not a drop to help it pass. Open visitation helps.'

Will nodded. 'I haven't got long.' Will winced at his own words, but Cole showed no reaction, just opened the door wide for Will to step through.

'Don't worry, I won't take much of your time.'

Will had never been able to be around people the way Cole was; even now, in a rehab centre, he was saying hello to the porters, the patients, addressing them all by name, always adding some knowledge of their lives with a sentence of small talk as he led Will through the corridors.

Outside, the neat vast lawns were lit up by floodlights, the edges bordered with shrubbery, while in the centre stood an oak tree that had sat in the same spot for over three hundred years. Will followed Cole down the steps towards one of the benches that surrounded the paths, Cole gesturing for Will to sit.

'I won't keep you, Will, it means a lot that you came.' Cole sat beside him, his close proximity making Will uncomfortable.

'So, how does this work?' Will asked, unable to keep the bitterness out of his voice. 'You tell me you kissed my wife and I forgive you, is that it?' Will waited to see how his words affected him, but Cole didn't seem shocked; he just scratched the back of his neck and nodded.

'She told you, huh?'

'She did.'

'I'm not going to tell you I'm sorry, Will, because that would be a lie, and being in here, it makes you want to face the truth.'

Will's eyes were drawn to the coin that Cole was running over his knuckles, his fingers bending and flexing as the coin ran from left to right.

'I'm not sorry I kissed Ella, Will.' He stopped the coin and held it in his palm before looking up. 'Because it set me free. There was nothing there, not even a glimmer of hope, she recoiled from my touch as though I was fucking poison.'

Will expected to feel something like satisfaction at Cole's words, but all he felt was a deep sense of sadness.

'Did she tell you what she said?' Cole continued.

Will shook his head and waited. The October air ran past

them, kicking up stray leaves, lifting the ends of Cole's hair as it hurried on.

Cole's eyes bored into Will. 'It's Will, Cole, it's always been Will.' Cole smiled sadly, shaking his embarrassment away. 'I've spent my entire life in love with her, waiting for a moment that would never come. Ella doesn't love me like that, Will, but I always thought she might, you know? Somewhere deep down. And if there was even a chance, no matter how small, I was going to wait for her. But I'm done waiting, Will, I'm done living my life wishing I was *you*, wishing I had everything *you* had, wishing you were dead or having an affair, wishing *you* had never saved me.'

Will let Cole's words wash over him, a flood of pain, grief, regret. He waited for the anger he always felt for Cole to surface: this was it, his one chance to tell the man in front of him how much pain he had caused him. But instead, Will felt an understanding. After all, hadn't he done the exact same thing? Hung around, waiting for Ella to choose him?

'I don't blame you for Jack's death, Cole.' Will zipped up his jacket and tucked his hands in his pockets. 'I did . . . For a long time, I could never understand why you got to live and he didn't.' Will blew out a plume of air. 'But it was an accident, a terrible, unavoidable accident.'

'It was my fault, though.'

'It was my idea to go to the river in the first place.'

'My choice to swing so high on that rope.'

'But it could just as easily have been mine or Jack's, or any other kid hanging around that day. It's taken me a long time to come to terms with that, but it really wasn't your fault . . . and it wasn't mine either.'

'Thank you.'

Will looked away from the tears glistening in Cole's eyes. 'And I understand why you would hold on to the hope that Ella would one day choose you. Believe it or not, I understand that more than you know. But I can't forgive you for hurting my son, and I won't put him or Ella through that again. It ends here, Cole.'

'It does,' Cole agrees, lifting his chin, feeling that lightness again, sensing his skin beginning to repair where the shackles had rubbed him raw.

Will stood and offered Cole his hand. 'Goodbye, Cole.' Cole's hand was warm and firm against his own and Will could feel a strength behind it.

'Bye, Will.'

Will turned and began walking away.

'And for what it's worth . . .'

Cole's voice made Will hesitate; he turned his head over his shoulder.

'I'm glad it was you.'

Will gave him a grateful nod as another jigsaw piece slid into place.

He returned to his bike, pushing away the strange feeling in his gut that made him question if he would ever see Cole Chapel again.

Chapter Forty-Three

Now

Ella

Sunday 30th October 2022 — 01:15am

I scroll down my screen and call Gwen. I know it's late, but something is wrong – I can feel it shouting inside my skull, feel it crawling along my skin. The phone rings out and I hang up in frustration. My fingers dial Will again, my brain somehow taking charge, acting rationally though inside I feel like my head is being held under water while my lungs are gasping for air. 'The mobile you have called is not responding.'

Fuck! Oh God, Will, where are you? The clock looks down at me, and with each second passing I feel like Will is being dragged further away. I turn up the volume on the radio as the happy travel reporter begins his report: 'Avoid junction two on the M54 where there is a broken-down lorry, and this just in, avoid the A129 after reports of a fatal accident involving a motorbike and two cars, both lanes are temporarily closed so avoid the slip road until further notice and that's your travel update, back to Helen with the news and weather.'

I try Gwen's number again, my hand shaking; this time she picks up, her voice still holding that doctor's receptionist tone; she still repeats the landline number like something out of the seventies.

'Gwen, hi, it's Ella. Um, sorry to call so late, but is Will there?'

'Will?'

'Yes, he was supposed to be here over an hour ago and I'm getting a bit worried.'

'Oh, well he went to see Cole, but that was some time ago . . .'

'Cole?'

'Yes, he's in a rehabilitation centre, he wanted to see Will, to apologise.'

'How, um, do you know where that is?'

'Hold on, let me go and find the letter, it had an address on. I'm sure they've just got carried away . . . yes, yes, that must be it, too busy chattering.'

I swallow down the fear that I can hear in her voice, the tell-tale signs of the woman I remember from our early relationship, catching on her repetition. It wasn't until I had Amber that she began to recover in earnest.

'Ah here it is, Severn Oaks Rehabilitation Centre, Hatlock Grove, Staffordshire.'

'Thank you, Gwen, they've probably lost track of time, got carried away chatting. I'll call you as soon as I know anything.'

My blood runs like ice through my veins as I bring up Google Maps, entering my postcode and that of Severn Oaks with shaking hands: the A129 is lit up by a blue line, a direct route from there to here. *Oh, God, no, no, no.*

I dial Cole's number, but he doesn't pick up. I pace the length of the lounge while checking the route again and searching on my phone for details of a crash, but nothing comes up. I try Cole again, chewing the side of my nail and fighting back the tears as it goes to voicemail.

'Hi, Cole it's me. Look, Will's not home and I know he

came to see you, and I'm really worried something has happened to him. Call me as soon as you get this, OK?'

I check the road again, willing a taxi to pull up.

My phone vibrates and I swipe the screen urgently.

'Ells?'

'Cole! Thank God. When did he leave? Will? When did he leave?' My voice is fast and filled with panic.

'About an hour and a half, maybe two? Why? What's going on?'

'He's not answering his phone, Cole, and there's a motorbike accident on the A129.'

'OK, Ells? Ells? Calm down. He could be broken down, it doesn't mean it's Will, it could be anyone . . .'

I blink back a flash of my memory, of the archway, of me standing there, the urgent look on my face, the desperation. I glance at the clock, the face challenging me, the second hand wagging its finger towards one-thirty: hurry up, time's a-wasting.

'You have to go and find him, Cole.'

He pauses. 'I can't, I have to stay here. Look, why don't you call the police? I'm sure they will be able to find out what's happened. They can help you.'

'I can't!' I shout, already reaching for my coat. 'I don't have time to talk to them, I've only got half an hour, Cole.'

'What do you mean?' His voice is apprehensive. 'Ells? What do you mean?'

'You know what I mean! I have to get to the fair! *This* is why I go back, I have to stop it, I have to stop Will coming to see you, don't you see? I have to *save him*.'

'Wait, Ells!'

But I've already hung up the phone. I yank open the door beneath the stairs, smacking my head on the corner of the door as I shove my feet into my boots. I touch my finger to my temple, a smudge of red against my fingertips. I reach for my scarf, wrap it around my neck and grab a piece of tissue from the downstairs loo. Above the sink, today's reflection and that of twenty-three years ago stares back at me: the worry, the nervousness, the graze at my temple . . . at least now I know, I know why I would risk my past and my future: I have to save Will's life.

Chapter Forty-Four

Then

As Ella was lighting the candles in her bedroom and admiring her new underwear, Will sat with his hazard lights blinking on the side of the A129. He tried to start the engine, but again, after a splutter and a nasal groan, it remained stubborn. Will climbed off, rain filling a large pothole by his boot with tar-coloured liquid; he unzipped his pocket, reaching for his phone. Droplets slid along the leather of his gloves and before he could react, the phone slid from his grasp, skimming along the surface like a skipping stone, landing in the path of an Asda delivery lorry.

And the phone that Ella would desperately be trying to ring in an hour's time was destroyed, sprayed along the tarmac with the hiss of wet wheels.

'Bollocks!' Will stood on the side of the road, his arms thrown up in disbelief as intermittent cars sped past, red taillights, full beams focused forward. The rain continued to fall from the sky, the stars already hidden from him by the streetlights punctuating the darkness.

Will had no idea that he was seven miles away from the nearest services or that the emergency phone three miles away would be out of order, or that his leathers and tall broad frame would put off any drivers who would in other circumstances have offered him help. But as he began the long walk to the nearest exit, he did know that he had little choice. He kicked up the stand and began to push the dead weight of the bike forward.

Cole turned the page of the crime novel, his attention somewhere deep in espionage and car chases as his phone began to vibrate on the bedside table. He folded his page and rolled over to retrieve it. Seeing Ella's name, he returned the phone to the bedside table. He took a deep breath, forcing himself to resist the temptation; instead, he waited until the missed-call message ran along the top of the screen. Will's words, 'It ends here', were still thick and rich in his mind. Cole took the phone and slipped it into his top drawer, retrieved his book and turned his back.

An hour later, Cole rolled back over, folded the page again and stared at the blue light flashing from within the drawer. With a sigh and an air of defeat, he slid the drawer open and pulled out his phone. Seeing there were now three missed calls, and noticing the time, he chewed his bottom lip before selecting the answerphone messages. In the first, Ella was calm, and he couldn't help the small warmth that spread through him at the sound of her voice, but that warmth soon cooled as he listened to the next message. She was agitated: he could hear that there was real fear in her voice as he listened, sliding the menu down, taking in the time, and a sickness filled his stomach. Will should have been home ages ago. Cole replayed the second message, his mouth dry as he scrubbed the back of his head with his knuckles, his thumb returning Ella's number.

Panic tapped firm fingers in the digits of his spine; it ran a hand around his throat and squeezed. 'Ells?' He listened to her voice, could hear the desperation in it. He swallowed hard. 'I can't leave here.' Cole knew he needed to be strong if he was to survive this time. He needed to stay where he was safe if he were to resist oblivion, and he knew he wasn't ready, not just yet. The thirst for whisky was already in his thoughts: he pictured himself walking out of here, finding Will, handing him back to Ella, and knew the pain that would cause him would be too much of a catalyst; he could see himself walking into the bar not ten minutes away; the temptation would be too strong. But Ella was begging and the fear in her voice was already beginning to mix with the feeling in his stomach, a concoction of worry and confirmation that she was right: this wasn't like him, something really might have happened to Will, and he couldn't be responsible for another death. Surely God or fate or whoever was in charge of this world he lived in wouldn't do it to him twice?

Cole pushed the image of the bar with its amber liquids away; he boarded it up, turned off the lights, locked the doors and emptied the shelves so that all that remained was an empty husk of a building with nothing more than dust and mice to fill the silence. Cole concentrated on Ella's words, somehow understanding her irrational plan. Rather than going to the police and waiting for their help, she was going to go to the fair: she was going to walk through the stands as they had done all those years ago; she was going to stand next to the archway. She didn't need to tell him what she would say if her plan worked: he knew, deep in his bones, that she would tell her younger self that Cole Chapel would ruin her life, that he would be the cause of her divorce, the death of her husband.

But if it didn't work, this was his chance to put things right.

Cole yanked on his jacket, feeling for the keys in his pocket, fingering the sobriety coin, and slammed the doors behind him.

'And what can I do for you, Mr Chapel?' Edna asked, dipping her Jammie Dodger into her tea.

'I need to leave, just for a couple of hours.'

Edna had heard it all before, and her heart sank as she looked at the man in front of her. They had all sorts here, but there are those that get under your skin, and Cole Chapel was one of them. Oh, beneath the sparkly eyes and the easy manner, she could see the darkness that addiction held, but she really had held high hopes for him.

'If you discharge yourself, it's against doctor's advice, do you understand?'

'I'm not discharging myself, I promise, Edna, would I lie to you?' Cole flashed her a smirk and a wink.

'You'd lie to Jesus himself, I have no doubt. Just wait here. I'll go and fetch Mr Singh, he'll need to sign the papers.'

'OK, but can you be as fast as you can?'

'Sure, honey.'

Cole waited for her to turn the corner, then let himself out of the building.

Chapter Forty-Five

Now

Ella

Sunday 30th October 2022 — 01:43am

The wipers of the windscreen are working furiously to clear the rain. I lean forward towards the screen, wiping away the tears that are blurring my vision, blinking them back and turning the air-con up to full, the cool air hitting my wet face, stinging my skin and making me alert. The radio continues in the background as I indicate towards the park; another travel update isn't due until two o'clock and by then it will be too late. 'Walking on Sunshine' dances through the speakers. I turn off the stereo; the upbeat tempo doesn't fit this scene. The image of Will's bike, of his lifeless body, crashes into my mind but I push it away. I can stop this; I can stop it from happening. The steering wheel slides between my palms; I clasp it tightly as the car dips and judders along the roughly laid carpark, the signs for the October Fair signalling the way. I yank the handbrake, slamming the door behind me, my boots sinking into the gravel and mud. Remnants of the fair lie on the air, the last of the smoke from the bonfire, burnt sugar, donuts. The embers are just visible on the horizon, a lazy flickering of light taking its time to go out despite the rain. I follow the path that Will and I walked hand in hand just a week ago.

I run past the abandoned ticket booth. There is no one waiting for me to pay for entrance; the blackboard with prices is folded away and propped against a makeshift booth. The place is deserted, no undercurrent of closing up, of boxes being filled, the scrape of metal doors being slammed shut and padlocked. I run through the stalls, there are no staff looking at me quizzically as I hurry by, my coat flying out behind me, past the stall with bags of pink candyfloss being taken off hooks, past the new and improved octopus ride, the lights no longer blinking along its tentacles. My throat is dry and my breath scorched. Devoid of pop music, of children, the air feels thick with the unusual. My fingers fumble in my pocket for my phone: eight minutes until two o'clock. I dig my chin into my chest and force my feet to run faster. I run past silhouettes of the dodgems – the cars paused, suspended in their last joyride – and the ghoulish sign on the Ghost Train. The forest at the back of the fair looms ahead. I flick on the torch from my phone, my other hand yanking back the branches as my boots pound against the bracken. The patter of the rain is different here beneath the trees, broken, the rhythm a mixture of slaps and crashes, the deep bass of my feet the only solid tempo.

The archway comes into view, thoughts, snippets of conversation echoing through the trees: *Your brain will find a way to protect itself, Ella, it won't let you see something that will cause you distress*; I must remember to start with gentle beginnings. I trip over a branch, my knees dirty and mud-soaked as I pull myself back up. Amira's voice rings out: *But you don't remember, do you? So that means whatever you say doesn't work. It's all relative, you can't change what's already happened.* I shake her voice away as the ruin opens up in front of me, my hand landing on the cool stone. I have three minutes until the clocks go back.

The wind takes hold of the branches in an age-old dance,

the swirl of leaves fanning out around me as the steps of time lead the way.

I close my eyes and picture myself in Robin's room; I try to ignore the dance of the forest, replacing the ancient hum with the warmth of his voice, breathing in and out slowly.

I need to be calm; I can't frighten her or she won't remember.

The image of Will's body next to his bike surges bile into my mouth, but I push it away. I close my eyes tighter: Robin's room, the softness of the sofa, the sound of the clock.

Robin's voice reverberates around me: *If I was eighteen and I was told by some old man that I was going to have to watch the woman I loved more than anything in the world go through that hell, that I would watch her crumble before my eyes, that I wouldn't want to live with myself once she was gone, I would run for the hills, Ella.*

Images of my life flash past like a deck of cards fanned out before me: Will on my bed; our young bodies nervous and eager; his voice asking me to stay; the room in France; Will onstage; me sitting on the edge of the bath, the pregnancy test in my hand; Amber's tiny face; the house; plaster falling from the roof; Cole opening the door to the lounge; the magical inside park and his impersonation of Britney . . . the memories come thick and fast. The alarm on my phone rings, startling me; a crow caws and flaps from a branch above. I'd set it so that Will and I could raise a toast to the clocks going back, to the magic hour. I turn it off, the rain stops, a mist rising from the floor.

I take a deep breath, push my hair back from my face, and try to control the panic inside as I step forward, my hands either side of the stone as through the archway a girl walks towards me, red plaits, denim jacket, her voice whispering through the branches: 'Hello?'

Chapter Forty-Six

Then

Sunday 30th October 2022 — 01:40am

As Ella's red Nissan Qashqai headed towards the uneven ground of the October Fair carpark, mud splashing up the rims while 'Walking on Sunshine' tried to sing through the speakers, Cole pushed his foot down harder on the accelerator and headed to the A129. Even though he knew that the chances of being able to get to the accident were slim, he had promised Ella that he would try. He fumbled with the dash, connected his phone and tried the police; his signal was intermittent, and he breathed out a breath of relief as the call connected.

'Hello? Hi, I'm trying to find out some information about the accident on the A129 . . . I think my friend might be involved and—'

'Hold on, sir, I'll just transfer you to the road safety department.'

The line began to play some classical music as Cole indicated and turned onto the road. He flicked his headlamps onto full beam, taking care to ease his foot off the accelerator as the car followed the unfamiliar twists and turns.

'Hello? How can I help?' A voice crackled through his speakers.

'Hi, I'm ringing about the motorcycle accident on the A129. I think my friend might be involved, he was due home about two hours ago and there is a good chance he would have taken that route.'

'Right, well I can see your cause for concern. Can I take your name, please?'

'Cole Chapel.'

'Right then, Mr Chapel, let me see what I can find out for you. Can I take your friend's name and date of birth, and the make of the vehicle, if you have it?'

Cole reeled off the details and was put on hold again as he continued along the road. He tried to think logically: if Will had broken down, if he hadn't been involved in the accident, what would he have done?

Cole drummed his fingers against the steering wheel as the car followed the road. It was quiet, with only a few cars passing on the opposite side. Cole leant in closer to the dash, looking for signs of Will's bike, of Will, because try as he might, he couldn't shake the feeling that Ella was right, that Will *had* been in an accident. A breakdown was unlikely: Will Roberts would have AA cover, and he would have called Ella. Will Roberts was not the type of man to run out of charge on his phone. Cole bet Will had a back-up phone in case of emergencies, and a first aid kit. Will Roberts was always the hero.

Time had passed slowly for Will. His legs burned and his back felt like it was on fire; there was a gradual incline to the road that he had never been aware of before. He had no idea how long he had been walking, but it felt like hours. He stopped, straightened his back with a wince and sat on the bike, reaching for the last of the water from his bottle. He drained it and rested for a while, getting his breath back. The bike was too heavy, he'd been pushing it for too long, and he had no idea how far away the nearest exit was. He didn't want to leave it on the roadside, but Will couldn't see that he had any choice. He would just have to walk the rest of the way and come back for it when he found help.

The pain in his calves burned as Will resumed his journey along the road. Sweat ran down his spine – beneath his leathers, his skin was slick – and the rain persisted, heavy fat drops soaking every part of his exposed skin. Wet rain, Ella called this type. He continued to walk, completely unaware of the accident that lay ahead, where a young boy of nineteen had just lost his life: a split-second decision to overtake a car in hazardous conditions had meant he lost control of his bike. Toby, the boy was called: he'd been on his way back from meeting his girlfriend's parents for the first time.

Cole's fingers drummed on the steering wheel.

'Hello? Mr Chapel?' The voice through the speakers brought him back.

'Hi, yes?'

'I have some news that may bring you comfort. The casualty in the accident was a young man, and the bike doesn't match your description.'

Cole let out a breath he didn't know he was holding. 'Thank you, thank you so much. I'll let his wife know.'

'I'm sure there will be a reasonable explanation, but don't hesitate to call back if you have any more concerns.'

Cole ended the call, but as he reached for his phone screen to call Ella, something caught his attention, his eyes focusing on the outline of a figure walking along the edge of the road. The figure was momentarily lit up by the backlighting of an oncoming car, the headlights not straight and steady but veering slowly to the left and back over to the right. Cole would have recognised that walk anywhere: the set of Will's shoulders, his chin dipped into his chest.

The car lighting up Will's silhouette was a white BMW and behind the wheel sat Steve. Steve had been awake for twenty-three hours and had been drunk for fifteen of them. As a travelling salesman, he was used to driving in the dark, used to late lunches that rolled into early dinners, followed by one for the road. It had been a long day, and as he shook his head, trying to sober himself, he knew that last double whisky had been a bad idea.

Cole's dark eyes widened as they tracked the gradual slide of the car rushing towards Will, the brief jerk back into the middle of the road when the driver corrected himself. Blood rushed in Cole's ears, the pounding of his heart knocking against his rib cage. He forced his hand hard on the centre of the wheel, the cool black plastic resisting the pressure as his palm forced down on it.

But as the sound of the horn screeched through the air, Cole knew that this would not save his friend.

The decision Cole arrived at was made in one second – one second to you, to Steve, to Will, to Ella, who was running through the fair – but to Cole, that one second felt endless.

On the road, where time ran freely, Steve was jolted awake by the sound of a horn, by the lights from the car in front of him: he must have dozed for a second, just a second, he thought to himself as he registered a person on the verge.

But it was too late for Steve to correct the car's impact.

And Cole knew; he knew this was his last chance. His chance to put right all the wrongs he had made, to give Ella back her freedom.

Time slackened, relaxed; the pin-sharp rain began falling softly like blossom from an apple tree on a gentle warm breeze; the wipers held still, their blades pointing to the right. The lights from the car behind Will shone brightly: a spotlight on a stage, Will's silhouette etched perfectly out of the background, frozen still, a snapshot before the scene had a chance to continue, his head turning to look behind him, his body mid-stride.

Cole smiled, with a deep sense of completion, of his life coming full circle. He could save Will, and for once in his life, he would get to be the hero.

Chapter Forty-Seven

Now

Ella

Sunday 30th October — 02:00am

My whole body is shaking as the cool fog envelops me. Through the archway and the grey-blue haze stands Ella Walker. Her body is like a character being broadcast from an old TV: the image is soft, it wavers, a re-run from a time before high definition and smart phones. Behind her and in the distance, the glow of a small bonfire, the silhouettes of Will, Cole and the others just visible further beyond. I'm lightheaded; my skin beneath my coat is alight with goosebumps.

It's real; it was all real. I can stop Will from going to see Cole.

My heartbeat pounds away: the seconds passing, my own internal clock. My time is running out; I need to make her listen.

'Ella? Can you hear me?' I ask, the words I recall from my sessions with Robin falling naturally from my mouth, as though I was always supposed to say them.

She nods. She looks so young; it's hard to believe that she is on the verge of motherhood.

I clear that thought away. 'Good, that's good.' I place my

hands either side of the air between us, but there is resistance in the atmosphere, like repelling magnets.

I look past her to where, beyond, I know that Will waits, and for a moment I forget myself; the need to run past her to take Will in my arms is consuming. I want to hold him, to tell him not to go and see Cole tonight, to come to me, to stay with me, where he belongs. I bang my fists against the air, the traffic-report jingle tinkling through the trees like a windchime, *a fatal motorcycle accident* screaming in my ears.

I take a deep breath. I need to do this right. I can see she is scared; her Doc Martens are edging backwards. Robin's voice is carried on the wind, weaving through the trees, through the crackle of leaves: *Our memories are clever things. People who have had a traumatic experience, for example, are protected from that memory – our mind suppresses it.* This was his warning not to rush in, not to scare my mind into hiding this information from myself. I need to make her remember.

But I don't, do I? My own voice this time, as the memory of my conversation with Cole pushes forward, then his words: *First rule of time-travel – if it's already happened, it's happened.* I shake the thought from my mind. I have to try to make her remember this time.

'There is nothing to be scared of, Ella. I'm here to help you have a happy life, a safe life. And do you know the best way to start? Have cake for breakfast.' I smile as she squints.

'I can't hear you.' She leans in, her words floating back at me. I repeat myself.

'Have cake for breakfast, every day.' I smile. 'Why wait for the end of the meal?' She steps closer, her dark almond-shaped eyes wide and searching.

She will hear these words, just not yet.

I look at her, this girl, and bite down on my lip. I used to think I was chubby, and yet the girl who stands in front of me now is curvy in all the right places. I hated my nose, still do really; but as she scratches it, I can see that it fits her face perfectly. The beauty spot that I tried so hard to cover with concealer sits in the curve of her cheek; she doesn't know yet how Will always touches his finger to it when he kisses me goodbye.

Tears prick behind my eyes at the thought of him. Is he safe? Is he dead? Is he waiting outside our house?

Ella Walker pulls at the cuffs of her jacket. I remember how awkward I had felt in it, how the Levi 501s that Mum bought me for my birthday never fitted like they should have, and yet as Ella Walker stands in front of me, I can see what they saw. I can see the girl Will Roberts fell in love with, the woman who plagued Cole's life, the woman she would become, if only I knew then what I know now.

'Why are you here?' she asks. The news story rolls into my mind, pushing everything aside: the image of Will lying by the road, his motorbike destroyed.

'I can't tell you, it's too soon, you won't remember. Ask Robin.' But then again, she doesn't know who Robin is yet. Is that why I chose him out of all the hypnotists I looked for? Was it there already, buried deep in my subconscious, the same way that having cake for breakfast was? If that was in there somewhere, then what if everything I say now is hidden deep down inside? Could I fix years of never feeling good enough for Will, of never being able to see how much he loved me? I take a deep breath. The wind blows stray wisps of hair around my face as I contemplate my words, think about everything I wish I had known about myself back then.

'I'm here to tell you how beautiful you are, Ella.' I smile. 'Just as yourself. I hope you can see that.' I wipe away a stray tear. 'You don't need to compare yourself to others, to try and impress them.'

Young Ella's image is obscured by the thickening of fog,

like a cloud passing in front of the sun. I rush on as the cloud moves forward.

'You have your whole life ahead, Ella, and it's a good life. Don't waste it worrying if you're pretty enough, if you're clever enough, if your nose is the right shape.' I swallow down the lump in my throat. 'Enjoy every minute with Will, let him take you home, cherish every day you get to hold him, to talk to him, to be with him because he loves you, Ella, you . . . you have to believe that.' I tap my hand over my heart, beating out I-love-you.

Around me I can feel a shift in the weight of the atmosphere, like the first pressure of an incoming thunderstorm, and I know that my time is running out. I rush on.

'You need to remember what I'm saying, Ella. And I know that when you wake up tomorrow, you will think none of this is real, but it *is*, Ella.'

I pinch the curve of the brooch as the words fall from my lips.

'When you leave Robin's office, you will be soaked by the number seven bus and you'll have to throw away your favourite pair of yellow suede boots. Oh! And the vase, you'll knock over the vase when you leave his office. This is real, Ella, you have to believe what I'm saying, because if you don't, then . . .' The dread of the accident prickles my skin, and I wipe away a tear with the heel of my hand. 'I don't know if you'll remember this, I mean I didn't remember it last time, so who knows?' I straighten my back and lean in closer. I remember the view from the other side, how the sound of my voice came and went. I clear my throat and speak louder; the pressure in the air builds. 'Something is going to happen, something that is going to change everything.' I try to smile; I try to hide the fear. 'The night this happens, there is an a—'

I'm about to say more but I stop.

My words circle my body like a tornado, whipping up the leaves as I stand on the edge of the storm. I want to tell her he might be dead, I want to tell her more, but if I do . . . I won't remember. I think of the brambles trying to stop me accessing this part of the night, the fractured sound . . . I have to remember some of this – if I don't, then tomorrow I might be faced with a life without him. The leaves fall back to the ground and I shake my head, trying to clear the jumble of thoughts rushing to be heard.

Blood pounds in my ears. Around me everything stills. The wind holds its breath, the birds in the trees sit motionless: the eye of the storm.

If I tell her I think Will might be dead, I could scare her. What if she never walks home with him? I think of the rest of my life without Will and it cuts through me like ice and glass, but then I think of a life without him in it at all, without our children, and the pain I feel is unbearable.

Isn't it better to have loved and lost than never to have loved at all?

If I tell her about the accident, we could lose everything we've ever had. If I scare her with the truth, she might never come to have the life I love; she may never have our children. I realise I would endure a thousand of Will's deaths rather than a life without them.

And so would Will.

But I can help her, if somewhere deep down she hears me. If somewhere deep down I remember this, I will be strong enough to fight for him, to stop him from leaving me, to have these last precious weeks, to learn how much he has always loved me.

The reality of why I'm here settles over me; a warmth fills my chest.

That's it. I realise I have to believe in myself enough to fight for him, to keep the last few weeks of our marriage alive . . . so we can learn how much we love each other. So that *he* knows it was always him that I loved; if something *has* happened to him, I want him to know that. That I would still always choose him.

I shake my head, desperate now. No. I can *still* stop it from happening, I don't have to tell her I think he's dead, but I could warn her to stop Will from going to see Cole tonight.

'I can't hear you,' Ella Walker says.

The wind stirs again; a branch cracks.

I have to help them; I have to help *us*.

'Something is going to happen, Ella,' I begin, 'and you will feel alone and scared, but you are strong enough to cope with it. Do you hear me? You are strong, beautiful, clever, and full of life, you have to believe in yourself. You are loved, Ella, so very much. Will Roberts loves you, much more than you think. You are brave enough to face what is about to happen, you *will* survive it all.'

The fog condenses, the air pressure pushes down on my head and Ella Walker's image begins to tilt from one side to the other. I panic, desperate words begin falling from my mouth. 'On this night, but a long time in the future, in 2022, you must stop Will from going to see Cole. Ella? Ella, can you hear me? Do *not* let Will visit Cole.' And then I have the same feeling as I did that night in 1999, of trying to stay upright on a ship's deck, before everything goes black and I fall to the floor.

I don't know how long I have been on the ground. My hair is matted, rain and mud clings to the side of my face, my fingers are white, my mouth dry, my lip bleeding. Next to me, my phone rings. My nails scrape mud and dirt beneath them as I grapple for it, turning it over – a number I don't recognise.

'Hello?' My voice is brittle. I sit myself up, hugging my knees, my body shaking. 'Hello?!' I shout. 'Will? Is that you? Will?!'

There is a voice, male, a crackle, but then all that follows is silence as the line goes dead.

Chapter Forty-Eight

Then

Sunday 30th October 2022 — 02:00am

As Cole's hand began to turn the steering wheel, as water sprayed up from the wheels beneath him, Cole thought of Ella: he thought of her gap-toothed smile as he chased her around the garden, her knees scraped from a fall off her bike; he pictured her looking across the fire at Will; he felt the weight of her as she sat on his shoulders at a festival, could feel the plastic from her wellies against his collarbone; he saw her pale and sick with Amber; he saw the kingfisher that flew away, taking his dreams of a life with Ella with it; saw himself dancing like Ricky Martin as he put the light back in her eyes and the sadness in her as she told him they would never be more than friends.

And then there was Will as a seventeen-year-old, water dripping from his hair as he leant over him, coughing and spluttering river from his lungs. Cole replayed the panic in his eyes as he asked where Jack was, saw Will at the funeral, head down, his mother's hand on his arm. The way Will looked at Ella when they were first together, like he was surprised to see her beside him, like he didn't deserve her.

Cole's foot pushed a little more fiercely on the pedal as he saw the damage he had done to their relationship: when Will would come home with a smile that dropped when he saw Cole in his place; his look of hurt and confusion when Jamie reached for Cole instead of him.

But now, he could fix it. He could fix it all.

Cole felt every moment of the impact of his actions, but instead of feeling pain as his whole body lurched forward, as his bonnet hit the side of the white BMW, careering it away from its trajectory towards Will, he pictured Ella opening the door, Will collapsing into her arms, the joy of having him home, the relief she would feel. And as the windscreen shattered, with each piece of debris that cut and scraped at his face, Cole could feel the pieces of their life being put back together.

From the side of the road, Will's body reacted to the speed of the car in front of him as it banked across the road. His thoughts were jumbled, panicked, instinct telling him to get out of the way, the realisation that Cole's car was somehow here and smashing into the white car heading towards him sending his mind spinning in confusion as his body dived out of the way. As Will's head hit the ground, a primeval screech of metal on metal tore through the atmosphere, tyres spinning and colliding, radiators hissing.

'Cole!' Will scrambled from the roadside. The white BMW was upside down, a man inside groaning and asking for help, but Will limped across the road, yanking open Cole's door. Will had never been close to an accident like this before, but nothing could have prepared him for what faced him as he opened the door.

Cole's eyes rolled in the back of his head. Blood covered one side of his face; he coughed, blood in his mouth, falling from his lips. Tears sprang unchecked in Will's eyes as he knelt down, the crunch of glass beneath his knees.

'Cole? Can you hear me?' He wanted to sound in control, but he wasn't; he had never felt more helpless in his life.

He thought of CPR, but Cole was still breathing; he thought of stopping the bleeding but there was debris lodged in his neck and he knew you shouldn't remove any objects; he knew he shouldn't move him in case of spinal injury. Will dragged himself to his feet, limping over to the BMW. He tried to open the passenger door where the driver lay still with his eyes closed. Will banged his fist against the glass.

But the driver of the car didn't respond. Will tried to prise open the other doors, but the whole exterior of the car was buckled and twisted, all the doors locked.

'Fuuuuuck!' Will banged against the driver's window but no response came from within. He limped back to Cole, crouching down, his hands hovering over Cole's body, wanting to help but not knowing what to do with them; instead he reached for Cole's hand, squeezing it tightly as Cole's eyes began to close.

Will's eyes scanned the inside of the car, looking for Cole's phone.

'Wake up, Cole! Wake up!'

Cole's eyes opened, his head turning a fraction towards Will.

That was it: he would talk to Cole, keep him conscious, that was what he should do. 'It's OK, you've been in an accident, you're going to get through this, mate, you're going to pull through.' His words tumbled from his mouth as behind him came the sound of an engine, a new set of headlights.

Flo was a red-headed mother of two and had been on her way home from a nightshift at a restaurant when she saw the accident. She slipped on her hazard lights, grabbed her phone and rushed to the man who was kneeling down beside one of the cars, seemingly unharmed.

'How can I help?' Flo asked, her eyes flitting over the upside-down BMW. 'Have you called an ambulance?'

Will shook his head. He wanted to say more, he wanted to

tell her this man had just saved his life, that he was a friend, that he had always been a friend. But all that came out was, 'No phone.'

'I'll ring now. Are you hurt?'

Will shook his head. In the background, he registered the woman's urgent voice on the phone; he could hear her talking to the man in the car behind. She was reassuring, calm.

'There's an ambulance on the way,' Will told Cole. 'And they will patch you up in no time. No time at all.' He looked up into the black sky: the stars were visible from here, the rain was beginning to stop, he observed with a strange detachment. He returned his gaze to Cole, who stared blankly back. 'You're going to be fine, Cole. Everything is going to be fine. Had to be the hero, huh?' Will's words hitched as he swallowed down the pain searing the back of his throat. He felt the lie on his tongue like a blister between his teeth. He knew everything was not going to be fine.

But Will was wrong. Because as Cole used every ounce of power left in his failing body, he squeezed Will's hand. And in the last moments of Cole Chapel's life, he looked deep into Will's eyes, and tried to convey everything he wanted to say: that he was sorry, that he was grateful, that he would miss them, that he was glad that he'd got to be part of their lives, that he wanted them to be happy. That he loved them.

As Will searched Cole's face, somehow he knew; he knew everything Cole was trying to tell him in that last look.

'I know,' Will replied.

And as the final piece of Cole Chapel's part in the jigsaw was placed, he was grateful that the last person he saw was Will Roberts, the man he'd always wanted to be.

His hero.

And for the first time in his life, Cole Chapel felt peace.

Epilogue

One Year Later

I slam the doors closed on the removal van and step back, Will's arms around my shoulders as we turn and walk back towards the house, the *Sold* sign swinging in the October sun. I tilt my head up towards him and he kisses me deeply.

'Ugh, seriously, can't you two at least do that when we're not around?' Amber scrunches up her nose while Jamie hides his eyes behind his hand. Will and I pull apart and grin.

'Are you finished?' Jamie asks, peeping from between his fingers.

'Yes,' I laugh.

'For now,' Will adds, winking at me.

'Thank God for that.' Amber pushes her sunglasses up her nose and tightens her ponytail, white-blonde hair swaying neatly behind her before Jam grabs hold of her scrunchie, letting her hair free.

'Ugh, why are you such a shit!' Amber yells, chasing after him as he holds the scrunchie above her head and out of her reach.

'Jam, stop tormenting your sister.'

'But it's so easy!'

Amber shrugs her shoulders and walks slowly over to his car, the red convertible that Cole left him in his will.

In the months after Cole's death, an emptiness surrounded us. Life without Cole Chapel felt broken, slanted; without the third edge of our triangle we didn't know how to exist, but we found our way: Will and I leant against each other and somehow the two of us were strong enough to stay upright.

In those months, I would often dream of waking up on the ground, dirt and mud in my nails as I scrambled for the phone. Sometimes I would hear Cole on the other end, telling me he was OK, not Will's voice as he finally got through to me that night, the one telling me he was safe, but that Cole was dead.

I would replay that night over and over again, analysing everything I said, questioning myself for not warning my younger self about Cole's alcoholism, for not trying to save him a life of torment, but then I would hear his voice: '*This is all me, Ella – there is nothing you can say or do that will stop me having a drink if I want one – it all comes down to me.*' Nothing I could have said would have changed Cole from going down that road; it was already written, the moment he swung on that rope swing. But that's the problem with hindsight, isn't it? You can only see your mistakes after you've made them. I'd always thought that Cole was the broken one in our relationship; it took losing him to show me that it was the other way around: he was the rock, he was my anchor. It's taken me a long time to forgive myself, for not doing more to save him, but I have, because the last thing Cole would have wanted would be for me to waste the life he has given me back on regrets.

Cole was more organised in his affairs than any of us expected. His will was up-to-date and with the sale of the garage, he was able to leave the kids a small nest egg and a car each. The rest of his estate was left to his mum and myself, but I have donated my share to a small refuge for alcoholics, where his money is being spent on helping others on the road to recovery. Amira volunteers there at the weekends. She has a young apprentice at the shop and is already designing new mood boards, wanting to 'mix things up a bit'.

Amber runs a manicured finger along the bonnet, side-eyeing Jamie, holding out her other hand towards the blue sky, flicking the end of her nails. 'You know, they're quite sharp really. Who knows what damage they could do to the paint-work of a car?'

Jam jogs over to Amber, hands up in surrender, before flicking her scrunchie back at her. 'Fine, you win.'

I had a call yesterday from Severn Oaks. As part of his recovery, Cole recorded apology messages to us both. The recordings were never meant to be seen by intended recipients; they were an exercise, to be revisited after a year to help with the longevity of recovery. Cole's video was stored away with the other patients' but he had signed permission for it to be released in the event of his death. It feels right somehow, to see him for the last time on the anniversary of his death. A year ago today, I told myself I was strong enough to survive what was ahead, and I was. Even though there were days when I couldn't lift my head from the pillow, or eat, or sleep, I survived because I knew I had Will, wholly and completely. When my mind wanders back to that night, I question if somewhere deep down the things I said to myself worked, if they gave me the self-belief to fight for Will when he asked for a divorce. If I hadn't seen Robin and allowed myself to access those memories, if I hadn't gone back and told myself those things – how strong I am, how much Will loved me – would I have let him go? Would I have just believed that I was never good enough for him?

We are both taking a sabbatical and have sold the house, putting everything in storage, and we are using the money to travel around Europe for a year, maybe two. Who knows? But before we go, we're going to see Cole for the last time.

In the back of Jamie's car, the boxes from his room are piled up. Amber has moved into a smart one-bed apartment, an easy journey between her medical school and the hospital she is due to start her placement at, using Cole's money for a deposit.

'Do you need a lift home?' Jam asks her as she pulls her hair back up.

'Please.'

He swings his keys around his middle finger and she rolls her eyes as Jamie grabs the few boxes he's taking to leave in Kenny and Caterina's spare room.

Kenny finally met his soulmate at a role-playing event: she was dressed as Guinevere and he stood on her toe; her first words to him were, 'I love your bow tie.' It was love at first sight. They moved into their house last month and baby Lance is due in the spring.

'So, how long until you're back?' Amber asks.

'Well . . .' I begin, 'we don't know really. We'll see how it goes.'

Jamie snorts as he slams the boot shut. 'Yeah, right. Come on, Dad, where is it?'

'Where's what?' Will replies, frowning.

'The itinerary . . . come on, I know it's hidden somewhere, there is no way you are going to "see how it goes".'

'He doesn't have an itinerary!' I laugh.

Amber pushes her lips together, meeting Will's eyes as he shifts from foot to foot.

'You have an itinerary?' I ask him.

'Noooo. Not as such.'

Jamie bursts out laughing.

I hold my hand out to him, palm up. 'OK, hand it over, Roberts. We're supposed to be flying by the seat of our pants, remember?'

He pulls out a folded piece of paper and hands it to me.

'Oh!' I say when I scan through his neat handwriting, opening and closing times beside each entry. 'These are all art galleries.'

'They are. I didn't want you to miss any.'

I wrap my arms around his neck and kiss him.

'And we're off,' Jam says as we pull apart.

Amber folds me into a hug, landing a kiss on my cheek. 'Have the *best* time and send me lots of pictures and messages.'

'I will.'

Jamie jumps on Will's back, their bodies practically the same height and build.

Will stumbles forward, but he's laughing. 'Get off, you pillock!'

Jamie plants a sloppy kiss on his cheek. Their relationship has changed since Cole's death. Jamie took it particularly hard, and they found their way to each other through the loss and sadness. I think Will was worried that Jamie was drinking too much on his own, so they began to drink together, then they started to not drink together, finding different ways to spend their time, tinkering on the car being one.

We follow our children as they climb into the car, the windows wound down and wishes of 'Have fun' and 'Don't do anything I wouldn't do' shouted with waving hands as they round the corner out of view.

It feels like the end of a chapter, like that feeling when you slot in the final piece in a jigsaw, that sense of completion, that after all the hard work you have the finished piece in front of you. And then you break it all up and start a new one. That's how this feels, like I'm about to start a new picture, a new puzzle, a new beginning.

'Ready?' Will asks, his forehead against mine.

'Ready.'

Then

29th October 2022

Cole took a last drag of his cigarette and crunched it beneath his boot. He'd decided he was going to give them up soon, try one of those vape things instead. Properly say goodbye to the man he was. It was the last Saturday in October and the smell of autumn was in the air. He thought of Ella and wondered if she would go to the archway after all. Would she go back and change all of their lives?

He jogged up the steps, tucking his lighter in his pocket and high-fiving Jonathon on his way past.

'Linda is looking for you!'

'Uh-oh. Better lock my doors, she can't resist my charms, that one!'

Jonathon shook his head. That Cole Chapel, what a character.

'And just where have you been?' Linda put her hands on her hips and shook her head, her large chest bouncing up and down with the action.

'Quick smoke, I know you like the bad boys.' He winked at her as she laughed.

'You could charm the birds out of the trees.'

'I know, I know, but I only have eyes for you, you know that!'

'Right well, you'll need those eyes for your recording.'

'Ah shit, is that today?'

'No it was yesterday, but you sweet-talked Lou into playing chess instead. You're not getting out of it again.'

Cole smirked as he linked arms with her. 'Tell me again why you won't marry me?'

'What, apart from the fact I'm already married and I'm sixty years old?' she replied as she led them into the small interview room.

'Pah! Minor details. And I love an older woman, more experience.' He winks as she shakes her head, laughing.

In the corner, a camera on a tripod and on the chair opposite, a small remote control.

'Now sit your behind on that chair, face the camera. And when you're ready, hit the red button, OK? And when you're finished, the green one. You can record as many as you want.'

'Yes, ma'am. I do like it when you're authoritative, you know.'

'Oh, shush, you save those smart words for the person who needs to hear them. You know what you have to do?'

'Apologise and take ownership of my wrong doings, yeah, yeah . . . although I might need another couple of days for that.'

'Just speak to the people you think about the most. You'll know who they are.'

Cole waited for the door to close and passed the controller between his hands, glancing between it and the screen, trying to think of all the things he wanted to say.

He stood and turned on the TV, the screen lighting up from black to blue. He stepped backwards, settling himself on the seat before leaning forward, his dark curls hanging loosely in front of his eyes as he picked up the controller, hitting the red button.

On the screen, Cole was faced with his own image. He coughed, smirked and tucked his hair behind his ear.

'Hi, Ells.' He grinned at the screen, his eyes filling briefly. 'Fuck, this is harder than I thought it would be. I doubt you'll ever see this, so I guess I should just go for broke, huh?'

Cole sat back and thought about all the things he wanted to say, how to begin to tell her how he felt. He took a deep breath and looked straight into the camera.

'I love you, Ella Walker. I've loved you all of my life.' He scratched the side of his face, feeling his stubble beneath his fingers. 'I loved you when you put that big fuck-off spider under my sheets . . .' he laughed, 'and when you puked 20/20 all over the bottom of my jeans . .' he shook his head, 'and when you stood in that church and married Will.' He looked down at his knee bouncing up and down. 'But I guess none of that is news to you any more.'

Cole reached into his pocket and brought out his lighter, flicking the lid of the silver Zippo, his eyes cast down as he considered what he needed to say. He looked back up at the screen.

'I'm sorry, Ells. I'm sorry I wasn't brave enough to tell you when we were young, I'm sorry that I've caused you so much pain by telling you now . . . but you know me, last orders have always been my speciality.'

He grinned and leant back in the chair, contemplating his words, pulling at his bottom lip.

'I should have left your side a long time ago.' Cole crossed his leg over his knee and stared back at the screen. 'You never needed me. Not really.' His dark eyes burned into the screen as he tried to put all of his feeling through the lens of the camera. 'I let you feel like you did, but . . .' He shook his head. 'You were strong enough to stand on your own.' He dropped his leg and leant forward, both his elbows on his knees, chin resting on his clasped hands. 'You've always been the strong one.'

'The truth is, Ells . . .' he looked down at the floor, at the stain on the grey tiles then back up. 'It was my fault. All of it. I tried to show off in front of Jack so he would see that I was more fun than his brother.

'I always wanted to be better than Will . . . no, not better, I wanted to be his equal, I wanted to impress him, but that's part of the charm of Will Roberts, isn't it?' He tilted his head. 'He makes us all want to be better than we are.

'It was my fault that Will felt like there was something more between us than there was. I mean, I practically moved into your house when the kids were small, bribed them with chocolate . . . well, not Bamber, she knew, I think . . . there was always so much going on behind those blue eyes.' Cole pointed his fingers across his eyes. 'She knew I was bad news. I wish I could tell her now how proud I am of her . . . a doctor, Ells, I mean, shit.

'And Jam . . . man, that kid kills me.' He laughed, sitting back up and dragging his hair back from his forehead, letting it drop back down. 'He's going to do big things, that one. I think he was the only one out of all of us that knew the real me and . . .' he blew out a mouthful of air, 'he fucking loved me anyway.

'But, Will . . . Jesus. He saved my life. And I tried to take *everything* away from him. He saved me when I didn't deserve to be saved.

'There is part of me that hopes that one day I'll be able to return the favour, to give you each other, to get out of the way, but let's face it, I'm the villain of this story, not the hero.'

Cole grinned up at the screen. 'Anyway, gotta go. I've got a hot date with a blonde who is a shark with a deck of cards.'

He clapped his hands together once, leant forward and tucked his hair behind his ear again.

'We made it though, didn't we, Ells? We made it to the end.'

Cole lifted the controller, winked and pressed the green button.

The TV screen fading back to black.

Acknowledgements

It's always hard to begin these things because there are so many people involved behind the scenes that help shape the book you have just read, but I would like to begin by thanking you, the reader. That's right, you, the person who has spent the last few days in the company of my imaginary friends, because without you, I wouldn't be here typing this in my pyjamas on a cold November morning. Without the wonderful messages I receive from you lovely lot, I can promise you, I wouldn't have had the will power to get my bum on my seat and put my fingers on the keyboard over the last year that we've had. Writing can sometimes be a lonely profession and it's the thought of this moment, when the final copy is being held in a reader's hands that gets me to the finish line. So from the bottom of my heart, thank you.

In the background of every book I begin, even when it is just a glimmer of an idea, is my incredible agent Amanda Preston ... think Buffy the Vampire Slayer but in literary agent form! She is there every step of the way, from the many (many, many!) ideas that aren't fully formed, to the belters that we will then discuss at length. Amanda has this knack of sniffing out a hook and a plot twist from my rambling pages and I don't think I've ever met anyone who has as many ideas as she does! She is there from the first draft, the second, the third, through the tears, the rants, the joys and meltdowns until we see the final novel. She is my biggest champion and a wonderful friend. Thank you, Amanda, you are my superhero.

Huge thanks go to my next hero, my editor, Jennifer Doyle. Jen has been my editor for all four of my books so far and has been there from the inception of this story, helping me right from the beginning and answering my numerous questions before I had even written the whole prologue. She is always there when I need her, guiding me through, cheering me on when I send the pages over and reassuring me when I'm worried about something (which is often!). And let me tell you, the hours she has dedicated to helping me choose this title are lengthy and long! Jen, you are amazing . . . and we made it, to the end.

Thanks must also go to Katie Sunley, who has now moved on to pastures new but who fell in love with Ella, Will and Cole's story right from my first and very rough pitch. Your enthusiasm and love for this book kept me going through some pretty tough days! I hope your new career is bringing you everything you deserve.

Wider thanks go to the Headline team! To Alara Delfosse, Jessie Goetzinger-Hall and Ellie Morley (who is now over at PRH). A special mention of thanks must also go to Sherise Hobbs who has been helping and supporting me behind the scenes in so many ways!

Thanks to the whole team at LBA for answering the many polls and discussions around the blurb and title! Extra thanks to Hannah Schofield too, who is not only building her own client list, but has been a huge support when I have bombarded my poor agent with countless ideas, blurbs and partial chapters!

Hugest of thanks to my social media followers who have shared their own stories about the things they would have said to their younger selves and for all of their comments about noughties nostalgia. An extra mention goes to Brigitte @bakingbree for her nose! @tilly.writes, for loads of nostalgia fodder, @melancholiet for Cole's dragon jeans, @adventuresinabookshop, for all of her support both on social media and at Telford Waterstones, to @mariasinclair3112 for her mention of the millennium bug, and also the hugely talented @tammyrobinsonauthor for sharing her memories of glittery eyeshadow with me.

Further thanks must go to the book blogging and Bookstagram community. These wonderful people spend their precious time reading and supporting writers; you are truly remarkable and I can't thank you enough. I must add specific thanks to Anne Cater and Linda Hill who have supported and read my books right from the beginning, @EmDigsBooks (who made me laugh so much on her live that I was left with cheek ache!), Claire at @Secretworldofabook for her endless support and to Jenna, the @book_club_momma for hosting the incredible Tasting Notes Live event.

I can't not mention two of my favourite FB pages too whose companionship and bookish chat keep me sane, so huge thanks as always go to The Fiction Café and The Savvy Writers' Snug.

Now onto my long-suffering friends and family.

To Nicki Smith, my oldest and dearest friend. For thirty years you have been there for me in my darkest times and brightest days, you are the River to my Phoenix.

Massive wine-fuelled thanks go to Emma Jackson, Claire Ashley (and her apple bottom jeans!), Julie Henry (for reading my draft and checking for timeline issues!), Louise Brindley-Jones and Teresa Merry who will get message after message with titles, blurbs, partial chapters and me wittering on and on about book stuff. I love you to the moon and back.

To Zoe Harrison, my Tuesday morning walking buddy. Thank you for keeping me sane and for the many, many skinny lattes! I would have been lost without our walks and chats over the past year, thank you for listening and for the laughs along the way.

Thanks must go to my writing tribe, who are always there at the end of the phone to talk me down, cheer me on, read my stuff when I think it's crap, and are just generally amazing in every way, so thanks again to Caroline Hulse, Josie Silver, Kim Nash, Natali Drake, Hannah Sunderland, Olivia Beirne and Katie Collins.

Massive thanks to my lovely mum who makes the best gravy in the world and to Chris for always topping up my wine glass! Further thanks to my brother, Dan, for championing me from the side lines and to Terry who married some bloke called Fred (Dad, I love you and your new name!).

Onto my wonderful extended family, the bonkers Evans gang, I love you all but an extra special thank you goes to the world's greatest mother-in-law, Jac, you really are the best.

And my brood . . . even though I'm guessing only one of you will read this! Thank you for putting up with a mum who seems endlessly attached to a keyboard or Kindle! Ethan, Ally, Max and Delilah, I don't quite know how a couple as scatty and disorganised as us managed to raise such kind, clever and thoughtful kids, but somehow we did. I'm endlessly proud and you are still all my favourites.

Finally to Russ who I met when I was eighteen. Thank you for making me laugh every day and making me feel like the most beautiful woman in the world even when I'm hungover and haven't washed my make-up off from the night before. Thank you for reading draft, after draft, after draft . . . without you, this book wouldn't have been written.

And an extra special thank you for coming up with the name for one of my most favourite characters ever – Cole.

If I could go back in time and tell my teenage self what I know now I would say, 'Don't change a thing. You are about to meet the love of your life and you're going to have four amazing children together . . . oh and never think you're not good enough to be a writer because one day, you will be writing the acknowledgements for your fourth published book. But maybe, don't eat the rest of that packet of digestives while you do it.'

If
I Could
Say
Goodbye

One minute Jen and her sister Kerry were
crossing the road to go to the shops and the
next minute life was changed forever. Jen lost her
sister in the accident that day, as well as a part of herself.

Jen is married to her wonderful (if slightly awkward)
husband, Ed, is mother of two perfect children
and living in a house like something out of a
Next catalogue. She has everything she has
ever wanted. But who is she without her sister?

As her memories of Kerry become her reality,
the further away she gets from her family.

Can she learn to say goodbye to her
sister before it's too late?

Available to order now.

REVIEW

The FIRST TIME I SAW YOU

Lost:
Six-foot-two Irish man who answers to
the name Samuel McLaughlin.
Has weak shins and enjoys show tunes.
If found, please return to Sophie Williams.

Sophie Williams has the perfect career and it's all she needs
to shut herself off from the rest of the world, and more
importantly, the secrets of her past.

Samuel McLaughlin is an open book. He lives for the
present and life for him is his big Irish family and his friends.

Against all expectation, Samuel breaks down the walls
of Sophie's ordered world and they spend the perfect
week together, but when Sophie discovers the terrible
truth, she is forced to leave.

But as Samuel begins searching for Sophie,
a life-changing event alters how he sees life forever.

And with each passing week, Sophie seems further
and further from his reach.

Available to order now.

The Songs of Us

If Melody hadn't run out of de-icer that day, she would never have slipped and banged her head. She wouldn't be left with a condition that makes her sing when she's nervous. And she definitely wouldn't have belted out the Arctic Monkeys' 'I Bet You Look Good on the Dancefloor' in assembly at her son's school.

If Dev hadn't taken the kids to the zoo that day, then the accident wouldn't have happened. He wouldn't have left Flynn and Rose without a dad. Or shattered the love of his life's heart.

But if they hadn't seen the missing person report that day, they might never have taken the trip to Cornwall. And, in the last place they expected, discovered what it really means to be 'Us'.

Available to order now.

REVIEW